The
VAN DIEMEN'S LAND

Thespian

The
Van Diemen's Land

TJ Lovat

ASHWOOD
PUBLISHING

ISBN-paperback: 978-1-7641254-6-8
ISBN-epub: 978-1-7641254-7-5

Published by Ashwood Publishing, Cradoc, Tasmania.
ashwoodpublishing.com.au
info@ashwoodpublishing.com.au

This is a work of fiction, and the persons, events, and locations depicted herein are either fictitious or, in the case of real locations, persons, or organisations, are used fictitiously.

Cover design: Susan Young.
Image: George Frankland, 'Hobart Town, Van Diemen's Land (c. 1827), Allport Library and Museum of Fine Arts, State Library of Tasmania: HA414. Used with kind permission.

A catalogue record for this work is available from the National Library of Australia.

The work of Ashwood Publishing is nurtured by the beautiful country of the Melukerdee people in the Huon Valley in southern Lutruwita / Tasmania. We acknowledge and pay respect to the traditional and continuing custodians of this place.

To Mum, a Clan Cameron lass

Author's Note

The Van Diemen's Land Thespian is a work of fiction built around several historical characters and events, including the key characters of Samson and Cordelia Cameron, pioneers of Tasmanian and Australian live theatre in the early 1800s. While I have paid attention to the bare historical records concerning matters such as their arrival in the colony, birthdates of children, places where they lived and performances they offered, the novel should be read principally as a creative work that attempts to tell the story of two immigrants from a well-developed British civilisation who travelled the globe to begin the art of western theatre in a land characterised mainly by a flagellated Indigenous civilisation and a harsh convict settlement, along with a fledgling European society. The motives, intentions and actions imputed to the main and other characters, some real while some are fictional, bear no necessary resemblance to their lived reality. The truth is that no records of such personal matters exist. On matters of daily life, I have made every effort to be historically accurate, but I have taken liberties at times where it enhanced the storyline.

One

'I wanted ye to see our new home,' Samson said as he helped Cordelia take the last step before reaching the deck. 'I think ye'll see it's better than ye expected.'

'Please don't use the word *expected*, Samson,' the heavily pregnant Cordelia replied. He helped to steady her as they stepped together across the slippery deck towards the handrail of the ship. 'Not until we're onshore, anyway.'

They looked out over the Derwent River towards the fast-approaching Hobart Town. The warm tailwind was blustery, hurrying the *Lochiel* to its destination.

'Well, the hill is pleasant at least,' Cordelia said, shading her eyes from the sun setting over the imposing mountain that stood like a fortress over the town. 'What's it called?'

'Wellington,' one of the officers who had overheard called out. 'Mount Wellington. After the famous duke.'

The Duke of Wellington had defeated Napoleon at the Battle of Waterloo not eighteen years beforehand.

Samson sniggered. 'I dare say it would have been called

something different if the French had landed here first.' But the officer was downwind of him and obviously didn't hear. As ever, Cordelia ignored her husband's feeble attempt at humour.

As the glare of setting sun gave way to a crimson ribbon stretching across the mountain top, the contours of the town itself came into view.

'It's bigger than I thought,' Cordelia said, stepping between Samson and the full force of the wind. 'See those large houses in the foothills.'

'Aye, I doubt they're for the convicts,' he whispered lest one of the officers take offence.

'Shush, Samson.' Cordelia pinched his arm. 'Let's not get off on the wrong foot before we even start.'

As the ship slowed and turned into the wind for docking, the fresh, salty smell of the sea was replaced with the stale odour of fish left too long in the sun, combined with human sweat and a whiff of alcohol.

'Ooh,' Cordelia said, reaching for her stomach. 'I hope we're not living too close to the dock.'

'I'm assured we're in a bonnie spot, darling. And if not, we'll move, won't we?'

Samson Pearce Cameron and his bride of a mere eight months, Cordelia nee Bouchier, had set sail from the Scottish port of Leith in April of the year of our Lord 1833. On this mid-September day of the same year, the *Lochiel* was steering them towards their new home, Hobart Town in the British colony of Van Diemen's Land. It was just thirty years since the first European settlement had displaced the Palawa, the Indigenous people who had inhabited the land for at least thirty thousand years. What stood in their place was one of the British Empire's most disreputable penal settlements. The name of Port Arthur, a penitentiary just sixty miles away, would become synonymous with the physical and mental cruelty of the convict era.

Within an hour, they were standing on the dock, being greeted in the twilight by nameless associates of their patrons who, with little ceremony, bundled them into a wagon.

'I was expecting something a little more formal, Samson,' Cordelia said under her breath.

'I expect they just want to get us to our lodgings before we jump back on the boat and go home.'

The wagon, loaded with all their goods, made its way along the dust-filled road, made even dustier by a wind that swirled around them, unable to escape the fortress of the mountain.

The wind, along with the strangely mixed odour of the dock, began to subside as the wagon turned into Harrington Street. Soon, they felt they had entered a windless, dry furnace, a heat neither of them had ever experienced.

'My Lord, what must it be like in the middle of the day?' Cordelia said, gripping her nose with a handkerchief. 'And what is that horrendous smell?'

'The smell of blood, sweat and tears, darling,' Samson replied, gazing at the labourers still hard at work under torchlight even at this late hour. Their convict-apparelled figures in motion were creating shadow puppetry on the outer walls of the diggings.

'Poor devils,' Samson mused. 'I wonder what they did to deserve this.'

'Broke the law, dear. Broke the law!'

'Mm, perhaps. Laws made to protect others. Not themselves, I dare say.'

'Seriously, Samson. I do wonder about you sometimes.'

'What? That yer ma might have been right?' Samson chuckled.

Cordelia turned away, tightening the grip on her handkerchief.

The further they inched towards the mountain, the more the workshops and warehouses of the docks and downtown were supplanted by some of the grander housing that Cordelia had spied from the ship.

'I didn't expect to see homes like this here,' she exclaimed, almost excitedly. 'It's a little like parts of Leominster – in a way.'

'Aye, just newer and a wee bit smaller.'

'Perhaps we can survive a while here, after all,' she said, casting a reluctant smile in his direction. 'So long as we're up here and not down there.'

Samson reached over and placed his bare hand on her silk glove. 'We can only hope, darling. We're a long way from home.'

She pulled her hand away and stiffened her body. 'Well, it will be on your head if we don't survive, Samson. You've assured me all is in readiness for us.'

They both went quiet as the extent of their journey from the other side of the world sunk in. The clip-clop of the trotting horse on the cobblestones put them both in a deeply reflective mood, Samson especially conscious of his responsibility for the woman he adored. How his life had changed in the two years since meeting her in rehearsals for a performance of *The Stranger*, that sometimes controversial play by the German playwright, Friedrich von Kotzebue. She was slightly older, already an established performer, and playing the main role of Mrs Haller. He, on the other hand, was nothing more than one of any number of young hopefuls, playing several minor roles. Besotted as he was, he scarcely dared to hope this 'goddess of the stage' could be interested in him. It was Uncle Roy MacTavish, a veritable man of the world, in whom he confided. Uncle Roy asked to know what she looked like.

'Dark brown wavy hair and deep blue eyes, Uncle,' he said, his own eyes glazing over. 'And skin like porcelain.'

'Well, with yer flaming red hair and hazel eyes, I'd say ye were a bonnie match, lad.'

'Aye, but!'

'But naught, lad. If ye love her, tell her. Lassies like a laddie who kens what he wants.'

So, Samson girded up his loins and found the right moment to tell her, and the rest was history. Having already broken her parents' hearts by taking to the stage instead of settling down to domestic duties as Bouchier daughters were meant to do, Cordelia tore them further asunder by accepting his proposal of marriage.

'A Scottish tradesman's son?' was her mother's first exclamation.

'Marry down if you must, dear' one of her last.

Cordelia's only condition was that Samson should accompany her to Van Diemen's Land, where she was commissioned to take up an as-yet-unspecified acting commitment sometime in the future.

'I was actually a little worried about going there alone,' she had confided. 'I've no idea what I'm stepping into and organising to go halfway around the world terrifies me.'

'Leave it all to me.' Remembering Uncle Roy's advice, Samson made sure to say it in a way that allowed no opposition.

And it worked. From that point on, Cordelia left all the organising to Samson. He wrote to the Van Diemen's Land authorities, laid out their conditions, negotiated salaries and living conditions, settled on dates, consulted shipping movements, and purchased tickets. His father was full of advice about the business side, while

Uncle Roy urged him to get as much acting experience as he could before embarkation.

'Ye need to be a *pair* of thespians, lad,' he said on one occasion. 'Dinna let the lass take all the limelight.'

'To be sure, women like to put men in their place,' on another occasion. 'But dinna let the place be too far below.'

With Uncle Roy's voice in his ear, Samson was constantly on the lookout for any chance to elevate his status as a performer. When Cordelia's co-star, Sir Richard Osborne, became ill during the Edinburgh performances of *The Stranger*, he seized the opportunity.

'You? In place of Sir Richard?' Cordelia scoffed. 'Samson, you're doing well and one day—'

'Then, let the day be today,' he pushed back. 'I know all the lines and who else do ye think will be playing Mr Solomon in Van Diemen's Land?'

'True, but I don't believe the Repertory here would abide it. They'll want someone of significance.'

'By tomorrow?' he shot back. 'Ye need someone to play Mr Solomon tomorrow.'

'Oh, all right. I'll speak with them about you filling in until they can find a better replacement.'

'Thank ye darling,' he said, reaching out to embrace her.

'Samson,' Cordelia replied, extending her arm so to prevent the embrace. 'Don't shame me, will you?'

Ye've done well, lad,' Uncle Roy said, tapping the entertainment pages of the *Caledonian Mercury* that Samson had handed to him, too afraid to read it for himself. 'Listen to this.'

The groan from the audience when Sir Richard's absence was announced softened to sweet accord as it warmed to Mr Cameron's admirable efforts to fill some big shoes. While understandably overshadowed by the unsurpassable Miss Bouchier, Samson Cameron proved that his desire to pursue stage performance is not altogether ill founded.

'I ken ye're a worthy match for yer famous fiancée.'

'All thanks to yer worldly wisdom, Uncle.'

'Lad,' Uncle Roy replied with a wink. 'When it comes to the fairer sex, a man doesna possess much ye could call wisdom.'

Samson's thoughts were jolted back to the present as the wagon stopped suddenly.

'This is the address, sir,' the driver said.

'Yes, it looks quite pleasant.' Cordelia cast a casual glance over the building. 'Not entirely unlike my parents' summer house.'

Samson smiled with satisfaction. It was all going to plan. Between his elevated status and all the backroom work in liaising with the Van Diemen's Land authorities, he felt a surge of confidence that they just might have arrived as the pair of thespians envisaged by Uncle Roy.

Closer inspection tempered his satisfaction somewhat. Their new home turned out to be just one of four one-bedroom flats in what Cordelia had initially thought was the whole house. She was none too pleased.

'Where on earth are we going to fit a child in here?'

'I'll speak with them as soon as I get a chance, darling. Anyway, we have a few weeks to sort things out.'

Two

THE FEW WEEKS TURNED OUT to be just two days after they disembarked, the 14th day of September 1833, when Cordelia gave birth to their first child, Elizabeth. The theatrical people arranged for a midwife to attend her in their new home. Mrs Garrett came by every day to help the new mother with a premature infant.

'Ye might have had her on the ship.' Samson attempted to lighten her mood some days later. 'Think of that.'

'At least there'd have been more room than in here,' was Cordelia's surly reply. 'We must get this child into something more congenial, Samson. She seems so delicate.'

In between the unfamiliar duties of parenthood, including dealing with an infant who seemed unable to take her mother's milk, they spent a few frantic months preparing for the inaugural performance due before Christmas. There were promises of better accommodation, but none of them ever came to bear fruit. As the opening night approached, Elizabeth's frail health faltered even further. The best doctors, nurses and others that Van Diemen's

Land could boast seemed incapable of arresting the slippery slope. Elizabeth died just two days before the show was to begin.

'Ye dinna have to do this, darling,' Samson said as the Reverend Archibald MacArthur turned towards the door of the upper floor flat. 'I'm told there's at least one very good actress in the town who could take your place for a week or so.'

It was the morning of the 12th day of December 1833, and MacArthur, Presbyterian chaplain of Hobart Town, had just officiated at the hurried funeral. By public order, all burials were to occur within twenty-four hours of death, owing to worries of disease spreading.

'Who, Samson?'

'Maria Taylor. I'm told she's been doing some recitals at the Court House, and it's been much appreciated.'

'What? Madame Dhermainville?' Cordelia spat back, her grieving look quickly transforming to one of obstinacy. 'There's no way I'd let that woman anywhere near Mrs Haller, though I confess she'd be far better suited to playing an adulteress than me.'

'I only thought—'

'I know what you thought, Samson,' she butted in, angrily snatching the handkerchief from her blouse and rubbing her nose vigorously. 'You thought you might try your luck as the Madame's latest dalliance, didn't you?'

'Oh, Cordelia, as if—'

'As if what, Samson? As if I don't know you're tiring of me, tiring of a wife who can't even give you a child that survives more than a few months!'

'Darling,' he said, moving to sit next to her.

'Stay away, Samson.'

'Darling,' he repeated, standing some feet away from her. 'If ye believe ye can get up on stage for the performance, of course that's what ye must do.'

'Samson.' She was on the verge of succumbing to tears again. He watched her as she raised a hand to her face and then looked up, her voice firm. 'I'd rather bury my grief as Mrs Haller. That way, I won't have to face my own … just yet!'

'Ye're a bonnie warrior, Mrs Cameron. The bonniest of them, to be sure.'

'Oh, don't be such a sop, Samson. What about you, anyway? She was your daughter too.'

'I know,' he replied, lowering his eyes to avoid her seeing them welling up. 'I can barely imagine life can be any worse than right now.'

'Well, would you rather cancel then?' she said coldly. 'The reverend mentioned that he'd help reorganise if we'd prefer.'

'No, heavens, no! Ye canna imagine the disruption, the disappointment. All the tickets have been sold. And, frankly, I'm not sure what else I'd be doing anyway. So, if ye can bury yerself in Mrs Haller, then *I* should be able to do the same in Mr Solomon.'

They had chosen to reprise their roles in *The Stranger* as the first performance because it was so fresh in their minds and where they had proven themselves as a pair of thespians by popular acclaim, at least as far as Samson was concerned. Cordelia was never convinced about the 'pair' element, but even she had to acknowledge the audience reception, especially in his hometown of Edinburgh. It played there to sell-out audiences for weeks, with Samson being compared more and more favourably with Sir Richard, if not always with Cordelia. In a subsequent Midlands tour, admittedly reviews had been less favourable, not only of Samson's prowess as understudy to Sir Richard, who happened to hail from the Midlands town of Leicester, but of the play in general. One Derbyshire village even cancelled remaining performances at the behest of the local pastor, citing a threat to public morality.

Such controversy often followed von Kotzebue's plays. His reputation as a playwright was for work that cut through social conformism. A product of the German Enlightenment built around candour, he prodded and poked at the niceties of the civil order. In the case of *The Stranger*, Mrs Haller's challenge to propriety was in her adultery as a married woman. There were those who considered this unsuitable if not seditious material for projecting onto the public stage. Nonetheless, in correspondence with the authorities, Samson had been assured that the residents of Van Diemen's Land were, like the Germans and Scots, a hardy people not easily shocked and quite given to candour. He was told this was particularly the case among the former convict class, largely Irish. He also heard that there was a particular thirst for public entertainment among this caste, something he and Cordelia would come to see for themselves, for good or ill.

Mr Cameron begs to announce to his friends, and the public of Hobart Town and its vicinity, that having engaged the new large room of the Freemasons' Tavern, it is his intention to give a series of Dramatic Amusements, and that no cost or exertion on his part will be wanting, to render the same worthy the approbation of the public. When it is ascertained, what number the room can conveniently accommodate, the necessary number of tickets will be issued, and no more.

So read the notice to be found here and there around Hobart Town. There was such excitement at the prospect of live theatre, the surest of veritable symbols of the town's acquiring a measure of civilised status, that tickets sold out in less than a day. The main feature was *The Stranger*, followed by a short satire, *The Married Bachelor*. In between the two, Cordelia sang a solo piece. The *Colonial Times* newspaper of the 24th day of December 1833 published a review of the first night's performance:

There was a full house, and such was the demand for tickets that hundreds were turned away. Mrs Cameron's 'Mrs Haller' was excellent, and the same character was never better gone through on any provincial stage in Great Britain and Mr Cameron acted in such style he is perfect master of stage effect. Between the pieces, Mrs. Cameron sang the 'Swiss Toy Girl'. There is a playfulness, and enchanting coquettishness in her voice and manner of address, which is highly pleasant – we would sooner hear Mrs. Cameron than any other vocalist in the Colony – she was of course encored.

'Well, they loved ye at least,' Samson said, placing the newspaper down on the small table next to his chair. 'Here we go again.'

'Samson, I thought the words about you were quite benign.'

'Benign?' He sniggered. 'When have ye ever had benign words said about ye?'

'Often,' Cordelia replied unconvincingly. 'Years ago.'

'Aye, many years ago, I dare say. Anyway, I'm pleased for ye, darling.'

'For us, Samson. For us.'

'Aye, for us.' He chuckled and and looked fondly into her eyes, hoping for the sign of recognition that they were at last a pair of thespians. She looked away.

The *Colonial Times* review was signed by Ken Norville, an upstanding member and frequent communicant of the Church of England. Some days later, the newspaper's main editorial, assumed to be written by the same Mr Norville, was devoted to them and their contribution to the town's development:

There is indeed a new Era in Van Diemen's Land. Public amusements have opened upon us in as great variety as in so limited a population could be possibly expected. This being then the commencement of a new Era, we shall devote more than the space we usually spare to such subjects to our notice of the opening of the Theatre on Tuesday evening. The proprietor is a Mr. Cameron, a gentleman of excellent family in Scotland – brought up and educated in a manner appropriate to his station in life. Mrs. Cameron is well remembered by many here as Miss Bouchier, the Star of the Norwich – Bath – and Cheltenham Circuits. They came out purposely to establish a Theatre here … Liberally indeed have they set to work, and we most sincerely rejoice to add, that there is every prospect of their spirited attempt being liberally remunerated … In conclusion, we may observe that never did performances go off better; nor was there ever so much interest excited.

In the same edition, the entertainment section included some of Mrs Haller's lines from *The Stranger,* apparently intended to underscore the point about Cordelia's 'versatility of talent' in how she delivered them:

In all that merits admiration, respect, and love, he was far, far beneath my husband. But … I thought my husband's manner grew colder to me … I thought he denied me pleasures and amusements still within our reach … The serpent tongue of my seducer promised everything … he fixed my belief that my lord was false, that the coldness I complained of was disgust to me and love for another. Maddened with this conviction, I left my children, father, husband, to follow a villain.

Taking it as a public condoning of adultery, the Christian Ladies' Guild, made up largely of women from the various Protestant churches, began to mobilise. Letters of protest were sent to the editor, whose wife was a friend of the wife of the Church of England's Colonial Chaplain. The editor instructed Norville to desist from reporting on the play 'until things cooled down'. And so, he did, at least in the *Colonial Times*. The Guild Ladies' self-congratulatory mood was short-lived. Just one day later, the *Hobart Town Theatre*, a fledgling but popular newspaper devoted to the arts, wrote a similar piece, including even more of the scandal-riddled lines from Mrs Haller. The piece was signed 'Ken Norville'.

The women realised they needed to call on the big guns. They asked for an urgent meeting with the Colonial Chaplain, the Reverend Philip Palmer.

The four ladies were led by Phyllis Birmingham, Head Lady of the Guild, an unusually large and angular figure. They were ushered into the meeting room in the chaplain's residence, arguably the finest home in Hobart Town at the time. The Reverend Palmer, remaining seated in a black mahogany armchair unsuited to his diminutive size, signalled to them to sit opposite on the far smaller, high-backed chairs on the opposing side of the massive, black wooden table. The table sat in the middle of a room whose walls were bedecked with what appeared to be the finest of wallpaper, with large portraits, heavily framed, of various royal and ecclesial dignitaries. The central and largest portrait was of King William IV, who appeared to be gazing out at the ladies atop the cleric's overly small head.

Agnes Gore, a newcomer to the Guild, could not contain her excitement at being invited for the first time to a residence that was the talk of the town.

'Oh, my. Look at those legs,' she blurted out.

The other ladies stopped in their tracks, scanning each other's legs and then their own.

'On the table,' Agnes guffawed. 'They're like tree trunks.'

'Yes, Mrs Gore,' Phyllis replied, resuming her normal pose of controlled indignation. 'Thank you for the observation.'

'Ladies, thank you for coming,' Palmer said, opening proceedings. 'What can I do for you?'

'Well, Reverend,' Agnes, leaning forward in her chair, began to speak.

'Thank you, Mrs Gore,' Phyllis jumped in. 'Please let me speak. I am, after all, the Guild's Head Lady.'

Agnes slunk back in her chair, an embarrassed smile flashing across her face.

'Thank you for seeing us, Reverend,' Phyllis continued, her steely gaze fixed on Palmer. 'It concerns this new performance at the Freemason's Tavern. Or what are some referring to it as now? Theatre Royal or some such impertinent title.'

'Oh, I hadn't heard of the Tavern referred to in that way but, yes, of course, the performance with the newcomers from back home,' Palmer nodded knowingly as he peered over his glasses, scanning the ladies' faces. 'Cameron? Is that the name?'

'We choose not to know their name, Reverend. By whatever name they go, this performance is a disgrace.'

'Oh, do tell me more,' Palmer said, resting the back of his head on the chair. 'A disgrace, you say?'

'Without doubt, Reverend,' Phyllis replied. 'Nothing short of glorifying womanly promiscuity. We know of course that the odd occasion exists when a woman of no virtue falls into sinful ways but it's a human excess that we need not have thrust upon us in this way.'

'Indeed, Reverend,' Florence Stirling-Mason added. 'Not merely thrust before us but proffered as though of some virtue.'

'Beyond proffered, I'd suggest,' Beatrice Inverarity thundered. 'Enjoined upon us as though such behaviour is essential to a woman's fulfilment.'

'Oh, my,' Agnes said, letting out a short giggle before restraining herself.

'It must be stopped, Reverend,' Phyllis finished off. 'Our precious town is being turned into Sodom and Gomorrah.'

Palmer flinched at reference to the two legendary cities of Old Testament mythology, noted for a level of wickedness that brought God's wrath upon them. It was every religious leader's nightmare to be held responsible for overseeing such a state. He looked over his rimless spectacles at the four amply fed, over-dressed, and uniquely unattractive women before him. His mind was momentarily distracted by pondering whether he would choose the fictional woman of no virtue over them if given the option.

He quickly put the thought out of his head.

'Well, this does sound serious indeed, ladies,' he said, putting on his most ecclesial face. 'Tell me, what did your husbands think of the play?'

'Oh, they were not there, Reverend,' Florence replied. 'As if we'd allow them to go.'

'So, you went alone?' Palmer asked, raising an eyebrow.

'Good heavens, no,' Beatrice replied. 'We weren't there, Reverend. What sorts of Christians do you think we are?'

'So, none of you actually saw the play yourselves, I take it?'

'No,' Phyllis, Florence and Beatrice replied in unison.

They all looked at Agnes, who had a sheepish look on her face.

'Oh, no, I haven't seen it,' she said, giving out a small chuckle. 'Not yet, anyway,'

'Not ever, Mrs Gore,' Phyllis thundered. 'Not ever, do you hear?'

'Oh, of course not,' Agnes replied, shrinking back in her seat, beads of sweat appearing on her forehead.

'So, how do you know about it then, ladies' – Palmer picked up the conversation – 'if neither you nor your husbands have seen it?'

'Well, we've read what the newspaper's saying,' Phyllis replied.

'Yes, and one of my neighbours was telling one of my friend's cousins all about it,' Beatrice added. 'And if you could see this neighbour, you'd know what sort of people are attracted to such perfidious pastimes.'

'So, just to be clear, ladies, you haven't yourselves seen the play nor had a close companion attend?'

'No,' Florence replied. 'But we haven't been to Hell either, Reverend. And we don't need to go there to know what it's like.'

'Of course. Of course. Well, thank you, ladies, for bringing the matter to my attention.'

'Please do whatever you can, Reverend,' Phyllis said. 'We have it on good authority that Mr Langmore will be petitioning the Governor – if not organising a demonstration of some sort. And we don't want the Methodists outdoing us, do we, sir?'

Palmer was aware of the tussle among the churches to be the leader of Christian morality in Van Diemen's Land. Palmer was often the butt of scorn for falling behind the Reverend John Langmore, superintendent of the Methodist Assembly in the colony. Langmore was unyielding on any human activity that he did not personally sanction, which meant just about everything beyond the Sunday service. Palmer, on the other hand, was inclined to appeasement, to reasoning things out. It was costing him not just a reputation but numbers of parishioners. An increasing number of Christians had stopped attending Church of England services and the majority of them were now to be found in the Methodist gatherings. Among other considerations, this was costing the Church of England money and influence, a matter Palmer's fellow clergymen were pointing out to him more and more.

'Of course, I'll do what I can, ladies. It's so good of you to have taken the time to come today.'

Philip Palmer took a deep breath as the last of the ladies exited his office. The relief was short-lived as his wife, Fanning, entered from another door.

'I suppose you heard all that, dear?' Palmer said, wiping his brow. 'We really must get a thicker door into the corridor.'

'I certainly did, Philip. I was tempted to storm in here and show my support for them.'

'Yes, I thought you might agree with them.'

'How could one not, Philip? Least of all a clergyman – which I presume you still are!'

'Yes, dear, last time I looked.'

'Well, what are you going to do about it?'

'Why don't you instruct me, dear?' Philip replied, standing in resignation. 'While I pour myself a Scotch.'

'No God-fearing Christian gentleman, *nor least a lady*, should submit their time to this torpor,' Palmer thundered to his congregation. 'I cannot imagine an image of godly womanhood more in contrast with the woman we honour during this holy season, she who bore the Son of God in her womb, as virginly as she was on the day of her birth.'

The occasion was the sermon on the Feast of the Epiphany, celebrated on Sunday 12 January in this particular year, 1834. The place was St David's Church of England in Hobart Town.

'Loyal servants of the Crown everywhere in this colony will rue the day these Jacobite heathens were allowed on our shores.'

Fanning Palmer sat in the front row, surrounded by the Ladies' Guild. She could hardly contain her excitement as her husband read, word for word, the sermon she had written.

It's doubtful that Fanning, or perhaps even Philip, knew much about Jacobites, other than it being a convenient way for the English to belittle a Scot, or at least attempt to. Personally, Samson took it as a matter of pride to be associated with the rebels who so nearly restored the Crown to the Stuarts, a Scottish clan, only to be vanquished at the Battle of Culloden in 1746. His own great grandfather had perished on the day, a story his father would recount on the battle's anniversary every April 16th.

'It's all right for you, Samson,' Cordelia spat out. 'The foolish man doesn't realise that we Bouchiers were among those who fought off the Jacobites. Without us, there might well be no Church of England, much less its overly pampered clerics.'

'Aye, darling, but at least he got the heathen part right,' he chuckled in an attempt to lighten the mood.

'Don't be ridiculous, Samson. My family are stalwarts of the Church of England in Leominster. I've never been so affronted. What are we going to do? Do something, Samson.'

Three

DESPITE HIS PINT-SIZED STATURE, WHEN Philip Palmer was at his thunderous best, he could outdo the Reverend Langmore's moral uppity-ness any day of the week. So, when the first protest happened outside the Tavern on the 16th day of January, the *Colonial Times* noted that the majority of protesters were Church of England members. It was a day of vindication for the Colonial Chaplain who, Samson and Cordelia were told by an informed source, would secretly have given his clerical collar to have attended the play.

Palmer would be saved from his self-imposed hypocrisy when a scuffle broke out that threatened to injure Cordelia. It happened as the audience was exiting the theatre. The pair of thespians had gone to the foyer to mingle with the audience. Cordelia was walking one of the ladies out the door when a protester pulled her by the arm, causing her to fall on the pavement.

'Are ye all right, darling?' Samson cried as he rushed her back to the dressing-room. 'Should I send someone for a doctor?'

'I'm fine, Samson. I believe I gave as good as I got. I'm just not used to the ferocity of these Christians.'

'Aye, I imagine they lost that page of the Bible where it says "ye shall know them by their love for one another".'

'Well, we were warned about the Methodists,' Cordelia said. Samson watched her feeling the back of her head. 'Ouch. Is there any blood there?'

'No, darling.' Samson seated her down and ran his fingers through her hair. 'Which is as well. I hadn't imagined I'd be up for murder so soon after arriving here.'

'Would you truly murder for me, Mr Solomon?' Cordelia attempted a smile.

'Ye know I would, Mrs Haller. That – and more.'

'Somewhat a romantic, aren't you, Samson?'

'A romantic Scotsman? Never let it be said! No, darling. Just an unromantic Scot totally besotted by his wife.'

Samson leaned over and gave her a hug.

'Righto, you two,' came a thundering voice as the dressing-room door flung open.

They both jumped, looking to the doorway and the menacing gaze of a policeman.

'Constable,' Samson said, stepping forward. 'Ye're a sight for sore eyes.'

'Don't go on with all that fancy talk, sir. I just need you to come down to the station with me. Both of you!'

'What are you talking about, Constable?' Cordelia butted in. 'Why aren't you arresting those vile people who caused this ruckus instead of us?'

'I didn't say I was arresting you, ma'am. Just to come to the station, please!'

'For what purpose?' Samson said, reaching his hand over to rest on Cordelia's shoulder. 'As my wife said, what are ye doing about the mob that started this horrid event? I hope they're behind bars as we speak.'

'You mean those good Christian folk out there with their placards?'

'No. I don't think there were any bonnie Christians here tonight, sir. Just some miserable Methodists who know naught about Christianity.'

'With respect, sir. My understanding is that they weren't all Methodists. Not even half. Most of them were from His Majesty's church, and the Reverend Palmer sent them – or so they say.'

'Church of England?' Cordelia thundered. 'I really don't think so, Constable. My father is a warden of the Church of England – and one of its most generous donors. Neither the Church of England patrons, nor those of the Church of Scotland for that matter, ever engaged in such behaviour in our home country.'

'Well, I wouldn't know about that, ma'am. But my instructions are to bring you two down to the station to answer some questions.'

'So, we are the ones being arrested, then, Constable?' Samson asked, staring down the policeman.

'As I said, sir, I didn't say you were being arrested. Simply that you need to come down to the station.'

'By whose orders?' Cordelia said.

'Ah, the sergeant's, miss.'

'Madam, if ye will, Constable. This is my wife ye're speaking with here.'

'Sorry, ma'am.'

Samson helped Cordelia to her feet. She winced, reaching for the back of her head again, while levelling her gaze at the policeman. 'I'm not worried about what you call me, young man. But

I am worried for your career if you think you can get away with arresting innocent people who have been set upon by an unruly mob. When my father hears about this, there'll be hell to pay.'

'Sorry, ma'am. I'm just following orders.'

Samson, holding Cordelia by the arm, took a step forward. 'Yer sergeant's orders, ye say? And who gives yer sergeant his orders, Constable? Why would he want us to come to the police station, rather than the instigators of the riot?'

'I don't know for sure, sir. But I believe he got a letter from the Colonial Chaplain. You'll have to take it up with him. Now, please, can we go?'

'So, Sergeant, are we to believe the Church of England chaplain is behind this?' Cordelia said as she strode quickly to the desk.

'Who told you that, miss?'

'Madam, Sergeant,' Samson chipped in. 'Ye're speaking with my wife.'

Sergeant Townsend's face hardened. 'Who told you that, ma'am?'

'Your constable here.'

'Constable Driscoll,' Townsend said, his eyes fixed on his underling. 'What did you tell these people?'

'Sorry, sir. I thought you said something about the reverend wanting to stop the play.'

'Thank you, Constable,' Cordelia said. 'It sounds as though we've uncovered the seat of the problem here. It seems that the Reverend Palmer is to blame for the events that unfolded tonight.'

'My wife is being too polite, Sergeant,' Samson added. 'The events were in fact a riot, one that could have killed someone.'

'And if that had happened, Sergeant,' Cordelia chimed in. 'It would have been on your head, and your best friend's head, the Colonial Chaplain himself.'

'Ma'am, hold your tongue,' Townsend said. 'The reverend's only concern is for the good of his people and the wellbeing of this town.'

'So, who was it who organised the lynch mob that almost killed my wife?' Samson asked as he stepped forward menacingly. 'Ye or yer priest friend?'

'Yes, Sergeant,' Cordelia jumped in as Townsend was opening his mouth to speak. 'My husband is asking who is responsible for sending a riotous mob to murder us? You or the good chaplain? We need to know before taking this matter to your superiors.'

'Ma'am. The Colonial Chaplain is not a friend of mine. He is the shepherd of his flock. God's representative for Church of England folk. As such, he has a role to play in guiding our moral standards. And that is what he has done.'

'So, he controls the police,' Samson said. 'Is that what ye're saying, Sergeant? The Colonial Chaplain is yer superior?'

'No, sir. I take my orders from the Superintendent of Police.'

'Well then,' Cordelia said, brushing the dust off her dress. 'May we speak with your superintendent?'

'I don't believe that will be possible, ma'am. Nor desirable.'

'Then we insist ye send a message to Mr Sotheby,' Samson shouted, banging his fist on the sergeant's desk, sending a tumbler of water crashing to the floor, the glass smashing into a thousand pieces.

'Sir,' Townsend shouted back as he stood to his full height. 'Damaging the King's property is an act of treason, you realise. I'll have you thrown in the cells for that action, as well as your part in the ruinous events of tonight. Constable Driscoll, take these two to the cells.'

'Will they share the same cell, sir?' Driscoll fussed.

'Of course not, Constable.'

'Very good, sir,' Driscoll said, saluting before turning to the soon-to-be guests of His Majesty. 'Ma'am, Mr Cameron, please come with me.'

'This is a disgrace,' Cordelia said, pulling her arm away from Driscoll's attempt to grab her. 'You will hear more about this, Sergeant. Much more.'

'Ye can be sure of it,' Samson added. 'And I doubt ye'll be a sergeant by the time this is all finished. I doubt ye'll even be a constable.'

'Well, we'll see about that.' Townsend sniggered. 'And who is that Mr Sotheby you mentioned, anyway? Not the—'

'Aye, the Colonial Secretary. He and my wife's da are the best of friends.'

'Truly?' Townsend said, visibly gulping.

'Yes, Mr Townsend,' Cordelia turned to engage the policeman with her full gaze. 'My father and Mr Sotheby are the best of friends. Lifetime friends, in fact.'

Four

QUENTIN SOTHEBY WAS CONTACTED EARLY the following morning by the Superintendent of Police. He urged the immediate release of the two actors, then quickly rode to Philip Palmer's house for an urgent meeting.

Sotheby strode into the chaplain's office, accepting the glass Palmer was offering from across the desk.

'Reverend, I urge you to put this matter to rest, and quickly,' he spat out as he took a seat opposite Palmer, still standing.

'Tell me again, Mr Secretary, why I should do that?' Palmer replied as he slowly sat in his own chair.

'Sir, Mrs Cameron's father is an extremely influential man, both in England and here in the colony. Mr Bouchier has friends in all the high places that matter, from Westminster to Lambeth.'

'Lambeth Palace?' Palmer said, bolting forward in his chair. 'The Archbishop of Canterbury's seat of power?'

'Yes, sir. Lambeth Palace itself,' Palmer said, nodding once, eyes afire. 'The Archbishop and Mr Bouchier go way back, I'm told. And their wives are even closer. Once Mrs Bouchier knows that her daughter spent a night in Hobart Town's cells, and that you were deemed responsible, I wouldn't fancy your own chances of ever being Archbishop of Canterbury, or even a village rector, to be honest. Can I be any clearer in my advice?'

Palmer slumped back in his chair. 'Oh, good heavens. I was only trying to appease some of my own flock who seem to have taken extreme umbrage at this wretched play.'

'*The Stranger?*' Sotheby spluttered. 'Have you seen it?'

'No. I wouldn't have thought it proper.'

'Oh, Reverend. You should see it. It's a brilliant mockery of all that needs mocking in our pretentious establishment. Quite Christian in its own way, I thought. I imagine the Lord himself would have been rollicking in the aisles, as we all were.'

'Truly? So, you didn't find it offensive?'

'Not at all. Brilliant. Poignant. Hilarious in spots. And Mrs Cameron gave such a remarkable performance. I agree with the review in the *Times* that it was as good a rendition as one would find anywhere in the Empire. And I should know. My wife and I saw the play twice at home, once in London and once in Birmingham.'

'Oh, please don't mention that word.'

'What word, sir?'

'Birmingham. Mrs Birmingham is the leader of the Christian Women's Guild. She's the one who led the delegation to my office. She virtually threatened to take her gaggle out of the church and set up shop with Mr Langmore.'

'Reverend, if I may,' Sotheby said, taking another sip of his dram. 'I think you and the Church of England would be enhanced if women like Phyllis Birmingham were to set up shop with the Methodists. The lady is nothing but a prude and a troublemaker.

She'd be at home with the Methodists, but you have bigger fish to fry.'

'Bigger fish? What do you mean?'

'Sir, there will be an official colonial church in Van Diemen's Land at some point, and the Church of England is the obvious candidate, especially once a diocese is established and the colony has its own bishop.'

Sotheby paused, watching Palmer process the implications of what he had just disclosed. 'Do I make myself clear, *Bishop* Palmer?' Palmer looked up to see Sotheby raising his glass in mock salute. Palmer shifted in his chair, unable to disguise his pleasure. Sotheby continued. 'I'm already planting the seed about all this with Westminster and Lambeth, and I know there have been discussions between the Home Secretary and the Archbishop of Canterbury about the matter of an official colonial church.'

'A colonial church? Of course, and surely, that will be the Church of England.'

'Well, from what I'm told, your archbishop is naturally enthusiastic that such be the case, but I gather the Home Secretary is more inclined to a *let's wait and see* approach – whatever that means. The man is not especially given to the Church of England, I take it. He's divorced and had some unpleasant experiences in his home parish. He even took up with the Congregational Church, would you believe?'

'What? So, are you seriously suggesting that the Congregational Church might become the colonial establishment? Surely not! Westminster wouldn't allow it.'

'We're a long way from Westminster, Reverend. In case you hadn't noticed.'

'Please don't remind me, Mr Sotheby. My wife recounts this deplorable fact every day – and night.'

'Mrs Palmer is not happy here, I take it?'

'To say the least, sir,' Palmer snuffed and watched as he swirled the liquid in his glass. 'Every time a ship arrives with mail, she asks if there's a letter appointing me to somewhere in England. Anywhere in England, or even Wales. She once said she'd be content to go to Ireland. That was her lowest moment, mind you. I doubt she'd ever be so desperate. But, no, to answer your question. She is most unhappy here at the end of the earth.'

'Then, again, Reverend, I earnestly recommend you do something about the current situation, lest you and Mrs Palmer expend your days here, as surely as the wretched inhabitants of Port Arthur.'

'What do you suggest, Mr Sotheby?' Palmer said, shaking his head and exhaling loudly.

'Make amends, sir. Apologise, grovel if you must, deny Mrs Birmingham's claims that her actions were done in your name. Whatever it takes.'

'But that would be a lie, sir,' Palmer said, looking up with a righteous stare.

'Is it, Reverend?'

'Well, there are witnesses.'

'Oh, well, that's a different matter.'

'I don't understand, Mr Sotheby.'

'Reverend, what I mean is it's up to you to determine the truth of matters – and what might constitute a lie. Who is in a better position than a servant of God to do that? In contrast, the matter of witnesses is another thing altogether.'

'Sir, are you suggesting that I could call a lie to be the truth but for witnesses to the contrary?'

'Reverend, I possess not the temerity to advise you about matters of such profound moral import. I am limited to advising you of what might serve your own, and your good wife's, best interests – and what most certainly will not serve them.'

'So, I should make amends with Mrs Cameron at any cost. Is that your advice?'

'At any cost, sir. And with Mr Cameron. I'm told they are very much a pair.'

'Dally with a Jacobite? What will Mrs Birmingham say?'

'Sir, it's what the Archbishop of Canterbury will say and, indeed, in all likelihood what the Prime Minister will say, that should be your supreme if not only concern.'

'Thank you, Mr Sotheby. I wonder if you might arrange a meeting with the Camerons in your offices.'

'Surely, sir, but why not meet them here?'

'Ah, well, to be honest,' Palmer lowered his voice as he cast his eye towards the door into his residence. 'This place has ears on the walls.'

Samson and Cordelia received a hand-delivered invitation to attend a meeting with the Reverend Palmer in the Colonial Secretary's offices on the following Friday. It was signed *Quentin Sotheby Esq, Colonial Secretary, Van Diemen's Land*. Samson was disinclined to go, but Cordelia's greater diplomatic sense prevailed.

'And I was so very sorry to hear of the loss of your beloved infant. The burden of such a loss can only have added to the grief caused by my wayward parishioners.'

'Thank you, Reverend. I appreciate your candour,' Cordelia replied. 'And I'm certain my husband feels the same.'

Palmer and Cordelia looked over to Samson, who had said

not a word in the ten-minute exchange between his wife and the purportedly contrite cleric.

'Samson, dear. You do feel the same, don't you?'

'I canna be sure, my dear. I'm afraid I learned a long time ago that ye canna trust a man of the cloth.'

They both looked at the chaplain, expecting a reaction, his steely gaze foreshadowing a seemingly inevitable dressing down. They waited and watched as Palmer's demeanour changed. He took a deep breath and looked at them, his eyes softening.

'I fully understand, Mr Cameron. I dare say you would feel an inability to trust me after the execrable incident you suffered. I can only apologise profusely and assure you once again that I in no way endorsed it. Why, I didn't even know it was occurring.'

'Thank ye, sir.' Samson stood as if readying to leave. 'Then there are two things ye could do to assure us, to use yer own words, of yer sincerity.'

'Certainly, and what are they?'

'Ye could pen a disclaimer in the *Times*, making it clear that the action was in no way done under yer authority.'

'Ah, yes, I'm sure I could find a form of words.'

'Which my wife and I would approve.'

'Ah, of course,' Palmer replied, swallowing hard. 'And what's the other thing I should do?'

'Attend the play. Ye and yer wife – in the front row.'

'Philip, you can't be serious,' Fanning Palmer spat at her husband. 'How would I ever face the Ladies' Guild again?'

'Dear, is the Ladies' Guild truly more important than getting us both off this dreaded island at some point?'

'Well, if it means ending up on the mainland, the answer is yes. On the other hand, if you can guarantee me passage home to England, then the answer is no. The Ladies' Guild is of no importance. Indeed, nothing is of any importance when compared to that prospect.'

'And that is precisely Mr Sotheby's point.'

'Thank ye for yer attendance, ladies and gentlemen,' Samson announced to the audience before the performance of the 30th day of January 1834. 'I'm sure ye'd like to know that we have some very important guests here tonight. The Reverend Palmer, Colonial Chaplain in this bonnie town, is in the front row, alongside his beautiful wife. I'm sure ye'd be wanting to welcome them.'

Samson put his hands together, clapping loudly as Cordelia joined him under the light of the single chandelier that marked the stage area. She joined in the applause, as did sections of the audience. The chaplain and his wife sat with their heads down as the applause lingered. The longer their heads were inclined to the floor, the longer and louder the clapping persisted. There were some final cheers and wolf whistles before Samson raised his hand to halt proceedings.

'Thank ye so much. I imagine the good chaplain and his wife are overwhelmed and I'm quite certain they'd be wanting to thank ye personally. Mr Palmer, I'm sure ye'll be wanting to say a few words. Would ye care to step up onstage and into the light?'

'Don't you dare,' Fanning whispered under her breath.

'It's all right my dear,' Palmer leant over to his wife, whispering. 'The Jacobite's a cunning fox, like all Jacobites.'

Palmer stood to another round of applause, making his way to the chandelier. The applause slowed as he walked to centre stage and stood beside Samson, beaming, according to Cordelia's later report. Samson extended his hand, which Palmer accepted. As he turned to face the audience, Cordelia stepped forward, held him by the arm and aimed a kiss at the cleric's cheek. As Palmer turned towards her, the kiss landed on his lips. The audience broke into extended laughter. There was an audible gasp from the front row.

'Oh, I apologise, Mrs Cameron, Mr Cameron,' Palmer said, his face reddening as his brow broke out in a sweat visible to the third or fourth row.

'Not at all, sir,' Cordelia said with a cheeky grin.

'It's fine, sir,' Samson said, unable to restrain his own wide grin. 'We're all friends here, are we no?'

Palmer stood awkwardly, gazing out at an audience sitting in semi-darkness below the dim light of several hanging gas lanterns. His mouth was agape, but nothing was coming out.

'Speech, speech, *speech*,' the audience began to clamour.

Palmer emitted a few words that no-one could hear, not even the two actors standing just behind him.

'Ladies and gentlemen,' Samson shouted as he stepped forward, raising his arm towards the audience. 'I'm sure we all want to hear what the good reverend has to say.'

The audience quietened bar several especially noisy patrons towards the rear of the theatre.

'Please,' Samson called out again. 'Don't ye good folk want to hear what this servant of the Laird has to say?

'Nah,' the rough voice could be heard. 'We ain't interested in the priest. Get on with the show.'

'Sir,' Samson called back. 'The reverend is an important man, dinna ye know? He is the Laird's representative in this town, and we all know he's a man of immense honour.'

'And great integrity,' Cordelia added, raising her voice and her arm. 'What my husband is saying is that the reverend must be respected. We all know that his beliefs come from his faith in the Lord who taught us to be truthful and fair in all our dealings.'

There were sniggers and chortling in sections of the audience.

'So please listen now to the reverend's words,' Cordelia concluded, extending her hand to Palmer who stepped forward, raising his voice this time.

'Dear people. I merely wish to say that my wife and I were honoured to receive Mr and Mrs Cameron's invitation and are delighted to be with you tonight. As some of you might have read in the *Colonial Times*, I sincerely apologise for any distress caused to Mr and Mrs Cameron arising from the actions of some of my parishioners, actions that I strenuously disavow. And as for any lingering notion that Mr and Mrs Cameron's performance is in any way an affront to Christian belief, I disavow that as well. I have it on the best authority, none less than from the Colonial Secretary, a man of immense wisdom born largely from his profound Christian faith, that the play we are about to see conveys some important Christian content. I trust the Secretary's judgement, which I have always found to be impeccable. As such, I reiterate that my wife and I are delighted to be with you tonight.'

All eyes in the first few rows were directed to Fanning Palmer, sitting immobile, her head still inclined to the floor. Samson and Cordelia glanced quickly in the same direction, stealing a wry smile as they turned back to face each other. Palmer had not the courage to look anywhere near his wife.

'So, thank you again, Mr and Mrs Cameron. And my sincerest

apologies once more for any distress caused unwittingly by my church.'

Palmer hastened from centre stage, reclaiming his seat next to his wife. He cast a steely gaze towards the stage while she persisted in mimicking a statue.

Five

'Are ye sure, darling?' Samson asked as Cordelia made a surprising move one night in bed.

'Do you want to or not, Samson?'

'Of course, I want to but would ye be prepared for the consequences?'

'Oh, you do have an elevated opinion of yourself, don't you? Do you think I might be so overwhelmed by your prowess that I would be transported to another state, or perhaps suffer a medical episode?'

'Well, ye do know what happened to Mrs Haller when her bonnie Romeo seduced her.'

'But, my dear Romeo, in this case it seems I'm the one doing the seducing. Now, do you have any other objections?'

'No objections, my darling. Only …'

'Only what, Samson? For heaven's sake, can't you face the prospect of a woman initiating? Must it always be the man?'

'I'm sorry, my darling, I just want to be certain ye'd be ready for another bairn, should it happen.'

Cordelia fell onto her back, letting out a huge sigh. Samson lay quietly next to her, waiting for an answer.

'Samson,' she whispered.

'Aye.'

'I'm not only ready. I want it. I need it. It's the only way I can imagine I'll stop thinking about Elizabeth night and day.'

'Sorry, I didn't realise it was as bad as that.'

'What? Just because I don't talk about it, night and day, you think I'm not tormented by it, night and day?'

'No, of course I know ye've been hurting inside, but everyone has said how amazing ye've been. Playing Mrs Haller without missing a beat. I mean, I suppose I thought somehow ye must be getting over it.'

'Getting over it?' Cordelia snapped, sitting up and peering into his face. He could see the contours of her head against a far wall catching a sliver of moonlight. 'Getting over losing my baby? Samson, I'll never get over it. Do you understand? Never!'

She collapsed on her back again, this time turning away and snuffling.

'I'm so sorry, my darling,' Samson said, extending one hand across her body and resting it on her stomach. 'I'm so sorry. I knew ye'd never really get over it, but I just wasna sure ye'd want to risk going through it all again.'

'Well, I do,' she blubbered, pushing his hand away. 'I do. I want to take the risk. I want a child, Samson. I want to have lots of children. My stage life is not enough. I want to be a mother.'

'And am I not enough either? Ye do have more than yer stage life, ye know?'

'Oh, Samson, don't be such a foolish child. I married you, didn't I? But a woman needs more. Any woman.'

'But ye're not just any woman. Ye're Van Diemen's Land's finest performer.'

'As I say, Samson. It's still not enough. And what about you anyway? Do you not miss our daughter? You loved her too, didn't you?'

Samson fell silent. Cordelia waited for an answer, her back still turned away. She turned over, lifted herself by her elbow and faced him. In the same moonlight, he knew she could see the glistening in his eyes.

'You do miss her, don't you? And you haven't been saying much about it either.'

She reached down to kiss him on the cheek. He brought her whole body down and nestled her into his arms.

'Aye, I dinna think I've ever felt so wretched.'

'Then why didn't you tell me? See, you've been bottling this up, just like I have.'

'I know ye're right. It's just too awful. So horrid.'

'It is, Samson,' Cordelia said, turning away and going limp in his arms.

He turned over and faced her. He could feel her trembling. He was searching for some words of comfort, but before he could find them, she spoke softly, haltingly.

'And so, it seems easier just to keep busy. In our case, to keep on being Mrs Haller and Mr Solomon.'

'Aye, as if we're them, instead of our miserable selves.'

'Then let's take the risk, Samson,' she said, lifting her head and looking down on him. 'We've nothing to lose. Everything to gain. What do you say?'

'I say ye've convinced me. And what a burden that'll be.'

'Well, if you don't want to,' she said, feigning indignation. 'I'm sure, just like Mrs Haller, I could find someone else.'

'No, Mrs Haller. Ye know ye're mine. All mine! No-one else will ever get their hands on yer bonnie body.'

'Now, that's more like the Samson Pearce Cameron I know.'

'And love?'

'I suppose!'

Six

OVER THE NEXT TWO MONTHS, Samson and Cordelia maintained a punishing performance schedule of four evening and two matinees per week. They offered a variety of plays, including *The Maid of Milan*, *The Gamester*, *She Stoops to Conquer*, and *The Honeymoon*, all regarded as 'popular melodrama'. To appease certain members of the Establishment who were worried about the increasing popularity of emerging theatre life among the poorer classes, they also offered some 'legitimate theatre', principally through Shakespeare's *The Merchant of Venice* and *Othello*. While Samson was happy to assist with legitimate theatre, he stood aside from performing, as did Cordelia.

'But did ye not play Desdemona against Sir Richard's Othello back home?' Samson said one night in bed. 'I'm certain I read about it before I even met ye.'

'It was never a favourite, Samson. To be honest, I find Shake-speare a little dull.'

Samson chuckled. 'Ah, I can hear yer ma saying *that's what happens when ye marry beneath ye.*'

Amidst the hectic schedule, it was von Kotzebue's *The Stranger* for which Samson and Cordelia saved most of their energies and for which all classes continued to clamour.

By late March of 1834, Cordelia was some weeks with child. The early stages of her pregnancy were filled with persistent unwellness, making for difficulty in her performing. Theatre management, now largely in the hands of several wealthy business investors, wanted the plays, especially *The Stranger*, to continue unabated for another three months, but Samson pleaded Cordelia's illness and negotiated a two-week break leading up to Easter of that year.

The unexpected cessation was interpreted by Mrs Birmingham's Christian Ladies' Guild, now well ensconced with the Methodists, as vindication for their ongoing, if less aggressive, protests. They were invited to meet with the Reverend Langmore, assuming he would be commending them for their actions.

The same four ladies were ushered into an office whose size and sparseness contrasted markedly with Philip Palmer's equivalent. Langmore's bulky figure sat overhanging a chair rendered invisible to the ladies' sight, with a small, unadorned desk between them and the four plain wooden chairs on which they were invited to sit at some distance away from the desk. Only two small portraits hung on the wall behind Langmore: one of King William, the other of John Wesley, the Methodist founder.

'Ladies,' Langmore began before they had settled properly into their chairs. Mrs Gore was still trying to squeeze herself into hers. 'I believe the play in contention will recommence in a few weeks.'

'We'll be ready for that, Reverend,' Phyllis Birmingham replied, shifting her bottom around in the hope of finding a modicum of comfort on the chair. 'Be assured, sir!'

'Well, ladies, I'm sorry but I've called you in to ask that you desist from any further protests.'

'But Mr Langmore,' Phyllis thundered. 'Surely you've not succumbed to the devil, like that wretched Church of England fellow.'

'No, madam. I assure you I remain opposed in principle to the nature of the Cameron play, as I do to theatre of any kind.'

'Then, surely, Reverend,' Beatrice Inverarity said. 'You can't be seriously forbidding our efforts to have it stopped.'

Langmore looked around at the four sets of eyes staring him down. He took a moment to tug on his beard with one hand, while tapping the desk with the forefinger of his other hand.

'Ladies,' he began again. 'Negotiating the shoals between one's most profound Christian principles and what most benefits the church is not always a facile task.'

Langmore paused, nodding his head as his eyes moved from one judgemental face to the next. Only Agnes Gore's was turned away, distracted as she was by the wallpaper.

'What are you saying, Mr Langmore?' Phyllis snapped. 'That we should learn to compromise with the Word of God? Surely the Bible makes it clear …'

'Madam, would you kindly let me finish?'

'Please do finish, Mr Langmore,' Phyllis replied, rearing her head upwards as if trying to accentuate her stature. 'But be snappy about it. Do you agree, ladies?'

Three of the four women nodded as they grunted their agreement. Agnes Gore looked around, seemingly confused.

'Thank you,' Langmore said, pulling out a handkerchief and wiping his forehead. 'What I'm trying to convey is the difficulty in maintaining a proper righteous anger while, at the same time, not unwittingly placing the church at some disadvantage.'

'What disadvantage, Reverend?' Florence Stirling-Mason asked, her brow furrowed with consternation. 'How on earth can the church be disadvantaged by morally proper people expressing outrage at iniquity?'

'Iniquity?' Agnes said, leaning forward to catch Florence's eye. 'What's that, dear?'

'Wickedness, Mrs Gore,' Phyllis interrupted. 'Evil. Mr Langmore is asking us to tolerate a work of the devil.'

'Why, Mr Langmore?' Agnes said, tears forming in her eyes. 'Why would you do that?'

'Indeed, sir,' Phyllis added, her piercing eyes staring down the clergyman. 'Why would you do that?'

'Ladies, please let's not make this more awkward than it is. I assure you I am not urging that you do anything of the sort. If you wish to continue protesting at this lurid performance, please feel free to do so.'

'Well, thank you, Mr Langmore,' Phyllis said, surveying her colleagues with a victor's gaze. 'Then we shall—'

'But please disassociate yourselves from the church,' Langmore spat out, as if courage to do so would otherwise be lost.

He looked at the women, his eyes afire. For a moment, they were stunned into silence.

Phyllis was the first to recover her voice. 'Are we then to be cast adrift from the church, Mr Langmore? From the barque of Peter, as it were! Are we effectively orphans before the church?'

'Mrs Birmingham,' Langmore raised his voice, banging the table with his fist. 'Your mind is addled. You are overstepping proper ecclesial boundaries here. Please allow me the licence to run the church as the presbyter I am, installed by the Lord himself, I should remind you. While you, madam, should revert to the role designated for you by the same Lord.'

'And what is that role, Mr Langmore?' Phyllis asked, resorting to the steely calm for which she was noted. 'What is that role?

To abandon godly ways so that I can better serve the church, or merely to salve your conscience lest it be addled by your own failure before the Lord?'

Langmore fell to silence. Agnes imagined she could see steam coming from his mouth and nose. She looked around nervously, wondering who would speak first. She noted the regal demeanour of Phyllis Birmingham, staring unmoved at the clergyman.

'Madam,' Langmore finally managed to say, scanning the faces before him. 'And ladies. The Lord's work is rarely dispensed without clamour. It was the same in the Lord's own days. The Gospels tell us of the many times he confronted the worldly wisdom of the pharisees and others, only to confound them with the wisdom that he knew came from his Father in Heaven.'

Langmore paused, seemingly for effect. Agnes was looking over his shoulder, apparently intrigued by the portrait of the King behind him. The others took their lead from Mrs Birmingham and stared implacably at the clergyman.

Langmore looked down at the desk and continued. 'What I'm trying to say, ladies. And might I also say that I do not expect it is within your remit to fully understand this. But my task before the Lord is to ensure the wellbeing of the institution he left in his name. And after much prayer and reflection, I have come to understand that the welfare of the church will be better served by your taking your protest elsewhere.'

'Could you explain what you mean, sir?' Phyllis said, without faltering or taking her eyes off her adversary across the room. 'For we are, as you say so well, merely women, lacking the divine remit that sits so burdensomely on your shoulders.'

'Madam, I'm not fully at liberty to say but I can tell you that the Camerons are well connected, in both London and Edinburgh. They carry some weight, including with the imperial government.'

'Are we meant to be impressed, Mr Langmore?' Phyllis replied. 'Many a villain has been well connected. Herod was well connected. Did that make his judgement to send the Lord to the cross a right and proper one?'

'Madam, I must insist that you restrain yourself from such impertinent nonsense. Why, I fear Mrs Cameron herself would be outdone by your own panache for the dramatic arts! What you must understand is that there are people in very high places who could do our church untold harm by the mere whisper that we are engaging in calumnious acts against others whom they cherish and might wish to protect.'

'Could do our church untold harm?' Phyllis scoffed as she rose, signalling that the other women should do the same. 'Or you, untold harm, Mr Langmore? Or you?'

With that, Phyllis turned towards the door, standing with her back to Langmore as she ushered her fellow Guild members out of the room.

'Hurry, Mrs Gore,' she said as Agnes returned to retrieve her reticule.

'Sorry, Mrs Birmingham,' she said, flustered. 'Goodbye, Mr Langmore.'

'Goodbye, Mrs Gore,' Langmore replied. 'Goodbye, Mrs Birmingham.'

Phyllis hastened to the door without turning back or uttering a word. Though Langmore saw the door was about to slam, he still jumped at the noise and its reverberations. He looked to the wall and his desk, fearing for a moment that something would be shaken loose and crash to the floor. When all was still in place, he drew a deep breath and pondered what might next befall him.

Seven

'WELL, SAMSON, I SUSPECT WE'RE becoming quite respectable around this town,' Cordelia whispered as they settled into bed one evening after performances had resumed. 'Even after their Easter celebrations, the zealous Christians were absent.'

'Aye,' he whispered back amidst a giant yawn. 'I thought they'd be out in force again, even with their leaders in our corner.'

'As I say, Samson. I think we have become quite respectable.'

'Boringly so.'

'Don't you like respectable, Mr Cameron?' Cordelia dug him in the ribs. 'Would you prefer to be a rebel all your life?'

'When respectable, as ye call it, means ye're in the same corner as clerics and the like, I canna be certain it's what I want to be.'

Cordelia turned over, her back to him. 'Oh, well, I'm sure you'll have more chances to be the Jacobite rebel. I doubt our newfound allies in the churches will be quiet forever.'

'Aye, with friends like them, who needs enemies?'

'I'm afraid I agree, Samson.' Cordelia turned to lie on her back. 'These church people can't be trusted. Once Mr Sotheby is out of the way, they'll revert to their prudish ways, for sure.'

'Aye, and then there's the papists. I imagine they've been keeping their powder dry.'

'Yes, what do you make of that?'

'Oh, I'm sure they'd think it was just fine to see the Protestants getting into trouble with the authorities. Ye know if the Church of England says *up*, the papists say *down*.'

Cordelia rolled over to face him. 'Do they really hate each other so much, these Christians?'

'Oh, aye. If that's what they are.'

'Christians?'

'Aye, I think they've forgotten more about Christianity than they remember. They're all the same. They're Church of England, Methodist, Catholic, anything but Christian.'

'So, it's not because the Catholics like what we're doing that they haven't bothered us?'

'I canna be sure, but I suspect it's more because they wouldn't want to be seen standing with the Protestants.'

'So, Mr Sotheby would have no influence there?'

'Heavens, no! The papists wouldn't care what's happening in London or Edinburgh. Only what's happening in Rome. It's all about what the Pope says.'

'And what do you think the Pope would think of Mrs Haller and Mr Solomon?'

'If they upset the Protestants, he'd probably think they were braw,' Samson replied, chuckling.

Cordelia allowed herself a small snigger as Samson turned over and placed his arm around her.

They had woken late, as there was no need to hurry on a rest day.

Cordelia stretched, only to burrow her hands under the bed-clothes again. 'It's cold!'

'Aye, well, it's late April, and that means winter will soon be upon us, down here in the Antipodes.' Through the window he could just see the first snow on the mountain above Hobart Town.

'What will you do, Samson, if Mr Langmore does come to the play?'

'I doubt he will, darling.'

'But word is he will.'

'Oh, well, I suppose we'll do something like we did for Mr Palmer.'

'What, you'd call him a prick too?' Cordelia taunted, clearly enjoying herself. Her all-too-rare playfulness lightened his spirits like nothing else could.

He chortled. 'I never called him that.'

'Well, you might as well have.'

'No, I was talking about his bishopric when he finally becomes a bishop. Which I'm sure the coot will one day. It's a term referring to a bishop's land.'

'Samson,' Cordelia said, raising herself on her elbow and looking into his eyes. 'No-one believes you. Certainly, the audience that night didn't think you were talking about land when you talked about his bishop *prick*.'

'Well, I canna be responsible for what the audience thinks,' he said, feigning innocence.

'And the look on poor Mrs Palmer's face made it clear that she knew exactly what you were referring to.'

'Do ye think poor Mrs Palmer even knows if her husband has a prick?'

'I dare say it might come as a surprise to her,' Cordelia replied with a snigger.

'Or to the poor fellow himself.'

They chuckled together momentarily as he pulled her head down and held his arms around her body.

'Mr Solomon,' Cordelia whispered, pulling away. 'What's that I'm feeling?'

'I've no idea, darling. I'm told it belongs to a bishop. He said I could borrow it.'

'Well, tell him he can have it back,' Cordelia said, as she flopped back down next to him.

'Are ye still not …?' he said as he reached out and held her by the arm.

'No, Samson, I'm not!'

Cordelia was some four months into her pregnancy. While her health had improved slightly throughout the break, her unwellness was by now overtaking her again. The rare moment of playfulness was short lived.

Eight

Performances had only one week to run before another two-week break. Theatre management had been offering two further three-month contracts, the first one involving a season of mixed melodrama and Shakespeare, with *The Stranger* still the constant centrepiece. It had proven itself to be the one play that engaged all classes of people. The second contract was to be negotiated around Cordelia's availability, granted her condition. Samson was concerned about her seeing out even the first three-month contract, granted her health seemed to be deteriorating and her disposition lowering by the day.

There was a knock at the door. He hastened out of bed and opened it.

'Mr Cameron?' the rotund gentleman asked, hat in hand.

'Aye,' Samson replied, bleary-eyed as he pulled the cord of his dressing gown around his waist, ''tis me.'

'Mr Cameron, my name is Robert Portleigh, and I represent the owners of the London Tavern in Launceston. I wonder if I might step inside. It's a little chilly out here.'

'Now, why would ye be wanting to step inside, sir? Why can ye no state yer business here and now?'

'Samson,' Cordelia called from the bedroom. 'Don't be rude. Ask the gentleman inside.'

'As ye can see, sir, my wife is the boss here, so I'll allow ye to step inside. But only because she says so.'

'Why, thank you,' Portleigh replied, stepping through the door. 'And my thanks to your wife, Mr Cameron.'

Portleigh began taking off his coat. 'Do you mind if I take off my coat?'

'Well, it's a wee bit late to be asking seeing as it's all but off yer back.'

'Oh, I'm sorry. I can put it back on.'

'Leave it off, Mr Portleigh,' Cordelia said, stepping into the room in her dressing gown, her hair brushed immaculately.

'Forgive me, madam.' Portleigh turned his head to face the other way.

'You're forgiven, Mr Portleigh,' Cordelia replied, standing her ground. 'And please forgive my husband's rudeness. He's Scottish, you understand. A self-styled Highlander, not noted for his gentility.'

Cordelia took Samson by the arm, looking up at him. 'Are you, Samson, dear?'

'If ye say so, darling. We all know ye're the boss around here.'

'As it should be,' Cordelia said, turning to the visitor. 'Don't you agree, Mr Portleigh? I'm sure your wife is the boss as well.'

'Oh, well.' Portleigh laughed, not sure where to look. 'I'm really not sure.'

'Well, she should be, sir,' Cordelia said, looking him up and down, stern-faced. 'She should be. Now, what can we do for you?'

Portleigh stood tall, still holding his coat and hat. He cleared his throat.

'Thank you again for your time and your graciousness. We've heard so many wonderful things about your performances, especially about you, madam.'

'I would think all this goes without saying,' Samson interrupted. 'My wife is the finest actress in the Empire. But how is any of this in yer interest, sir?'

'Samson,' Cordelia scolded. 'Let the man talk. I'm always happy to be offered a little praise. Please do go on, Mr Portleigh. You say *we*. To whom are you referring?'

'As I said to your husband at the door, madam, I'm representing the owners of the London Tavern in Launceston.'

'And who are they?' Samson interrupted again.

'A range of eminent people, sir. Several businessmen have invested in the tavern. They have formed a board under the chairmanship of Sir Albert Guilfoyle. I'm sure you've heard of him.'

'I dinna believe so,' Samson replied, turning his head away as dismissively as he could. 'Who would he be, then?'

'Oh, one of Van Diemen's Land's most distinguished officers. A retired army colonel. Fought in the war of '83, won a Military Service Medal for bravery. One of the British Army's youngest officers to be so honoured. Then went on to distinguish himself in the stoush with Napoleon in 1815. Won another string of medals. Came to Van Diemen's Land to advise the local corps and has now set up several business ventures in the colony.'

Portleigh took a breath, looking like the cat that ate the cream as he peered at them, clearly hoping for a reaction. Samson made sure his face was as expressionless as possible.

'So, ye believe that makes him ... what did ye say? *Eminent?*

How many innocent folks did he kill to win his Military Service Medal?'

'What? I—' Portleigh stuttered. 'I really couldn't say, sir.'

'Because that's not important to ye? Is that it, Mr Portleigh?'

'I'm sorry, Mr Portleigh, but my husband is not impressed with the good colonel's achievements, as you may have noted. But please do tell us why you're here, and I assure you we will listen,' Cordelia turned to her husband. 'Won't we, Samson?'

'Of course, darling,' he replied, rolling his eyes in full view of their visitor.

Portleigh stared at Samson, clearly unsure whether to continue speaking or leave before he was thrown out.

'My husband says he will listen, please be assured.'

'Thank you, Mrs Cameron, Mr Cameron. I'll go straight to the point, if I might.'

'Please do,' Samson said, holding his hand over his mouth as he yawned and stretched as conspicuously as possible.

'Well, Sir Albert and the London Tavern's investors have liaised with the Launceston Town Council and, together, they wish to invite you to spend some time in our fair town, especially performing the play that has been such an outstanding success in Hobart. *Strangers*, I believe it is called.'

'*The Stranger*,' Samson said. 'I gather yer board doesna know von Kotzebue's plays.'

'Who?'

'The playwright, Mr Portleigh,' Cordelia said. 'Friedrich von Kotzebue is the writer of *The Stranger*.'

'Oh, I see. I'm certain some members of the board would know him. I myself am not an advocate of live performances. I find them too difficult to comprehend.'

'I wonder if that might say something about yer level of

comprehension, Mr Portleigh?' Samson spat out as rudely as he could manage.

'Samson,' Cordelia cast a serious frown in Samson's direction. 'Hush now. We promised not to be rude, remember. Do tell us more, Mr Portleigh. When would your board like us in Launceston and where would the play be performed?'

'And what would they pay us?' Samson butted in.

'Of course,' Cordelia said. 'Why don't we start there? The Tavern management has been most generous to us here in Hobart Town, with salary and accommodation, so we would want something at least as generous.'

'Oh, of course, madam. This is one of the matters I was commissioned to negotiate with you. Could I ask what your conditions are here?'

'Aye,' Samson jumped in. 'We have free bed and board here in this establishment and we're paid half a guinea each for each performance.'

Cordelia's mouth was open ready to speak. She closed it and glanced briefly at Samson before turning back to face Portleigh.

'Yes, that is correct, Mr Portleigh. Could you match that?'

'Or do better, even?' Samson said. 'If we were to put ourselves to the inconvenience of moving, I imagine we'd want something better than that.'

'My goodness,' Portleigh said as he peered at the ground. 'I'd have to ask the board, of course.'

'Well, why don't you ask them if they would be prepared to pay us one pound ten shillings for each performance?' Cordelia said. 'That would cover both of us, so you could make it sound like a bargain.'

'And bed and board at least as good as this,' Samson added. 'Or even better, if ye could manage it.'

'Well, I—'

'Mr Portleigh,' Samson interrupted. 'I sense ye just might have caught us at the right time. Ye might know we're about to sign a six-month contract with the Tavern here, so if ye really want us in Launceston, I think ye need to get there and back to us as quickly as ye can.'

'Yes, indeed, Mr Portleigh,' Cordelia added, smiling. 'You'll need to be quick. It will help if you have a contract drawn up for us. At least six months, and where did you say the play would be performed?'

'Umm, I hadn't said but I believe it will be at the tavern itself.'

'Well, I think we'd need to see the tavern before we could enter into any agreement,' Samson said, rubbing his chin. 'Perhaps ye could arrange transport to take us there to see it for ourselves.'

'Ah, yes, I'm sure that could be arranged.'

'Very good, then,' Samson said, gesturing to the door. 'So, if ye've nothing else to say, ye probably should be on yer way.'

'And we'll look forward to hearing from you, Mr Portleigh,' Cordelia added.

'Yes, madam. Thank you so much,' Portleigh said as Samson pushed him towards the door. 'And thank you, sir.'

'Thank ye, and do give my greetings to yer brave Colonel what-was-his-name?'

'Sir Albert Guilfoyle.'

'Aye, Mr Guilfoyle. Do give him my regards,' Samson said, ushering Portleigh out the door and closing it behind him.

'Well, you were in a mood with that poor man, weren't you?'

'Ye know how I hate being disturbed on our rest days. Especially now that ye're over yer morning sickness.'

'Oh, for heaven's sake, Samson. It's almost midday and we haven't even had breakfast.'

'So, what do you expect will happen when Mr Portleigh finds out we only get half a guinea between us?' Cordelia asked as she stirred the porridge on the fuel stove. 'Not *each* of us.'

'I doubt he'll find out. If the Launceston folks are as keen as he says, they'll not be asking too many questions of our Hobart Town friends. They'd be too worried they'd outbid them.'

'But what if they do?'

'We'll just say Mr Portleigh misunderstood us.'

Cordelia lifted the stirrer for a taste test. 'And what then?'

'We'll just say it's still our price.'

'So, do you really want to go to Launceston or not?'

'Aye, I think I do. It'd be braw for both of us to have a change.'

Cordelia placed a ladle in the pot and reached for a bowl. 'All right, then, let's see what happens. I must say I'm quite content here, especially as we're now so respectable.'

'Well, I think we should move on before we become too respectable.'

'It doesn't fit your Highlander blood, does it, Samson?'

'What?'

She handed him a bowl, steam pouring out. 'Being too respectable.'

'No, I've learned ye canna really trust respectable folks.'

'Perhaps the Colonial Chaplain was right when he called you a Jacobite.'

'Aye. And proud of it.'

'Which means then you're a Catholic at heart.'

'Oh, Laird, no! God forbid!'

They would never know if Robert Portleigh checked on the accuracy of the Hobart Town salary. All they knew was that he wrote to them a mere ten days after the meeting, the second day of their two-week break.

'Who was that?' Cordelia asked. She had heard the knock on the door but had fallen back to sleep while Samson went to answer it.

'It's a letter from Portleigh.' He held it out for her to see, but she kept her eyes shut.

'That was quick,' she said sleepily. 'What does it say?'

'They're offering to carriage us to Launceston at a time of our convenience.'

'Just to look, do you mean? Is there anything about a contract?'

'Ah, aye, I think there might be.' Samson surveyed Cordelia's supine form and sat down just out of her reach. 'There are some other papers here.'

Cordelia sat up, wide awake now. 'Let me see them.'

'Dinna be so impatient,' he said, turning away from her outstretched hand and rifling through the contents.

'Don't speak to me like I'm a child, Samson. I don't appreciate it.'

'Ah, listen to this,' he said, ignoring her castigation. '"Please find enclosed the offer of salary should you agree to enter into the six-month contract, also enclosed."'

'That sounds promising,' Cordelia replied. 'And the offer?'

'Aye, it's an official document from the trustees of the London Tavern signed by our friend, Mr Guilfoyle.'

'Sir Albert, if you will, Samson,' Cordelia replied, still smarting from having been ignored.

'If ye insist,' he said, turning over the pages until alighting on the last one. 'Aha. I think they're offering us what we asked for.'

'A pound and ten?'

'No, darling. Even better. A guinea each.'

'Each?'

'Each.'

'Well, that's very good, isn't it? When can we start?'

'Well, I think we should keep our powder dry. Who knows? We might even get more out of them.'

'I don't need any more, Samson. It's not wise to stick our necks out too far.'

'Just trust me, my darling. Have I not done well by ye so far?'

'You're proving useful, I'll admit,' Cordelia replied with a wry smile.

'I'd call that high praise from ye, Mrs Cameron,' he said, beaming.

'Perhaps, but don't come to expect it.'

Nine

Samson and Cordelia accepted the Launceston offer to travel and meet the London Tavern investors. It was the first opportunity to explore Van Diemen's Land outside a township. The hired carriage, pulled by two horses, was quite comfortable but insufficiently so to make for a smooth journey on the rough, sometimes boggy road weaving in and around the many mountains and valleys on the only route between the two main towns. It was a three-day journey, with stops on the way. On the second night they stopped at the settlement of Campbell Town. Their driver, a former soldier, was known at the garrison, and they took lunch at a long bench with three soldiers. He introduced them to his former supervising officer, Lieutenant Angus Fraser, a Highlander who was filling them in on the history of the settlement.

'We saw several work gangs on the way in.' Cordelia was holding the large tankard of tea with two hands. 'Are they all convicts?'

'Aye, ma'am. There's no employed labour in this town.'

She took a sip and screwed up her face.

'Is the tea not to yer liking, ma'am?' Fraser was chuckling. 'How about yerself, sir?'

'Aye,' Samson replied. 'It's like the brew my grand da used to make.'

Samson and Fraser, who hailed from Inverness, began swapping notes about life in the Highlands.

Cordelia, who had given up on the strongest tea she had ever tasted, interrupted. 'But I didn't see any soldiers guarding them. Aren't you worried they might escape?'

Fraser chuckled. 'No, ma'am. They ken there's nowhere to go.'

'And you have no fear they might attack someone? They looked quite wild to me.'

'To be honest, ma'am,' he lowered his voice. 'I'd be more worried about some of the settlers.'

Samson laughed along with Fraser. Cordelia could not hide her disdain while butting in. 'And what of all the natives? Aren't you worried about them? I understand they can be quite violent.'

Fraser's face hardened. 'Once upon a time, perhaps. Poor devils!'

'Poor …?' Cordelia scoffed. 'Surely …!'

'Surely what, ma'am?'

'Surely you have no sympathy for them. Why, from what I've heard—'

'No sympathy for the violence, ma'am,' Fraser jumped in, holding his soup spoon aloft. 'But for losing their land? Well, perhaps if ye were a Scot, ma'am.'

Cordelia was silent for the rest of the lunch, her distaste for which she could not hide. Samson and Fraser went back to their discussion about the Highlands, its history, the food and music they missed.

Their first stop was to view their proposed new lodgings, a two-bedroom cottage in the lower reaches of Tamar Street. They were in the hallway, a room to either side with a kitchen at the end.

'It's a wee bit small,' Samson said as Portleigh stood watching them explore the cottage.

'Small?' Portleigh replied, raising an eyebrow.

'Yes, Mr Portleigh,' Cordelia cut in. 'I agree with my husband. You mightn't realise we're about to start a family.'

'Oh, of course. Well, I'm sure Sir Albert would be happy to look at something bigger. It might be further out in the hills but I'm sure they could find something.'

Samson had wandered into the kitchen. 'In the hills?' he snapped, stepping back into the hallway. 'Do ye truly think I'd take my wife and a new family to the hills? No. We must be close to the town.'

'Of course, sir, I'll … I'll—'

'Mind you,' Samson cut him off. 'There are other ways we could be compensated for its size.'

'What do you mean, sir?'

'Well, perhaps we could be paid more.'

'I'm afraid I don't understand, sir.'

'Mr Portleigh, my husband is saying that our salary might be increased and that would make up for the inconvenience of having to squeeze into this small dwelling.'

'Oh, I … ah … I'm not …'

'Or we can re-sign the contract in Hobart Town,' Samson interrupted. 'Ye realise we're under quite some pressure to do that.'

'Oh, oh. Let me speak with Sir Albert.'

'That'd be braw, Mr Portleigh. If ye can let us know by tomorrow before we leave for Hobart Town. Once we're back there, I imagine we'll be asked to re-sign.'

'Of course. Of course!'

'Did you really think it was too small?' Cordelia asked as she powdered her face in front of the mirror.

They were in the executive suite of the London Tavern, preparing for the dinner to be held in their honour by the tavern's directors and the local business association.

'No, what did ye think?'

'I thought it was very sweet and just right for us.'

'Well, why did ye not say so, then?'

'Because I thought you were merely playing games with the poor man, trying for a better deal.'

'Ye're an even better actress than I thought, darling,' he said, chuckling as he grabbed her from behind and tucked his lips into the back of her neck. 'I thought ye really thought it was too small.'

'Samson, you'll ruin my make-up.' Cordelia pushed him away. 'You can thank me later.'

Samson withdrew his unrequited affections – yet again – and returned to the task of straightening his bow tie, looking at the mirror over her shoulder.

'I hate these infernal things,' he said, undoing the tie and making a third attempt to do the job properly.

'How can you hate a bow tie, Samson?' Cordelia replied, busy rubbing rouge on both cheeks. 'You wear them all the time in the play.'

'Aye, but those ones are stuck to the shirt. I've never had to tie the real ones.'

'Well, it was nice of them to supply you with a suit, anyway. They're obviously keen for us to take up the contract.'

'We'll see how keen they are tonight. Or how good a negotiator our friend, Portleigh, is.'

'Just be civil, won't you, Samson?'

'Civil? I've no idea what ye mean,' he replied, winking at her in the mirror. At last, he had that infernal bow tie looking right.

Cordelia huffed and shook her head as she returned to her task.

Cordelia smiled and squeezed Samson's arm as they walked into the dining room.

'Isn't it wonderful?' she whispered. 'I hadn't realised how much I've missed these things. I used to go to this kind of lavish event with my parents in Leominster. One time, I even stood in for my mother as my father's partner for the night. Now, here we are as the honoured guests. What fun!'

'Aye,' he whispered back, hoping the tremble in his voice was not too apparent. Cordelia's familiarity with such events only highlighted his own extreme discomfort. Fun? He was filled with terror.

They were escorted to the most elaborate dining table, stocked full of cutlery, glasses and flowers, all atop a starched white table-cloth. Two young waitresses, attired in black dresses with stiff white collars and bonnets, showed them to their places, men on one side, women on the other.

The first course was miniscule fish on a small plate. Samson reached for the regular fork to the left of the setting but fortunately was sufficiently cautious to glance Cordelia's way to check. The glimpse of a scowl on her face told him of his error.

Samson's eyes darted from the other culinary items to Cordelia and back again. He felt a flush creeping up his neck. She should have taken a few moments to tutor him in what to expect! Aye, and she was probably regretting her oversight now. There was the smallest of opportunities for them to communicate as the other guests' gaze was on the maître d' welcoming the guests to his establishment. 'That one,' Cordelia whispered almost inaudibly as she pointed to the tiny fork to the right of his setting. Her smile affirmed his success.

'And, finally,' the maître d' said, wrapping up the welcome, 'I must say, the London Tavern is honoured to have Mr and Mrs Cameron with us tonight. We in Launceston have heard so much about you and do hope to see much more of you in the near future.'

'Indeed,' Sir Albert Guilfoyle butted in. 'Thank you so much, Mr Wilkins, for your hospitality, and I endorse your sentiments that it is indeed such an honour to have Mr and Mrs Cameron here with us tonight. I am certain I speak on behalf of Mr Walsh from the Business Association and his good wife, and all here present from the Town Council and Tavern Board, in welcoming one of the Empire's most famous thespians.'

Sir Albert began the applause. Samson sat and watched as the single pair of hands extended to those of the eleven others around the table. All eyes were on Cordelia, who was busy nodding and mouthing thanks as she turned her head to take in the assembly.

Samson banged his knife on the glass until the applause began to subside.

'Ah, Mr Cameron,' Sir Albert shushed the remnants of applause. 'I believe you might wish to speak to your wife's fame. Please do, sir.'

'*Moran taing gu dearbh*,' Samson blurted out as he stood quickly and carelessly, his seat overbalancing and all but crashing to the floor. '*Tha thu nas coibhneil.*'

The table guests gasped and stared at him, then around at each other, some tittering, some reaching for a drink.

'Oh, jolly good,' one of the councillors said, holding up his glass. 'Latin is such a beautiful tongue.'

'My husband is merely thanking you and telling you how kind you are,' Cordelia said, her face flushed with embarrassment. 'In his native Highland tongue. He gets a little carried away when he is overwhelmed by kindness.'

'Oh, of course, of course,' Sir Albert replied, rubbing his brow with his handkerchief. 'And a fine tongue it is. Don't we agree, ladies and gentlemen?'

There was chatter mixed with grunts of approval and some tittering. Samson crashed down, the legs of his seat banging on the timber floor. Was his face as full of perspiration as he could feel around his collar? He would ask Cordelia later in the evening.

'And thank you for the translation, Mrs Cameron,' Sir Albert said, chuckling and raising his glass. 'Well, it is as I say a great honour to have you here with us in our fair town. We do hope your travel from Hobart Town was felicitous and that the lodgings we hope you will accept are to your liking.'

Cordelia opened her mouth to speak. Samson put his hand up to stop her.

'I think I can speak for my wife and I, sir. The cottage is nothing more than what we Scots would call a *taigh-osda*, a pleasant-enough outhouse. I'm sure ye must know that we are about to start a family.'

He grabbed the wine glass in front of him and sculled half the contents before banging the glass on the table. He stood shaking visibly. Cordelia leant forward to take in the reaction of the guests.

'Thank you for asking, Sir Albert,' she said, smiling. 'My husband is merely suggesting that the cottage, lovely as it is, might be a little small, granted pending events. By outhouse, he really means a flat, such as one might find in the yard of an estate.'

'Madam,' Mrs Cornwallis, the young wife of one of the councillors, called out from her seat next to Mrs Guilfoyle at the far end of the table. 'I fear you might be giving us the polite version of a most impolite allegation. For your information, my grandfather was a Highlander, and we used to laugh whenever he referred to the outhouse as a *taigh-osda*. It is not, as you suggest, a flat in the grounds of an estate, but, as I'm sure you know, somewhere one goes to relieve oneself.'

Mrs Cornwallis slumped back in her chair, her head in the air, clearly aggrieved. The group fell to grunts and grumbles. The ladies looked to each other, shock and dismay written on their faces.

'I apologise for my husband, ladies and gentlemen.' Cordelia said, looking around the table and then scowling in Samson's direction. 'I'm sure you all understand that Mr Cameron is merely concerned for my welfare. As you now know, I am with child. My second child, in fact. You might not be aware that our first child, our darling Elizabeth, died suddenly in December. She was but a few months old.'

Cordelia paused. She reached for the napkin on her lap and held it over her eyes. There was silence around the table. Sir Albert, sitting at the head of the table, looked to his wife directly opposite as if asking her to intervene and comfort their guest. She remained unmoved, seemingly out of sympathy for her colleague, Mrs Cornwallis.

Samson stood again and walked around to Cordelia's side.

'Are ye all right, darling?' he asked, choking on the words.

'Oh, my,' Sir Albert said, standing and looking pleadingly at the other women who, he might have assumed, would be better equipped to intervene in such a situation. When no help came, he turned to look at Samson leaning over Cordelia with his hands firmly on her shoulders. 'I'm sure we are all moved by your situation, sir, and can only commend you for your care and attention towards your wife.'

'Thank ye, sir,' Samson replied, straightening and looking in his direction. 'Ye canna imagine how difficult it's been. Our wee bairn died only a month or so after we arrived here.'

'Ah, yes, of course,' Sir Albert said, looking again at Mrs Cornwallis for the smallest hint of compassion.

'Oh, it has been …' Cordelia choked on the words. Her welled-up, reddened eyes were revealed to all for the first time. '… so very difficult. I'm sorry. We're so sorry. I'm sure neither of us intended that our pent-up emotion should spoil your evening.'

'Oh, not at all,' Sir Albert said. 'Not at all. I'm sure we all understand.'

'Nonetheless,' Mrs Guilfoyle spoke for the first time. 'Mrs Cornwallis is rightly offended by having her cottage, so splendidly restored, referred to in such a foul way.'

'Oh, I'm sure Mr Cameron didn't mean what he said,' Mr Cornwallis said. 'My wife is just upset because the renovations were done under her watch. Isn't that the case, dear?'

'No,' his wife snapped back. 'It's not the case. The cottage was built by my father, as you're all well aware. It was a labour of love. And to have it referred to in such a derogatory way. Well, I'm just glad he's not here, God rest his soul.'

'We're so very sorry, madam,' Cordelia said, wiping her eyes, then looking up to Samson, standing over her. 'Samson, please apologise and retract what you said. Mrs Cornwallis's father built that cottage. It's not his fault that it's so small. Besides, I'm certain it would accommodate us until the baby is born.'

'Well, to be frank about it, Mrs Cameron,' Mrs Cornwallis said. 'I was raised in that house, as were my five siblings. Admittedly, it was a squeeze for us, but it was all my parents could manage in such a new settlement, and we were content. I frankly can't imagine why you would need more, even after the baby is born.'

'Oh, Mrs Cornwallis,' Cordelia replied. 'I'm sure a loving family like yours would have been more than content with whatever your parents could provide. I myself was brought up in a modest house in Leominster, far more modest than most of my friends, but we had a bedroom each and we were happy with that.'

'How many in your family, Mrs Cameron?'

'Eight bairns,' Samson butted in, having returned to his side of the table. 'Eight bairns, plus the ma and da, and the maid and butler had a room each as well.'

'Oh, my,' Mr Cornwallis said. 'I see why my wife's family residence would seem a little too small.'

'Indeed,' Sir Albert said. 'Let's not fuss about the residence any longer. Should you take up our offer, I guarantee you we'll find something more suitable.'

'Oh, how lovely,' Cordelia replied. 'In the same area?'

'Well, I can't be sure of that, Mrs Cameron. Most of the houses in that area are around the same size, you understand. We might have to look out of town.'

'Oh, how disappointing,' Cordelia said, casting her eyes down and reaching for the napkin.

'Aye. My wife must be close to the tavern, especially in her condition.'

'Well, perhaps we could compensate for the cottage's

inadequacies in some other way,' Sir Albert proffered. 'Do you think we might find some room for negotiation?'

'Aye, sir. I imagine we might.'

'Wonderful. And perhaps we can discuss the issue of theatre management at the same time.'

Samson smiled in a way that betrayed his self-satisfaction. 'Aye, I'm sure ye must know I have experience in such things.'

There was an air of awkward silence. Samson took note of the men shifting in their chairs, while the women looked to each other as if deciding who should speak first. Mrs Guilfoyle broke the silence.

'Well, the women have prevailed upon their husbands to ask if Mrs Cameron might undertake that role – in time, of course. She is after all the more renowned performer.'

Samson could not hide his reddening face, a mix of embarrassment and fury. Cordelia glanced at him, then looked straight at Mrs Guilfoyle. Cordelia's demeanour was a study in control.

'Thank you, ladies, gentlemen. I would be delighted.'

By the time they left Launceston the next morning, Sir Albert and the Camerons had agreed on a sum of one pound, five shillings for each performance for each actor, and five shillings extra for Cordelia when she began in the theatre management role. Pending was the issue of larger accommodation being found close to the London Tavern.

'In all honesty, Samson, I love the cottage,' Cordelia said as the carriage pulled away.

Samson was silent.

'And you do too, don't you?'

'Aye.'

'And we got everything we asked for, didn't we?'

'Aye.'

'And I'll be the first female theatre manager in all the colonies I'm told. So, it was a successful evening, wouldn't you say, Samson?'

'Aye,' he shrugged.

Ten

THE LAST CAMERON PERFORMANCE IN Hobart Town was on the 24th day of May 1834. It was a sell-out, as were all performances once the word was out that they were moving on. Under duress from the management, they agreed to do three extra sessions during the last week.

'A guinea *each*?' the theatre manager screeched as he turned to walk away.

Samson stood his ground and called out after him. 'I think ye know about my wife's condition, sir.'

'Surely, though …' the manager turned back to face him.

'Take it or leave it, as ye'd say, sir.'

'What did he say?' Cordelia asked as Samson walked through the front door.

'Aye, he said it's a bonnie deal.'

'Liar,' she replied, scoffing and repressing a smile.

They arrived in Launceston on the 30th day of May. The first performance at the London Tavern, in the space hereafter to be known as the Royal Olympic Theatre, was to be on the 5th of June, beginning a three nights per week season of *The Stranger*, described in the press as their 'best piece', along with a popular farce, *The Citizen*. For the first month, an experienced stage manager from Melbourne, John Meredith, had been hired by the Tavern Board to serve as theatre manager until such time as Cordelia was ready to undertake this responsibility.

By coincidence, around the time that the Camerons moved to Launceston, there was a meeting there of senior Church of England leaders. Colonial Chaplain Palmer spoke with the rector of the Launceston church, the Reverend Cecil Cottesloe, advising him about the town's new arrivals and especially of Cordelia's family connections that went all the way to the Archbishop of Canterbury. Cottesloe made it his business to secure tickets to a showing of *The Stranger* for his wife and himself. They sat in the front row, having made a show of their arrival. Cottesloe's ambition for higher duties in the Church of England was exceeded only by that of his wife.

At the end of the performance, they made their way backstage.

'We're so pleased to make your acquaintance, Mrs Cameron,' Mrs Cottesloe gushed as she grabbed Cordelia's hand. 'We naturally know of your reputation in our common homeland.'

'Thank you, Mrs Cottesloe,' Cordelia replied, trying to maintain equilibrium as her hand was being throttled. 'That's most gracious of you. Perhaps you've heard of my husband as well.'

Cordelia turned towards Samson, busy divesting himself of Mr Solomon's garb.

'Well, I never knew of him back home,' Mrs Cottesloe whispered loudly enough for him to hear. 'There are occasions when the woman's fame overwhelms that of the husband. I'm sure you agree.'

'Oh, are you speaking of your own situation?' Cordelia replied, looking into Mrs Cottesloe's eyes before turning to the rector.

'Oh, goodness, no,' Mrs Cottesloe said, her face reddening. 'My husband is a man of great reputation. He was Dean of Worcester Cathedral before being summoned to the colony.'

'Well, sub-dean at least, my dear,' Cottesloe said as he extended his hand. 'I'm most pleased to meet you, madam. Wonderful performance.'

Cordelia took Cottesloe's thin, bony hand and turned back to face her husband.

'Samson, come and meet Mr and Mrs Cottesloe. Mr Cottesloe is the Church of England rector in Launceston.'

Samson ignored her, being entirely caught up with shedding his character's clothes and wiping make-up off his face. He was taking the opportunity to scold one of the stage boys for some misstep he had made during the performance.

'Samson.'

'Aye, darling,' he turned to face Cordelia, unaware that the unbuttoned fly of his trousers was now visible to all. 'Do ye need me?'

'Oh, my,' Mrs Cottesloe uttered as she turned her head away.

'Samson!' Cordelia said sternly. 'Please cover yourself up and come over here. We have some important guests.'

'Oh, I see,' he replied, re-buttoning the fly as he walked over to join them. 'A clergyman, I see. What flavour of Christian are ye, sir, if I may ask?'

'Church of England flavour, sir,' Cottesloe replied, his free hand extended. The other one was still wrapped around the back of his wife's neck, her face buried somewhere near his shoulder. 'I do hope that meets with your favour.'

'I'm not sure my favour would matter at all to yer good self, sir,' Samson said, taking Cottesloe's free hand and squeezing as hard as he could. 'One clergyman is as good, or bad, as another.'

'Oh, indeed, indeed,' Cottesloe replied, pulling his hand away as the pain showed on his face. 'May I introduce you to my wife?'

'Certainly. Good evening, ma'am,' Samson said, wresting her hand from her husband's side. 'I'm pleased ye have the chance to meet me at last, inferior as I am to my wife's fame.'

'Oh, it's my pleasure, sir,' Mrs Cottesloe replied, red-faced and casting a furtive glance in the direction of his fly.

'It's all right, ma'am. I'm decent,' he said dismissively. 'Insignificant but decent.'

'Oh,' Mrs Cottesloe said, not sure where to look. 'I didn't mean to …'

'We do apologise,' Cordelia said, trying to save the embarrassing moment. 'Once the show is over, we do tend to treat the dressing-room as if it was our own bedroom.'

'Of course, of course,' Cottesloe said. 'We are the intruders here. And most grateful ones I add. It's such an honour to be invited back here, and on your first night as well.'

'But who invited ye, sir?' Samson said, continuing to shed parts of his costume.

'Samson,' Cordelia said, noting the startled look on the

Cottesloes' faces. 'Don't be so rude. Surely you remember the Reverend Palmer telling us about the Cottesloes.'

'No. I canna recall that.'

'Well, he did, Samson. And I was the one who said they should come backstage whenever they came to the show. I did tell you, dear.'

'Oh well, there ye go, ma'am,' he replied, looking squarely in Mrs Cottesloe's eyes. 'Insignificant and stupid.'

Samson turned away and stepped behind the modesty screen to shed the final garment. They watched as he threw the trousers over the top.

'Perhaps we should go, Cecil,' Mrs Cottesloe said, looking up at her husband.

'Of course,' Cottesloe replied. 'I'm so sorry, Mrs Cameron. We've obviously caught you at an inconvenient moment.'

'No, you haven't. And please do stay. My husband and I would love to chat with you about the town. The good things we should look out for. Things like that.'

'Well, that won't take long, my dear,' Mrs Cottesloe said, clearly relieved to have something else to talk about. 'Beastly little town. We're only here because my husband was prevailed upon to help bring some Christian civility to the place.'

'And no doubt ye've both done a bonnie job,' Samson called from behind the screen. 'I canna imagine how they survived before ye came here.'

The Cottesloes looked at Cordelia without saying a word. Restrained nodding and smiling were sufficient accompaniments to their heading for the door.

'Thank you again for coming this evening,' Cordelia said as they walked out. 'And please do let us know when we might meet again.'

Cordelia was in the process of closing the door when she

stopped, opened it fully and called to the Cottesloes, by then some ten paces away.

'Oh, and did you enjoy the show?'

'Indeed,' Cottesloe replied. 'I loved the music.'

'And Mrs Cottesloe?'

'Entertaining,' she replied without looking back.

'Samson, would you really rather we have the churches holding protests?' Cordelia scolded as they prepared for bed.

'Aye. Frankly, aye. I canna look myself in the mirror when the clergy are on my side.'

'But is it truly so bad?' Cordelia snapped, throwing her dress down on the bed. 'Surely, you can see there are good and bad among them, like anyone else. What has that poor Cottesloe gent ever done to you? Wasn't he just being friendly, or don't you understand friendly?'

'He was only being friendly because that Palmer coot told him to.'

'Perhaps, but what's so bad about that?'

'Cordelia, he's just looking to his own skin, like they all do. Why do ye think Palmer suddenly wanted to be our friend? Because he really liked us? Because he approved of the play?'

'Because Mr Sotheby told him about my father's connections,' Cordelia replied, hastening to the washstand to remove her make-up.

'Exactly,' he said, throwing on his nightshirt.

'So, what's wrong with that, for heaven's sake? It's the way the world works, Samson. No-one's beyond being able to be bribed by who knows who.'

Samson laughed. 'Even though the clergy are supposed to be beyond all that?'

'So, is that what's bothering you?' she said, turning to face him, washcloth suspended in the air. 'You think clergy should be beyond worrying about what's good for themselves?'

'Aye.'

'Oh, what a sweet, innocent, little purist you are, Samson Cameron,' she scoffed. 'Do you actually believe they should be what they say they are?'

'Aye! Is that such a stupid idea?'

'Dear little Mr Innocent, I learned long ago that clergy are like the rest of humanity. No better, no worse.'

'Well, I learned long ago that they're worse.'

'But why worse? Why?'

'Because they think they're better, but they're not. That makes them worse.'

'I don't follow you, Samson. They think they're better so that makes them worse. That makes no sense.'

'Well, I think it does. Did the Laird no say "listen to what they say but dinna do what they do?"' Why did he say that? Because they're the worst kinds of hypocrites, that's why!'

'So, they're the worst hypocrites because they say one thing and do another?'

'Aye.'

'Well, aren't you the pious one, my dear?' Cordelia turned back to face the basin and continued to rub her face furiously. 'Quoting the Bible and all?'

'Aye, I like the Bible. I just dinna like the church and its hypocritical clergy.'

'Fine, Samson, have it your way, but I'd still rather have them with us than against us. It's just been so much more pleasant without the protests. And then there's safety to consider, especially with the new little one on the way.'

'Aye, I understand, but I canna help feeling that I'm doing something worthwhile when the churches are against us.'

'Well, I'm sure you'll get your chance, but let's just keep things peaceful until the baby is born.'

'Aye, we'll keep doing *The Stranger* then whenever we can. That should flush out any of those Lady Guild types in this town.'

'And then?'

'And then we might give the Reverend Cottesloe and his wife something to really think about.'

'Oh, the wife?' Cordelia laughed. 'I'm not sure she has the wherewithal to think.'

'Aye, well now we have something we can agree on,' he said, turning back the covers and slipping into bed.

'Personally, I thought we always agreed, dear,' Cordelia replied as she slid in next to him.

'Aye, darling, when I think the same as ye do yerself.'

'And isn't that all the time?' Cordelia said, pinching his arm under the covers.

'Of course, darling.' He turned and wrapped his arm around her.

'Anyway, let's get some sleep,' Cordelia said, and rolled to face the other way. 'I'm exhausted. I'll be so relieved when this baby comes.'

After a one-week winter break, Cordelia took over as theatre manager, supported by Samson.

'Are you sure you don't mind, Samson?' It was the evening before the season was to recommence.

'Having my wife as my boss? Why would I?'

'You'll have your moment, Samson. I know it! I'm sure I'll need to hand over to you when the baby comes – for a short while, at least.'

'A short while,' Samson snuffed as he turned over in bed to face the other way. 'Anyway, let's get some sleep. We both need it. Ye especially with yer new responsibilities.'

Cordelia poked him in the back.

In the second part of the season, *The Stranger* was rested while a new play, *The Bandit of the Rhine*, took its place. The author was a New South Wales–born playwright, Evan Thomas, who had contacted Samson from Sydney some time beforehand. It was the Camerons' first venture into local thematic scene-setting, in this case one centred on bushrangers. Cordelia played the role of the heroine, Rubina, opposite Jonathan Leigh, an Irish former convict turned controversial performer. He played Feudlams, the anti-hero, at the insistence of Mrs Guilfoyle, who had known him years before in England.

> Mrs Cameron (as she always is) was perfect in her part … Leigh did justice to Feudlams.

So reported *The Examiner* of 1 August 1834.

'*Did justice?*' Samson sniggered as they sat across the table at breakfast. 'I ken they're toadying to yer lady friend again. The man canna act to save himself.'

Cordelia smiled as she took the last sip of her tea. 'Mrs Guilfoyle is not my lady friend, Samson, but I agree Jonathan has a few things to learn and I also agree that you would have surpassed him in that role.'

'Jonathan?' Samson held the slice of bread aloft. 'Aren't the two of ye getting along well?'

Cordelia stood up, ignoring him. 'Are you coming to rehearsal this morning?'

'No, I dare say ye can get on without me today.'

The second part of the season ran until early September, by which time Cordelia was almost eight months pregnant. There was a two-week break before a reprise of *The Stranger* was to herald a new season.

'I think it's going to be too difficult for ye, darling. I'll speak with Guilfoyle.'

Cordelia had been unwell throughout the break. She had gone to bed early the night before the new season was to begin.

'No, no. You mustn't, Samson. I'll be all right. I just need a good sleep and I'll be fine.'

Samson shook his head and began to pace the floor.

'And please start to call him Sir Albert, Samson. I fear you'll end up calling him Guilfoyle in public sometime.'

He sniggered. 'Or worse.'

'What could be worse, for heaven's sake?'

'Oh, I can think of a few other things I could call the bleeding dandy.'

'Like that, you mean.'

'No. Much worse than that.'

She let out a weak chuckle. 'I think I can see why the English and Scots have fought so often over the years.'

'Why?'

'Because you're just so different.'

Samson sat on the edge of the bed and looked her in the eye. 'Difference, as ye say, has naught to do with it. It's just that we're always right and they're always wrong.'

Cordelia raised herself slightly and adjusted the pillow. 'So, you're always right and I'm always wrong, is that what you're saying?'

'No, my darling. I dinna see ye as a true Sassenach.'

'What? I'm not English? What on earth am I, then, if I'm not English?'

Samson reached out and squeezed her hand, 'Ye're an *Al*bannach. A Scot.'

'How can I be a Scot if I was born in England?'

'Because ye're married to me. Ye're my wife.'

Cordelia pulled her hand away. 'So, because I'm your wife, I lose my ancestry and inherit your Scottishness. Is that what you're saying?'

'No, it's even better than that,' he replied, a broad grin on his face. 'Ye're now a *Ghaidheal*.'

'What on earth is that, Samson?' Cordelia said, the look on her face suggesting she was not sharing her husband's state of amusement.

'Ye're a Highlander!'

'A Highlander?' she shrieked. 'How ridiculous! I've never even been to the Highlands. The furthest I've travelled into Scotland is to Glasgow, and I was only a child then. I've little memory of it.'

'It doesn't matter, darling. Being my wife means ye inherit all of it.'

'And do you inherit my ancestry, then? Are you an Englishman because you're my husband?'

'God forbid!'

'So, I inherit your ancestry, but you don't inherit mine.'

'Of course.'

Cordelia slumped back on the pillow, letting out a sigh. 'And that's that? Does it not occur to you that this might be a little unfair, unequal even?'

'I canna see what the trouble is. Aren't ye Mrs Cameron? Am I Mr Bouchier?'

'Yes, of course. And, no, I didn't insist that you be Mr Bouchier. But we might have agreed to be Mr and Mrs Bouchier-Cameron. It's not unknown, you know?'

Samson scoffed. 'Perhaps, but it'd be strange, would it no'?'

'Not strange at all, Samson. Unusual, perhaps. But these things are happening. Including in Scotland. I'm sure you've heard of Mrs MacDonald-Fraser from Aberdeen.'

'Canna say I have.'

'Truly. She's a fellow playwright. Quite famous. I met her in Preston when one of her plays was on at the Playhouse Theatre. She married Thomas Fraser, the Inverness newspaper man. You know who I mean?'

'Aye, I think I've heard of him.'

'Well, when they married, they agreed to combine their names. They're now known as Mr and Mrs MacDonald-Fraser.'

Samson shook his head, conscious that he was losing his customary cool. 'Do they have any bairns?'

'I believe they do.'

'So, what are they called?'

'MacDonald-Fraser, I imagine.'

'Strange!'

'Why? Why strange? They're two prominent names. Mary MacDonald was quite famous before she married. Why should she lose her fame just because she's married?'

Samson was feeling frustrated that the light-hearted argument he had begun was becoming so heavy, not to mention one he was losing. '*Because* she's married, my dear. That's just the way it is. The wife takes the husband's name. When Margaret Tudor married King James, she became Margaret Stuart. It's just the way the Laird ordained it.'

'Oh, so, suddenly, you turn to religion. When in a tight spot and losing the argument, you call on the Lord?'

'I'm *not* losing the argument, darling.'

He could sense that Cordelia was enjoying the downturn in his mood. 'I think you already have, Samson dear. Margaret Tudor remained Margaret Tudor until the day she died. Even as Queen of Scotland, she never abandoned her maiden name.'

'Oh, well, it's just as well we're not royalty, then, isn't it?'

Cordelia closed her eyes, silent for a moment. 'Well, there are those who say we are theatre royalty. You and me.'

'Do they?'

'Yes, Mr Bouchier-Cameron. They do.'

'Is that right, Mrs Cameron-Bouchier?' he replied, smiling.

Cordelia opened her eyes and flashed a begrudging grin in his direction.

'So, do ye think if I was Mr Bouchier-Cameron, they might have asked me to be the theatre manager?'

Cordelia fell back on the pillow, closing her eyes. 'That really does irk you, doesn't it, dear?'

'No, darling. I'm proud of ye.'

'Truly?'

'Aye.'

'Well, let's face it, Samson, you might well end up doing it if I can't find a little more energy.'

'Aye, time for ye to rest now, darling.'

'Only if you do too, Samson.'

'Is that an invitation to lie with ye, Mrs Haller?'

'No, Mr Solomon,' Cordelia replied. 'You can rest on the couch. I can't have any distractions if I'm to be ready for the stage tomorrow.'

Eleven

CORDELIA'S UNDERSTUDY WAS AT STAGE side just five minutes before the evening performance of *The Stranger* on October 7th. It was the beginning of a five-night run of the play, brought back by demand after a two-week rest. Cordelia touched her on the elbow.

'It's all right, Grace. I feel fine.'

'Are you certain, Mrs Cameron? I can do it.'

'Perhaps tomorrow night, dear,' Cordelia said in a way that trucked no opposition.

Samson noted Grace's crestfallen look, a little like the small child who has just been chastised. I know how she must be feeling, he thought.

'That was ye at yer best, darling,' Samson said as they divested their costumes.

'Thank you, Samson. I thought so too.'

'It just goes to show how much people know. They all thought ye wouldn't make it past September.'

'By "all", I think you meant Grace, didn't you? She seemed rather anxious that I shouldn't make it through tonight.'

'I dinna believe that's the case,' Samson replied gently. 'I'm sure she just wants to make sure she's ready to fill yer big shoes.'

'Samson, you don't know women like I do. Most especially ambitious young actresses.'

'I'm quite certain I don't, darling, but she does seem like a pleasant young lass to me.'

'Mmm,' Cordelia murmured, back turned as she rubbed off her make-up. 'Just be careful, Samson. You're not an unattractive man, you know?'

'I'm not sure I've heard ye say that before, darling. I think playing Mrs Haller might be rubbing off on ye.'

'Don't be foolish,' she spat back, disposing of the damp cloth, then wincing as she grabbed her extended stomach.

'Are ye all right?' Samson rushed to her side.

'Ooh,' Cordelia clutched at her stomach and bent forward.

'Darling.'

'Samson, I think I saw Mrs Crawford there tonight. She mightn't be too far away.'

'Don't go anywhere, darling.' Samson was running towards the door, still half attired as Mr Solomon.

'Of course, I won't be going anywhere, you silly man.' Cordelia fell back on the nearest settee.

They had met Mrs Crawford just once, at her house. She had been recommended as an experienced midwife. Samson was readying to run in the direction of her house, beating his way through the small crowd at the front of the tavern when he all but knocked her off her feet.

'Is everything all right, Mr Cameron?' Mrs Crawford was steadying herself.

'I'm sorry, ma'am. I think my wife needs ye.'

'Son, go home and get my bag,' Mrs Crawford called to the young boy as Samson was yanking her in the direction of the dressing room. 'And bring it here – quickly.'

'Yes, Ma,' young Crawford shouted back as his mother disappeared into the alleyway as quickly as Samson could pull her.

It was a little after one o'clock in the morning on the 8th day of October that Mrs Crawford ascertained that she was faced with a breech birth. Her son's second duty of the night was to ride the short distance to the settlement of Invermay, on the Tamar River, to fetch a more experienced midwife.

'Surely there's someone closer to hand,' Samson protested.

'Yes,' Mrs Crawford replied. 'But not one with Miss Rusdon's experience in these things.'

'These things?' he said, his eyes strained, his head shaking.

It was then that Samson was told about the anticipated breech birth and some of the challenges.

'Now, Mr Cameron. I really think it would be best if you stepped outside.'

'No, no, please, Mrs Crawford. I want my husband here.'

'Well, it's most unusual.'

'Aye,' Samson said as he stepped forward and held Cordelia's hand. 'They say that about thespians, ye ken.'

Mrs Crawford ignored him and went about her business.

A bleary-eyed Miss Rusdon stepped into the dressing-room around two o'clock in the morning.

'Good morning, Mrs Crawford.'

'Good morning, Miss Rusdon. You're a sight for sore eyes.'

'Who is this gentleman and why is he here?' Miss Rusdon scowled in Samson's direction. 'Please tell him to step outside. It's no place for a man. And that's that!'

'This is Mrs Cameron's husband.' Mrs Crawford raised her eyebrows. 'She says she wants him here.'

'Step aside, man.' Miss Rusdon pushed Samson away from Cordelia's outstretched hand. 'Well, the woman's clearly delusional.'

Miss Rusdon peered into Cordelia's bloodshot eyes and rubbed her puffed up cheeks.

'Trust me, dear, you'll thank me later that your husband wasn't here for the worst of it.'

Mrs Crawford and Samson looked at each other. Crawford cast her eyes towards the door. Samson took three steps in its direction.

'No-o, *no-o,*' Cordelia screamed. 'Stay, Samson, stay. I want you to know what I have to go through.'

He hurried back to the bedside, squeezing his body between the wall and the midwife.

'I'm here, darling. And I dinna care what this wretched woman says. I'm staying.'

'Good Lord,' Miss Rusdon exclaimed. 'I've never—'

'With respect, Miss Rusdon,' Mrs Crawford said. 'I think it might be best to let them have their way.'

Miss Rusdon huffed and puffed her way to the business end of delivering a baby. She continued to say nothing, bar a few basic instructions to push, take a deep breath, push harder, interspersed with manipulating the infant's position. The whole body was finally freed from Cordelia around two thirty. Hence, a son, John

Pearce Cameron, was born in the early hours of the 8th day of October 1834.

Miss Rusdon quickly washed and headed for the door.

'I'm sure you can take things from here, Mrs Crawford.'

'Ah, yes, thank you again, Miss Rusdon.'

As she reached the door, she stopped and looked back.

'I'd suggest you take things easy for the next few days, Mrs Cameron.'

'Thank you, Miss Rusdon,' Cordelia whispered with what seemed like a dying breath. 'Thank you so much.'

'That's perfectly all right. Now, I have only one thing to ask of you. Please tell no-one I let the husband stay. Heaven knows where that might lead.'

'Your secret is safe with us,' Mrs Crawford said as the door was swinging shut.

'Thank you again, Miss Rusdon,' Cordelia called breathlessly as the door slammed. 'Samson, please go after her and thank her.'

'Aye, darling. I'll see to it later.'

'I'll be fine, Samson,' Cordelia said from her bed on the late afternoon of the same day. 'Mrs Crawford has offered to look after the baby. She's been a mother seven times and it will only be for a few hours.'

'No, darling. I forbid it.'

Cordelia raised her head, staring him down. 'Forbid? Samson, what are you saying?'

Samson stood his ground at the foot of the bed. 'I'm saying I forbid it. Ye had a harrowing time of it and ye need yer rest. Ye heard what Miss Rusdon said.'

'Oh, so suddenly the "silly old cow", as you described her, knows what she's talking about. Is that it?'

'I suppose. But it's only common sense. Just have a look at yerself in the mirror. I doubt ye'd make it through the first act.'

Cordelia's head slumped back down on the pillow. 'Oh, but I hate missing a performance. You know that. And Grace …'

'What about Grace?'

'Well, she's so inexperienced.'

'Aye. And I know why. Ye never give her a chance to prove herself.'

'I suppose so, but if I agree, it will only be for tonight. Is that clear?'

'Aye, darling. Understood!'

'The role of Mrs Haller will be played by Grace Bellingham,' John Meredith announced a few seconds before the pianist struck the first note.

The music was quickly drowned out by the din coming from the audience. Howls of protest were sprinkled through the crowd, some standing on their seats and shouting berated accusations with others trying to haul the seat-standers down, beseeching calm.

The ringing shot of a pistol finally brought a moment of silence. It was quickly overtaken with shrieks of alarm. People began clambering over each other headed for the back door. A second shot rang out.

'Order. *Ooordeeer*,' the constable shouted. 'Can everyone please sit back down?'

'I paid good money to see Mrs Cameron,' one man shouted back.

'And we're not staying unless she's here,' the woman next to him called.

'Then I suggest you leave,' the constable called back.

'But what about our money?'

'I'll be happy to refund anyone who wants to leave,' Meredith announced from the stage area.

Amidst much mumbling and grumbling, half the audience took their seats, while the other half slowly made their way towards the door, most of them glaring through fierce eyes at the constable.

'Ladies and gentlemen.' Samson's voice boomed out from the stage area.

Bit by bit, people began looking in his direction, including those on the way out who stopped in their tracks and turned to see who was speaking.

'Ladies and gentlemen,' he repeated in a less booming way. 'Do ye not see what ye're doing?'

The shuffling and murmuring ceased.

'No, Mr Cameron,' a single voice called. 'Do tell us what we're doing.'

'What ye're doing is stamping on my wife's good graces. She's the one who's put Miss Bellingham before ye tonight because she wants to leave something of herself here when she finally leaves. That's how much she cares for ye all, that she wants to leave the best of herself with ye and she thinks Miss Bellingham is the best of herself. By turning yer backs on her, ye're as good as turning them on Mrs Cameron. Could ye think about that before ye walk out into the street?'

The murmuring began again, then died as the audience members moved back to their seats. Only a handful took the opportunity to walk out.

Thank ye, ladies and gents,' Samson said. 'My wife will be forever grateful for yer kindness.'

'Please send her our best wishes,' one member called out.

'And our love,' a male voice shouted. 'Send her our love, Mr Cameron.'

'He just means our affection,' a female voice sounded from the same vicinity. 'Don't ye, love?'

A chuckling rippled through the members as they were reclaiming their seats.

'Aye, yer love and affection. I'll let her know. Thank ye, ladies and gentlemen. And I'm certain ye'll not be disappointed.'

As the members sat down, a lone clap was followed by loud clapping from all corners of the theatre. Samson retreated behind the makeshift curtain that began to open for Act One. Grace Bellingham stood mid-stage, teary-eyed and sweating, as the opening bars from the piano were heard.

'Good on you, Gracie,' an audience member shouted.

Another round of clapping was overwhelmed by shushing. The constable's shushing, pistol in hand, was the loudest and most effective. Finally, silence and the pianist began the opening piece for the second time.

Twelve

'How was it?' Cordelia whispered as Samson stepped into the bedroom that evening.

'Darling, I really thought ye'd be asleep,' he replied in full voice as he sat on the edge of the bed and threw his boots on the floor.

The baby stirred. 'With a newborn? You've obviously forgotten. So many things you forget, Samson,' Cordelia spat back, shaking her head as she tried to restore the baby's calm. 'And can you please come in more quietly in future?'

'Sorry, my darling,' he reached over and placed a hand on the baby's head.

Cordelia shushed the baby until he fell back to sleep. She whispered, 'Anyway, tell me. Did Grace do all right?'

'Grace? Aye, well enough,' Samson replied as he casually reached under the pillow for his nightshirt.

'Meaning what?' Cordelia said sternly. 'Sensational or was she merely all right?'

'Somewhere in between.' He threw the nightshirt on and

slipped in next to her. He looked down at the tiny bundle in her arms. 'And how is wee John then?'

Cordelia ignored him. 'So, better than all right?'

'Aye,' he replied absently as he focused on the baby.

'But not sensational?'

'No.' Samson hadn't missed the tension in her voice. He smiled extravagantly at the baby. 'He's a braw wee lad, aye?'

Cordelia leant closer to catch his attention. 'So, I shouldn't be worried that I'm superfluous to need?'

He sighed. *Well that didn't work.* 'No, darling. Ye could never be that.'

'Good.'

'But how are ye? And the bairn? That's more important.'

Cordelia slumped back on the pillow. 'Oh, all right, I suppose. Still sore and a bit groggy. Me, I mean.'

'Well, I'm not surprised. I think ye'd have to know now that ye couldn't have performed tonight?'

'I didn't say that,' she snapped. 'Are you sure Grace wasn't better than something less than sensational?'

Like a dog with a bone. 'Absolutely, darling. She filled in well.'

'So, the audience liked her, did they?'

Samson was cooing at the sleeping babe.

'Samson!' Cordelia demanded.

He looked up. 'Oh, aye, I think they thought she was more than adequate.'

'But not sensational?'

'No.'

'How long did the applause go?'

'I dinna know, darling, but not as long as yers, be assured.' Samson lay back on the pillow and closed his eyes.

'But how long? I mean compared to mine?'

Samson opened his eyes and looked up at her. 'I didna count, darling. Maybe half?'

'Half as long? Only half? Are you sure?'

'Roughly.'

'You're not sure, are you?'

Will she never be reassured? 'I wasna watching the clock, Cordelia. All right?'

'Well, so long as it wasn't as long as mine, I suppose I'm safe turning up tomorrow night.'

'Tomorrow night? Do ye really think ye'll be well enough by then?'

'Of course, Samson. I'm not missing two nights in a row. Unless there's something you're not telling me. Just how good was Grace?'

'She was more than adequate, darling, but nowhere near as good as ye are.'

'You're sure?'

'Aye. I'm sure. Now, can I get ye anything before I go to sleep?'

'Perhaps a glass of milk?'

Samson stepped out of bed and headed for the kitchen. *Let's just hope the* Advertiser *critic doesn't write about the loud applause and wolf whistles when Grace took her final bows.*

'Samson, we need more milk and eggs,' Cordelia called from the bedroom the following morning. 'Could you?'

'Not at all. I'll go now.' Samson took the last gulp from his teacup.

She hasn't asked for the newspaper. He smiled as he grabbed his coin purse and hastened to the door.

'And don't forget the *Advertiser*,' he heard as he was about to pull the door shut.

Samson strode down the hill to the corner shop, rehearsing the lines he might need in case the story of Grace's overwhelming success had made it to the paper.

'Thank you, Mr Cameron,' the shopkeeper said, pouring the silver and copper change into his hand.

He turned and walked to the far corner near the groceries stand. Placing the milk and eggs on a rack, he turned the paper to a small entertainment section at the back. The only entry was about the non-compliant lion at the circus the night before and whether the event should have been set up at some more suitable venue.

Saved! He grinned and strode out of the shop and into the street, a renewed spring in his step.

'Anything about last night in the paper?' Cordelia called from the bedroom.

He walked in to see her re-positioning John's mouth over her nipple. 'I havena had a chance to look, darling,' he lied. He handed her the paper and bent to kiss her cheek, rubbing a hand over the baby's head.

He walked the milk and eggs to the cupboard and stood in silence until the rustling of the newspaper stopped.

'Mmm.' He heard her murmur. 'What would you think about Grace doing one more night?'

'Are ye not feeling so well?' he replied, hastening back to the bedroom.

'Just a little tired. I thought perhaps another night off might be a good idea. Or will the audience be too upset, do you think?'

'I'm sure they'll be fine, darling. Yer health is all that matters.'

'Very well, then. Would you mind letting Grace know? And thank her for me and tell her I'll definitely be back tomorrow night.'

'Aye, I'd best let her know immediately. Should I go now? Are ye all right with the bairn?'

'Perfectly all right, Samson. John really is such a treasure.' Cordelia looked up from the baby to glance in her husband's direction. 'Just like his father, I suppose you'll say.'

'Not at all. I'm sure he takes after ye, dear. Ye're my treasure.'

'Off with you now,' Cordelia said, grunting and offering the smallest of smiles in his direction. 'And do thank Grace for me.'

'Aye, I'm sure she'll be delighted,' he said, throwing on his coat and heading for the door.

'Yes, I've no doubt about that,' he heard her mumbling as he closed the door behind him.

Samson strode off to take him the half mile or so to Grace's lodgings. He was congratulating himself on negotiating the shoals of a difficult situation. If Cordelia knew of the raucous applause Grace had received the night before, she would have insisted on doing tonight's performance. And if she had, the audience might actually have been disappointed. Grace was one of them, after all.

Aye, well, at some point this shoal might still win the day but at least he'd avoided it so far.

Samson was feeling weary by the time he made it to the guest house, grabbing the railing that took him up the ten steps to the front door. He rapped on one of the frosted, cracked glass panes and waited until the shadow of an inhabitant could be seen hastening towards the door on the other side. The slender figure told him it might well be Grace.

'Mr Cameron, what are you doing here?' she gushed excitedly as she opened the door. 'Do come in and please excuse the mess.'

Samson couldn't hide the look of shock as he stepped into the hallway to see the peeling paint and wallpaper, the torn and tattered carpet, and to smell a dankness that spoke of long-term mould.

'Oh, Grace, I…'

'I know, Mr Cameron. I'm hoping to get something better when I …' She choked on the words.

'When ye can afford it,' he said, finishing her sentence.

She nodded and smiled as she ushered him to the common sitting room and pointed to the one large, shabby, upholstered chair with massive arms. She pulled up a small stool and sat opposite him, suddenly letting loose a torrent of babble about how she hadn't expected him and was sorry about her unbrushed hair and how she would have had something prepared if she had known he was coming.

Samson sat quietly, smiling on the inside as he took in her beaming expression and the refreshing vision of youth that sat in such stark contrast to her execrable lodgings. Grace's auburn hair and green eyes would go unnoticed in Scotland, he thought, but, heavens, they did stand out here in the Antipodes.

'Of course, Mr Cameron,' she replied when he told her the purpose of his visit. 'I'd love to do it. Is Mrs Cameron not well?'

'Just a wee bit tired. It was not an easy birth.'

'When do you think she'll be back then? I mean able to perform?'

'Oh, I think she'll want to be back tomorrow, but ye'll have tonight to prove that last night was no fluke.'

'Is that what you think, Mr Cameron?' Her bright eyes dimmed with self-doubt. 'That it was a fluke? Do you really think I'm not very good?'

'No, Grace. I'm not saying that at all. To be honest, I think it was a near perfect performance.'

'Truly?' her eyes widened, and her smile lit up the room. 'Do you mean that? Was I truly as good as that?'

'Aye. Grace, ye could not have been any better.'

'But you don't mean I was as good as Mrs Cameron?'

Samson hesitated, glancing towards the floor.

'Oh, Mr Cameron, I'm sorry. That was so rude of me. Are you all right?'

'Aye, Grace,' he replied, looking into those contrite eyes that would haunt him for some time to come. 'Let's just say ye were a very good second best. The best second best.'

'Thank you so much, Mr Cameron,' she said, bounding off the stool and reaching down to give him a hug.

Samson involuntarily pulled back and to one side, causing her to stumble forward. Before either of them could stop it, she was half sitting on his lap.

'Oh, I'm so sorry, Mr Cameron!' Grace quickly lifted herself off and stood before him, face fully blushed and eyes tear-filled. 'I didn't mean for that to happen. Oh, I'm so embarrassed. It's just that, coming from you, that means so much. So very much.'

Grace lowered herself back onto the stool, looking up at him from underneath her long eyelashes, as if appealing for forgiveness.

'That's perfectly all right, lass. I was just not expecting it. After all, it's not every day that a bonnie young thing like ye throws herself at me.'

'Oh, sir, I... I didn't... I...'

Another feeble attempt at humour, Samson thought.

'Anyway, Grace. We'll see ye tonight, then?' he said as he stood and eased his way towards the door. She was still sitting on the stool, head now in her hands. He briefly placed his hand on her shoulder as he moved past her, the strands of her hair gently tickling his small finger.

'Mr Cameron,' she called as he was about to let himself out. Samson stepped back to the open door of the sitting room and craned his head around to see her. 'Please don't tell Mrs Cameron about this.'

Samson walked down the steps and onto the pathway. He found himself staring at the gravel beneath his feet as he trod along, remembering that last pleading gaze on her face. Brushing an auburn strand out of one of her glistening eyes, choking on the words of entreaty. He saw for the first time her vulnerability, like a small bird he could crush unless taking great care.

He stopped in his tracks, tempted for a moment to go back and reassure her. *But would I be doing that for her or for myself?* He was snapped out of his indecision by sounds of what might be an omnibus behind the tree line ahead. He was tired and keen to get home as quickly as possible. Once beyond the trees, he saw it was a private carriage. May as well keep walking for now. He could use the time to think anyway. Why did he have this feeling of unease?

'Good day, Mr Cameron,' a voice jolted him into the moment.

'Oh, good morning,' he replied to the unknown gent with outstretched hand.

'Wonderful performance last night,' he said, grasping and shaking Samson's hand with verve. 'And what a find is Miss Bellingham.'

'Aye, she's doing very well for a newcomer.'

'A newcomer, you say?'

Samson was trying to withdraw his hand, to no avail. 'Aye, she's only done amateur work until now.'

'Well, you certainly wouldn't know, would you?'

'No, indeed. She shows much promise. I really think she'll be a fine performer in time.'

'More than fine, young man,' a female voice came from behind.

'Oh, Mr Cameron,' the man said, finally releasing Samson's hand. 'This is my wife, Mrs Livingstone.'

Samson turned around just in time to steer away from Mrs Livingstone's lips heading for his cheek. He pulled his head away, causing her to stumble forward. It seemed this was the day for such awkward manoeuvres! One look at Mrs Livingstone told him that this one would not haunt him in the same way, though the smell of cheap perfume would linger.

'I'm so thrilled to meet you, Mr Cameron,' she said as she steadied herself. 'We so love your work. I appreciate it more than most, of course, because I was an actress myself for some time. But my husband has some appreciation for the theatre even though he's more the business type, you understand. Don't you find it frustrating how so few understand what it's like for people like you and me, who are courageous enough to get up in front of an audience and share our talents …?'

Samson backed away and collided with Mr Livingstone, who yelped.

'Oh, my heavens!' Samson turned and looked down at Mr Livingstone's damaged shoe.

'That's all right,' Mrs Livingstone continued. 'My husband is so clumsy. Anyway, as I was saying …'

'Aye, it's lovely to have met ye but I must get back to my wife. We have a new bairn at home, ye know?'

Samson turned and hurried away.

'Oh, we know,' Mrs Livingstone called after him. 'That's why that wonderful Miss Bellingham was on the stage last night. Did you read that splendid review in the *Advertiser*?'

Samson stopped in his tracks, turning back to face the Livingstones now hot in pursuit.

'I didna think there was a review.'

'Oh, yes, I have it here,' Mrs Livingstone said, pulling the newspaper from her string bag. 'It was in the later edition. Here, you can have it.'

'And please don't wait here on our account, Mr Cameron,' Mr Livingstone said, catching Samson's eye as he came up behind his wife. 'We know you have to get home.'

'Thank ye so much,' Samson said as he took the newspaper. 'Do I owe ye anything?'

'Oh, no,' Mrs Livingstone said. 'Being a fellow actor, I know it can be a struggle sometimes – financially, I mean. And you with a young family …'

'Thank ye again,' he said, turning and walking swiftly away.

'And do let me know if I can assist,' Mrs Livingstone called after him. 'We live in the same street as Miss Bellingham.'

'Thank ye. If we need any help with the bairn, I'll know where to find ye.'

'Oh, I don't mean that,' she raised her voice, so a passer-by stared at her. 'I mean on stage, me being an actress and all.'

Samson raised his hand and waved as he strode away as fast as his legs could carry him. Once around the corner, he looked for a safe place to stop and scour the newspaper. He spotted a small grassy patch with a bench seat. He noticed an elderly couple walking towards the seat.

Dinna sit there, he willed. *Please!*

The elderly couple kept walking.

Thank the Laird.

Samson reached the bench able to accommodate three persons, sat in the middle and pulled the *Advertiser* from under his arm. An aroma of cheap perfume wafted into the air and up his nose, causing him to sneeze three times before reaching for a handkerchief.

Having dispatched the handkerchief to its home in his trouser pocket, he commenced the task of leafing through the paper, starting from the back. Where was it? Five pages in, the words leapt out.

A Star is Born.

Samson rubbed his eyes and focused. He had been meaning to purchase some spectacles, but life had been too busy. Now, with the glare of the afternoon sun on the paper, his eyes were failing him.

No doubt, Grace Bellingham surpassed Cordelia Cameron through her fine portrayal of Mrs Haller.

His heart sank, his mind turning to a desperate scheme by which he might keep the story from Cordelia. Giving up on that idea, he was scrambling to find the words needed to pacify her.

Of course, Grace didna surpass ye.

How ridiculous!

There's no-one alive who could do that.

It's only a newspaper.

It was the clip-clop and rattle of the omnibus that jolted him from his all-consuming rehearsal.

I have to get to her before anyone else does. He rose and hastened towards the sound. The omnibus came into view. He raised his arm to signal the driver. As the horse came to a stop, he noticed a handful of passengers already aboard.

'Where ye headed, guv'nor?' the driver called.

'Lower Tamar Street.'

As Samson stepped up, he tipped the brim of his hat in the direction of a kindly-looking woman sitting opposite a spare seat. She nodded in acknowledgement as he sat down.

Seated now in the shade of the omnibus, he opened the pages of the newspaper again.

No doubt, Grace Bellingham surprised Cordelia Cameron through her fine portrayal of Mrs Haller.

As he held the newspaper closer to his straining eyes, blessed relief overtook him.

Surprised, not surpassed.

He was tempted to ask his fellow passenger to confirm what he hoped he had read. He looked her way. She glanced up.

'Did you need some assistance, young man?'

'No, thank ye.' Samson smiled.

'It's good to see you smile, young man. I must say you looked as though you had the weight of the world on your shoulders when you got on.'

'Aye. I ken for a moment that I did.'

'Oh, you're Scottish, aren't you?'

'Aye.'

'Oh, I love the accent. You remind me of that wonderful man who's in the play in town.'

'At the London Tavern?'

'Yes, have you seen it?'

'Many times.'

'Oh, I say, you are *he*, aren't you?'

Samson nodded, blushing.

'How silly of me. And that wonderful actress. She's your wife, isn't she?'

'When did you go?' he asked, fearing his problem was about to be exacerbated.

'Two nights ago.'

'Aye, that was my wife,' he replied, beaming smile all over his face. 'She's wonderful, isn't she?'

'Oh, the best, the very best,' the woman replied, letting out a chuckle. 'She certainly is. My husband and I come from Melbourne. We go to concerts whenever we can, and we agree that she is the best singer we've heard anywhere.'

'Well, I'll be sure to tell her.'

'Oh, please do. We're just down here visiting our daughter. When she suggested taking us to the theatre, we weren't very keen. We frankly didn't imagine anything in Launceston would be worth going to. But fortunately, she persuaded us.'

'Your stop, ma'am,' the driver called as the vehicle slowed.

'Well, this is where I get off, young man.' The woman reached up for the strap hanging from the side of the vehicle. 'It's been lovely meeting you. And please do tell your wife how much we admire her talent.'

'I certainly will.' Samson stood and helped the woman onto the running board. 'And thank ye again.'

'Goodbye, young man,' she replied as she stepped away.

'Farewell, ma'am.'

'Oh, I love it,' she said, giggling. 'I just love that brogue. I'm so excited to tell my husband I met you.'

Samson waved as the omnibus began moving. Sitting back down, he felt the weight of the world had been lifted. There was no need for further rehearsing of lines. A single word had saved the situation. *Surprised?* Yes, of course, Cordelia might have been surprised at how well Grace had done. He could manage that conversation. *Surpassed*, on the other hand, would have meant a conversation quite beyond him.

And then he could tell her about the lady from Melbourne as well.

There was a spring in his step as he alighted and made his way to their lodgings. He was halfway down the pathway when the screeching and wailing sounds forced him to stop. He stood still, listening intently, head whirling. It was Cordelia doing the screeching, barely audible over the baby's cries.

Who was she shouting at? Samson's heart sank again. He slipped back into rehearsal mode as he slowly made his way to the door.

'How dare he?' were the first words he heard clearly. 'Doesn't he know I've performed in the best theatres in England? Grace is nothing more than a young upstart!'

By the time Samson turned the handle on the door, he knew what awaited him.

'Samson, thank God you're here.' Cordelia strode towards him, babe in arms.

'What's the trouble, darling?' Samson hoisted young John out of her arms. The baby began a new round of wailing.

'Ask her what the trouble is!' Cordelia spat out, turning, and pointing with the finger of her now spare hand to the shadow standing behind her. 'Ask *her* what the trouble is! She's the one making trouble.'

Samson's eyes were still adjusting to the dim light in the front room. He was struggling to make out the identity of the woman whose shadow gradually came into focus.

'Good afternoon, Mr Cameron.'

'Mrs Guilfoyle, is it?'

'Yes, Mr Cameron. It is.'

'How can we help ye, Mrs Guilfoyle?'

'By getting on a boat and going home,' Cordelia shouted. 'Apparently!'

'Mrs Cameron, we're not saying that at all. You must know how pleased we've been with all you've done for us.'

'So pleased you want to sack us? Or is it just me you want to sack?'

Cordelia rushed to the settee in the corner. She slumped down, beckoning for young John to be returned to her arms. Samson could see that she was half sitting on a copy of the *Advertiser*. She reached down with her free hand and threw it to the floor. She shoved the baby onto her breast and proceeded to bury her face in his neck, weeping audibly.

'What's the trouble, Mrs Guilfoyle?' Samson turned to face their visitor. 'Why are ye here?'

'Mr Cameron, as I was trying to explain to Mrs Cameron, my husband has asked me to take some interest in the younger players. You know some of them are a long way from home. I simply came here to suggest that Grace take Mrs Cameron's place for a while to give your wife the chance to recover from the difficulties of giving birth and, at the same time, to give Grace a chance to advance her theatre skills.'

'Advance her theatre skills?' Cordelia shrieked, the baby jumping in fright. 'From what I'm reading, they're already more advanced than they should be for a young vagabond like her.'

'Now, now, darling,' Samson said, kneeling down in front of her. 'Grace did well last night but I was just speaking with a lady in the omnibus who said how wonderful ye are. She often goes to concerts in Melbourne, but she said she has never heard a better voice than yours.'

'Oh, so the lady in the omnibus knows better than that vile critic from the *Advertiser*. Have you seen what he said?'

'Ah, aye, I did read that but all he said was that ye might be surprised at how good she was. Well, ye were surprised, weren't ye?'

'We were all surprised,' Mrs Guilfoyle said. 'She really was quite remarkable. You must agree, Mr Cameron.'

'Well, do you, Mr Cameron?' Cordelia said, her piercing eyes staring at her husband on bended knee.

'She was good,' he said, touching the baby's cheek. 'I told ye that, darling.'

'Samson, I asked you to be honest with me. But you weren't, were you? From what that foul critic said, not to mention the foul wife of Sir Albert standing here, she was better than I. Do you think she was better than I? Answer me truthfully, Samson.'

'Foul?' Mrs Guilfoyle said in an affected tone as she turned towards the door. 'Why, I've never been so insulted. Wait until I tell Sir Albert.'

'Please, Mrs Guilfoyle,' Samson said, bouncing to his feet. 'Ye know my wife has just been through a difficult time. She doesna always know quite what she's saying.'

'I believe she knows exactly what she's saying on this occasion. And she's right. This foul woman agrees with the foul critic. Grace was far and above a more convincing, vibrant Mrs Haller than your wife could possibly be.'

'Mrs Guilfoyle,' Samson said with a pleading look. 'Please listen.'

Mrs Guilfoyle took a step towards the door before turning back to face them. 'No, Mr Cameron. You can listen. And when your wife is in a more civil mood, perhaps she will listen too. If it were up to me, I would ask you both to leave Launceston as soon as possible, but I know my husband will have a different view on that. Even after I tell him what I've endured today, he will no doubt tell me that he is obligated by contract to keep you on. And if that's so, I just want your wife to know that the only reason she will be tolerated in this town is because she is your wife.'

'Mrs Guilfoyle,' Samson tried again, taking one step towards her.

'Your wife, Mr Cameron.' She put her hand up to signal he should not come any closer. 'That's why she will remain here. Not because she is a fine actress because, frankly, we now have a finer actress in the person of Grace Bellingham.'

'Mrs Guilfoyle,' Cordelia called as she stood and pulled the baby around to rest on her other shoulder.

'Yes, Mrs Cameron. If you wish to apologise, then please do it quickly. I'm a busy woman.'

'Perhaps busy body would be a better phrase, madam.'

'Well, I never,' Mrs Guilfoyle spat back as she turned again towards the door.

'Do not go out that door, Mrs Guilfoyle,' Cordelia shouted. 'You need to hear me on this.'

'Hear what?' Mrs Guilfoyle said, looking back at Cordelia as she turned the doorknob.

'I will be performing tonight, Mrs Guilfoyle. Be sure to tell that to Sir Albert. I will be Mrs Haller tonight and every night we are in this godforsaken place. And the moment anyone tries to change that, we will close the theatre altogether for breach of contract.

'You cannot do that,' Mrs Guilfoyle said, continuing to swivel the squeaky doorknob.

'Oh, but we can, Mrs Guilfoyle. And we will. Now, good afternoon. I must rest before tonight's performance.'

Thirteen

'Are ye sure this is a good idea, darling? Ye look a wee bit frail.'

'I'm fine, Samson,' Cordelia replied harshly as she began to step onto the stage. 'It's not only a good idea. It's the only idea. We cannot let these people win.'

'Aye, I know ye're right, darling. Just be careful. Ye dinna look as well as I'd like.'

Cordelia moved to the chair in the middle of the stage and gave the signal for the curtain to open, then launched into her speech.

'Why, oh why, have I trodden the path of turpitude?'

Samson's attention was fully on Cordelia as he listened for the slightest pause or gravelly voice that might give away her unwellness.

'I'll go home, sir,' Grace was whispering in his ear.

He turned to see her tear-filled eyes reflected in the candlelight from the stage.

'Oh, Grace, I canna say how sorry I am.'

'It's all right, Mr Cameron. I know it's not your fault. I'm just grateful for the opportunity you gave me.'

'One that ye took with both hands, lass. Ye deserve all the braw things people have been saying.'

'Thank you, sir.'

'But please know,' he said, winking as he pressed her hand, 'ye canna tell Mrs Cameron what I said.'

Grace's eyes lit up as she suppressed a chortle with her other hand before placing it on his arm.

'I would never do that,' she whispered.

They smiled at each other as she turned to leave.

'Grace,' he called in a loud whisper.

She turned back and tiptoed towards him. Her eyes widened in appealing an explanation.

'Grace, could ye stay a while?' he said, having to speak above the now noisy stage banter.

'If you wish, sir, but why?'

'I think ye just might have to be on stage. Listen to Mrs Cameron.'

'But why, good sir, do you dally when you should hasten?'

'She's saying the opposite, sir.'

'Aye, and that's the second time she's got it wrong. I dinna think she's well.'

'And her voice doesn't sound normal either. What are you going to do, sir?'

'Aye, I doubt she'll be able to sing but that's not until Act Two. Do ye think ye could fill in after that?'

Grace's eyes lit up. 'Of course, sir, but do you think she'll let me?' She reached out as if to grab his arm again before quickly withdrawing her hand.

'I'm not sure, Grace. I'm really not. Just be ready, could ye?'

'Of course, sir.'

During the final ten minutes of Act One, with Grace by his

side, Samson watched and listened as Cordelia's voice became less and less audible and her diction more incomprehensible. Those on props, lighting and curtains assembled on both wings of the stage, seemingly ready to run on and save Cordelia should she show more worrying signs of collapse. The minutes seemed like hours until, finally, the makeshift curtain was lowered for the end of Act One. They had less than five minutes to make the change that all knew must happen.

Samson was the first to reach Cordelia, who was sitting on the chair and waving a fan furiously around her face.

'Ye're not well, are ye, darling?'

Samson was confident that she would acknowledge her struggle and relent. He placed his hand under her elbow and began to lift her.

'I'll get someone to take ye home.'

Cordelia pulled away, sitting back down with determination. 'Home? Why would I be going home?'

Samson leant down, hand on her shoulder, and spoke softly close to her ear. 'Do ye really not know, darling? Ye were getting yer lines wrong, and yer voice sounds bad.'

'I was *not*, Samson,' she replied loudly. 'There was only that one line where I got things back-to-front. That happens – even to you occasionally, my dear. And my voice is fine.'

'Darling, I know ye know. Just ask anyone here. We're all worried ye might collapse.'

Cordelia turned her head quickly to face the wing where Grace was standing. 'Oh, so by anyone, you mean Madame Bellingham standing over there, hoping I'll collapse?' She turned back to face Samson and lowered her voice. 'Well, you can tell that smug little piece that she can go home. *I'm* Mrs Haller tonight, and that's that!'

Samson opened his mouth to speak, but nothing came forth. Cordelia, eyes afire, looked again towards Grace and then to him standing over her.

'And, speaking of which, are you ready, Mr Solomon?'

'Aye,' he replied, drawing the deepest of breaths.

'Is Mrs Cameron going on, is she?' Grace asked as he hastened past her, heading for the dressing-room.

'I'm afraid so, Grace, but it'll be good if ye can stay all the same.'

'I will, Mr Cameron.'

'Ye're a bonnie lass, Grace, dear,' he called back as he closed the dressing-room door.

Grace turned to face the stage, a satisfied smile on her face.

Mrs Cordelia Cameron's performance last night reminded us why we were so exulted on the previous evening with Miss Grace Bellingham's rendition of Mrs Haller. Those of us who cherish the theatre can only hope and pray that Mrs Cameron accepts that her time has come. Indeed, it might well have come some time ago.

The *Advertiser* review went on to exhort the Tavern Board to remedy the situation as quickly as possible, even at the expense of losing both the famous thespians.

Miss Bellingham has reminded us of the talent being bred in the colonies without the need to look to the Motherland. If she can better Mrs Cameron's Mrs Haller, as was so clearly the case, we can only wonder how many fine young actors are currently waiting in the wings to replace Mr Cameron's Mr Solomon.

'What did I say?' Mrs Guilfoyle threw the newspaper across the breakfast table. Sir Albert grabbed his teacup lest its contents spoil the tablecloth.

'She obviously should not have performed last night,' Sir Albert replied, his eyes darting across the table to see if any damage had been done. 'I'm not sure why she did. I know Mr Cameron made a special trip to Miss Bellingham's house to ensure she was available.'

'Of course, she shouldn't have,' Mrs Guilfoyle spat out. 'The woman is a vixen. You need to get rid of them both.'

'As you've said a few times, dear. I'm not quite sure what it is about Mrs Cameron that riles you so. I don't suppose you know why she performed last night. You did go to see her yesterday, didn't you?'

'I did and I've no idea. The insolent woman is beyond redemption.'

'So, you do know why she got out of a sickbed to perform?'

'I didn't say that, Albert.'

'I can't go on tonight.' Cordelia slumped in her chair, baby John attached for his morning feed. 'How could I face that vile man after this?'

'Who?' Samson replied, looking up from the newspaper.

'Mr Stewart.'

'The journalist? He's the least of our worries.'

'The least of yours, perhaps. If he's there tonight, he'll be looking for the tiniest stumble. The smallest crease in my blouse. Anything to fill his rotten story for tomorrow's edition.'

'I'm sorry, darling. I truly am.'

Cordelia moved the baby from one breast to the other and

adjusted his blanket. 'You did try to tell me, didn't you, Samson? Why didn't you force me off the stage?'

Samson moved from his chair and went to kneel in front of her. 'Force ye? Me and whose army, darling?'

Cordelia chuckled. 'Surely, I'm not that bad. Am I really so stubborn?'

'Oh, I wouldna say stubborn. Just determined, perhaps.'

'Determined?'

'Aye.'

Cordelia placed her spare hand on his shoulder. 'You're very patient with me, aren't you, Samson?'

'Well, I'm not sure everyone would describe me as patient,' he replied, unsure how to handle the rare compliment.

'Perhaps because they don't know you like I do.'

'True. No-one knows me like ye do, let's face it!'

'I'm proud to be the one who knows you best,' Cordelia said as she peered down at her baby's sleepy eyes. 'I just hope you're half the fine gentleman that your father is, little one.'

'Gentleman?' Samson scoffed, resorting in his confusion to the default humour. 'Dinna curse the wee lad.'

'And what's wrong with being a gentleman?'

'Well, it just makes me sound too much like a Sassenach.'

'Are only Englishmen gentlemen? Can't you be a gentleman and a Highlander?'

He chuckled. 'Perhaps, but unlikely.'

'Well, I'll have to take you at your word, I suppose. But it's disappointing.'

'Is one of those spare, Mrs Haller?' Samson said, persisting with the feeble attempt to lighten the mood with humour.

'What?' She looked up disdainfully to see him pointing at her bosom. 'Don't be ridiculous.'

Fourteen

'The role of Mrs Haller will be played tonight by Miss Grace Bellingham,' the theatre manager announced.

Cordelia, standing next to Grace in the wings, heard the rapturous applause and stamping of feet.

'I'm sorry, Mrs Cameron,' Grace said, barely turning her head towards the older thespian. 'It's just that I'm new.'

'And I'm old. Is that what you're saying, Miss Bellingham?'

'Oh, no ma'am. I didn't …'

'That's all right, dear. You just do your best tonight. Off you go, now. Quickly!'

Grace moved to centre stage, arriving a split second before the curtain began to open. Samson stepped forward to take Grace's place beside his wife.

'Are ye all right, darling?' he whispered.

Cordelia sniffed. 'After that applause? I still think I should be the one out there.'

'I know, and ye will be.' He placed his hand on Cordelia's arm. 'Just give it a wee bit of time.'

'Time for them to totally forget me?' she said louder than intended. 'A brilliant plan, Samson. Simply brilliant!'

Cordelia stormed away, her footsteps audible to those in the front rows – and those on stage. Grace jumped mid-sentence.

'*… why Mr Haller, I ask?*'

Peals of laughter rang out in the audience.

'*I mean, Mr Solomon.*'

'Are you sure, Grace?' someone shouted from the second row.

Raucous laughter followed.

'Tell us more about Mr Haller, Grace,' someone called out from further back in the audience.

More laughter, followed by shushing.

'Give the girl a chance,' someone screeched.

'Yes, could you do any better?' a woman from the fourth row stood, turned around and shouted to those behind her.

Grace lowered her head, silent, overcome. Samson strode onto the stage and held his arms up to quieten the crowd.

'Oh, it's Mr Haller,' someone called out.

More laughter and shushing from the now completely restive audience. Grace lowered her head even further.

'Ladies and gentlemen,' Samson shouted across the din.

The crowd slowly settled.

'Ladies and gentlemen. I implore ye to be kind to this bonnie lass. She's been good enough to step in for my wife who, as ye know, has just given birth to our bairn. And, as ye also know, Miss Bellingham did a wonderful job two nights ago. She doesna deserve the ribaldry ye're throwing her way.'

The audience quietened.

'Thank ye. I think we should begin again,' he said, turning to Grace. 'Are ye all right with that, lass?'

'Thank you, Mr Cameron,' she blubbered, accepting the handkerchief that one of the stagehands was offering.

Samson walked over to her, resting his hand on her shoulder.

'Ye know Mrs Haller wouldna let these coots win, d'ye no?' he whispered, leaning close to her ear.

Grace looked up at him, smiling through her moistened eyes. The glistening reminded him of his feelings of two days ago, having left her guest house. He quickly turned and walked to the outer stage, signalling for the show to begin.

'*Why, oh why …*'

'So, it was a shambles, I gather?' Cordelia hurled at Samson as he walked into the bedroom later that night. She was propped up in bed, the baby asleep in her arms.

'It was a difficult beginning.'

'Oh, the poor girl must be shattered. I suppose I should do tomorrow night after all.'

'That'll not be necessary, darling,' he said as he sat on the bed and began taking off his shoes. 'She performed well – in the end.'

'Well, it didn't sound that way when I left. I was half expecting someone to come running and ask me to step in.'

'Aye, it was a challenge, but she's a bonnie lass.'

He stood to undo his shirt and trousers.

'You're quite smitten, aren't you, Samson? I've told you to be careful there.'

He turned to face her.

'I'm not smitten, darling. But I admit I do like the lass.'

'Just "like"?'

'Aye, and I admire her. She hasn't had the start in life that ye've had. Ye should see the place where she's staying.'

He rummaged in the chest of drawers, knowing that she was scrutinising his reactions. 'What's the house to do with anything? You're smitten, Samson. I know you, remember!'

He turned to face her again. 'Darling, I like her, but not in the way ye're implying. All I'm saying is I admire the way she's been able to overcome her circumstances to be up there with the likes of ye who've had such a start in life.'

Cordelia looked at him sternly. 'Oh, so I've just ridden on my father's coattails, have I? No talent, no determination, no seizing opportunities. It's all been handed to me on a plate. But Grace? Dear, sweet little Grace. She's had none of my lazy fortune but she's up there, as you put it. Up there with me.'

'I thought it a compliment, Cordelia. To ye, I mean. Up there with ye is as up there as a person can be.'

'So, she really is as good as me. That's what you're saying, isn't it?'

'No, I'm not. She's not as good as ye. For the Laird's sake, who could be? Anywhere in the Laird's world – much less here at the bottom of it.'

Samson watched as the tensed look on Cordelia's face rolled away. He noted the first deep breath she had taken since his arrival.

'Thank you, Samson,' she said, tears forming in the corners of her eyes. 'So, what do you mean by up there with me, then?'

Samson leant in close to her. 'Darling, she stepped into yer shoes. She followed yer lead. Ye're her heroine. Surely ye know that. Ye're everything she could ever hope to be.'

Cordelia's head fell forward as she let out a piercing cry. Samson moved quickly around to her side of the bed, knelt and cradled her head to his shoulder. His spare hand rested on the baby's back.

'All's well, my darling,' he whispered. 'I love ye so much, ye know?'

'I'm such a fool,' she blubbered, struggling to get the words out. 'A jealous fool.'

'Ye're not a fool!'

'Yes, I am, Samson. A jealous, ungrateful fool. Poor Grace. How can she ever forgive me? How can you forgive me?'

'There's naught to forgive. Ye're just a wee bit emotional after having the bairn.'

'But I've no right to be emotional, Samson. Especially not the nasty way I've been with Grace. I don't know how you can say you love me when I'm such a wretched woman.'

'Well, I do love ye all the same, my precious darling. I adore ye.'

Cordelia let out an involuntary guffaw, fighting her tears.

'Thank you for saying all that, Samson.'

The sleeping baby jumped with the noise of the laughter. He began to cry.

'Could you take him, Samson?' Cordelia handed the baby over. 'I need to get up and start getting my house in order.'

'Of course.' Samson took the baby in his arms – awkwardly as ever – and stood up. 'But what do ye mean, getting yer house in order?'

'I mean I need to come to grips with myself; I need to accept that I'm too worn out to perform just now. I need to speak with Grace and apologise. And I need to work out if I can stay in this town.'

'Stay in this town? What do ye mean? Where else can we go?'

'I want to go home, Samson.'

'To Hobart Town?'

'No, to England.'

Fifteen

It was almost a year after Cordelia's expressed desire to leave the colony, a desire that became ever more persistent, if not a matter of some obsession. Samson was by this time fully ensconced in the theatre management role. Every effort to get her back into it, or even on stage, was thwarted by a bout of illness on the part of their child or Cordelia herself. Even when Grace had to return urgently to her home to attend to a family matter, Cordelia refused to fill in for her.

'Oh, so now I'm the understudy. Is that what you're saying, Samson?'

Rather than thrust someone else onto the stage, least of all in the key role of Mrs Haller that Grace had increasingly made her own, Samson organised with the Tavern Board to rest the regular performances and replace them with a series of recitals. Cordelia agreed to feature in several of them. They received satisfactory reviews, buoying her spirits – for a while. A letter from Grace, telling Samson that she would not be able to return for several more weeks, provided an opportunity to reprise *The Bandit of the Rhine*. Reluctantly, Cordelia agreed to play the role of the heroine, Rubina, receiving similar plaudits for her 'perfection'. Her confidence was returning, but when Grace came back earlier than expected, she chose to step down, allowing Grace to take up the role for a short time until the next season of *The Stranger*, with Grace again in the lead role of Mrs Haller.

'Mr Sotheby,' Samson said, extending his hand. 'How good to see ye, Mr Secretary. What are ye doing so far to the north?'

The Colonial Secretary had attended the play that evening, mid-October of 1835. He entered the dressing room as Samson was divesting his stage apparel.

'To the north? Or do you mean south? I'm just back from Sydney.'

'I didna realise. I thought ye'd been in Hobart Town all this time.'

Samson put on his coat and invited Sotheby to sit on a settee. The two men sat at either end as the actors and stagehands scurried around them.

'I've just been escorting my wife. Mrs Sotheby insisted on travelling home to England for a time. She misses her family terribly.'

Samson sighed and looked away, absentmindedly taking note of Grace in the distance. 'Aye, I understand how she must feel.'

'Oh, are you homesick, Mr Cameron?'

'No, but my wife very much wants to go home.'

'Permanently?'

Samson turned to Sotheby and nodded. 'Aye, I think that's what she means.'

'Oh, that would be such a loss.' He lowered his voice, glancing towards Grace. 'That young girl tonight was quite good but nowhere near Mrs Cameron's superlative standard.'

'Thank ye, sir. I'm sure Mrs Cameron would be pleased to hear that. Others have not been as kind to my wife.'

'Truly?'

'Aye. Well, young Grace Bellingham has developed quite a following in this town.'

He stole another glance at Grace as she was exiting through the side door. She was turning to say goodbye to one of the players when she noticed him looking at her. She blushed, smiled and waved. Then she was gone.

'Oh, I had no idea!'

Samson was distracted. 'Sorry, Mr Sotheby. No idea about what?'

'That the young woman had developed a following.'

'Oh, aye. Ye see, she was merely Mrs Cameron's understudy who had to fill in when Mrs Cameron was indisposed.'

'Goodness, big shoes to fill for the poor girl!'

'Aye, I agree,' Samson moved closer and lowered his voice to a whisper. 'But there are some who clearly think Grace is as good as, perhaps even better than, Mrs Cameron. Even one of the newspapers has said as much. It's quite distressed my wife at times. Some days, I even find it hard to get her out of bed.'

'Goodness. I had no idea. Mrs Sotheby will be devastated to hear this. She truly thinks your wife is a goddess.'

'Aye, as do I, sir!'

Sotheby looked concerned at the stress Samson was displaying. He moved closer and placed a hand on his shoulder.

'Never fear, Mr Cameron. Perhaps some beneficent stars are aligning. I just might have a solution for you. I take it you yourself are happy here?'

'Well, aye. At least until all these things started to happen.'

'And you were happy in Hobart Town?'

'Aye.'

'And Mrs Cameron?'

'Oh, aye. At first at least!'

'Well, how would you feel about returning there for a period of time?'

'Truly?'

'Yes, are you interested?'

'Perhaps. I need to know what ye're proposing.'

'And how was Madame Bellingham tonight?' Cordelia muttered as Samson slipped between the sheets.

'Fine, darling.'

'Just fine? I doubt that, Samson. I fear she has well and truly supplanted me – in all ways.'

'What do ye mean, darling? "In all ways"?'

'To be honest, Samson, I fear I'm losing your affections as well as my career.' Cordelia turned away. Her sniffling and snuffling became steadily more audible.

'My affections?' Samson reached an arm around her waist.

She pushed his hand away.

'I've seen the way you look at her, Samson. I'm not a fool, much as you might think I am.'

'The way I look at her? When? Where?'

'Tonight. You were looking at her the way Mr Solomon looks at Mrs Haller. And we both know what that led to.'

'Ye mean on the stage? During the play? Were ye there?'

'Yes, I was, and I know you'll say you were just playing the role, but you know what we've said to each other before about that.'

'What have we said, darling?'

'That the play is just an extension of what we have between us. That it would be hard to play the role without the feeling being real.' Cordelia choked on the words before catching her breath. 'That you can lust after Mrs Haller because you lust after me.'

She moved her body further away and buried her head in the pillow. Samson rolled onto his back and stared at the shadows that the street lantern was casting on the ceiling.

'I really don't know how ye could even think such a thing.'

'Well, I do. I'm frightened I'm losing you. I'm terrified that every night you walk out to go to the play, it will be the last time I see you.'

'Oh, my Laird. Is that why ye came tonight?'

'Yes.'

'With the bairn? Or did ye leave him here on his own?'

'Of course not! See, that's how badly you really think of me, isn't it?'

'No, of course not. But who looked after the bairn, then?'

'Mrs Townsend.'

Samson sat up and leant over her. 'The charwoman?'

'Yes. Is there a problem with that?'

He lay back down. 'No. I suppose not!'

'Are you sure? You seem to disapprove.'

'No, I'm just a wee bit surprised.'

'Surprised? Why on earth? She's a mother several times over and always so good with John. I wouldn't just leave him with anyone, you know!'

'I do know, darling. Of course, I know that.'

'Why surprised, then?'

'That ye'd come to the play without me knowing. What did people say when they saw ye?'

'No-one saw me.'

He sat up again and placed his hand on her shoulder. 'How could they not see ye?'

'I dressed up. I'm quite practised at that, you know.'

He could hear her chuckling.

'Dressed as what?'

'An old woman. Mrs Kerridge, in fact. Mrs Kerridge from Melbourne.'

'Who is Mrs Kerridge?'

'No-one, silly man,' Cordelia said as her head sprang from the pillow, and she faced Samson. He could see that she was smiling, thanks to the light from the street lantern reaching through the window. 'As made-up as Mrs Haller, dear.'

'Why Mrs Kerridge, then?' he said, feeling some relief from the lighter mood.

'It just came to me when someone asked who I was. Mrs Kerridge was a neighbour back home in Leominster.'

Samson burst into laughter as he pulled Cordelia down and into his arms.

'Oh, I do love ye, Mrs Cameron. Truly, I do. I couldna live without ye. How could ye possibly think otherwise?'

Cordelia snuggled into his shoulder, squeezing her arms around his body.

'You haven't said anything like that for a long time, do you know that?'

'I thought I had,' he whispered. 'I'm sure it's not such a long time.'

'Well, it seems a long time to me.'

'I'm sorry. I suppose I just thought ye weren't in the mood for such frivolities.'

'Oh, so it's my fault, is it? Always my fault.'

He lay in silence, breathing deeply, pondering on the brevity of the lightened mood.

'So, say something, Samson.'

'I dinna know what to say. Except that I love ye. I could never stop loving ye. And I suppose I'm a wee bit hurt that ye'd not know that.'

She snuggled in more tightly.

'I'm sorry, Samson. I've just been so sad. I feel as though everything is falling apart. My career, my marriage, my child.'

'Yer bairn? What do ye mean? He's fine, isn't he?'

'Yes, but after Elizabeth, I just fear I'm going to lose him as well.'

'Well, ye won't lose him, d'ye understand? Dinna even think it! And dinna ye talk anymore about losing me, d'ye hear?'

'But are you sure, Samson? You do seem very fond of Grace. You looked truly convincing as the adulterous pair on the stage. Honestly, I came home tonight and couldn't get it out of my head. And then you were late home, so what was I to think?'

'Well, that's what I was going to talk to ye about – before ye started on all this madness.'

'What?' Cordelia said, raising her head from his shoulder and staring down at him. 'About you and Grace?'

'No,' he said, snorting in frustration. 'About why I was late!'

'Oh, so why were you late?' Cordelia was looking intensely at him in the dark.

'Well, how would ye feel if we went back to Hobart Town?'

'For how long?'

'Oh, six months or so.'

'Samson, you promised we could go home after we're finished – well, *you're* finished – in this wretched place. And by home, I mean England, as you promised!'

'Aye, I know, but Mr Sotheby was there tonight.'

'The Colonial Secretary? Why?'

'Well, to be honest, he came to see ye. He was disappointed when ye weren't there.'

'That's nice. Did he say what he thought of Grace?'

'Aye. His exact words were, "that young woman was quite good but nowhere near the standard of Mrs Cameron".'

'Well, that's lovely of him. But what's this to do with going to Hobart Town?'

'Well, ye know they're building a new theatre there?'

'They were talking about that when we were there. Are they actually doing it?'

'Aye. He says they've dug the foundations, but he wants us to come and oversee the building.'

'Why? We're not builders.'

'No, but we know what a theatre should be, what it should look like, what sort of stage, how high the ceiling, the acoustics. All those things. Think how often we grumbled about the Free-mason's Tavern and how if we could ever build a proper theatre, what we would do.'

'Yes, but …'

'But nothing, darling. This is our chance. And I haven't even told ye the best part.'

'What?'

'That they'd put us on a contract. He said perhaps even ten guineas a week. More if we ask for it.'

'And a house? I don't want to go back to that awful flat. Not where Elizabeth died.'

'Aye, he knows we want a proper house.'

'What do you mean by a proper house? With a garden? A fence? A veranda?'

'Aye, just like the one ye grew up in as a bairn, darling. What do ye think?'

'I suppose so. For a while, at least. But I do want to go home then. I really do, Samson.'

'Aye, I know. I promise. We will.'

'So, how long will it take to build the theatre? And what do we do in the meantime? Does he want us to perform at all?'

'Oh, aye.'

'Not at the Tavern, surely?'

'Well, perhaps for some performances but the other exciting news is that the Argyle has been renovated, and he believes he could use his influence to allow us to perform there.'

Samson and Cordelia had made attempts to use the Argyle, a former hotel turned into music rooms by John Philip Deane, one of the first musicians in the colony. Samson and Deane had fallen out before the venture transpired.

'So, am I to assume Mr Deane is no longer calling the tune?'

'Aye, so it seems. Anyway, he says the people he's been talking to want us to perform whatever we wish, be it in the Tavern or the Argyle, along with helping in the design of the new theatre and then, once it's open, to begin with a season of *The Stranger*. He says the people have been clamouring for it. And, what's even better, another play of our choosing after that.'

'And no Grace?'

'No, darling. Mr Sotheby made it quite clear they want ye and ye alone!'

Cordelia rolled over on her back. The baby stirred. She lowered her voice to a whisper. 'Well, it's tempting, I must say, but how long will all this take? Did he say?'

'He thinks it will take four to five months to finish the theatre, so we could perform whatever we choose in the meantime, as long as *The Stranger* is included here and there. We do that for a few months and then a brand-new play of our choosing, so …'

'So, it could be a whole year before we go back to England?'

'Aye, perhaps, but …'

'But that's fine, I suppose. And, of course, I will choose my understudy if I need one.'

'Aye, darling.'

'One less attractive than Grace,' Cordelia said, sitting up and staring at him in the dark.

'Well, that'll be almost impossible, won't it?' he replied, sniggering.

'You're such a poor liar, Samson,' she said with a reluctant chuckle.

'Aye, someone who'd do anything for ye, darling. Even lie.'

'Anything? Are you sure?'

'Aye, I'm sure!'

'Then, don't move, Mr Solomon.'

'Why, Mrs Haller, what do ye mean?'

She snuggled in and pressed herself against him. They made love for the first time since the birth of their second child.

In December of that year, 1835, while Samson was wrapping up the season at the London Tavern, Cordelia was buoyed by being asked to offer three farewell performances at Launceston's Freemason's Tavern.

'That's wonderful, darling, but would ye not like to do a final performance at the Tavern as well?'

'No, Samson, I'd rather go where I'm appreciated.'

Cordelia offered a variety of songs to an especially appreciative group of patrons, the highlight being *Song of the Swiss Toy Girl*, for which she always received the highest of praise.

Hence, both Samson and Cordelia left for Hobart Town in the week before Christmas full of hope for the future.

Sixteen

'I CAN ONLY SAY AGAIN how sorry I am, sir.'

'It's not yer fault, Reggie. Ye canna build if there's naught to build with.'

It was soon after Easter of 1836, and the promised theatre in Hobart Town was still just that. From the beginnings of the new year and up until Easter, the Camerons had been settling into their new home, a two-bedroom cottage in the foothills, while offering a series of recitals at the Tavern and the occasional performance at the Argyle. The decision had been made to wait for the new theatre, initially thinking it would be complete by Easter, before performing any plays, including *The Stranger*. The walls and roof of the theatre were in place, along with the makings of a stage and graded flooring. But the interior was bare. Even the choir loft was incomplete, nothing was painted and no sign of the many backstage artefacts, a curtain or even one seat for an audience that was meant to number over three hundred. The two men stood in the middle of the stage makings, Samson trying to envisage what to make of what lay before his eyes.

'Mr Chisholm says we only have to wait to the next committee meeting and the money will start to flow,' said Reginald Gardner, the building foreman.

'Aye, Reggie, and where have we heard that before?' Samson said, shaking his head in disbelief.

'Yeah, I know Mr C. A few times. But Mr Chisholm seems a decent enough fella.'

'Aye, except he's a politician.'

'True. Anyway, Mr C, we've still got some of that paint that Mr and Mrs Guilford donated. D'you think we should start painting?'

'I'm not sure, Reggie. Shouldn't it be the last thing ye do?'

'I s'pose so, Mr C. Anyway, don't you worry no more. We'll be ready to get stuck into it as soon as the money's flowing again.'

'Thanks, Reggie. I think I might as well take Mrs Cameron away for a wee while. I really dinna want her seeing this the way it is.'

'How is Mrs C, sir?'

'Not as good as she should be. She always gets sick when she's expecting a bairn.'

'She's such a wonderful actress, sir. We saw her a couple of times when you were here last. Voice of an angel, we used to say.'

'Thanks to ye, Reggie. I'll tell her ye said so. Aye, she's the finest of women, but I do sense she needs to get out of town just now.'

'Oh, good idea, sir. P'raps by the time you get back, the theatre'll be finished.'

'Oh, aye, and hell will have frozen over,' Samson said, placing his arm on Reggie's shoulder.

They laughed as Samson turned and walked away.

'Do you have the scripts, Samson?' Cordelia called out.

Cordelia and John were seated in the carriage while Samson was standing next to it, holding the reins, and the driver was securing the bags.

'Aye, I think so. Can ye check my valise?'

'John, darling, can you pass me Daddy's bag?' Cordelia said as she reached her outstretched arm across her two-year-old son, seated next to her. 'The black one, darling.'

They watched as John tried to lift the valise, but his toddler arms were not up to the task.

'The lad'll not be strong enough, Cordelia,' Samson said in a voice more scolding than intended, while hoisting himself up on the running board. 'He's not even two.'

'I know how old he is, Samson. I'm his mother, you know. Stand up, John. Let me get it.'

The parents' hands seized on the valise handle at precisely the same moment. They pulled on it as though playing a game of tug o' war.

'I've got it,' Cordelia roused, pulling so hard on the handle that the valise pounded into the toddler's side, knocking him off his feet and hurling him forwards as Samson stumbled backwards off the running board.

'Samson,' Cordelia shouted, dropping the valise, and grabbing the arm of her son, who was about to fall between the carriage and the horse's hindquarters.

'Mummy. Mummy.'

Cordelia was holding the lad by one arm, trying to reach over to gain a better grasp. Meanwhile, Samson leaned into the breach between the carriage and the horse to rescue him before he fell. In the instant Samson was able to push him back towards Cordelia, the horse let out a piercing snort and bolted forward, cannoning the carriage into Samson's shoulder and knocking him sideways to the ground. The sudden forward movement threw John back into his mother's arms. She grabbed him with one arm and the side of the carriage with the other as the vehicle hurtled forward at a rapid pace.

'Mummy, Mummy,' John squealed as he clung his arms around his mother's neck.

'I've got you, darling. Hang on tight. Don't let go.'

Cordelia loosened one arm from John's side and reached forward for the reins that were, by now, being thrown around and threatening to be lost somewhere beneath the carriage. She managed to retrieve one of them, pulling as hard as she could. The horse responded to being pulled to one side by turning quickly in that direction, still galloping at the same speed. The carriage, unable to take the turn as quickly as the horse, slewed sideways before tipping on its side, throwing mother and child to the ground and forcing the horse to a stop.

'Cordelia!' Samson shouted as he ran to catch up as fast as his bruised hip would allow.

By the time he and the driver arrived at the scene, several passers-by were standing over Cordelia and John, two of them crouching over in attendance.

'Don't move, madam,' a gentleman in a dark blue suit said. 'I'll get help.'

'You can let go of your little one, love,' an elderly lady was saying as she lifted John into her arms. 'I've got him.'

'Daddy,' John hollered as he saw Samson limping onto the scene. 'Daddy.'

'Are ye all right, lad?' he said, grabbing one of the boy's outstretched hands. 'Stay with this bonnie lass while I see how yer ma is.'

Samson rushed past the lady holding John, kneeling to examine

Cordelia, still lying where she had fallen. The driver was steadying the horse while a passerby helped to uncouple the carriage.

'Are ye all right, darling?' he said, reaching forward and laying his hand on her cheek. 'Don't move, will ye?'

Cordelia's eyes were flickering. She blinked several times and then closed her eyes.

'Is John all right?' she asked, eyes still closed. 'Is he hurt?'

'He's fine, darling. But what about ye?'

'I don't know. My head hurts.' Cordelia closed her eyes as she lifted her hand to her forehead. 'And I can't see.'

'What do ye mean ye canna see?'

'I mean I can't see, Samson. I *can't see!*'

Cordelia, blinking rapidly, began to weep uncontrollably. She tried to sit up.

'Oh, my Laird. Dinna move, darling.' Samson rested one hand on the back of her head and lowered it with the other hand.

'Is she all right, sir?' a male voice was heard from behind. 'I'm a doctor.'

'I don't know, Doctor. She says she canna see.'

'Let me look at her.' The doctor knelt next to Cordelia. 'Good day, madam. I'm Dr Cornbleth.'

'Doctor,' Cordelia whispered, grasping his spare hand. 'I can't see anything.'

'Nothing to worry about, madam,' Cornbleth said, casting a glance in Samson's direction, one that belied his words. 'It often happens after a shocking event such as you've just had. Just stay calm. Sir, may I borrow your jacket?'

Samson took off his coat and handed it to Cornbleth. He folded it and placed it gently under Cordelia's head, then ran his thumb around her eyes and forehead.

'Could you try and open your eyes, Mrs …?'

'Cameron,' Samson butted in.

'Cameron?' Cornbleth said, staring wide-eyed at him. 'Is this …?'

'Cordelia Cameron.' Even in these circumstances, Samson could hear the pride in his voice.

'The actress. Of course. I'm sorry I didn't recognise you both.'

'I dare say I'm not looking my normal self,' Cordelia said, emitting a small chuckle.

'Now, that's a good sign.' Cornbleth flashed a look of relief in Samson's direction. 'Mrs Cameron has not lost her sense of humour.'

'Aye,' Samson replied, squeezing Cordelia's shoulder. 'Any wee blessing is welcome right now.'

'Indeed.' Cornbleth turned back to his patient. 'Now, eyes open if you can, Mrs Cameron. Try one at a time. The left one. Can you open it?'

Cordelia's left eye opened and shut, opened and shut, then flickered.

'Good. Can you see anything at all?'

'Just a bit of light.'

'Good. Any colours?'

'No.'

'Now try the right eye.' Cornbleth placed his forefinger gently below Cordelia's right eye. She opened and shut it repeatedly before flickering and settling it.

'Oh, I can see better with this one. Everything is blurry but I can see some blue in the sky, and something green over there. Is that a tree?'

'Indeed, it is, Mrs Cameron. I'm confident your eyesight will gradually come back to normal, but it might take a while. Now, let me check the back of your head if I might.'

Cornbleth lifted Cordelia's head slightly off the folded coat, holding her head aloft with one hand while the fingers of his other hand pressed into the back of her head. Cordelia flinched.

'Does that hurt, Mrs Cameron?'

'Yes, Doctor. Excruciatingly!'

'Mmm. I think that's the problem. You've given yourself quite a knock there and I would predict you might be concussed.'

'Concussed? What do ye mean?' Samson asked.

'Merely that she has had a severe blow to the head, and it will leave her a little the worse for wear for a while. In her powers of concentration, I mean.'

'But she'll be all right?'

'I think so but that's just my pavement diagnosis, I believe she needs a more thorough examination and at least some days of total rest.'

'Well, we were hoping to have a few days away,' Cordelia said, rubbing her eyes and wincing. 'In fact, that's where we were going before all this happened.'

'Tell me, Mrs Cameron, why did you wince just then? Is it that spot on the back of your head?'

'I just felt a stabbing pain. Every time I try to speak. Like right now. Oh! Ouch!'

Cordelia grabbed at her stomach.

'Let me see,' Cornbleth said as he ran his pressed fingers across parts of Cordelia's stomach.

'Good heavens, are you pregnant?'

'Aye,' Samson said, unable to hide his annoyance. 'I really thought ye'd know that. Ye're a doctor, aren't ye?'

'Well, I believe so, but I'm sorry, I was paying more attention to your wife's head.'

'Please forgive my husband's rudeness, Doctor,' Cordelia uttered exhaustedly.

'That's quite all right. I understand he's just concerned for you. Look, in light of this, I think you should delay your time away and stay here for several days. I'll see if I can get you into a place I know in Liverpool Street.'

'What's that?' Samson asked.

'It's a private rest home quite nearby. She'll have a nurse on standby and I can call in there regularly.'

'Do ye really think that's necessary?'

'Samson.' Cordelia was clutching at her stomach. 'Let the doctor do his job. He knows best.'

'Aye, whatever ye think, but ye know what I think of nurses and …'

'Darling!' Cordelia said, wincing in pain. 'Can't you see I need some help?'

'Aye, darling.'

Cornbleth spoke to a passerby who then ran off towards Liverpool Street.

'Someone is arranging for a cart to get you to the home.'

'A cart? I could arrange—'

'*Samson!*'

'It's a special cart, Mr Cameron. Made for carrying the infirm.'

'Samson,' Cordelia cried. 'For heaven's sake!'

'Aye, my darling. Whatever the doctor thinks best.'

Twenty minutes later, the horse drawn cart arrived at the scene. By this time, John was back in his father's arms. The drivers lifted Cordelia onto a stretcher, following Cornbleth's instructions, and onto the tray of the cart. Samson lifted John onto the tray and hoisted himself up.

'Mummy,' John cried as he lay down beside her. 'Mummy, Mummy, Mummy.'

Samson placed the boy on his knee and cuddled him.

'Yer ma'll be fine, lad. The doctor said so.'

'Mummy.'

Seventeen

It was several days after the accident. Dr Cornbleth, who had taken a personal interest in his patient, had delivered the news that Cordelia was to remain at the rest home for three weeks and then rest at home for a further six weeks. He advised against her returning to the stage before the anticipated birth in September.

'It's as much for the unborn child as any other consideration,' Cornbleth said in response to Cordelia's protestations.

'I'm sure the doctor's right, darling,' Samson had added.

'Of course he's right,' Cordelia snapped back. 'But it doesn't make it any easier, does it? I was looking forward to being back onstage and putting the past where it belongs.'

'I'll leave you two to talk through the implications,' Cornbleth said as he exited the room.

'I know what you're thinking, Samson.' Cordelia turned her head away.

'Is it all right with ye, darling?'

'I suppose so. What choice do I have?'

'Well, at least Grace knows the part, does she no?'

Cordelia did not reply, her face fixed on the window.

'Mind ye,' Samson continued, ignoring her ignoring him. 'I dinna know if she'll be able to do it. She could be in Melbourne by now for all we know.'

'Following her dreams?' Cordelia murmured carelessly.

'Aye, well she is a bonnie performer, no doubt …'

'Samson. Enough!' she snapped, turning to gaze at him. 'Don't you think I've heard enough about Grace and how good she is? How much better than me she is?'

'Darling.'

'Oh, just go, Samson. Write to her this afternoon. If you want her here in a month or so, you'd best write quickly – and send it the fastest way you can.'

'Aye, I just …'

'Samson. Go! And please see if Dr Cornbleth is still here.'

'Why?'

'Because I'd like to see him, that's why.'

'Ye and yer beau seem to get on well, d'ye no?'

She stared at him, stern-faced. 'What do you mean, Samson?'

'I think he's quite taken by ye. That's what I mean.'

'Don't be ridiculous, Samson. Are you jealous?'

'No more than ye are about Grace.'

Cordelia turned away in disgust. 'Oh, go away with you, you silly man. Go write to your sweetheart'

'She's not my sweetheart.'

'And Colin is certainly not my beau.'

'Colin?'

'Dr Cornbleth,' Cordelia said, blushing ever so slightly.

Dear Mr Cameron,

I'm so sorry to hear about Mrs Cameron's misfortune. I had actually read about it in the paper. There remains great interest in both of you here in Launceston. I'm honoured yet again to be asked to fill in for her but I'm afraid I have made a commitment to perform a season of Romeo and Juliet which begins here in two days' time.

Please forgive me, Mr Cameron. I would dearly have loved to work with you again. I think you know how much I valued our time together and would have cherished the opportunity I must now decline.

My best wishes to Mrs Cameron and my fondest best wishes to you,

Grace Bellingham

It was nearing the end of June, and it looked as if the new theatre might be ready sooner than expected. Cordelia had been out of the rest home and in her own bed for a week. They had employed a Miss Annabelle Walters, a mature spinster, as a nanny and maid until such time as Cordelia could be back on her feet, possibly until after the birth.

'So, you finally heard back from her?' Samson had just entered the bedroom.

'Aye, the letter was addressed to the Tavern.'

'Why not to here, Samson? Does Grace not know our address?'

'I canna say, darling. Perhaps I forgot to put it on the letter.'

He was rifling in a drawer, looking for something.

'Perhaps you did, Samson. Anyway, I'd like to see it.'

'Why?' he turned to face her. It doesna say anything that I'm not telling ye.'

'Still, I'd like to see it. Bring it home next time.'

He walked over and sat on the edge of the bed. 'Aye, darling, but what do ye think we should do?'

'Surely there must be another actress in Hobart Town.'

'Aye, but not one who can do Mrs Haller with such short notice.'

John ran into the room and jumped up on the bed next to Cordelia. She pulled him in to give him a cuddle. 'Well, you'll just have to cancel the season. Tell them we'll start in October.'

'We canna do that. They'll cancel our contract.'

'Well, do you have a better idea, then?'

'Perhaps!'

'Tell me, then!'

He hesitated, then leant in towards her, speaking softly as if he did not want his son to hear, or at least understand. 'Darling, who knows Mrs Haller better than anyone, except for ye, of course?'

'You, I suppose, but you can hardly do it.'

'Why not?

'Samson, are you mad?' she placed her hands over the toddler's ears, looking with pleading eyes at her husband. 'What? You would dress as a woman and then what? Play both parts?'

'No, Gerry Milford's been desperate to play my part.'

'Gerry Milford? He can't even play the pathetic part he's supposed to do now – and he's only on stage for a total of two minutes.'

John wriggled free of his mother's grip and ran out of the room. He left the door open.

'I'm sure I could train him up quickly. He knows the lines and Mr Solomon's only on stage for a quarter of the time Mrs Haller is. Hers is the role that carries the play – and I can do it.'

'Samson, shush. Shut the door.'

Samson strode quickly to the door and closed it.

'Including the singing?' Cordelia pleaded.

'Aye, ye know I was a soprano as a lad.'

'When you were ten years of age, you mean? I'm not sure you've noticed that a few things have changed since then, dear.'

'Aye, I know, but I can still sing falsetto.'

'Samson, you're mad. Simply mad.'

'So ye'd rather Grace be here?'

Cordelia went quiet. She looked him in the eye, giving way to a wry smile.

'Well, if you do it, I want to be there – in the front row.'

'Surely, sir,' Milford replied. 'It'd be the honour of my life. But who'll play Mrs Haller?'

Samson confronted him after an evening of recitals. Milford and Constance Blake, another younger player, had been performing a series of duets.

'Well, lad, I hope ye dinna mind if it's me.'

Milford was looking at him, clearly confused. 'You, sir? But …'

'But what, lad?'

'Nothing, sir. It'll be my honour.'

An awkward silence followed. Samson could see the discomfort on Milford's face.

'Are ye worried about the kissing, lad?'

'Ah, well. I …'

'Dinna concern yerself, lad. We can change it to an embrace if ye'd prefer.'

'Well, perhaps. You know my family will probably be there and …'

'Surely, lad, but ye do understand ye'd be kissing a woman,' Samson guffawed. 'A beautiful woman, if I might say!'

'I'm sorry, sir. A woman?' Milford looked even more puzzled.

'Me, Gerry. Do ye doubt that I can act so well?'

Milford blushed. 'Oh, no, sir. I'm in awe of your acting skills. You know that, sir. It's just—'

'Of course, it'll be a challenge,' Samson interrupted. 'But it'll be as much a challenge for ye as for me. We'll both be out of character and that's the real beauty of acting.'

'How so, sir?'

'Well, I can only do so much, Gerry! As well as I might do, it'll be up to ye to convince the audience that I really am a beautiful woman. Do ye see that?'

'I think so, sir.'

Samson placed his hand on Milford's shoulder. 'Remember, lad, ye're in love with this woman. If the audience senses ye're not really in love – indeed in lust – then it won't work.'

'Oh, my!' Milford said, looking away, trickles of sweat appearing on his brow.

'Are ye up to it, lad? If ye're not, it's best to say so now.'

Milford pulled a handkerchief from his pocket, wiped his brow, and looked Samson in the eye.

'I'm up to it, sir. All of it.'

'Ye're a bonnie lad, Gerry.' Samson drew Milford into a brief embrace.

'Thank you, sir. I won't let you down,' Milford replied as he buried his head on Samson's shoulder.

Samson struggled to pull away. Milford finally lifted his head and released his grip. Samson could see the tears in the boy's eyes as he stepped back to a safe distance.

'First thing on the morrow, then, lad. We dinna have all that long to get this right.'

'I'll be there, sir,' he said as he watched Samson turn and walk away.

'And, sir,' Milford called after him.

'Aye, lad?' Samson looked back over his shoulder.

'I think we should kiss.'

'The lad wants to kiss me.'

Cordelia raised her eyebrows. 'Well, I definitely want to be in the front row when that happens. When's this new theatre supposed to open?'

'The Theatre Royal, you mean? Heaven knows, but they want *The Stranger* on before then anyway.'

'Theatre Royal? Is that the new name? How original!'

Samson chuckled. 'Aye, I suggested The Caledonian but they didna seem to like that idea.'

Eighteen

This newspaper has offered unfettered support to the Cameron ventures in public theatre since they began over two years ago. Our support has extended to defending Mr and Mrs Cameron against charges of indecency and sedition brought by members of the public, including from members of our esteemed churches. It is therefore with the greatest regret that we announce today that this newspaper can no longer support these thespians regardless of their contribution to theatre in this town. Last night's performance of *The Stranger* included the lewd spectacle of a man dressed as a woman and that same man kissing another man, not once but several times and with the appearance of a passion that went beyond any requirement germane to the play. It was a foul spectacle that transcends the need for any religious authority to condemn on moral grounds. For the sake of our citizenry, and especially the incorrupt future of our children, we call on the sponsors of this abomination to desist and, if necessary, for certain of its most corrupt artisans to depart this city in shame.

The Colonial Times editorial, 31 July 1836.

'Have you read the *Times* today, dear?' Fanning Palmer asked as the Colonial Chaplain stepped into the house for lunch.

'I have, my dear.'

'So, what are you going to do about it, Philip? Go tonight and be humiliated all over again? And humiliate me in front of my associates? Again!'

He moved to take his place at the table. 'Hardly, dear!'

Fanning stood rigidly at the other end of the table, refusing to sit until she had his full attention.

'Then what, Philip? You can't ignore it. You can be sure Mr Langmore will be making his disapproval known as we speak, perhaps stealing even more of our congregation.'

'I don't know, dear. I'll try and make contact with Mr Sotheby and see what he thinks. Now, could you let the maid know we're ready?'

Fanning ignored him. 'Philip, we know what Mr Sotheby thinks, don't we? Isn't it because of Mr Sotheby's advice that we went to the wretched play in the first place.'

Palmer lifted the knife and fork, tapping them on the table. 'Perhaps he'll see it differently after this, dear.'

'After a public display of sodomy, you mean! One would certainly hope he would see things differently.'

'I really don't think it was sodomy, dear,' Palmer scoffed. 'Not from what I've heard anyway. There were just some inappropriate acts of affection.'

'Two men kissing, salivating over each other? You call that inappropriate affection? Truly, Philip, I do wonder about you sometimes.'

'I know, dear. I know.'

'Please, Philip. Do get to the bottom of this and quickly. Your disposition for smoothing everything out has run its course. This is a matter that requires leadership. And even if it means offending Mrs Cameron's friends in high places, whoever they might be, then we'll just have to deal with that.'

Palmer placed the knife and fork down, levelling his gaze at his wife. 'Even if it's the Archbishop of Canterbury and we're stuck in this island at the end of the earth for life? You'll be content with that?'

'If the Archbishop of Canterbury thinks it's fine to have two men cavorting as they were on a public stage, then frankly I don't care what he does to us.'

Palmer took a breath. 'Darling, from what I gather, they weren't cavorting, as you say. Mr Cameron was playing the part normally played by Mrs Cameron, who is indisposed. He was naturally dressed as a woman and the role required that he and the man playing the part he normally plays engage in acts of affection. It is a play, dear. Theatre! These things happen!'

Fanning stood in silence. Her face was white, her breathing heavy.

'Really, Philip. I wonder sometimes why I ever married you.' She hurried out of the room. Palmer went to the door and called the maid.

'Well, you've really done it now, Mrs Haller,' Cordelia said, smirking, as Samson walked into her room at the rest home. Dr Cornbleth had ordered her back into the home after difficulties in her pregnancy were detected.

'I'm guessing ye've read the *Times* then.'

'Indeed, I have. One of the nurses brought it to me. She thought I should know in case I wanted to have you barred from the home.'

'Barred? Oh, for heaven's sake!'

Cordelia sniggered. 'I think she thinks you might be a rapist or something.'

'Oh, my Laird!'

'Well, you must admit the way the newspaper conveyed it, you and Gerry were close to copulating on the stage. And to think I've been worried about Grace all this time.'

Cordelia gave way to a giggling Samson had rarely witnessed, holding her stomach. He sat heavily on the side of the bed, unable to join in her mirth.

'Oh, my Laird, what a disaster!'

'Was it really, though, Samson?' Cordelia said, suppressing her giggle and extending a hand to rest on his closer arm. 'Are you quite sure you didn't enjoy it?'

'Aye, darling. Quite sure!' he replied, grimacing. 'It was wretched. All of it!'

'Just because of the kissing, you mean?'

'No, the whole thing has become awkward.'

'In what way?'

'Well, I think Gerry is really enjoying it all. I said all we need is a wee hug and a pretend kiss. You know, we could turn our heads away from the audience, as performers would normally do, and make sure our lips don't touch.'

'And?'

'Well, that's what happened in the rehearsal but, then on stage, he went for my lips, and he wouldn't let go. Even when the audience was gasping, he pressed in even harder.'

'So, what did you do?' Cordelia asked, chuckling as she held her side.

'I had to push him away.'

'So, the second kiss?'

'Same. I had to push quite hard.'

'What do you think's going on?'

Samson shook his head, face down. 'I really dinna know. I tried to speak to him afterwards, but he just smiled at me.'

'Smiled?'

'Aye, a wicked kind of smile. A wee bit like the cat that ate the cream.'

'Oh, do you think Gerry might really be …?'

'I dinna know. Perhaps! I really dinna care so long as he doesna bring his ways onto the stage.'

'His ways?' Cordelia doubled over in mirth. 'It takes two, darling.'

'It's not funny, Cordelia. Ye're not the one enduring all this.'

'Oh, I'm sorry. I'm just annoyed that I wasn't there last night.'

'Aye, ye could've jumped up on the stage and saved my virtue.'

'Or just enjoyed watching you lose it.' Cordelia fell to a new round of giggling. 'To Gerry, of all people.'

'Well, it's all fine for ye, darling, but not for me.'

'Anyway, you say that wasn't the only problem. Tell me all of it.'

Samson took a moment before turning to look at her, his eyes betraying puzzlement. 'Well, Gerry was just hopeless playing Mr Solomon.'

'Hopeless? In what way?'

'I don't know what to say. He was just distracted the whole time.'

'Like a man in love, you mean?' Cordelia said, muffling another giggle.

'Oh, stop it. The poor lad has a problem. I knew he wasna the best actor in the world, but he was good enough at what he did. But as Mr Solomon, he was just awful!'

'You say distracted? What exactly do you mean? Give me an example!'

'Well, ye know when Mr Solomon and Mrs Haller are shouting

over each other. How wild it gets, with them butting in on each other all the time. The words are tumbling all over the place when ye and I do it.'

'Yes, I love that part, especially when Mrs Haller so clearly wins the argument.'

'Well, he was forgetting his lines and just staring at me in silence. I had to steal some of his lines to keep the whole thing going.'

'Goodness, that must have been awkward. And so that happened a lot?'

'All the way through. He was just dreadful.'

'And you?'

'What about me?'

'As Mrs Haller?'

Samson looked at her, self-satisfaction all over his face. 'Well, I thought I was superb!'

'As good as me?'

'Well, yes, frankly!' he said, twinkle in his eye.

'And Grace?'

'No, of course not,' he replied, ducking his head lest she throw something at him. 'Not that good.'

'Oh, if I wasn't tied to my bed, I'd hit you, Samson.'

'If ye weren't tied to yer bed, I wouldn't have said it, darling,' he replied, reaching over and kissing her on the cheek. He smiled at seeing her in such good humour. Such moments between them had been all too rare of late.

'Infuriating man, you are,' Cordelia replied, pushing him away. 'So, why do you think the *Times* didn't mention this superb performance you believe you gave?'

'Probably because they were only interested in the kissing.'

'Mmm, I'll be interested to hear what others thought about all that.'

'The kissing?'

'No, your performance. And Gerry's, of course. No doubt I'll hear. This place seems to have ears on its walls.'

'I'm sure everyone will have thought the same. Milford appalling. Cameron magnificent!'

In the circumstances, it must be said that Mr Gerry Milford, called on with little notice to fill the role, gave an adequate performance as Mr Solomon. Mr Cameron, on the other hand, filling in for his wife as Mrs Haller, was appalling. Whatever possessed him to think he could fill the gap rendered by Mrs Cameron's illness is beyond comprehension. His costuming was ludicrous, his singing voice execrable and the timing he normally displays in the opposite role completely abandoned him. On several occasions, I was cringing for poor Mr Milford in his vain efforts to carry the day. It remains merely to say…

The Hobart Town Theatre, 2 August 1836

'Honestly,' Samson said, flinging the newspaper across the room. 'No-one reads that rag anyway.'

'Well, I wouldn't say that, darling. *The Hobart Town Theatre* is regarded as the best arts publication in all the colonies. Haven't I heard you say that yourself? Including to Mrs Guilfoyle in Launceston when you thought she was criticising you?'

'Aye, well, it's obviously deteriorated since then.'

'How? Same play, same critic? How has it deteriorated?'

'Oh, I dinna know,' Samson huffed. 'Truly, between the two newspapers, it seems all is lost. What can we do?'

'I don't know, Samson. Short of me stepping out of my sickbed. Do you seriously think I should?'

'No, ye canna do that. The bairn is our number one concern.'

'Well, you're going to have to think of something quickly. You can't go on with this fiasco any longer. You've had three nights to get it right and it seems things are only getting worse.'

Samson slumped in the chair next to the bed, head in hands. Cordelia roused at him for jiggling his feet so ferociously that it was making the bedside table rock and rattle. There was a gentle knock on the door and a nurse stepped into the room.

'Excuse me, Mrs Cameron, there's a young lady who's asking to see you.'

'Did she give you a name?'

'Ah, yes, Miss Bellingham, I believe.'

Samson lifted his head and stared in disbelief.

'Did ye say Bellingham, nurse?'

'Yes, sir, I believe that was the name.'

'Grace Bellingham?'

'I don't believe she gave me her Christian name, sir. Shall I show her in?'

'Yes, thank you, nurse,' Cordelia said. 'By all means show Miss Bellingham in.'

'Dinna bother, Sister, just show me where she is,' Samson said, bolting out of the chair and hurrying the nurse out the door as Cordelia was forming the words.

'Samson, wait.'

It was too late. He was out in the corridor, virtually pushing the nurse in front of him. He heard the door to Cordelia's room close behind him.

'Grace,' he said, rushing forward to the bench where she was sitting. 'What a sight for sore eyes ye are.'

She stood, looking at him, smiling, blushing, arms by her side. 'Mr Cameron, I …'

Samson took her in his arms. Grace nestled her head on his chest.

'Grace, I canna believe my eyes.'

Her arms found their way around his back. *How can a young, petite lass possess such a strong grip?*

'I'm here, Mr Cameron. I had to come,' she said breathlessly, her face buried in his chest. 'I don't know why. I just had to come.'

'I dinna care why,' he said, stepping away and looking into her tear-filled eyes. 'Come and greet Mrs Cameron, will ye no?'

'Of course, sir,' she replied, blushing even more and turning back to pick up her valise and reticule. 'Just give me a moment.'

He watched her back as she reached into the reticule – tending to her eyes and face, he supposed. Having finished whatever-it-was she felt compelled to do, she turned and smiled a smile he had rarely seen in his life. It was as though they had known each other forever, including all their secrets. *I'll always remember this moment.*

They hastened together down the corridor and into Cordelia's room.

'Look who I have here, darling.'

It was obvious that Cordelia had composed herself, finding comb, lip rouge and presumably a mirror. In no time, she had transformed from looking tired and without make-up to the thespian she was, ready for a performance.

'Grace, how lovely to see you,' she said, smiling broadly, pushing some things under her blanket.

'Thank you, Mrs Cameron. I'm so sorry—'

'No, lass,' Samson cut in. 'Ye've naught to be sorry for. I swear the Laird of all creation has sent ye to us. But I thought ye were supposed to be starring as Juliet in Launceston.'

'Oh, I have been, sir, and I've been enjoying it. But, after I sent that letter to you, I couldn't get the idea out of my head of how wonderful it would be to play Mrs Haller again in a fine new theatre in Hobart Town – and being on stage with you, sir. Well, I just knew what I had to do. So, I gave my notice and decided I would come and see if the part had already been taken, and if so, well, that's what was meant to be. But I just had to give myself the chance to.'

'To be on the stage with my husband,' Cordelia interrupted.

'Ah, yes, ma'am. He's such a fine gentleman, and an inspiration to me, and such a wonderful actor.'

'Yes, that will be enough, Grace. I understand your level of affection for my husband. Only too well. I must say you obviously haven't read today's *Hobart Town Theatre*.'

'Ah, no. I haven't. I don't read it normally. Should I?'

'That won't be necessary,' Samson said, looking sternly over Grace's shoulder at Cordelia. 'Not necessary at all.'

'No, I suppose not,' Cordelia said, lowering her eyes. 'So, Grace, are you prepared to step straight onto the stage? Because that's what's required, you understand?'

'Oh, I didn't think I would be performing immediately. I assumed there must be someone else playing Mrs Haller and perhaps I would replace her some time in the next few days, or whenever she can suitably be replaced. I wouldn't want to put anyone out or offend anyone, or—'

'Dear Grace,' Cordelia cut in. 'So very sweet! I assure you the current Mrs Haller can be suitably replaced at a moment's notice.'

'Oh, truly? Who's been playing the part if I may ask?'

'You may indeed, dear,' Cordelia replied, taking a larger than normal breath. 'If you look behind you, you'll be staring at Mrs Haller.'

'Oh,' Grace said as she turned slightly and looked over her shoulder.

'Grace,' Samson said with a sheepish smile.

'Mr Cameron.'

Nineteen

IN MID-AUGUST, DR CORNBLETH ADVISED that Cordelia should remain in the rest home until the baby was born. He was paying a visit almost daily.

'So, ye dinna think he just wants ye here so he can visit ye every day?'

Cordelia was seated in bed. She placed the crochet she was working on firmly on her lap and looked Samson squarely in the eye. 'No, Samson, I don't think that. Colin ... Dr Cornbleth is merely doing what doctors are meant to do – look to the best interests of their patient. One would have hoped that husbands might want the best for their spouses as well.'

'I'm sorry, darling, I shouldna ...'

He took a seat on the chair beside the bed.

'Indeed, you shouldn't, Samson. You know I'd be up, and on that stage tonight if I could. But imagine if I did and something happened to the child. I'd never forgive myself – or you if you'd forced me.'

'Of course, darling. Of course, I'd never force ye!'

She picked up the crochet and continued to work the hook. 'Besides, it gives you an excuse to keep Grace here. I thought you'd be delighted with that prospect.'

'Well, if she can stay. She says she has to go home at some point. Her ma is still not well, and …'

Cordelia stopped her work and looked at him sternly. 'Samson, if you ask her, she'll stay.'

'Perhaps but she's as disappointed as the rest of us that the new theatre is taking so long. She keeps talking about how much better it was in Launceston, and—'

'Samson, let's not pretend.'

Samson hesitated. 'What do ye mean, pretend?'

'Samson, I'm not a fool. I see the way that girl looks at you. Unfortunately, I haven't been able to see how well she kisses you this time, but I can imagine. I'm quite sure she does just as well as Gerry at that. Indeed, I dare say Gerry is quite jealous every time he sees you two at it on the stage.'

'Oh, darling. Grace's a bonnie wee lass, for sure, and, aye, I do think she's quite fond of me, but …'

'But what, Samson?'

'She's not half the woman ye are, darling. Not half. And I miss ye on stage.'

'Even when you're kissing her?'

'Especially when I have to kiss her.'

'Oh, so you'd rather have Gerry back, would you?' Cordelia said, smirking.

'No!'

'So, Grace is not such a bad kisser then?'

'Compared to Gerry, I think ye could say that,' Samson replied, looking away from Cordelia's piercing glare.

She looked back to her crocheting. 'All right, Samson, I shouldn't torment you. It's just so hard lying in this infernal bed when I so want to be back on that stage.'

'I know, darling. I know. And ye will be. But, for now, we have to accept yer beau's advice.'

She stopped and took a deep breath. 'He's not my beau, Samson. He's my doctor. Please don't say that again.'

'Aye.'

'Go away with you. See if Grace can stay.'

'And if not?'

'Then you'd better get Gerry ready to fill in,' Cordelia scoffed as a wry grin formed. 'And pucker up!'

'I'm sorry, Mr Cameron, but you might have to choose,' Dr Smithers said.

'Choose? I don't understand.'

Smithers looked to Cornbleth, appeal for help written all over his face.

'Samson, what Dr Smithers is saying is you might have to choose between the life of your wife or your child.'

It was the late evening of the 9th day of September 1836. Cordelia had been in labour for thirty-six hours with little to show for it.

'Well, there's naught to choose.'

'You mean?' the two doctors echoed.

'Ye know what I mean.'

'We'll need you to sign a note to that effect, Mr Cameron,' Smithers said, attempting to engage with his frenetic eyes.

'Aye, but can I go back in now?'

'Ah, yes, but you do understand about the note?'

'Aye, whatever ye need to do to save my wife. Just let me back into the room.'

Samson hurried the few yards to Cordelia's door. He was about to grab the handle when the door flung open, the handle crashing into his outstretched hand.

'I'm so sorry, sir,' the nurse said, trying to grab the hand he was wringing.

'It's all right, Sister,' he said, pulling his hand away, lest she do any further damage.

'Dr Smithers. Come quickly,' she called, pushing past him.

'What is it?' Smithers approached her, Cornbleth hot on his heels.

'I think the baby's coming.'

'What?' Cornbleth said. 'But …'

'I know, Colin,' Smithers said, turning to his friend. 'But I told you castor oil might just do the trick.'

The time and date of birth of William James Cameron was recorded as 12:37 a.m. on the 10th day of September 1836.

'Congratulations, Mr Cameron, you have a perfectly healthy son,' Smithers said, an obvious glee in his exaggerated, slightly apologetic smile.

'Thank ye, Doctor, but I canna understand why ye'd be laying yer wicked lies on me not an hour ago.'

'I'm sorry, sir. I don't follow you.'

'Ah, I think ye do, sir. Ye quacks are all the same. Ye think there's naught better than making out ye know more than the rest of us. Do ye have no idea what that does to ordinary folk?'

Smithers' smile evaporated. His gaze hardened as he looked to the ground.

'Samson,' Cordelia whispered with what seemed her final breath. 'Samson, for heaven's sake, apologise. These good doctors have just delivered us a son.'

'Aye, but ...'

'No buts, Samson,' she said, drawing the baby's head in closer as he stirred. 'You owe these men an apology.'

'I'm not sure of that, darling, but if ye say so.'

'I do, Samson. I do,' she spat out angrily. 'Dr Smithers, Colin, and your wonderful nurses, please accept my husband's apologies and our deepest gratitude for all you've done.'

'Thank you, Mrs Cameron,' Smithers replied as he wiped his brow with a handkerchief. 'I, I—'

'I think what Dr Smithers wants to say,' Cornbleth interrupted, 'is that we understand your husband's concern.'

'Concern?' Samson blurted out. 'Concern? Wouldn't ye be concerned if someone told ye ye'd have to choose between killing yer wife or killing yer bairn?'

'What?' Cordelia said, clutching the baby even tighter as she gazed at the two doctors. 'What on earth are you talking about? Colin, please tell me my husband has completely lost his senses.'

'Well,' Cornbleth replied, shifting from one leg to the other. 'It wasn't quite like that.'

'No?' Samson levelled his eyes on Cornbleth. 'I think it was just like that. Ye told me I'd have to choose – my wife or my bairn.'

'Is this true, Colin?' Cordelia said, looking sternly at Cornbleth. 'Is this true?'

Twenty

Cordelia's displeasure with their time in Hobart Town had gathered pace after the birth of William. She had been laid low by the difficulty of the birth and her trust in Dr Cornbleth had taken a blow by her perception that he might have stood by while Dr Smithers put her life in peril in order to save the child.

'I think ye know he fancied ye, darling,' Samson said one way or another on several occasions. 'But now ye know he's just a typical dandy quack who cares more about himself than his patients.'

It never ceased to irritate Cordelia.

'Samson, I did not think he fancied me, as you say. And he was not a regular dandy quack, as you say. He was just someone who understood me. Someone I could relate to. Unlike …'

There was a pause. Cordelia turned and walked towards the bedroom.

'Well, perhaps ye couldna see the obvious because ye fancied him.'

This persistent jibe irritated her even more. She turned back to face him.

'Samson, I did not fancy him. How ridiculous! I'm just disappointed that he let me down and deceived me. Why would he not have told me that I might have lost my life? Was he ever going to tell me?'

Samson knew that he should have bitten his tongue, but he was threatened by the level of respect, even affection from Cordelia that Cornbleth had enjoyed, something he still yearned for. All his baiting achieved was to turn Cordelia further away from him, becoming increasingly moody. Sometimes, a sullenness that lasted for days. Once, for longer.

'Are ye never going to speak to me again, Cordelia?'

She simply turned, walked away, heading back to the bedroom where she spent most of her days.

'Back to yer cave now, darling.'

She turned and strode towards him. He thought she was about to hit him when she stopped and grabbed him by his lapels.

'That cave, as you call it, is where our children spend most of their days as well. Would you like to be cooped up there day and night?'

'Darling, I've said we can get ye some help.' He attempted to draw her in for a hug, but she pulled away.

'And that we can't afford things even as they are because the rest home was so expensive and I'm not working. Don't you tell me that constantly?'

She walked swiftly towards the bedroom.

'I have to go, darling,' he said as she retreated.

She stood at the bedroom door. 'So early?'

'Aye, Grace has an idea for tonight's performance.'

'A longer kiss, perhaps?' She walked into the bedroom and slammed the door.

The baby cried.

'See what you've done,' she shouted as she opened the door and quickly slammed it shut again.

Despite the promise of a new theatre, life in Hobart Town had become all too challenging at a personal level for the pair of thespians. So, when a gentleman named Isaac Clifford arrived unannounced and offered them a contract to perform in Sydney, it seemed like a godsend. Especially for Cordelia, whose mental anguish was seemingly endless. Samson saw the first spark of her old self when getting out of Hobart Town looked like a real possibility. He knew he should have behaved himself better, but Cordelia's unexpected change of mood and apparently instant rapport with Clifford combined to impel a certain skittishness in him.

'Well, ye'd have to change the name of the theatre, ye realise.'

'Change the name?' Clifford's eyes widened.

'Aye, His Majesty's?' Samson sniggered. 'Do ye really think I'm that fond of yer rotten king.'

'Well, I, I—'

'Mr Clifford, please ignore my husband,' Cordelia interrupted, flashing an affected smile in Clifford's direction. 'He's a Scot, as you might have gathered.'

'Ah, I … I did gather that, Mrs Cameron. But I thought we were all loyal subjects – even the Scots!'

'Well, ye thought wrong, didn't ye?' Samson said, ignoring Cordelia just as she had so steely-like ignored him.

'Ah, I'm really not sure, sir.'

'Mr Clifford.' Cordelia butted in, eyes still affixed on the visitor.

'Please be assured we are all loyal subjects of His Majesty. Even cantankerous Scots like my dear husband. Aren't we, Samson?'

'If ye say so, darling,' he replied while determinedly avoiding any side glances in her direction.

'Well, I must say I'm relieved to hear it. Granted this offer is coming with endorsement from Government House, I dare say it is important that the authorities are assured of your loyalty to the Crown.'

Samson chortled without saying a word, still avoiding the glare from Cordelia that he could now detect out of the corner of his eye.

'I can assure the authorities that this is so, can I not?' Clifford stared hard in Samson's direction.

'Samson,' Cordelia said sternly.

'Mr Clifford, could I ask ye to step outside while my wife and I have a wee chat?'

Clifford consented and let himself out. He wandered to the gate some yards from the front door and lit a pipe. He pulled the collar of his coat up to cover the back of his neck, shivering in the wind off the mountain.

Meanwhile, in the house, Samson turned to his wife to plead his case. 'Darling, we're committed to the new theatre. We canna leave until we fulfil that commitment.'

Cordelia scoffed as she fell into the settee. 'Oh, for heaven's sake, Samson, you mean the theatre that should have been finished months ago! Weren't we supposed to be on a boat heading home by now? Speaking of commitments, wasn't that your commitment to me?'

'Aye, but—'

'But nothing, Samson,' she butted in. He could see the exasperation in her eyes. He feared what she was about to say.

'I'm going to Sydney even if you don't. At least it's a bit closer to home, and there's more boats going from there than here.'

Samson leant back against the door, head down. He took a deep breath. He knew that the next few words might make or break his marriage.

'What about the bairns?' was all he could manage.

'I'll take them, of course.'

'Without me?'

'That's up to you, Samson.'

'Could I join ye later? Once I've done the right thing here?'

'"The right thing."' She snuffed, shaking her head. 'Samson, if your commitment to these incompetent people is more important than your commitment to me, perhaps there'd be no point.'

Samson paced the floor, hand on his furrowed brow. 'Can we at least think about it?'

Cordelia was wiping her eyes. She blew her nose and looked up. 'You can think about it if you wish, but I'm signing those papers while Mr Clifford is here. Heaven knows if there'll be another chance.'

'Darling …'

'Don't, Samson.' She choked on the words. 'Can't you see that I'm desperate to get out of this place? More desperate than I've ever been.' She buried her head in her hands.

Samson walked swiftly to the door, opened it and invited Clifford to join them. 'Mr Clifford, kindly let the good English Governor of New South Wales know what braw servants of the Crown ye discovered in Van Diemen's Land. I dare say he'll be pleased.'

'Good,' Clifford said, taking a letter from his pocket and unfurling it. 'We might then go over the contract.'

Cordelia had quickly gone into the bedroom to compose herself.

She re-entered the room and she and Samson gathered around the table that served as both a desk and for dining, she at one end, he at the other, with Clifford seated between them.

'Oh,' Clifford said, looking directly at Samson. 'Governor Bourke is an Irishman, I thought you should know.'

'Well, why didn't ye say so, lad,' he replied, smirking and winking cheekily at Cordelia who turned her head away.

Clifford ignored the exchange, sitting gruffly on the chair, dipping his quill in the inkwell he had placed carefully next to the papers before him.

'Just before you sign, Mr Clifford,' Cordelia said, reaching for his arm, so to prevent the quill hitting the paper. 'We are firmly agreed that we will have no professional interactions with Madame Dhermainville. Is that so?'

'I'm sorry, Mrs Cameron. I don't know who you are talking about.'

'You might know her as Maria Taylor.'

'Oh, you mean the Queen of the Sydney Stage. That's what they call her, you know?'

'Frankly, Mr Clifford, I don't care what they call her. I simply wish to have nothing to do with her. Is that understood?'

'As that is your wish, madam, I offer my undertaking.'

'Thank you,' Cordelia replied, releasing her grip on Clifford's arm and turning her head to nod in Samson's direction.

'So, we'll see you in Sydney in ten weeks' time,' Clifford said as he stood after they had signed. 'Be assured, everything will be laid out for you as we have agreed.'

'I've been asked to perform at the Court House, Samson,' Cordelia said as Samson opened the door after a nightly performance just ten days or so after they had signed the Sydney contract. 'And I've said I would.'

Samson saw the mix of strain and excitement in her eyes.

'Truly? When does it start and for how long?'

'In four weeks' time, and just for eight weeks.'

'But we're supposed to be in Sydney by then.'

'Oh, I'm sure the Sydney people will be happy to wait.'

'I dinna know, darling, and even if so, do ye truly think …?'

'Yes, I do, Samson. I want to do this, and I don't want you saying anything to spoil it. Jonathan Leigh himself came around to ask me. I'd forgotten how lovely he is, Samson. Such a gentleman. It's so uplifting to have someone who appreciates me, and …'

'Ye mean the same Jonathan Leigh who couldn'a act to save himself? The convict who only got on the stage because Mrs Guilfoyle fancied him?'

'Samson, she didn't fancy him, as you say. She felt sorry for him, as do I. I've told you before that he was charged with starting a fight in Dublin when he was really trying to stop it. But when the perpetrators got away, Jonathan ended up bearing the cost. Most unfair, unjust. His poor parents were heartbroken.'

'And ye believed all this?' Samson scoffed, shaking his head. 'Ye believed an Irishman who, from all I've heard, has kissed the blarney stone once too often.'

'I should have known it was no use trying to talk to you.' Cordelia turned and walked away. 'It's all right for you to have your career, but I'm supposed to be happy sitting at home looking after a baby and a toddler while you and your lady friend charm all of Hobart Town.'

'Darling.' Samson caught up with her and grabbed her by the arm. 'Listen to me. No-one could be happier than me to see ye back where ye belong – on the stage and wooing the crowd as ye've always done so beautifully.'

'Then, why are you so negative, Samson?' she replied, wiping her nose with her handkerchief and looking everywhere except at her husband.

'Well, it's just a shock, I suppose. Ye've refused almost every opportunity to go back on stage with me, but all of a sudden, ye've been seduced by Jonathan Leigh, of all people, to take to the stage with him.'

'How dare you use that language, Samson. I am not … How rude!'

'Anyway, isn't Maria Taylor meant to be coming back to work with him?' Samson interrupted, ignoring her offended appearance.

'He explained all that,' she replied gruffly. 'Apparently, there's been some tension between them, and …'

'His latest lovers' tiff,' Samson scoffed. 'Not to mention hers. Ye know they both have a reputation, d'ye no?'

'Samson, he explained all that too. He said he had discovered she was having an affair with some cad in Sydney and so he had told her not to come back here. He told her that he wanted me anyway. That he thought I was a better actress than she. Can you imagine the look on that vixen's face when she read that in a letter?'

'Mmm.' Samson rolled his eyes. 'It seems this Jonathan Leigh really is the conman everyone says he is.'

Cordelia pulled her arm free and strode into the bedroom, slamming the door behind her.

'And what are we supposed to do about Sydney, then?' Samson called through the door. 'Ye know we've signed a contract.'

'You go, Samson,' she screamed back at him. 'And take your little darling with you.'

Samson wrote to Isaac Clifford and pleaded for a three-month stay on the Sydney undertaking. Meanwhile, he had been procrastinating in informing the Hobart Town authorities about the Sydney move, so determined that he could fulfil his commitment there, after all. The only one in whom he had confided about the move was Grace.

'I'm so excited that you're staying, Mr Cameron,' Grace said, reaching out as if involuntarily and hugging him tightly.

'Thank ye, lass. I'm glad someone is happy about it.'

'And how exciting it will be to know that Mrs Cameron will be back on stage, even if it's at the Court House.'

'Aye, well, we'll see, won't we?'

'Oh, are you not happy about that, sir?'

'Well, frankly, Grace, the Court House is hardly Drury Lane, nor even the Theatre Royal, one might say, and there is some question about Mr Leigh.'

He took note of Grace blushing and looking to the floor. He watched her raise her head and smile.

'Ye do know what I mean, Grace?'

'Please, Mr Cameron. It's not for me to say. I'm sure Mrs Cameron will be able to manage Mr Leigh's, aah ...'

'Advances?' he said firmly, staring her down.

'Please, sir, I don't mean to ...'

'It's perfectly all right, lass. Tell me what ye know.'

'Well, if I'm to be honest, Mr Leigh's reputation is not entirely unfounded.'

'Thank ye, lass. I appreciate yer trusting me with yer frankness.'

'Oh, I do, sir,' she said, blushing anew, her eyes welling up. 'I'd trust you with my life, Mr Cameron.'

'Darling, I do want ye to be careful.'

'Careful. Why?'

'With this Leigh character. I canna be sure about his virtue.'

'Samson, I told you all about that,' she replied sharply, her wild eyes staring him down. 'The poor man has been maligned all his life. Hounded by the constabulary, used and abused by heartless women of ill repute, including our Madame Dhermainville. He assures me he has learned his lesson and is now a much wiser man.'

'Perhaps, but Grace did say—'

'Speaking of women of ill repute!'

'That is so unfair, Cordelia,' he said, his anger spilling over. 'If ever there was a picture of innocence.'

'Oh, Samson, you are such a fool. You honestly can't see what's staring you in the face.'

'I wonder what ye canna see, darling,' he said, turning away.

Twenty-one

'I WILL NOT PERFORM WITH her, Samson. I've made that perfectly clear from the beginning.'

Samson had gone to the Court House to speak with Cordelia about the opening night of the new theatre, now only a few weeks away.

'You know how I feel about Madame Dhermainville! How could you let that happen?'

'Maria Taylor, darling,' Samson replied, shaking his head in exasperation. 'Because ye made it plain that ye wouldna be available. So, when Captain Wilson and Mr Degraves said they wanted her to be part of the opening night, I had to say aye.'

'Anyway, I thought she was in Sydney.'

'They're bringing her down especially.'

'Why on earth?' Cordelia was distracted by Jonathan Leigh appearing from behind the stage curtain.

'Are you ready, dear?' Leigh called.

'In a minute, Jonathan.' Cordelia blushed.

'"Dear"?' Samson asked, cocking an eyebrow.

'He calls everyone dear,' Cordelia said, brushing it off. 'Anyway, it has nothing to do with me, so you enjoy your Madame.'

'Darling, it has everything to do with ye. We're in breach of contract if ye're not part of it. Think of the bairns.'

'The bairns,' she scoffed. 'The bairns you barely know, or care about.'

Samson was about to say something. His eyes betrayed his anger. He took a deep breath. 'Well, darling, if ye care about them, ye'll think about it.'

He turned and strode out, his boots clamouring on the floorboards of the Court House.

On the 6th day of March in the year 1837, the new Theatre Royal finally opened its doors. Two pairs of thespians, Mr and Mrs Cameron, along with Mr and Mrs Taylor, graced the stage that evening. On the 10th day of March, the *Hobart Town Courier* ran the story:

> This theatre was opened to the public, for dramatic performances,
> on Monday evening last, with Morton's humorous comedy of
> *Speed the Plough*, and the laughable farce of the *Spoiled Child* …
> A prologue was delivered by Mr Cameron.

Cordelia agreed to participate, on the condition that she could perform the *Spoiled Child*, which was scheduled the following week for the Court House. She demanded that part of Samson's prologue should serve to advertise the fact. She was miffed nonetheless when Maria Taylor performed in *Speed the Plough* before the interval, while her own performance was in the second half.

Samson was relieved to see the unexpected level of civility between the two actresses.

The Camerons went their various ways over the next six weeks or so. Cordelia was performing at the Court House, while Samson was spending every day at the 'Royal', mainly directing and coaching younger players, as well as performing. He was also filling in occasionally at the Argyle. Grace was constantly by his side.

To keep the household going, they had re-employed Annabelle Walters in a full-time role as nanny and maid. She would arrive early and leave as late as needed, occasionally staying over. They had set up a makeshift bed in the front room for those occasions.

'Miss Walters is coming to know our children better than us,' Samson commented quietly but wryly one morning at breakfast.

'I have to go.' Cordelia stood hastily, leaving most of her breakfast uneaten.

Samson stared at the bacon rasher and half-eaten piece of toast on his plate. He was breathing heavily, unable to finish his own breakfast.

Even on their days off, when they might have spent some time together as a family, Cordelia always had an excuse to be otherwise occupied, normally with Jonathan Leigh.

'Oh, don't be foolish, Samson. We have a new interpretation we want to include. It's what professionalism demands, you know?'

Samson was aware that Cordelia was spending more of their cash than usual, with little or nothing to show for her work at the Court House. Any effort on his part to bring up the topic was met with a brick wall.

'Can you not be a little more patient, Samson? Jonathan is

working on a new production, and you should know better than anyone how expensive that can be.'

April 21st of the year 1837 would live in Samson's memory as the worst day of his life. He had come in late the night before. As was their custom when he was late, he slept in a small room off the kitchen, so to avoid disturbing the rest of the household. An unusual noise woke him early. When he went to investigate, he found that Cordelia had already left the house. He knew that on a Friday, the rehearsal schedule for the weekend performances was heavier than normal, sometimes demanding an early start. *But this early? And without even telling me?*

He went to tend to the children, who by now were sleeping together in the second bedroom, only to find that they were not there.

He was standing in the room wondering what to make of it when Miss Walters walked in behind him.

'Where are your babies, Mr Cameron?'

He turned to see her look of concern deepen as she took in the shocked look on his face.

'Have ye no idea, Miss Walters? Did Mrs Cameron say naught about what she was doing this morning?'

'I'm afraid not, sir. Has Mrs Cameron taken them with her?'

'She didna tell me, but perhaps I've forgotten,' he replied, trying as much to calm himself as her. 'She's occasionally taken them for an early morning walk. I'm sure she'll be home soon.'

Samson made himself a quick breakfast of tea and a slice of bread and jam. He almost cut his finger as he sliced the loaf, distracted by the sense of confusion about his family's whereabouts.

He was deep in thought, mindlessly chewing on the bread, when Miss Walters approached him again.

'I'm sorry to disturb you, sir, but I was wondering about my wage.'

Cordelia normally left her wage on the kitchen table every Friday before leaving the house. She had taken to managing the house accounts ever since they had needed to hire the extra help.

'I'm sorry, Miss Walters. I assumed Mrs Cameron would have left the envelope in the usual spot.'

It was then that he was told there had been no envelope for the past three weeks.

'Good heavens. Have ye spoken with Mrs Cameron about this?'

'Yes indeed, sir, several times. Mrs Cameron always said she would attend to it immediately, but I was not paid.'

Samson went to the locked box in the bedroom cupboard where they kept their cash, only to find it empty. He excused himself and hastened to the Court House. Finding it locked, he hurried around to the Theatre Royal.

'Mr Cameron, you're early.' Douglas Crisp, one of the attendants who kept an eye on the place out of hours, hurried over to him.

'Good morning, Mr Crisp. I wonder if ye might have seen Mrs Cameron.'

'Mrs Cameron? But I thought she was working at the Court House. Is everything all right?'

Samson brushed off his concern and walked out onto Argyle Street. He needed time to think. He wandered the streets and found St David's cemetery, the burial ground somewhat neglected, almost deserted. He found a rock wall and sat on it, taking in the calming surrounds of autumnal trees shedding their leaves, laying a carpet of crimson and yellow over the ground, the distinctive call of a single magpie nearby.

There'll be an explanation. I canna but trust. I gave my heart to Cordelia long ago.

Refreshed and strengthened, he stood up and strode back towards the theatre. Halfway along Davey Street, he saw two constables hurrying towards him.

'Stop, sir,' one of them called as he picked up his step.

Samson stopped in his tracks, certain then that something dreadful had befallen Cordelia and the children. His head became a scramble of possible disasters. He felt some relief when the constables reached him so he could hear the truth, however challenging.

'Tell me, constables. Whatever it is, just tell me.'

'Mr Samson Cameron,' one of them replied, reaching inside his coat. 'You are under arrest.'

'Oh, Mr Cameron, I just can't believe it,' Grace said, reaching across the table in the prison yard to rest her hand on Samson's. 'How could she do this to you?'

'No touchin' the prisoner, miss,' the guard called out. 'Anymore of that and I'll 'ave to escort you out of 'ere.'

'I'm sorry,' she replied, looking back over her shoulder before turning her head back to Samson. She was shaking, her eyes red and tearful. 'I'm so sorry, Mr Cameron. How can you stand being in here?'

Samson shrugged. 'It's not easy, lass, I'll admit. I just dinna understand what's going on. How are people taking it all?'

'Shocked. They're all so shocked. And angry with Mrs Cameron. They ...'

'Oh, we dinna know, lass. No-one knows what really happened. I canna believe—'

'That you've been betrayed?' Grace spat out loudly, her eyes suddenly fiery in a way he hadn't seen before, her whole body shaking so the table bounced on the cobblestone ground.

'Miss,' the guard called again, taking a step in their direction.

'I'm sorry,' she replied, looking in his direction. 'I'm sorry. It won't happen again.'

'Lass …'

'Mr Cameron,' she interrupted, the fire in her eyes replaced with welling tears. 'Please forgive me. I'm just so upset. And I don't know how you can be so calm. How you can be so forgiving.'

'Grace, lass. I love my wife. I believe in her. And I'm certain there's an explanation. My wife is not a thief. Perhaps Mr Leigh is, but I know my wife is not. And I know she wouldna place our bairns in harm's way. So …'

'You're such a wonderful man, Mr Cameron,' she said, head down, lashes shielding her eyes from him. 'Mrs Cameron is so very fortunate.'

'Thank ye, Grace. But I'm the fortunate one to have such a friend, ye dear, sweet lass.'

Grace buried her head in her hands and wept. Samson stole a moment while the guard's head was turned away to reach out quickly and press his hand into her arm. Her own hand was on his before he knew, clenching it tightly.

'I said no touching,' the guard shouted as he strode towards them. 'That's it. Your time's up, miss.'

None of the circumstances of his arrest were fully explained to Samson. It appeared that a considerable sum of money had gone missing from the Court House coffers to which Jonathan Leigh had access. Someone reported seeing Samson loitering around the Court House that morning, so there was an immediate assumption that he was a suspect, or one of them at least. Meanwhile, Leigh and Cordelia, with the children in tow, had been seen boarding a ship bound for South Australia in the early morning. When the police were alerted, they first searched Leigh's place and found nothing. They then came to the Cameron home, where Miss Walters told them the story of the missing funds and that they would likely find Samson at the theatre. They went to the 'Royal', only to be told that he had been there earlier on, asking about Cordelia. In the end, it seemed Samson was the only suspect able to be apprehended.

In his first court appearance, Samson was grilled to within an inch of his life by the prosecutor, who appeared adamant that he was up to his neck in the disappearance of the funds. Having no-one to argue his case, he was charged and committed to what was called 'debtor's prison' for an unspecified time, dependent on recovery of the funds or further facts coming to light that might prove him innocent.

In Samson's second court appearance, further charges were brought against him by theatre management related to losses resulting from cancelled performances and, just to make sure the man on his knees was kicked again, by the performers in relation to their lost wages. Again, he had no-one to call on, least of all afford to defend him.

'I want you to know I had absolutely nothing to do with this, Mr Cameron,' Grace said on a visit said to be conditional on her good behaviour. 'I'm appalled that these people would put all the blame on you.'

'Thank ye, lass. I really dinna know what I'd do without yer trust in me.'

'Oh, I do trust you, Mr Cameron, sir.' Her eyes filled with tears. 'I said I'd trust you with my life and I meant it.'

Samson wanted so much to reach out and touch her again. But the guard was watching them.

'Ye know if we weren't here, I'd give ye the biggest hug, do ye no, lass?'

'I know,' she said, smiling through wet lashes. 'I know, sir.'

'Thank ye, Mr Heath, but ye know I canna pay ye.'

'That's perfectly all right, Mr Cameron,' the tall, elegantly dressed gentleman replied. 'That's all being taken care of.'

Preston Heath, a Melbourne-based lawyer who occasionally practised in Van Diemen's Land, was sitting opposite him in the prison yard. Samson reflected for a moment that he was sitting in the very spot where Grace had sat on her last visit.

'By whom, may I ask? I really didna think I had any friends left, least who might pay for a lawyer to defend me.'

'Well, sir, I've been asked to maintain privacy around that matter.'

Samson could see that Preston Heath was not the kind of man to dishonour a pledge. Although he would have wished to know who his donor was, Heath's honourable stance provided him with some assurance that he would do the right thing by him. He had been in the debtor's prison for almost five weeks. While he was told to be grateful for the relative comfort and freedom, compared to the prison's inner sanctum, he was nonetheless beginning to feel despondent about his future.

'Now, Mr Cameron, tell me everything.'

As it turned out, Preston Heath was as much a private investigator as a lawyer. In only a matter of weeks, he and his contacts had tracked Leigh and Samson's family to Adelaide. Leigh had been arrested, and Cordelia and the children were on their way back to Hobart Town.

'Mrs Cameron will testify on your behalf,' Heath assured him. 'I'm told she is most distressed at everything that has happened and is returning with the stolen goods.'

'I'm sorry for what happened, Samson,' Cordelia said on their return home from the courtroom. 'But I refuse to be treated like a criminal.'

'I dinna think ye're a criminal, Cordelia. I just need to know what happened and that the rumours have no substance.'

'What rumours?'

'Well, that ye ran away with Leigh,' he said, hesitating until he gauged her reaction. 'That …'

'What?'

'That ye did a Mrs Haller with him.'

Cordelia slumped into a settee, visibly upset. She looked up at him, her teary eyes betraying a mix of anger and remorse. She opened her mouth to speak.

'I'll be going now,' Miss Walters called from the doorway behind where Cordelia was sitting. 'The children have been fed and are sleeping.'

'Thank ye, Miss Walters. Ye're a godsend.'

'Not at all, sir. Wonderful to see you home again, Mr Cameron. Might I say, I never believed a word that people were saying about you, sir.'

'Thank ye for saying that. It's much appreciated.'

'Goodbye, then, sir. Just let me know when you need me.'

'Goodbye, Miss Walters.'

Miss Walters turned and let herself out. Cordelia sat rigidly in her chair, her head down. Samson took note that Miss Walters had not even acknowledged his wife's presence.

'I can only wonder what that woman must think of me,' Cordelia said finally, her head downcast.

'I dinna care what people think, Cordelia. I only care about what I believe, what I know. Please tell me everything.'

'Samson, you heard what I said in the courtroom. It was all a terrible mistake. I had no idea that Jonathan had stolen money, or that he was going to take us to Adelaide. No idea at all!'

'So, he kidnapped ye, then?'

'In effect, yes!'

'In effect? What does that mean, love?'

'It means I was kidnapped. The children and me. How else do you want me to say it?'

'I dinna know, darling. What about our money? Why did it disappear? What were ye doing with it? Ye know that's what caused all the problems with the theatre and the staff?'

'Samson, just give me time,' she replied. 'My head is killing me. The main thing is I'm here. The children are here. The money's been returned. Your name's been cleared. What more do you need right now?'

'I dinna know, love,' he said, choking on the words, lowering his head. 'I—'

'Samson,' she cut him off.

'Aye?' He looked up at her through tear-filled eyes.

'I do love you, you know.'

The wells of a woman's heart run as deep as the ocean. Samson had heard the saying somewhere. Unanswered questions remained but, as time went on, he found it best to leave them that way.

Preston Heath was able to give him some reasonable reassurance.

'I'm convinced of your wife's innocence in all this, Mr Cameron. In spite of appearances, might I say? There's no doubt that Mr Leigh put his theatrical skills to good use. A professional shyster is what we would call him.'

'But a ship to Adelaide? How could that happen?'

'Sir, my understanding is that she had no idea the boat was going that far or going anywhere for that matter. But your wife would know more about that. Perhaps you should ask her.'

'I have, Mr Heath,' Samson said, shaking his head. 'Believe me, I have.'

Heath paused, as if pondering on what he might say that fitted the moment.

'Mr Cameron, it's beyond my brief but if I might say I believe your wife has suffered much through all this. Reports from Adelaide were that she was extremely distressed when she realised what had transpired. Perhaps it's best that you give her time to recover.'

It was good advice, Samson decided. Best look to the positives. The various cases against him were formally dismissed, issues with the theatre and the staff were resolved, and he had his family back with him. And the greatest positive of all? His profound love for Cordelia. If forgiveness was needed, what else could he do but forgive? And trust. The alternative was too bleak to contemplate.

'Isaac Clifford has replied from Sydney. He says the offer still stands.' Samson scanned the letter in his hands. 'But we need to be there quickly.'

'I should have thought so,' Cordelia replied, lifting her head out of the book. 'But why so quick?'

'He says there have been moves to commission Eliza Winstanley and her company to supplement or even replace us.'

'I'm not worried about them supplementing us,' she said, looking back to the book. 'I actually wouldn't mind performing with her.'

'Truly?'

'Well, at least I know she's spoken for – unlike Madame Dhermainville.'

Twenty-two

'I REALLY THINK IT'S FOR the best.' Samson was hoping Grace wouldn't notice the sadness in his eyes.

They were standing, some distance apart, in the shabby parlour of her guesthouse. He had slipped out to say his goodbyes.

'I understand, sir. But I'm going to miss you so much.'

'Me too, Grace. Dear Grace,' he said, reaching towards her and resting his hand on her elbow. 'I've come to think of ye as the daughter I've never had. The daughter I might have had if Elizabeth had lived.'

'As a daughter?' Grace cast her head down and away from his gaze.

'Aye. Is that all right?'

Grace said nothing, her head still turned away. She removed her hand from his grip.

'Did I say something wrong, dear? Did I offend ye, by any chance?'

'No, Mr Cameron.' She turned her head back to face him with

a look of renewed resolve. 'Nothing wrong. I'm honoured that you think of me as a daughter.'

Samson saw again that knowing smile, the gaze that seemed to see straight through to his soul.

'Oh, I think I have said something to offend ye, lass.'

'No, sir. Not at all,' she said, looking down again, hiding her face from him.

'What is it, then, lass?'

'All right, then, Samson,' she said, staring into his eyes. 'I'm sorry. I mean Mr Cameron.'

Samson could feel a querying grin betraying him. They both knew it was the first time she had called him by his first name.

'Does Mrs Cameron look on me as a daughter?' The smile was gone, her eyes unusually cold.

Now, it was his turn to look down and away. He took a deep breath, hoping to find the right words.

'Aye, partly!'

'Partly?'

'Aye, lass.'

'And the other part?'

'I'm not sure, Grace.'

'Oh, I think you are, Samson. I'm not the foolish young thing you think me to be, you know.'

'I dinna—'

'Don't, Samson. Please don't patronise me.'

Samson took a step back. He paused for a moment. 'Grace, no matter what Cordelia thinks, ye know there's naught I'd love more than for us to stay as professional partners.'

'Meaning what?' she scoffed. 'That I come to Sydney with you?'

'Aye.'

She stepped further back, half turning away.

'I don't think so, Samson.'

'But why not?'

Grace turned to face him, an unusual determination in her eyes. 'Samson, I'll say it if you won't. Your wife is threatened by me. She sees me as a rival.'

'Well, lass, ye're a bonnie actress, a mighty good one. Ye canna blame anyone for being a wee bit threatened, as ye say. Why, the way the audience—'

'*Samson,*' Grace said sternly, looking down and taking a deep breath.

He watched her in silence. *Ah, here it comes.* Was he dreading or a tad excited by what she was going to say? He couldn't tell.

'Samson, it's not all to do with my theatrical skills. You know that. Let's not fool ourselves.'

It was his turn to take a deep breath. Hers to watch in silence.

'Lass, I'm not sure exactly what my wife thinks,' he said slowly, smiling and looking into her eyes, hoping to re-kindle the warmth he had come to expect was the norm between them, a warmth he was disarmed to be missing so much right now. 'But, aye, I imagine she might see ye as a *boireannach glic,* as my old ma would have said. She—'

'Samson,' Grace cut in, her voice harsh and eyes afire. 'Samson, for God's sake speak to me in a way I can understand. I know you like to hide behind your ridiculous Highland front when you want to avoid the truth, but this is not the time. Do you understand, sir? It is not the time.'

Grace half turned away again. She was dabbing her nose with a handkerchief.

Samson stood unsure where to look, mouth involuntarily agape. He could scarcely find the words or the look the occasion seemed to demand.

'I'm sorry, lass. I'm sorry. But it's difficult.'

'Samson,' Grace turned back to face him, tears forming and, as quickly, receding as she gathered her strength and stared him down. 'Samson, your wife thinks I'm trying to steal you from her.'

'Grace …'

'Stop. Please stop and let me finish.'

He took a step back and rested his bottom on the arm of the settee behind him. He sensed he might fall over without some support.

'Your wife clearly thinks I'm in love with you. These are things that women understand about each other. And I am a woman, Samson. I'm a woman. Not the silly little girl you think I am.'

'I've never …'

'*Samson!*'

'Sorry, lass.'

'I'm right, aren't I, Samson? Admit it!'

'Grace, aye, she thinks ye fancy me. A wee bit infatuated … but ye have to understand she's not so well and I know ye're not infatuated. Why would ye be, lass? Ye could have any man ye wanted. Ye're the finest lass. Ye—'

'She's right, Samson.'

He stopped talking and stared at her.

'She's right,' Grace said, pausing to wipe her eyes. 'I'm sorry, Mr Cameron. I feel such a fool. I can't believe what I'm saying.'

Grace began to sob. She stood immobile, holding the handkerchief over her face. Samson lifted himself up from the arm of the settee, stepped forward and pulled her head onto his shoulder. Grace pulled away.

'Don't, Mr Cameron. Please don't. I'm so sorry.'

She stepped back and sank onto a pouffe behind her.

'There's naught to be sorry about, lass. I'm just a fool. Cordelia has been telling me this for a long time, and I've just put it down to her being unwell, imagining things.'

He turned on his heels and faced away from her, looking out the window at a blossoming rose bush, hoping to find a calm that seeing her was disallowing him right now.

'Such a fool,' he muttered.

'You're not a fool, Samson. Please don't say that. You're too good for her. Can't you see that?'

Samson spun back and faced her.

'What? What on earth are ye saying, lass?' He was now feeling an anger that was loosening his befuddled head and tongue. 'Mrs Cameron is far beyond me in every way. I couldna believe my luck when she agreed to marry me. She was a famous actress, and I was nobody.'

Grace sat motionless, staring down at the handkerchief she was wringing through her hands.

'Do ye hear me, lass?'

'Yes, sir. I'm sorry,' she sobbed, wiping her eyes. 'It's just …'

'Just what, lass?'

'Nothing.'

'Tell me, Grace.'

'I see how she treats you, sir. She has you on a string. She's like the puppet master and you're the puppet, running around trying to please her when she can never be pleased. And you don't deserve it. You're such a wonderful man. She doesn't know how lucky she is.'

Samson stood, scarcely believing his ears, trying to process what he had just heard. He opened his mouth to speak.

'And she and that Jonathan Leigh,' she spat out.

'Now, Grace. Please. They are just rumours, and—'

'Oh, of course, Samson. Just rumours! And what about that doctor, then?'

'What doctor? What are ye talking about, lass?'

'Don't tell me you don't know, Samson. The whole of Hobart Town has been talking about it. Well before Jonathan Leigh arrived on the scene.'

'Ye mean Dr Cornbleth?'

'Yes, I believe that's his name.'

'He's been very kind and attentive to my wife. That's all.'

'*Attentive?*'

'Aye, attentive!'

'Well, that's one way to put it, sir.'

'I dinna know what ye're suggesting, lass. I think I'd best go.'

Grace stood up slowly. She took a step towards him.

'Dinna come any closer, Grace,' Samson stepped around her. 'Please.'

She stepped aside to allow him to pass. He reached the door and stopped, turning to face her.

'Tell me, Grace. What is it people are saying?'

She stood motionless, looking down and giving her head a slight shake. She lifted her head, took a step towards him and looked him squarely in the eye.

'Do you really want to know, Samson? Or do you just want to go?'

'I want to know.'

'Then, sit back down,' she said, motioning to the settee.

'I need to see Dr Cornbleth,' Samson said over the reverberations of the slamming door.

Unable to confront Jonathan Leigh, he felt he could at least take out some of his frustration and hurt on Cornbleth.

'Ah, and your name, sir?' the receptionist replied, glancing around to see who might assist if this man was as agitated as it appeared.

'Cameron. Samson Pearce Cameron.'

'I don't believe you have an appointment, Mr Cameron,' she said, leafing through the register.

'I doubt I'll need one, lass, if ye could just tell the doctor I'm here.'

'Well, the doctor is with a patient at present. Can you wait?'

'Certainly.'

'Good, would you care to sit down, then?'

'No, thank ye. I'll stand right here.'

Some twenty minutes passed, and he was still standing by the receptionist's desk, occasionally turning his back to it, then turning around again, every so often banging his open hand on the top of the desk. The receptionist would look up. This time, she jumped.

'Would you mind not doing that, Mr Cameron? It startles some of the patients. And me, if I'm to be honest.'

'I'm sorry, lass. It's just … when do ye think the doctor will be free?'

'I imagine it won't be long. Are you sure you wouldn't like to sit down?'

'No, thank ye.'

The door to the surgery opened and an elderly woman stepped out. She approached the desk.

'Ah, would you excuse me for a moment, Mrs Gordon?' the receptionist said as she stood up. 'I just need to see the doctor for a moment.'

'Lass, best ye attend to Mrs Gordon,' Samson said, heading for the surgery door. 'I'll see myself in.'

'Oh, Mr Cameron, please—' But Samson reached the door a split second before the receptionist. He opened it and stepped in. There was Cornbleth, sitting at his desk, peering towards the commotion.

'Mr Cameron,' he said, eyes wide and staring at Samson. 'I don't believe …'

'I'm so sorry, sir.' The receptionist stepped forward. 'Mr Cameron insisted.'

'It's all right, Rose. Just tell the next patient I'll be a few moments. Do come in, Mr Cameron. Please take a seat.'

'No need, sir. I dinna want to steal any of yer time.'

'Well, what is it, then? Is Mrs Cameron all right after her experience?'

'I thought ye might be able to tell me more about my wife than I can, sir.'

'I beg your pardon.'

'Sir, do ye know naught about the rumours around this town?'

'Rumours? About your wife and Mr Leigh?'

'No, dinna worry about Mr Leigh. I mean about Cordelia and yerself.'

'I've no idea, sir.' Cornbleth stiffened. 'Please tell me.'

'That ye and my wife have been seeing each other.'

'Seeing each other? Well, of course we've been seeing each other. She's been my patient. I would have thought you of all people would know that.'

'And is that all there is to it, sir? That's what I need to know.'

'Absolutely, Mr Cameron. I … I'm simply speechless. Have you spoken with Mrs Cameron about this?'

'Well, no. I … I didna want to bother her with it. With everything else going on. And she's not been well, as ye know.'

'Indeed, she's not been well. But, in light of these rumours you're speaking of, perhaps you should speak with her. Don't you think?

'Aye. I'm sorry. We've all been a wee bit stressed. What with all the goings-on, and preparing to move to Sydney – and Cordelia's illness, and …'

'I understand,' Cornbleth said, looking down at the papers on his desk. 'But if I might be bold enough to say …'

'Say?'

'Without breaking patient confidence, that is. I would need you to understand that this is in the strictest confidence. Not even your wife should know I told you.'

'What?'

'Do I have your word?'

'Aye, sir.'

'Well, your wife has confided in me that she is worried about you and your co-star, the young girl who has replaced her.'

'Grace?'

'If that's her name, yes. She's been worried that you're overly fond of her and, more so, that she is more than overly fond of you.'

'Oh, my Laird! Has she really told ye this?'

'She has.'

Samson sat in silence for a moment, taking in the weight of everything that had befallen him recently.

'Mr Cameron.' Cornbleth broke the silence. 'I believe your wife has been suffering from several stress-related matters, physical and mental, and your relationship with this young girl is certainly one of the latter. I suspect it might even explain some of these recent goings-on with Mr Leigh.'

'Surely not!'

'Sit down, Mr Cameron,' Cornbleth said sternly, waving his hand towards the empty patient's chair beside his desk. 'Sit down and listen. I don't know for certain what's been going on, but I do know what has been playing on her mind. The last time we spoke about it, she told me that whenever she brought up the matter of you and this young Grace that you would ignore her and change the subject. I suggested that she should be more persistent – for her own mental state, you understand – but then she said that she didn't want to push you away, that she feared you might leave her and that she felt old and unwell and unable to compete with such a young and attractive girl, unable to maintain her career while yours, and this Grace's, are soaring. These are the words she used, Mr Cameron. Can you see that she has been suffering in a seriously debilitating way?'

Samson opened his mouth to speak, albeit unsure just what he was going to say.

'And that you don't really care,' Cornbleth jumped in. 'That you've as good as given up on her.'

'Oh, my Laird!' Samson looked to the floor, shaking his head.

'So, you see, Mr Cameron. It seems you and your wife need to have a good talk. A good, open and honest talk. I mean, is there any truth to her concerns?'

'Not really,' Samson replied, head still inclined to the floor, pondering on his recent interchange with Grace.

'Not really, you say! So, it's perhaps not altogether Mrs Cameron's vivid imagination?'

Samson sat in silence, wringing his hands. Out of the corner of one eye, he could see Cornbleth watching him as he slowly stood up, muttering something apparently inaudible to the doctor.

'I'm sorry, Mr Cameron, did you say something?'

'Aye, I think it's well and truly time we got out of this town.'

Twenty-three

BECAUSE OF THE DELAY CAUSED by Samson's sojourn at His Majesty's pleasure, by the time they sailed into Sydney Cove in early September 1837, the Irish-born Governor of New South Wales, Richard Bourke, had already sailed out of the Heads on his way home. This was most unfortunate because he was to be replaced by the very English-born George Gipps, a man with far less interest in theatre and the arts than his predecessor. Furthermore, as they would come to see firsthand, Gipps' lack of interest was only exceeded by that of the Lieutenant Governor, who was keeping the seat warm until his arrival.

'I'm very sorry about this,' Isaac Clifford said as he escorted them to their rented accommodation, a far less salubrious place than had been promised. He was helping them to carry their luggage down a dank alleyway leading to the front door. 'It's just that Acting Governor Snodgrass doesn't want to make a decision before the next governor arrives.'

'But we were assured the decision had already been made,'

Samson protested as they entered a dark hallway, leading to a narrow, steep staircase. 'Did we not hear ye say so?'

'Well, it was what I believed at the time.' Clifford was bounding up the stairs with a valise in each hand. Reaching the top, he turned back to face them. 'But, of course, you weren't here on time, and with one delay and another, much has changed.'

Samson helped Cordelia, carrying William, up the stairs while, with his other hand, helping John, who seemed insistent on seeing how much he could complete the task by himself. When they arrived at the top, Clifford was standing in the open doorway.

'If so much has changed, why did ye not inform us, so we could at least be prepared?'

'I agree with my husband, Mr Clifford.' Cordelia spoke for the first time since they had stepped from the cart. 'This is an appalling state of affairs. We were promised accommodation with a view of the sea. The only water we can see from here is the filthy overflow in the gutter.'

'Yes, I can only say again how sorry I am about this. I—'

Cordelia cut him off. 'Well, I will be taking it up with the Governor when he arrives. I believe the reception is later this month. Is that correct?'

'Ah, reception …? What reception would that be?'

'In the letter accompanying our contract, we were told we were to be invited to a reception at Government House where we would be introduced to the Sydney establishment.'

'Were you? Who signed that letter?'

'Well, I don't recall,' Cordelia said, walking over to the assembled suitcases. 'Now, I wonder where it is. I know, I think I put it in here.'

Cordelia lifted a chequered valise and placed it on a small side table. She opened it and began fossicking through its contents.

'That's all right, Mrs Cameron,' Clifford said as he turned towards the door. 'It will do no good anyway. I'm afraid there'll be no reception at Government House at least until the next governor is in place. He's not due until late October.'

'Ye mean we'll be in this place until then?'

'At least until then,' Clifford called back as he walked out the door.

'Wait, wait, wait,' Cordelia shouted as she ran after him. 'Who can we speak with about all this?'

'I'll get back to you, Mrs Cameron,' Clifford said as he hurried down the stairs, heading for the outer door.

'When?' Cordelia shouted.

'Soon,' Clifford shouted back.

Twenty-four

December of 1837 came around, and still Isaac Clifford had made no contact. When all efforts to meet with him failed, Samson decided they needed to move to accommodation more suitable to their number.

'But we can't even afford this place,' Cordelia said when he told her of his visit to Woolloomooloo Hill on Sydney Cove's southern shores, known even then as one of the town's more affluent areas. 'Our savings are almost gone, and I can't ask for any more from my father.'

'Darling, as ye know, I never wanted for ye to bother yer da. I can provide. It's for me to take care of ye and the bairns.'

'But how, Samson? We have no work. We've been lured here under false pretences, and neither of us is fit for any purpose other than theatre.'

'Well, I think ye might be wrong on that front, Cordelia. Ye know I worked for my da in Edinburgh when I was a wee bairn.'

'A thousand years ago!' Cordelia sounded even more shrill than normal. 'And what did you do anyway, you foolish man? It was a shoe factory, wasn't it? Are you going to start making shoes? And with what? We don't have an ounce of leather, nails, hammers … and whatever else you'd need … and we don't have the means to purchase any of it. For heaven's sake, man, talk some sense or don't talk at all!'

'Well, I'll talk sense if ye stop for a wee moment and listen. Is that not too much to ask?'

'Fine,' Cordelia huffed, folding her arms indignantly. 'Talk to me.'

'Thank ye,' he replied, taking a deep breath. 'No, I won't be making shoes. Frankly, I was never much good at that side of the business anyway. Two left thumbs, Da used to say. But—'

'Well, your father and I agree on that score.' Cordelia threw her head back in mock laughter. 'Remember the time I asked you to hang that painting on the wall in Launceston?'

'Oh, I thought I did all right with that.'

'What? Wrecking the wall? If that's what you mean, I couldn't agree more.'

'Well, when ye've had all yer fun for the day, darling, let me finish.'

'I'm sorry, Samson. Just what is it you can do, other than make shoes?'

'I learned how to do the books. That's what! Da used to say I was a natural with numbers. Ye'd know that from the way I run the playhouse.'

Cordelia smirked and lifted an eyebrow. 'Well, yes and no.'

'Aye, I acknowledge there've been a few lapses, but we've always come through, have we no? Except when people have run off with our money.'

Samson regretted instantly bringing up this bubbling sore of an issue. There was silence while he waited for her response.

'Well, have we no?' He decided to cut off the potential castigation.

'By the skin of our teeth, perhaps,' Cordelia replied, giving nothing away. 'We've come very close to being out on the street. And if we're to be honest, we would have been on the street a few times without my parents' help.'

'Ye give me such wee credit, Cordelia. Is it so impossible for ye to be a wee bit more generous?'

'I'm sorry if that's the case, Samson. Anyway, go on with your story. How are you planning to pay for this new residence?'

'All right, then. From what I can see, there's a shortage of accountants in the colony, and I know it's something I can do.'

'You mean like you knew you'd be so good at playing Mrs Haller. That sort of knowing?'

'Oh, ye're a cruel woman, aren't ye?'

'Well, you must admit that was not your finest display of good judgement, now was it, Samson?' Cordelia said, glaring at him askance. 'Although I acknowledge that Gerry might well disagree with me.'

'Can ye never forget that, Cordelia?'

'No, Samson. I promise I will never forget it. Nor will I let you forget it.'

'If ye insist. But that was all sorted out quickly.'

'Oh, by re-hiring your sweetheart?'

'Grace was never my sweetheart. Let's not start all that again. Or would ye like to talk about yer Mr Leigh and yer doctor friend?' He grimaced. He could have kicked himself for letting that slip out in anger.

Cordelia stood, expressionless. 'Let's not go over all that again,' she replied as she turned and walked away.

'At last, we agree on something.'

Towards the end of the following week, Samson received a letter inviting him to attend an interview for a job in the Scots Church Offices in Surry Hills, a few streets away from their accommodation.

'You, working for a church?' Cordelia scoffed. 'I truly never thought I'd see the day.'

'Just as an accountant. Accounts are accounts, ye know.'

'Oh, no Samson. I think you should go all the way. You know, become a preacher. Why not? I don't think the pay is all that good, but I'm sure you'd look resplendent in black.'

Samson grinned. These wee moments of levity between them were rare enough these days. 'Ye're quite the comedian, aren't ye, dear? I ken ye should be on the stage.'

But his attempt at lightness was dashed before he had time to enjoy it.

'And, of course, you're so good at taking the moral high ground,' Cordelia threw at him as she retreated towards the bedroom.

Samson ignored the challenge and followed her. She was tending to the sleeping baby while he began to undress.

'Seriously, Samson,' she said after a moment. 'Is it something you really can do? I know you've managed some of the accounts for theatres and shoe factories, but for a whole church?'

'I'm sure I can.' *Good, she's back to normal.* 'It wasna just one factory, ye know. Da had several shops across Scotland, and even parts of England.'

'I never knew that, Samson. Why have you never told me?'

'I suppose we had better things to talk about, darling.'

'I suppose we did,' Cordelia said softly, casting her eyes down at the baby. 'Once upon a time.'

Oh aye? 'Aye, so there's hope for us then, is there no?'

Samson waited, facing the wardrobe. Would she say more? When nothing came, he turned and slipped into the bed. Cordelia came to bed soon afterwards and surprised him by snuggling up to him.

Twenty-five

By early March of the year 1838, they had moved to the rented flat in Woolloomooloo Hill with a view of the expanses of Sydney Cove. It came some weeks after Samson had taken up the position as Assistant Business Manager in the Presbyterian Church Offices. On a day in mid-April, the Moderator's secretary knocked on his office door.

'Aye.'

'Mr Cameron,' Emily Masters said as she stood at the open doorway.

'Aye, Miss Masters,' he replied, peering at her over his reading spectacles.

'Mr Lang wonders if he could have a word with you.'

'Mr Lang? By all means, Miss Masters. When? Now?'

'No, Mr Cameron. I'll let you know.'

Samson went back to the papers on his desk. He had been making notes on a proposal from the Methodist Church for a joint outback mission between the two churches. He started reading back over them but found himself distracted by wondering why the Moderator would want to see him. Had he done something wrong? Had someone complained about him? Had he not held his tongue as Cordelia advised – demanded?

Try as he might, he could not concentrate, reading and re-reading the same page several times.

An hour or so later, there was a knock on the door.

'Aye.'

'Mr Lang will see you now, Mr Cameron,' Emily said as the door swung open.

'Thank ye, Miss Masters.' Samson stood quickly and followed her out the door. 'Ye've no idea why Mr Lang wants to see me, I suppose?'

'No, Mr Cameron.' She was inviting no further exchange.

They walked in silence down the long corridor and up the stairs at the end. He had never ventured this far into the building. The dingy mustiness that he had become accustomed to about this place of work worsened with every step.

Why do churches always end up in places like this?

After what seemed like an endless journey into the underworld, Emily Masters opened the outer door to her office, stepping in and inviting him to follow.

'Please take a seat, Mr Cameron.' She pointed to two high-backed, black wooden chairs on the far wall.

'Thank ye,' he replied, moving nervously to one of the chairs. He sat down and adjusted his cravat, ensuring it was straight and tightly tucked in where it belonged. If he was to be laid off, at least he would look his best.

Twenty minutes or so passed. He could hear muffled male voices – perhaps two or three – coming from the adjoining office with 'Reverend J. Lang, Moderator' etched into the nameplate just beneath the frosted glass on the upper part of the door. Emily Masters sat at her desk, moving her eyes between two large ledgers, occasionally dipping her quill into the ink bottle and making an entry in one of them.

Suddenly, the muffled voices turned to raucous laughter. Samson looked anxiously towards the frosted glass – was there finally some movement? Miss Masters sat rigidly, as though she had heard nothing, continuing her eying of the two ledgers, administering the occasional entry.

The Moderator's door half opened. The portly stomach of Robert MacTavish, Business Manager and Samson's immediate supervisor, protruded.

'Could you ask Mr Cameron to join us, Miss Masters?'

Samson's heart sank further. He was certain now of his fate.

How will we pay the rent? What will become of us? What will Cordelia say when I tell her we have to move again?

'He's right here, Mr MacTavish.' Miss Masters smiled politely and gestured towards Samson's chair.

'Oh, I'm so sorry, Mr Cameron,' MacTavish said, leaning his head forward and turning to face him. 'I didn't realise you were here already. Could you step inside for a moment?'

'Certainly, sir.'

Samson stood and walked towards the open door, following MacTavish's directions and entering the Moderator's office. He took in the tall ceilings, the expanse of floor in front of him.

Ye could fit my pokey office in here six or eight times. The darkness in the room had him squinting to find focus. Every stick of furniture, desk, chairs, bookcases, was black, heavily polished timber of what appeared to be the best kind. The only colour in the room was in the deep burgundy carpet made of what he felt assured was the finest wool available in the colony.

'Gentlemen,' MacTavish said. 'Please let me introduce Mr Samson Cameron, my new assistant.'

'Welcome, Mr Cameron,' the deep Glaswegian voice emitted from the shadows of the far side of the desk. 'I'm Reverend John Lang. We've heard much about you.'

Samson hadn't known anyone was sitting on the chair from which Lang emerged. Dressed in black, with jet black hair and a matching beard that covered most of his face and stretched halfway to his midriff, he had blended perfectly into the large black armchair from which his oversized frame was now rising.

'Very pleased to meet ye, sir,' Samson replied, as the hugest hand he had ever seen or touched enveloped his own.

'And I'm Dr Samuel Wilkinson, President of the Methodist Mission,' Wilkinson said, standing from a chair on the near side of the desk and extending his hand. Wilkinson's long white hair and shaven face made for a stark contrast with the darkness of the room.

'Pleased to meet ye, sir,' he replied, taking the extended hand and shaking it carefully. His hand was still smarting from its encounter with Lang.

'Is that a Highland accent I hear?' Lang said. 'I thought ye were from Edinburgh.'

'Ah, aye, sir. I was born in Edinburgh, but my kin are from Duthil.'

'Duthil?' Wilkinson said. 'Where's that?'

'In the Scottish Highlands,' Lang replied.

'Ye know the town?' Samson asked.

'I do know that town. My ma was from the Cairngorms. She had a large family – huge – all the way from Inverness to Aberdeen. We often travelled there for weddings, funerals, things like that.'

'Ah, it's braw up there,' Samson said.

'So, ye spent some time up there, did ye, Mr Cameron?'

'Aye, my da's heart was in the Highlands.'

'My mother's heart was always there too,' Lang said. 'She used to say "if only the Scots had won at Culloden".'

'Aye, my da and ma were the same. They firmly believed there'd be another rebellion at some time.'

'Ah, there will be one day, for certain,' Lang said. 'But not a Jacobite one. There was one huge problem with that rebellion.'

The other three paused, looking expectantly at Lang.

'It was Catholic,' Lang said, letting out a raucous laugh as he slapped the desk with his two outstretched hands.

'Oh, aye, but my da never saw it that way,' Samson replied, joining in the laughter.

'Now, now, you two,' Wilkinson intervened. 'We're all supposed to be friends now, remember, Mr Lang. Catholics and Protestants. One big happy Christian family.'

'Oh, so sorry, Mr Wilkinson, how could I ever forget? Why didn't ye remind me, Mr MacTavish? Ye know that's yer job?'

Samson was enjoying the banter, sensing with each chortle that this was not a meeting for sacking anyone. Perhaps not even for grilling him about the proposal, the one main job that MacTavish had given him. *I want a detailed report on this proposal for a joint mission*, MacTavish had said. *It's not something we have done before, and Mr Lang is hesitant to commit to it.*

Not only had Samson not completed the report, but he had not even taken in the proposal details as well as he might have. He'd been so consumed by the worry of being sacked. Which could still happen, he thought, once they realised how poorly prepared he is for this meeting.

'Well, actually,' MacTavish said. 'This is what this meeting is all about, in a sense, isn't it, sir? Reminding us about our Catholic friends, that is?'

'Yes,' Wilkinson replied. 'In a sense.'

Samson was intrigued. *A meeting about Catholics. Why would I be here?* He looked around at the three men, smirking silently as they surveyed each other as though sorting out by osmosis who should speak first.

'Cameron, I suppose I should explain,' MacTavish said, breaking the silence. 'Please do sit down.'

Samson moved to the large dark leather armchair to which MacTavish was pointing. At the same time, Wilkinson was sitting back down in his own matching chair, and MacTavish settled himself in a hard-backed chair to the side of the Moderator's large and imposing desk.

'Mr Cameron, we need to trust in your discretion,' MacTavish said. 'Can we so trust?'

Samson took the first deep breath he had taken in hours.

'Absolutely, sir.' Samson sensed an inability to hide his quizzical look.

'Mr Cameron, do you recognise my name? MacTavish, I mean?'

'Aye, my ma was a MacTavish.'

'Indeed, so you might have memory of a Roy MacTavish. Your uncle, I presume?'

'Aye, I do. He was the one who introduced me to theatre.'

'In Edinburgh?'

'Aye. He was an old man, a wily *auld dhuine*, as my da used to say. Wily and *nas buige* than most *dhuines*.'

'What?' Wilkinson pleaded. 'What are you saying?'

'That he was wilier and smarter than most men,' MacTavish said.

'Just like all the MacTavishes,' Lang said, chortling.

'You're too kind, Mr Lang,' MacTavish replied, smiling and blushing as he turned back to face Samson. 'Well, old Roy was my father's cousin.'

'Truly,' Samson said. 'I recognised yer name when we met, sir, but I'd no idea we'd be related.'

'Well, Samson, I dare say we are, however distantly so.'

'It's a small world indeed,' Lang said. 'But we'll leave ye two to catch up on all that at some later time. For now, we'd like to talk with ye, Mr Cameron, about something a wee bit more delicate.'

Samson's sense of intrigue was peaking. He looked straight at Lang, who was shifting in his chair as he cleared his throat. Wilkinson and MacTavish glanced towards each other; tiny smirks suppressed as quickly as they appeared. They looked back in Lang's direction, as he began to speak.

'Mr Cameron, you might know we're under some pressure to accommodate our *Caitleageach braithrean*, as we'd describe them where you and I come from.'

'Could we all speak English here, please,' Wilkinson interrupted. 'Remember we've not all been blessed with a Scottish education.'

'Said with such sincerity, too, Mr Wilkinson.' Lang chuckled. 'Pardon Mr Cameron's and my occasional indulgence in God's own tongue. I was speaking of our Catholic brethren and the new Governor's injunction that we should welcome them into our Christian flock.'

'Yes, well,' Wilkinson replied, forcing a smile. 'As I say, let's not be distracted from our main task here.'

'Indeed,' Lang said, snorting and shaking his head. 'Perhaps we'd best stay with English lest we end up having to speak Irish once these Romans take over the colony.'

'Precisely,' Wilkinson replied. 'Perhaps I could explain our thinking to Mr Cameron, and why we wanted him here.'

'Please do.' Lang nodded, waving his upturned hand.

'Well, Mr Cameron.' Wilkinson leaned forward in his chair and lowered his voice. 'There are two reasons we wanted to speak with you. First, we have been led to understand that you were to meet with Governor Bourke when you arrived in Sydney.'

'Aye, sir. We were told by a Mr Clifford that we'd be invited to a dinner at Government House.'

'And,' Lang interposed, 'that never happened because Governor Bourke had returned home by the time ye arrived. Is that correct?'

'Aye, sir. And it's not the only promise we're still waiting for.'

The three men looked knowingly at each other.

'Indeed.' Wilkinson continued. 'Mr Clifford has what we might refer to as a reputation for making promises he doesn't fulfil.'

'Truly?'

'Aye,' Lang interrupted again. 'Mr Clifford had an unfortunate influence on the previous governor, possibly one that even explains why he resigned earlier than expected.'

'I didna know any of this.'

'Indeed, most people don't, Mr Cameron,' Wilkinson cut back in. 'Have you seen the scoundrel since you arrived?'

'Only once. We've not seen hide nor hair of him since he scurried away with my wife shouting at him to stay and explain himself. We were promised a six-month contract to run a series of plays, with a house looking over the Cove, and—'

'Yes, well I think you'll find that Mr Clifford has lost favour with the Sydney establishment, including Government House,' Wilkinson cut Samson off again. 'Which is a blessing for the rest of us but probably explains why he is avoiding you.'

'We're so sorry, Cameron,' MacTavish said. 'You really have been the victim of circumstances beyond your control. But I must say the theatre's loss has been our gain. We've been so delighted with your work here in the office.'

And I was worried I was walking in here to be sacked.

'At the same time,' Lang butted in. 'We do think ye're a wee bit underutilised, Mr Cameron.'

'I dinna understand, sir.'

'Well.' Wilkinson jumped in, glancing in turn at his two colleagues with a *remember I'm telling this story* look. 'That's the second reason we wanted to speak with you. What Mr Lang is saying is that we think we can make some good use of your other skills, your theatrical ones, the skills you came to Sydney to effect. I'm sure you must be desperate to get back on the stage. Surely that's the case!'

'Aye, Mrs Cameron and I would be thrilled if we could.'

'Well, we do have a plan,' Wilkinson said. 'But let me start at the beginning and then Mr MacTavish can fill in some of the details.'

Twenty-six

SAMUEL WILKINSON UNVEILED IN DETAIL all about Isaac Clifford's dealings with an illicit alcohol trade run by an infamous Irishman who went by the name of Padraig Flannery. Flannery had come to the colony in the early years of the century as a convict, having been charged and found guilty of conspiring to kill the then Chief Governor of Ireland, an Englishman named Dunrossil. Flannery was a radical republican implicated in several kidnappings and ransoms of English officials, and other assorted assaults on the English establishment. He was already on the run from the English army when he was caught red-handed with a gang of republicans plotting to invade Government House in Dublin and kill Lord Dunrossil. All members of the gang were tried, found guilty and hanged. For reasons unbeknown to anyone, Flannery's life was spared, but he was sentenced to life in the penal colony. In 1834, again for reasons no-one seemed able to explain, he was given a provisional pardon by New South Wales Governor, Richard Bourke. The provision was that he had to remain in the colony and abstain from further criminal activity.

'Now, why do you think the Governor would offer any kind of pardon to someone like that, Mr Cameron?'

'I've no idea, sir.'

'Neither do any of us, and that's where the intrigue begins. The scoundrel obviously had some friends in high places right from the beginning. He should have been hanged along with the rest of them.'

'So, where is he now?'

'Oh, as to be expected, he immediately became a pest, implicated in several illicit activities but never convicted. Apparently up to his neck in what we might call "bootleg liquor", frightful stuff, rot-your-gut alcohol. But a lucrative trade nonetheless, especially with the Irish.'

'Who canna afford anything else,' Lang interjected.

'Precisely,' Wilkinson added. 'Yet, despite all this, he remains free, and this is where we have started to put two and two together. What do you know about our now blessedly departed Governor Bourke, Mr Cameron?'

'Not a thing, sir.'

'Did you know he's Irish?'

'Oh, I think I did hear that, but I wasn't sure it was correct. I had assumed all governors would be Sassenach.'

'Sass …' Wilkinson said, his face contorted with confusion.

'English, Samuel,' Lang said. 'It has a bonnie derisory tone about it, ye know?'

'Oh, I …,' Wilkinson replied, clearly taken aback. 'Anyway, he is Irish and—'

'Pardon me, sir,' Samson cut in. 'Ye dinna think Bourke was in cahoots with this Flannery?'

'No, no. Please don't get me wrong – and may I repeat that this is where we must be very careful in any insinuations we make? We can only assume that from the Governor's point of view, pardoning someone who had been here for thirty years or so was an act of some largesse. But the more interesting aspect of all this concerns the role that Isaac Clifford played.'

Wilkinson then recounted the history of Clifford's associations with the Irish cause. He had used his position as a government officer in England to promote Irish independence. Everyone had assumed the motive was benevolence until rumours started to spread that he was benefitting from some black-market trading run by Irish gangs, and especially ones involving Flannery.

'So, you see, Mr Cameron, people are now starting to wonder whether Clifford had some untoward influence on the Governor, using the fact that he was Irish to encourage him to favour the Irish, even the likes of Flannery.'

But what has all this to do with me? Samson wondered, nodding politely.

'So, I imagine ye're wondering what all this has to do with ye,' Lang said, seeming to read the confusion on Samson's face.

'Well, aye, sir.'

'Perhaps if Mr MacTavish could take it from here,' Wilkinson said.

'Certainly, Reverend.' MacTavish leant forward in his chair. Looking directly at Samson, he went on to explain the connection between Governor Bourke's favouring the Irish and his advocacy for the Catholic Church to be given equal status with the other churches. It had been eight years since the Catholic Emancipation Act had been passed in England, so recognising the church as an official organ in the country for the first time since the English Reformation some three hundred years before. This meant that the Catholic Church in Australia was also recognised, officially at least.

'It's appalling,' Wilkinson butted in. 'Their clergy are no better than the convicts they're tending to. The idea that they should mingle and mix with our clergy is offensive.'

'Mind you,' Lang said, looking across at Wilkinson and then MacTavish. 'I think Bishop Polding is not a bad fellow.'

'Oh, I agree,' MacTavish said. 'He seems quite civilised.'

'Well, he is English, you know.' Wilkinson smirked. 'But he's really in the wrong church. Imagine trying to manage those Irish clergy. It would be easier to run a zoo.'

'Indeed, Samuel!' Lang guffawed as he banged the table. 'Give me the zoo any day.'

'Anyway, Cameron,' MacTavish said. 'We need your help to persuade the new Governor, Sir George Gipps, to take a – what shall we say – less enthusiastic attitude to letting the Catholic Church into the fold.'

'Me? I dinna understand.'

'Well, it's quite simple,' MacTavish continued. 'Let's go back to our Uncle Roy. What do you recall most about him? What do you remember, I mean?'

'Ah, he was larger than life. Quite bold, as I recall.'

'What do you mean by bold, Samson?'

'He didna care what anyone thought about him.'

'Why do you say that?'

'He said what he meant; not what others wanted him to say.'

'And what about his theatre work? What were his plays like? Do you recall anything about them?'

'Well, I was only a wee bairn when we first met and he'd retired from theatre by the time I'd grown up, but I think he liked to antagonise.'

'That's right, Cameron.' MacTavish began to warm to his task. 'Uncle Roy loved to stir the crowd. He was never afraid of a fight – which often happened with his performances, especially about religion.'

'Oh, aye, I remember he often got into trouble with the Catholics.'

'Now you're with us.' MacTavish turned to the two clergymen with a self-satisfied look. They nodded as he turned back to face Samson. 'My father used to talk about one of Roy's favourite plays, one called *Neo-mhothachadh Popery*.'

'*Popery Nonsense*,' Lang said, slapping his thigh and chuckling. 'I love it.'

'Aye, I think I've heard of it. But I'm not really sure what it was about.'

'Well, I am,' MacTavish said. 'Because I have a copy of it.'

'Of the play? I didna know it was ever written down.'

'Well, it was, Cameron. When Roy died, my father inherited all his earthly goods because Roy had no children. There wasn't much, mind you, but his plays were the most valuable things he left. There are several that lampoon Catholicism, but the best of them is *Neo-mhothachadh Popery*. It makes an absolute ass of the Catholic Church, from the Pope down. No wonder there were so many riots whenever he put it on.'

'And we want you to perform it right here, Mr Cameron,' Wilkinson said. 'Here, in Sydney, in front of the new Governor.'

'I …I …Why?'

'Because,' Wilkinson replied, a cheeky grin flashing across his face, 'because we know how the Catholics will react, especially with Flannery stirring things up and Clifford orchestrating things in the background.'

'Precisely, Cameron,' MacTavish butted in. 'They won't be able to contain themselves.'

'And that's what we want the Governor to see, do ye see?' Lang finished off. 'Then he'll have grounds to stop all this nonsense about the churches all being one big happy family. Imagine how John Knox would have reacted to such an idea.'

'Or John Wesley,' Wilkinson added.

'Indeed,' Lang said excitedly, almost jumping out of his chair. 'We have a duty to our noble church founders to fight this nonsense as fiercely as we can.'

'So, ye want me to start a fight? Is that it?'

'Yes, Cameron. That's about it. Does that worry you?' MacTavish replied. 'I mean, causing some unrest, perhaps even a riot like the ones your Uncle Roy endured – and enjoyed.'

'I know all about riots. We had a riot in Hobart Town when the Ladies' Guild took offence at the role Mrs Cameron was playing.'

'Ah, yes, well, we've heard the Hobart Town Ladies' Guild has a reputation for protesting,' Lang said. 'Haven't we, Wilkinson?'

'Ah, yes, indeed. My colleague, Mr Langmore, has spoken of them. But what was so offensive about your wife's role, Mr Cameron, if I might ask?'

'She played a loose woman, sir.'

'Loose?'

'An adulteress, I believe,' MacTavish added. 'Is that right, Cameron? The main lady commits adultery, doesn't she?'

'Aye.'

'Well, I'm not surprised there was a riot,' Wilkinson said. 'Indeed, I'd have been leading the riot if it were to happen in my town.'

'Aye, well, Samuel,' Lang said casting a smiling glance in Samson's direction. 'Let's give the Catholics something to riot about that ye would definitely not be leading.'

There was a moment of silence while Wilkinson collected

himself, and Lang and MacTavish looked to each other as much as to say *where to from here?* Samson laid his hand on his fidgeting leg – a sign he was feeling pressured. Another riot? Not if he could help it. These people were out to use him to serve their own ends, with no consideration for his needs, least of all his family's best interests. The relief that he was not to be terminated was being overtaken with a new foreboding. He had no desire to be in another riot – Cordelia would be furious! But could he say no to these men who held his fate in their hands?

'So, this is the plan, Cameron.' MacTavish spoke in a way that suggested the decision had already been made. 'I will hand over your Uncle Roy's script, so you can learn the lines and begin rehearsing. In the meantime, we'll make arrangements for you to meet the Governor.'

'Meet the Governor?'

'Oh, aye,' Lang jumped in. 'We want the Governor to feel as though he's watching a friend, a trusted ally, when he watches you perform.'

'Perform? But where? How?'

'Leave all that to us,' Lang said, looking around and winking at the others. 'Just leave that to us.'

'I don't like the sound of it, Samson,' Cordelia said, stirring the soup on the stove. 'The last thing we need is to be in the middle of a religious war.'

Samson was seated at the table, sipping a glass of whisky. 'I know, darling, but I doubt we'll get on the stage in any other way.'

'In cahoots with the Methodists? Of all the churches,' she carried on, ignoring him. 'They were some of the ones who were so wretched to us in Hobart Town. The Catholics were actually the nicest to us, remember?'

'I know, but things change. And I canna say I'm any admirer of Catholics anyway.'

'I know you don't admire them, Samson, but there's a difference between disliking them and starting a war with them.' She placed a bowl of soup in front of him. 'Why can't we just do *The Stranger* again? That's what we thought we were coming here to do.'

'I know. I know. And the Irish were the ones who loved it most, but that's not what Lang and Wilkinson want. They want to rile them, not entertain them. And besides, they seem to have the power over theatre in this town. I'm not sure why.'

Samson blew on the spoon, emitting steam that got in his eye.

Cordelia was back at the stove filling her own bowl. 'How odd! Are they the reason our contracts have not been honoured?'

'I dinna know, darling. But I suspect it might be so.'

'But we were led to believe it was the Governor who was somehow behind all the arrangements. That's what Mr Clifford was telling us.'

'I'm coming to think we canna believe anything that Isaac Clifford tells us, Cordelia.'

Cordelia sat down opposite him. 'Oh dear. This is all too much. We don't want another riot. We have our children to be thinking of now. John, William and …'

'And?' Samson repeated, looking her in the eye expectantly.

'And perhaps a third, Samson. I think I'm with child again.'

Twenty-seven

NEO-MHOTHACHADH POPERY WAS A ONE-MAN show. Samson had never seen Roy MacTavish play the role of the mythical Pope Urban IX but could recall him talking and laughing about it. Samson had picked up enough about it to know it was designed to mock and insult Catholicism. What he lacked in fine detail about it, Robert MacTavish was able to fill in. Over the weeks leading up to the first performance, MacTavish took on the role of producer and director of the play, a role that blurred uncomfortably for Samson with his other role as Samson's workplace supervisor.

'The hide of that man,' Cordelia spat out, shaking her head. 'He has no sense of propriety.'

'I know, darling, but there's naught I can do. They have me by the *goirid agus curlies*, as my da would say.'

'Is that what I think it is?' Cordelia was outdoing her normal look of disapproval. 'I imagine the *curlies* gives it away.'

'Aye, I know now what it'd be like to have them in a vice.'

'Don't be vulgar, Samson. It's unbecoming.'

'Unbecoming?' he muttered, shaking his head.

'What?'

'Nothing, dear.' Samson turned and began to walk away.

'Samson, come back here now.'

Samson turned and walked slowly back to where Cordelia was sitting, as if in state.

'Aye, dear, what is it?'

'We don't have to do this, you know. I'm perfectly happy for us to take our chances back in Hobart Town. Or there is that opportunity in Adelaide, remember?'

'Aye, but Sydney offers the best chance for us to really establish ourselves and, to be perfectly honest, I really dinna want us to go to Adelaide.'

Cordelia examined her sewing. She appeared to him to be feigning the need for an especial moment of concentration, so to ignore his professed distaste for Adelaide.

'Besides, if I do this for them, they've promised to let us have our head in any future work. *And the theatre will be yours.* That's what Mr Wilkinson said.'

'What?' she looked up from her stitching. 'Even to do *The Stranger* again? Do you really think Mr Wilkinson would abide that? Risk the ire of his Ladies' Guild?'

'I think he would. He almost promised.'

'And you'd take the word of a Methodist clergyman?'

'I know, darling.' Samson looked over and sniggered. 'I know that sounds foolish after everything.'

'To say the least.' Cordelia dug the needle into the coat she was mending as if into the clergyman himself. 'Personally, I wouldn't trust him as far as I could throw him. I'd rather we escape while the going's good.'

'Where to?'

'Anywhere? Why not write to that gentleman in Adelaide?

He seemed enthusiastic about starting up a theatre there. And I rather liked it there. No convicts!'

'Except one!' It slipped out before Samson could contain himself. He braced for the response.

Cordelia stood up and threw the coat onto the settee. She walked away, ignoring him again.

'Yes, no convicts there,' she muttered as she walked into the bedroom. 'Unlike here and everywhere else in this godforsaken land.'

Except one convict, Samson thought, but forbore to say it out loud a second time.

'Ah, Mr Cameron,' Governor Gipps said, extending his hand. 'A most interesting portrayal of Romanism.'

It was Samson's first meeting with the Governor, the one promised by Lang and Wilkinson coming to nothing.

'Thank ye, sir,' he replied, taking the hand and giving it a firm shake. 'I'm pleased ye approve.'

'Well, I didn't say I approved,' Gipps replied, a tiny smile curling on his lips as he withdrew his hand. 'To be honest, Cameron, theatre is not my favourite pastime, but I must say I'm pleased that the colony now has somewhere people can come for this sort of thing.'

The Governor turned and rushed away, leaving Samson stranded like a beached whale. He watched the regal figure, and his retinue, push through the crowd and disappear into the foyer of the hastily refurbished warehouse now referred to as the Royal Victoria Theatre after the new monarch, Queen Victoria. Samson felt a hand grabbing him by the elbow.

'What did the Governor have to say?' Wilkinson was asking. 'Did he like it, do you think?'

'I canna be sure.' Samson continued staring at the spot where he last saw the Governor's back. 'I really dinna know!'

'Why not, man? Surely, he said something.'

'Aye. He said he liked the new theatre.'

'Oh, well, that's good, isn't it?'

'I suppose so.'

'Well, I have to say, personally, I found it brilliant. Just what we wanted.'

'Braw performance, Mr Cameron,' Lang was saying as he approached, hand extended. 'We could not have wished for more.'

'Brilliant, Cameron,' MacTavish was patting him on the back as Lang's extended hand finally reached its target. 'I'm so proud of you.'

'Thank ye, sir. Thank ye.'

'I saw Gipps speaking with ye,' Lang said. 'What did he say, lad?'

'He said it was interesting.'

'Wonderful. Wonderful. So, he approved?' Lang's eyes were wide with excitement.

'I'm not entirely certain, sir. I thought he said something about not approving.'

'Not approving? But I thought ye said …'

'Aye, I'm a wee bit confused, I admit.'

'Confused?' Wilkinson jumped into the conversation. 'What are you talking about, man?'

'Mr Cameron,' the shouting Irish voice cut through the din.

Samson turned in the direction of the voice, as the din reduced to a murmur.

'Ye should be ashamed of yerself, sir. A loathsome, godless performance. The devil himself could've done no better.'

Samson surveyed the crowd but could not see where the voice was coming from.

'We're up here,' the voice said. 'Looking down on ye the way the Laird himself will be looking down on ye tonight. The way the Laird will be looking down on ye the day he casts ye into Hell's fire.'

'Who are ye, sir?' Samson called, peering upwards towards the balustrade above.

'It's none of yer business who we are,' a companion Irish voice replied. 'All ye need to know is that tonight's blasphemy is yer last chance to blaspheme.'

Samson was struggling to see the faces against the glow of the chandelier candles. He looked around to see Lang, Wilkinson and MacTavish all looking up in the same direction.

'Ye do understand what we're saying, Mr Cameron, standing there with yer heathen Protestant friends?'

'I'm sure ye know the play only goes for ten nights,' Samson called haplessly in the direction of the faceless voices.

'And that's nine too many, Cameron,' a third Irish voice from an angry face finally visible. 'Be sure, sir, that two will be too many.'

'Pay heed, Cameron. Don't be fooled by yer Protestant friends. They'll never stand by ye when things go bad.'

'Excuse me, gentlemen.' Wilkinson was shouting into the abyss. 'Are you threatening Mr Cameron just because you've clearly taken offence at the nature of his performance?'

'Ye know ye canna make idle threats,' Lang called out. 'If there's any more, I'll be calling the constable.'

There was silence from above as the band of Irishmen melted into the crowd on the second floor.

'Who were those men?' Samson was turning to his patrons for succour.

'I've no idea,' Wilkinson said. 'Did you recognise anyone, Mr Lang, Mr MacTavish?'

'I'm certain the ringleader was Flannery,' MacTavish replied. 'And I think I recognised someone else standing in the shadows behind him.'

'Who?' Lang was looking MacTavish in the eye.

'Clifford,' MacTavish snorted. 'Isaac Clifford.'

'I think we might have sown the seed, gentlemen,' Wilkinson whispered, grinning at his companions.

'Indeed,' Lang whispered back.

'Good work, Mr Cameron,' Wilkinson said, turning to Samson and extending his hand again. 'Good work indeed!'

'I told you this would happen, Samson.' Cordelia was handing him a dram of whisky. 'The Irish have no forgiveness.'

'Aye, darling. They were so riled.'

She sat down next to him on the settee. 'And to what end? It's so pointless. We have nothing against the Catholics.'

'I know, I know. But I have to see it through.'

'God knows what will come of it, Samson. I'm genuinely frightened. For us and especially the children.'

'Ah, I dinna think they'd really try anything. Lang and Wilkinson said they'd speak with the police to make sure I'm safe.'

'The police?' Cordelia spluttered. 'You do know what they call the New South Wales police, don't you?'

'No. What?'

'The Irish Mafia,' Cordelia replied, throwing her head back and raising her arms. 'The Irish Mafia!'

'Mafia? What's that?'

'Samson, dear, where is your head? It's an Italian crime organisation. A gang. My father had some most unpleasant dealings with it through his business interests in Naples.'

'Why have I never heard of it?'

'I don't know. Perhaps because you're too innocent, or …'

'Or what? Too stupid?'

'Stupid? No, Samson,' Cordelia huffed. 'As if I would say such a thing.'

'No, just think it.'

'Well!' Cordelia moved closer and patted him on the cheek. 'Let's just stay with innocent, shall we? And blessedly so. I only know about these people because Papa had business interests there. And from all I heard, best not to know anything about them.'

'So, what are ye saying about the New South Wales police? Are they all crooked?'

'Oh, I'm sure they're not all crooked. But apparently, they are all Irish – or a great number of them – at least in the ranks if not the officers. But Irish or not, Papa told me before we left that they can't be trusted. Perhaps you've heard about the history of the New South Wales Corps?'

'No. What's that?'

'Oh, my innocent dear one! The New South Wales Corps were the first police in the colony. They came out in the First Fleet in 1788. They were rotten to the core if you'll pardon the pun. They became the patrons of the rum trade. Some even called them the Rum Corps. And when Governor Bligh tried to sanction them, they sacked him. There was a coup. The British government had to send a new governor, Lachlan Macquarie, with his own soldiers, to take back the colony.'

'Oh, my Laird. Why did I never learn any of this?'

'Probably because you didn't have my papa as a father.'

Twenty-eight

Against all of Cordelia's urging, Samson returned the next night for the second performance. Leaving home early, he moved through back streets until he caught the first sighting of the Royal Victoria, looking on the outside to be every bit the old warehouse it was. He could see a few people, suspiciously not like theatregoers, standing near the entrance. With Cordelia's cautionary words ringing in his ears, he slipped down a side street and into the alley that led to a side door. He banged lightly on it. Nothing. He banged more loudly.

'Hey, lads,' the Irish voice rang out at the end of the alleyway.

Samson turned towards the voice to see a roughly dressed man beckoning to unseen companions as he himself began to sprint down the alley. Samson banged repeatedly on the door with all his might.

'Mr Cameron,' the usher said as the door was opening. 'What are you doing here?'

'Quick, lad. No time.' Samson pushed past him and slammed

the door, quickly slipping the large bolt in place. 'Are the front doors still locked?'

'Yes, sir. But—' The young lad jumped as the banging from the outside of the door began. The din increased as different fists arrived at the door.

'Open up ye cad … ye bleedin' heathen … Protestant scum!' were among the more decipherable oaths to be heard.

'What's going on?' The usher was standing inert, eyes wide with fright, hoping against hope the door could withstand the pounding. 'Will I …? Should I?'

'Call the police? Absolutely, lad. Are ye able to get out without being seen?'

'Ah, yes, sir. There's another way out.'

'Then run for yer life, lad. Do ye know the way to fetch the constable?'

'Yes, sir, and my father is a magistrate.'

'Then go get him too, lad.' Samson held him by the shoulders and looked squarely into his eyes. 'Anyone who can help us.'

'Yes, sir.'

'Is there anywhere I can hide?' Samson was looking around at a corridor filled with racks and ropes and bits and pieces of props. 'Anywhere at all?'

'Ah, yes, sir. Follow me.'

The usher, whom Samson would learn in time was named Clive, led him through several doors and into a narrow corridor where a flight of steps took them to a basement. Clive strode to the centre of the room and rolled a carpet away, revealing a tiny trapdoor which he proceeded to open.

'Down there, sir. Quickly.'

Samson peered into a black hole through the small opening.

'How, lad? I dinna think I can fit.'

'You'll fit, sir. I've seen larger men than you go down there. Just hold onto that ladder.'

'Ladder?' Samson was peering further into the hole. 'Oh, aye, I see it.'

Clive held onto Samson's arm as he placed one foot carefully on the wooden ladder attached to the inner wall of the space below.

'What's down here, lad?'

'I've no idea, sir. I've never been down there.'

Once Clive had closed the trapdoor, Samson found himself in a dank, dark, airless, and noiseless place. He rested his back on the wall, one hand holding tight to the ladder, lest he lose the only bridge to normality. He heard only the occasional muffled sound, enough to coax him away from the temptation to climb the ladder and take his chances.

He crouched at the foot of the ladder for more than an hour, battling his emotions. He should be able to negotiate with the Irish mob, he thought. *We're all Celts, after all.*

But the ice-cold fear in his veins reminded him that these Celts were trying to beat down the door to tear him apart.

Eventually, having heard not a sound for a while, he clung more tightly to the arm of the ladder and pivoted his body around so to find the bottom rung with his left foot. Slowly, he climbed, one rung after another.

He cursed. *Why didn't I count the rungs on the way down?*

When it seemed that he was close enough to the top, he reached up in the hope of feeling the bottom of the trapdoor. Nothing! Another rung. Nothing!

Don't fall, ye fool!

Finally, he felt the timber of the trapdoor against his outstretched hand. Applying just enough pressure to lift it, he hoped for a sliver of light so he could see if anyone was there. There was no light because Clive had replaced the carpet over the trapdoor.

Bless ye, lad.

As he raised the trapdoor further, so the carpet began to lift from the floor, the first sliver of light became apparent, along with the first clear sound of voices in the distance. A cacophony of sounds, harried, anxious, aggressive voices very unlike the placid murmurs of an audience awaiting its performance.

Samson stepped further up the ladder, pushing the trapdoor upwards until it was sufficiently open to allow him to slither out from the hole, carefully and quietly lest the source of the voices hear him and wish him some harm. He lowered the trapdoor quietly and carefully until it met the floor and replaced the carpet. Then tiptoed towards the door and opened it.

'But we didn't mean to,' were the first words he heard. *Irish!*

'Save your excuses for the magistrate,' were the second words. *Yorkshireman!*

Sufficiently emboldened by the assurance that some authority was in control, Samson pursued the voices. Moving through the long, cluttered corridor, stopping behind a clothes rack or prop here and there to assure himself it was safe to go further, he finally came to the scene of the altercation.

'Put your hands up!' The man with the Yorkshire accent was moving quickly in his direction, shouting as he strode.

Samson took a step backwards. 'I'm Samson Cameron, the actor.'

'I said *put your hands up*,' the policeman repeated, raising his baton. 'I don't care who you are.'

'But, but...'

'You heard me, mate. The man's eyes narrowed, baton now over his shoulder, ready for action.

'All right,' Samson said, placing his arms in the air. 'But ye're making a big mistake.'

'Save your talk for your Irish friends,' the officer said, turning Samson around and securing handcuffs to his hands behind his back.

'Please, sir, I'm a Scot. I have no Irish friends.'

'You're all the same to me. Traitors and rebels, the lot of you.' Hands ran roughly down Samson's upper and lower sides. 'As if an actor would come to the theatre in that state. You must think I was born yesterday.'

It was then that Samson looked down and noted the dust on his shoes and the debris over his coat and pants. He turned his head to one side to see in a dark corner of the foyer several men seated on the floor, all with their hands behind them, and three or four policemen standing guard over them.

'You,' the officer called, beckoning to one of the seated men as Samson was shoved towards them. 'Do you know this man?'

Samson thought he recognised the Irishman who had raced towards him in the alleyway.

'Flannery,' the officer repeated, as he pushed Samson even closer to the seated men. 'I said, do you know this man?'

So, here I am face to face with the Irish nemesis I've heard so much about.

'Aye,' Flannery replied, a sardonic grin flashing across his face. 'It was all his idea.'

'Just as I thought.' The Yorkshireman shoved Samson into the arms of one of the guarding policemen. 'Keep him over there until the wagon comes.'

'He's lying,' Samson said breathlessly as he was being thrown to the floor. 'Are ye stupid enough to believe anything this Irish thug tells ye?'

'What did you say?' The Yorkshireman turned and strode back to Samson, reaching again for his baton.

'Oh, Paddy,' Flannery called out. 'Ye canna fool the police. They're too smart, ye know.'

'There's some good advice for you, Paddy,' the officer said, looking Samson in the eye. 'You should listen to your friends.'

Samson bowed his head and took a deep breath. What was Cordelia going to say about all this?

He was not sure how long he was sitting there but it was long enough for him to take in the horrifying thought that he was about to have his second experience in a colonial prison.

And I won't have a leg to stand on once they find out about my record in Van Diemen's Land.

'Sir, let this gentleman go,' Wilkinson said as he burst through the door of the theatre. 'He is a much-respected performer. Good heavens, man, what are you doing?'

'Begging your pardon, Reverend,' the Yorkshireman replied, taking a step backwards. 'But these Irish thugs said he was their ringleader.'

'And you would believe an Irishman, would you, Sergeant?' Wilkinson stepped forward towards Samson. 'Least of all Mr Flannery here. It shows you still have a thing or two to learn about the Irish. Who are you, anyway?'

'Sergeant Wright, sir. Please don't get too close to the prisoners. Might I ask who you are, anyway, sir?'

'You may!' Wilkinson stood at his full height. 'I am the Reverend

Wilkinson, Head of the Methodist Church in New South Wales, and a very good friend of Superintendent Windsor. I dare say you've heard of him.'

'I apologise, sir.' Wright turned his head to face Samson. 'And to you, sir.'

Samson raised his tired head and smiled in the direction of Wilkinson.

'Are you all right, Mr Cameron?'

'I've been better, sir.'

'Indeed, this is all most embarrassing.' Wilkinson reached out to help Samson to his feet. 'As if it's not enough to be harassed by these wretched Catholics, without our constabulary adding to your duress.'

The handcuffs made it impossible for Samson to stand up, even with Wilkinson's assistance.

'What have they done to you? Tied your hands behind your back. Really, Sergeant!'

'Constable, uncuff this man,' Wright shouted to a young police-man, who rushed over to follow his orders.

'Truly, Sergeant, was this absolutely necessary?' Wilkinson was making a second effort to help Samson to his feet. 'Does this man look like a danger to society to you?'

'Well, no, sir, but the gentleman over there told me that he was their ringleader … as I said, sir.'

'You mean this Irish Catholic hoodlum?' Wilkinson glared in Flannery's direction. 'Do you know anything about the history of this place, Sergeant?'

'I believe I do, sir.'

'In that case, do you know how many Catholics came out here of their own free will?'

'I'm not sure of the number, sir.'

'Well, there's a good reason for that, Sergeant. Because the number is nought.'

'I'm not sure that's correct, sir.'

'Well, I do, Sergeant Wright, and I'm quite certain Superintendent Windsor will know that as well.'

'If you tell him so, I'm quite certain he will,' Wright said, looking fiercely at the clergyman.

'And what's that supposed to mean?'

'Nothing, sir.'

'Come, Mr Cameron. I have a carriage outside. I'm quite certain you're allowed to go. Is that so, Sergeant?'

'Mr Cameron, I'm happy to release you into the care of the good clergyman here, but I need to warn you that this matter is far from resolved. I'm sure there will be a hearing, and I have at least one witness who has given testimony that you were involved with this gang. That's what I'll be writing in my report and the court will have to decide on its truth or otherwise.'

'Really, Sergeant!' Wilkinson was helping Samson towards the door. 'I'll be speaking with Superintendent Windsor about this entire matter.'

'As is your right, Reverend.'

'And we'll be speaking with the Governor about it,' Wilkinson said, turning his back on Wright and winking at Samson with a self-satisfied look.

Twenty-nine

'You do realise you'll get the blame for all this,' Cordelia said, scolding Samson as she might a child.

Samson was slumped on the settee, head down, a dram resting precariously on his lap. 'Surely not, darling. Surely, they'd not be so dishonest.'

'Samson, listen to yourself. These are clergymen. Their middle name is dishonest.'

He slumped even further, lifting the glass casually to his mouth.

'Even so, I canna believe they'd do that. MacTavish will speak for me, for sure.'

'Samson, look at me. Look at me, man.' She stood over him. 'Even if it means his job? I don't think so!'

'Then what should we do? I clearly canna go back on the stage in this town.'

Cordelia sat down heavily next to him, taking the glass from him and forcing him to face her. 'I don't think you need worry about that. Lang and Wilkinson will disown you, for sure. So, all those promises about a season of *The Stranger* have just gone up in smoke.'

Samson wrested the glass from her and took a sip. 'Then perhaps we do need to leave. Would ye like me to write to that gentleman in Adelaide?'

'Adelaide?' Cordelia replied, feigning disinterest. 'Perhaps. What was his name again?'

'Goodfellow!'

'Well, let's hope he is a good fellow,' she said in a rare moment of levity.

Samson sat up straight, a mix of relief and excitement in his eyes. 'Aye, and if he is, we could be there in a few weeks.'

'A few weeks?' Cordelia said, suppressing her laughter and rubbing her stomach. 'We might have to wait a little longer, Samson.'

'Oh, I'm sorry, darling. I forgot ye'd not be able to travel yet.'

He slumped back on the settee and drained the glass.

'Not for quite a while unfortunately,' she said, raising her eyebrows and shaking her head.

'So, I'll have to keep working here. But, if ye're right, Mr Lang won't want me around.'

'Perhaps he will if …'

Samson turned to see the look of inscrutability he expected. 'If what, darling?'

'If you fall on your sword.'

'Fall on my sword?' His face was screwed up in puzzlement. 'What on earth do ye mean?'

'Well, from what I hear, your clergymen friends' little plot has backfired badly. The Governor is onto their scheming and blaming them for the riot. Is that what you've heard, Samson?'

'Aye, Mr MacTavish told me on the quiet that Gipps is even making overtures to the Catholics to quieten them down. If they really wanted to turn the Governor against the Catholics, then "backfired badly" is putting it mildly.'

'Serves them right,' Cordelia scoffed. 'And much as I don't wish to see them squirm out of their mischievous undertaking, I think we can do ourselves a favour by coming to their aid.'

The look on Samson's face settled. The trust in Cordelia's inscrutable ways was back. 'Aye, tell me then!'

'Well, what about if you were to take the blame for it all? Say it was all your idea, and you talked Lang and Wilkinson into it? That you were the one who wanted to upset the Catholics and Lang and Wilkinson were innocent bystanders.'

Samson shook his head. 'But how would that help me keep my job? Tell me!'

Cordelia moved closer. She placed her hand on his shoulder. 'Do a deal with them. Speak to them. Offer to write to the Governor taking the blame in exchange for keeping your job for, let's say, six months.'

'Do ye think we can trust them?'

'Get it in writing.'

'That's very decent of you, Mr Cameron,' Wilkinson said, scanning the letter that Samson had drafted for the Governor.

'Aye, it's braw,' Lang endorsed. 'And ye'll have it sent today, lad?'

'Aye.'

'A wonderful gesture, Cameron,' MacTavish added.

'There's just one wee – what would ye call it – condition?'

'Speak up,' Lang said, looking around at Wilkinson and MacTavish.

'Well, ye know Mrs Cameron is due to have a bairn later in

the year, so we have to stay here for now. Could I have yer word that I can keep my job until, let's say, Christmas?'

'I'm certain that can be arranged,' Lang replied, looking in the direction of MacTavish. 'Ye can arrange that, can ye no, Mr MacTavish?'

'Indeed, Reverend,' MacTavish replied.

'Thank ye, sir. And would ye mind putting that in writing?'

'Oh, I believe my word is sufficient, Mr Cameron.' Lang was smiling as he sat forward and focused on the papers on his desk. 'Quite sufficient!'

'I'm sorry, darling,' Samson said as he handed Cordelia the letter a week or so later.

'What is it, Samson?'

'Just read it.'

Cordelia read the letter twice. The shaking of her head increased with each line.

> *Dear Mr Cameron,*
>
> *In light of the prevailing circumstances, we regret to inform you that your employment with the Presbyterian Church Offices has been terminated. Your last full day of employment will be on Saturday, July 20th, 1838. At ten minutes to noon on that day, you should report to the Head of Accounts to receive your final pay and return any goods that belong to the Office. We wish you well in your future work.*
>
> *Yours sincerely,*
> *R. MacTavish Esq*
> *Manager of Business*

'I know ye told me to get it in writing.'

'Yes, I did, Samson, but even I was fooled – yet again – in believing that the word of a clergyman would stand for something. And Saturday? Two days' time?'

'Aye, one would have thought they'd at least give me a week. I'm so sorry, Cordelia. I dinna know what to do.'

'So, who is the Head of Accounts?'

'MacTavish.'

'So, the Manager of Business is telling you to report to the Head of Accounts, who happens to be the same person?'

'Aye.'

'And this same person, who you believed was a friend, indeed a relative of some sort, has said nothing to you?'

'No!'

'When did you last see him?'

'A wee few hours ago.'

'And he said nothing? Even while this letter was being written, he said nothing?'

'Not a word!'

'What a snake in the grass!'

'Aye, and that's unfair on the snake!'

Thirty

'YE WERE THERE, MR MACTAVISH,' Samson said, hands outstretched, exasperated. 'Ye heard Mr Lang make a promise. A man of the Laird, no less.'

'I know, Cameron, I know, but my hands are tied.'

'Should I try to see him?'

'I wouldn't advise it. Mr Lang was adamant.'

'Adamant? Is that English for being a liar?'

'Now, now, Cameron. Mr Lang is an honourable man.'

'Sassenach honour? I suppose. But he's a Scot – or supposed to be. My da used to say "Laddie, a Scot's word is his bond", so I believed I had his bond when he told me I could stay until Christmas.'

'It's complicated,' MacTavish replied, his lips tightening. 'The Governor is still blaming Mr Lang – and Mr Wilkinson – for what happened. You can imagine the impact this could have on their churches. Why, Sir George is even threatening to declare the Roman church as a national religion to appease the Catholic bishop. To give it a standing alongside the Church of England – and leave the Presbyterian and Methodist churches in lesser positions. I'm sure you can see …'

'Oh, I can see that I'm the – what would ye say? – scapegoat in all this. So, these two braw Christian men of the Laird are telling the Governor it was all my doing. Is that the case?'

'Um, well, yes. After all, that is what you wrote in your letter to the Governor, so they are merely confirming its truth. I'm sure you understand.'

'What I understand, Mr MacTavish, is that if I wrote that letter, my job was to be guaranteed until Christmas.'

'Yes, well the Governor wasn't certain that you hadn't been coerced into that, so he demanded that your employment be terminated as a way of testing Mr Lang's resolve.'

'And, so, Lang's word to me meant naught in the end?'

'Oh, it did, Cameron. It did. Privately, he felt bad about the way it's all happened.'

'Not as bad as he'll feel when I tell everyone the truth.'

'Oh, I wouldn't do that, sir. That would be most dishonourable.'

'Dis …?' Samson snorted. 'I'll let the Governor decide who's being dishonourable.'

'Mr Cameron, as if the Governor would take your word against two men of the cloth.'

'I think he just might if it came from the Catholic bishop.'

'You wouldn't,' MacTavish said, staring him down. 'You wouldn't, would you?'

Samson turned away.

'Cameron,' MacTavish called, turning back towards his desk. 'What about your pay? Your final pay? I have it in the drawer.'

'My two days' severance?' he sneered, looking back over his shoulder. 'Tell yer honourable man of the cloth he can keep it.'

'You what?' Cordelia was busy at the stove. John and William were fighting over a rubber ball. 'Boys, be quiet. Go into your room.'

John ran into the bedroom and shut the door, leaving William, just learning to walk, in his dust. He hollered.

'I said he could keep it.'

Cordelia walked over and picked up William, depositing him in the bedroom. 'Now play quietly or you'll both go to bed without tea.'

Samson had followed her like a lost puppy. 'I said he could keep it.'

Cordelia hastened back to the stove and continued stirring the stew. 'Samson, we need it.'

'I know, but …'

'But nothing, Samson. I understand how you feel but think of the children. We're going to need every penny we can get.'

'It just seems like blood money.'

'Blood money for bread, milk, butter, dear!'

'I know, I know.'

A rapping on the door halted the exchange. Samson opened it to be greeted by the young doorman he recognised from work.

'Henry, what are ye doing here, lad?'

'Hello, Mr Cameron. Mr MacTavish asked me to deliver this to you personally.'

Henry extended his hand to reveal a brown envelope.

'What is it, lad? Do ye know?'

'No, sir. I've no idea.'

'Please would ye tell Mr MacTavish, I don't—'

Cordelia swooped between them, snatching the envelope and whisking herself away.

'Do thank Mr MacTavish, Henry,' she called out from the depths of the house.

'I shall, ma'am. Good day, Mr Cameron.'

'Aye, Henry,' Samson replied as he closed the door.

'Where are ye, darling?'

'In here,' came the voice from the bedroom. 'Move the pot from the hot plate and come in here.'

Having done what he was told, Samson walked in to find Cordelia sitting on the bed, rifling through a bundle of green and brown notes.

'What are ye doing?'

'Counting, my dear. Counting! Samson, what on earth did you say to Mr MacTavish?'

'Naught really. Except that I might tell the Governor who was really behind the riot.'

'Is that all?'

'Oh, and that I might go to the Catholic bishop with my story.'

'You? Go to the Catholic bishop?'

'I know. I know. It was a ridiculous thing to say.'

'Well, ridiculous or not, it worked, my dear. It worked. Look at all this money. How much do you get a week?'

'Two pounds thirty-eight.'

'So, for your two days' severance pay, you should have …?' Cordelia counted the notes.

'A wee bit under a pound, I suppose.'

'So, that's not quite as much as twenty-two pounds, is it?'

'Ye're jesting.' Samson walked over and started picking up the notes. He leafed through the bluey green pound notes first, placing each one back on the bed and counting as he went.

'Sixteen pounds.' He placed the last pound note on its pile

and reached for the brown ten-shilling notes still in Cordelia's possession. 'Plus, one, two … twelve. Twenty-two pounds!'

'I told you!'

'I know but I just canna believe it.'

'Well, you might if you read this,' Cordelia said, handing him a piece of folded paper.

He unfolded it and read its contents. A wry smile began forming, followed by a loud snuff of disgust. He turned to face Cordelia.

'Now, I understand.'

'Whatever you said – or didn't say – to Mr MacTavish obviously worked to …'

'Aye, what do people call it? Buy the silence?'

'Buying the silence, Samson. Buying the silence.'

Thirty-one

Late on the 8th day of August, Cordelia staggered into the front room where Samson was reading.

'I thought ye were asleep,' he said casually before looking up. 'Oh, my Laird, are ye all right?'

'My waters have broken, Samson.'

'Oh, darling.' Samson jumped up, noting the trail of water on the floorboards as he rushed to take her by the elbow. 'Come and sit here.'

'Towels, Samson. The towels.' Cordelia was waving her hand, pointing to the bundle of towels sitting on the sideboard.

'Aye, towels, towels,' he stammered, rushing over to the bundle. He pulled a towel from the top and started the journey back to the settee.

'All of them, Samson. *All of them.* And the sheets next to them.'

'Aye, dear. Aye, dear.' He turned on his heels and headed back to the bundle.

Shaking, Samson laid the sheets and several towels across the settee and set Cordelia down, lifting her legs and ensuring her head was comfortably laid on the armrest.

'What should I do, darling?'

'Samson, we've been through this a thousand times. Remember? Go fetch Mrs Cartwright in number six! Hurry!'

'Aye, but the lads?'

'They're fine. They're asleep. Just hurry, please!' Cordelia was grimacing in pain.

'Aye. Dinna go anywhere, darling.'

'Go, Samson. Just go!'

By the time Samson rushed back into the room with the midwife in tow, Cordelia was standing, gripping onto the arm of the settee with both hands and emitting a deep groan. 'Well, Mrs Cameron. How are we this fine night?' Mrs Cartwright was untying her shawl and making a beeline to Cordelia. 'Lie down, dear, and let's see what's going on here!'

Cordelia lay back down on the settee. 'Thank you, Mrs Cartwright. We're so sorry to disturb you at this hour.'

'That's what I'm here for, dear.' Mrs Cartwright placed her extended palms firmly on Cordelia's stomach, moving them around the body of the unborn infant.

'Mmm, this baby is almost here.'

'Almost here?' Samson collapsed onto a chair.

'Don't sit there, man. I'm going to need you to get a few things.'

'Aye.' He jumped up as fast as he had gone down.

'More sheets, pillows – and boiled water if you can, as much as you can get – and be quick.'

Samson was back in the room in a matter of seconds with his arms full of sheets and pillows.

'Thank you. Now, hot water, even if it's not quite boiled. Your wife's going to need it.'

'Is everything all right?' Samson was looking closely at Cordelia's face, hardly distinguishable from the white sheets around her. 'She looks awfully pale.'

'Just go fetch the water, man. Be as quick as you can!'

The embers in the stove were still smouldering. Samson threw two more logs in and moved a pot of water over the hot plate. In between darting back and forth from the front room, he managed to get the first bubbles of a boil in the water. *She said not quite boiled would do.* He poured a pitcher and raced back to the midwife, noting the beads of sweat dripping off Cordelia's face. She was gasping.

Samson placed the pitcher on the floor next to the midwife. 'Is … Is she …?'

'Do you know where Dr Smart lives, Mr Cameron?' Mrs Cartwright spat out.

'Ah, I'm not sure!' Samson fell to his knees next to Cordelia and placed his hand on her cheek.

'Is she …?'

Mrs Cartwright turned her head to face Samson. He noted the steely gaze that signalled her concern. 'Mr Cameron. Do you know Dr Smart's house or not?'

'No.' He turned back to take in again Cordelia's deathly pale face. His eyes filled with tears. 'Is she …'

'Mr Cameron,' she said, grasping him firmly by the arms and forcing him to face her. 'Your wife's and your child's welfare depend on you paying attention to me. Do I have your attention?'

'Aye.'

'Dr Smart lives in Lodge Road; do you know where that is?'

'Aye, I think so. But is she …?'

'Stop blubbering, man. Your wife needs you. Do you know where the brewery is in Lodge Road?'

'Aye.'

'Of course, you do. What man wouldn't? Now, imagine you're standing facing the brewery. Do you follow me?'

'Aye.'

'Then two doors to your left, you'll find a three-storey terrace with a white picket fence. Do you follow?'

'Aye.'

'That's Dr Smart's house. Go and bang on the door until he wakes up. Sometimes, that takes a bit of banging – depending on how many pints he's had – tell him to come here immediately.'

'What if he won't?'

'Tell him he'll have me – Marion Cartwright – to answer to. Have you got that?'

'Aye,' he replied, standing up and looking down again at Cordelia, whose paleness was being overtaken by a yellow tinge. 'Darling…'

'Just go, Mr Cameron. Travel like the wind.'

Samson took what he feared might be his last look at Cordelia, her face and arms blending into the linen around her, sweat dripping from her face like a gentle waterfall.

'I … I …' he stammered, backing towards the door.

'What is it, man? Just go! Now!'

He opened the door and was stepping from the room.

'Oh, and Mr Cameron.'

'Aye,' he replied, poking his head back through the door.

'Do you have a priest?'

'A … What do ye mean?'

'Never mind, man. Just go!'

Samson ran like the wind, as instructed. *Thank the Laird MacTavish took me to that brewery that one time.* Striding on past it, he arrived at the gate of the picket fence. He hurried to the door, banging on it furiously until a flicker of candlelight became evident through the frosted glass to one side of the door.

'What is it, for the Lord's sake?' a pompous, agitated voice could be heard as the bolt on the door was turning.

'Dr Smart?' Samson blurted out as the door opened to reveal a portly gentleman standing in his nightshirt.

'It is I. What seems to be the problem?'

'It's my wife, sir. Can ye come *gu luath*?'

'What? What are you saying, young man?'

'It's my wife. She needs yer help. Please come quickly, sir. I think she's dying.'

In what seemed like days but, he was later told, was less than an hour after Samson had left Cordelia, he stumbled back up the stairs of their building, closely followed by the portly doctor, puffing loudly. A baby's cry greeted them as he opened the front door of the flat. Samson rushed over to the settee, Dr Smart hot on his heels.

'What kept you, Doctor?' Mrs Cartwright said, suppressing a smile.

Cordelia was half-lying, half-sitting, with the tiniest and palest of infants nestled to her breast, lying limply, not moving. The once pristine white sheets were stained with blotches of blood. Samson hurried over to the new mother and babe.

'Darling, are ye all right?'

'I think so, Samson,' Cordelia whispered exhaustedly. 'I think so.'

'And the bairn?' he said, placing his hand gently on the baby's head. 'Is it?'

'It's a girl, Samson. A very tiny little girl. She's …'

Cordelia choked up. She looked down at the babe, rubbing its cheek with her finger.

Meanwhile, the doctor and midwife were whispering at the end of the settee. Samson noticed the look of concern they were sharing.

'What happened, Mrs Cartwright?' He cut into their conversation. 'Did ye not need the doctor, after all?'

'I thought I might, Mr Cameron,' she replied, turning her attention away from the doctor. 'As it is, Mrs Cameron found the strength I was doubting she had.'

'Your wife has clearly lost a lot of blood, Cameron.' Dr Smart was lifting the sheet to examine Cordelia's lower body. 'Mrs Cartwright did the right thing in calling for me. Things could have turned quite nasty.'

'Of course. I didna mean to question ye, Mrs Cartwright.'

'Quite right,' she replied discourteously. 'Anyway, I'm pleased the good doctor is here because he'll be able to get your wife and child into a home far faster than I could.'

'A home? Is that really necessary?'

'You're a rather impertinent chap, aren't you, Cameron?' Dr Smart stood up and faced Samson, who noted the look of disdain. 'Scottish, I take it? Ever the rebel, eh?'

'No, sir. I'm no rebel. I just want the best for my wife, ye know?'

'And for your infant, I presume.' Dr Smart was looking back to the midwife. 'The child is premature and very delicate. I'll arrange for a carriage to take them both to a rest home first thing in the morning. In the meantime, Mrs Cartwright will stay here and try and get the child to latch on. She desperately needs some sustenance. Is that all right with you, Mrs Cartwright?'

'Of course, Doctor. Of course.'

'Very good, then.' Dr Smart made a move towards the door before turning his head back. 'Oh, and congratulations, Cameron, Mrs Cameron.'

Samson followed Dr Smart to the door, catching him as he stood in the hallway.

'I'm sorry, Doctor.' Samson took the doctor by the arm. 'Can ye say if they'll be all right?'

'We'll do everything we can, Cameron.' Dr Smart wrested his arm away. 'But it's in God's hands, so if you're a praying man …'

Samson stepped back inside and returned to the makeshift bed. He was about to speak when the door opened again.

'One more thing, Mrs Cartwright.' Dr Smart was standing in the doorway. 'What was the time of birth? I'll need to record it.'

'Two thirty-eight a.m., Doctor.'

'Thank you. And is there a name?'

'I think we'll need to get back to ye on that, Doctor,' Samson replied.

'Well, I will need a name for the register.'

'It's all right, Samson,' Cordelia whispered exhaustedly. 'Her health is all that matters. You can choose the name.'

'Are ye certain about it, darling?' he whispered in her ear. 'It's only because it was my gran's name, ye know?'

Cordelia nodded again as she slumped back on the pillow, closing her eyes.

Later that morning, Dr Smart recorded the birth of Grace Cordelia Cameron as 2:38 a.m. on the 9th day of August 1838. At Cordelia's insistence, she would be known thereafter as Gracie.

Thirty-two

'Are you Church of England, Reverend?' Cordelia asked the tall, thin, dark-haired man dressed in black with an unfamiliar back-to-front white collar. He was standing near the end of the bed in the rest home. Cordelia had been in there for ten days, her own and the baby's health improving by the hour.

'No, madam. I'm a Catholic priest. Father Charles Lovat is my name. Reverend Brigastocke is unwell, so he asked if I might look in on his faithful. Is that all right with you?'

'Yes, Father. Certainly. It is a little unusual, though. Or does this sort of thing happen regularly in the colony?'

'You mean Catholic and Protestant clergy covering for each other? Well, no! Sadly, no, but Charles Brigastocke and I have our own views about these things.'

'Can I say, Father, that I think that's wonderful, and I'll say that to the reverend if I get to see him.'

'Oh, would you? I believe he would be very grateful. As you might know, not everyone agrees with Christians being civil to one another.'

Cordelia noted the twinkle in the priest's eyes, deep, brown and caring.

'Well, Christians loving each other,' she replied, letting out a small chuckle. 'What next, Father?'

'Indeed,' her visitor said, taking a step closer. 'Anyway, how are you after your ordeal?'

'You mean the birth? Oh, I'm recovering, Father. Thank you.'

'Good, good. And your little girl?

'Yes, her strength is improving, thank God.'

'Wonderful. You must be very excited. Is she your first?'

'No, Father. We have two little boys, and we did have a girl. She was our first, but she died at three months.'

'Oh, I'm so sorry. You must have been devastated.'

'More than devastated, Father. I know you'll think me terrible when I say this but there was a time there when I truly couldn't believe in a God who would snatch a tiny child away like that.'

'I don't think that's terrible at all, Mrs Cameron. Not at all!'

'So, you really don't think I'll go to Hell for thinking like that?'

'I'm quite certain of it. I'm sure I would feel the same.'

'Truly, Father? You surprise me.'

'Surprise you that I would be heartbroken and angry with God if I lost a child?'

'Well, yes. I suppose it's not quite what I've come to expect of a priest.'

'Would you prefer that I scold you for doubting God's plan?' said Father Lovat, smiling. *That glint again!* 'I can do that if you really want me to.'

A faraway look came over the priest's eyes, a sadness, as Cordelia would later report it. *A compassion I hadn't seen before in a clergyman, Samson.*

'Oh, no, Father,' she said, shaking her head. 'I'd rather you say what you want to say. Have you lost someone close to you?'

'Why do you say that?' Father Lovat smiled wistfully.

'I see the sadness in your eyes. I hope I'm not being rude when I say that.'

'No, not at all.' He cast his eyes to the floor. 'I lost my younger sister some years ago and ...'

Cordelia would later tell Samson of the tears she saw forming in the priest's eyes.

'I'm so sorry, Father. Were you very close?'

The priest chuckled and looked Cordelia in the eye. 'Oh, I loved her dearly though I regret not getting to know her better. I was a little too busy getting to know God.'

'Well, that's another thing I had never thought I'd hear a priest say.'

'Oh, I am shocking you today, am I not?'

'Not at all, Father. I'm loving hearing all this. And you were about to say something else.'

'Yes, I also lost one of my brothers. I only received the letter a month or so ago.'

'Oh, I am so sorry.'

'Thank you so much.' Father Lovat placed his hand gently on her shoulder before quickly withdrawing it. 'Anyway, I'd best move on. I only came to see if you needed anything.'

'Will you come back again, Father?'

'Probably not. I dare say Reverend Brigastocke will be back on duty.'

'I'm sad to hear that, Father. No offence to the reverend, but I do wish you would come back. I feel as though we have much to talk about.'

'Well, I'll see how I'm placed. I'm really only filling in here for

Father Flynn anyway,' Lovat smiled, suppressing a snigger. 'He's a much better priest than me.'

Cordelia let out a loud laugh, then fell to a fit of giggling.

'You're a card, Father Lovat. You should be on the stage.'

'Like you, I gather?' He was backing towards the door.

'Oh, you know about me, then?'

'And about your husband.' Charles Lovat smiled broadly as he exited the door.

'How are you coping with the boys?' Cordelia asked as Samson handed her the flowers.

'Bonnie. I'm a better mother than I ever thought I'd be,' Samson said with a wide grin, as he took the flowers back from her and placed them in the vase on the bedside table.

'Well, you did have some practice as Mrs Haller,' Cordelia replied, matching his grin. 'So, Mrs Cartwright has them at the moment?'

'Aye, she's braw with them.' He sat on the edge of the bed and gazed at her. 'Darling, I have to say ye look happier than I've seen ye in a long while.'

'Yes, well, I met a wonderful priest today, Samson, and it was so lovely talking with him.'

'A priest?' he replied, reaching over to kiss her and cradle the baby's head with his hand. 'I've never heard ye say something like that before.'

'Well, no. I don't believe I've ever met a priest like him before.'

'I dinna think they even call them *priest* out here.'

Samson was surveying the walls bedecked with paintings of various flora.

'What do you mean, Samson?'

'Mm, I doubt they had Redoute paint these for them,' he sniggered.

'Who? What on earth are you talking about?'

He gestured towards the walls. 'These paintings, Marie-Antoinette would have had Redoute's head if he'd produced them.'

Cordelia grabbed him by the arm. 'Samson, answer me. What do you mean they don't call a priest a priest out here?'

Samson wiped the smile from his face and held the hand now firmly ensconced on his arm. 'I mean the Church of England is very different from what ye'd be used to in Leominster.'

'Well, he's not Church of England anyway. He's Catholic.'

'*Catholic?* Why would ye be talking to a Catholic priest?' Samson said more loudly than intended.

Cordelia removed her hand from his arm and rocked the now restless infant more tightly. 'Shush, shush, shush. He was just filling in for the Church of England chaplain. What's wrong with that?'

'*Filling in?* Darling, the Church of England thinks the Catholics work for the devil. And the Catholics think all the Protestants are going to Hell. So, I canna imagine one would be filling in for the other.'

'I know it doesn't sound normal, but he assured me that he and the Church of England chaplain are friends.'

'Well, that's certainly something different.'

'Anyway, I thought you might like to meet him.' Cordelia looked down at the now sleeping infant.

Samson stood up and began to turn for the door. 'I dinna think so, darling. As ye know, I've had enough of clergymen to last me a lifetime.'

'Oh, but he's not like those ones you've been dealing with. He's a really lovely man.'

He turned to face her again. 'They're all the same, darling. I assure ye they're all the same.'

'No, Samson, I don't believe he is like the others. When I told him about Elizabeth, I could see the sadness in his eyes.'

Samson took a step back towards the bed. He looked at her sternly. 'Why were ye telling him about our bairn? It's none of his business. None at all!'

'I don't know, Samson. I haven't talked about it with anyone. You and I don't even talk about it. But when I told him, I felt this weight being lifted. A relief I haven't felt since she died.'

Samson shook his head and lowered his eyes. He knew Cordelia's pain – the pain he tried to avoid.

'Well, we don't, do we?' Cordelia said, nudging him out of his silence.

'Do what?'

'Talk about it. Talk about her.' Cordelia choked on the words. 'She'd be five, you know.'

'Next month,' Samson said softly.

'Next month.'

'Does the chaplain come every day?' Cordelia asked the nurse who was overseeing Gracie's feeding.

'Depends which chaplain,' the nurse replied offhandedly.

'What about Father Lovat? He visited me yesterday.'

'Don't know him, ma'am. He must be new,' she replied, as the baby's mouth was rammed into Cordelia's nipple. 'That's it, lift her head more. Like this!'

'Thank you. I do have some experience, you know.'

'Well, if you don't want my help, ma'am, there are others who do!'

'I'm sorry,' Cordelia said, forcing a smile. 'I appreciate your care.'

'Right then.'

'So, Father Lovat is new, is he? Who normally comes for the Catholics?'

'Oh, there's a few of them papist types. All Irish. Not my cup of tea, the Irish!'

'I don't think Father Lovat is Irish. He sounded more English.'

'Doubt it. If he's Catholic, he'll be Irish. Think they're God's chosen ones, they do. Don't like any of them.'

The following day, Cordelia was dozing after lunch, the baby lying across her chest. She was wakened by a strong hand shaking her shoulder.

'Mrs Cameron,' the Irish voice commanded. 'The nurse said you wanted me to call.'

Cordelia looked up to see a short, white-haired man dressed in clerical black.

'Ah, no, I don't think so,' she said, forcing her eyes open and comforting the now clearly disturbed babe in arms.

'Well, she said you wanted the Catholic priest. Are you a Catholic, madam?'

'No, Father. I'm Church of England but Father Lovat did visit me a few days ago.'

'I don't think so, ma'am. That would have been Reverend Brigastocke.'

'Yes, but Father Lovat was filling in for him,' Cordelia said, lifting herself higher against the pillows. 'He told me so.'

'Filling in for a Protestant?' the priest replied. 'I'll be telling Father Lovat's bishop if that's the case. Are you certain?'

'Perhaps I made a mistake, Father. I have been a little delusional since the birth.'

'I should hope so, Mrs Cameron. Delusional like your husband, I wager. What a disgraceful performance all that was. I hope you weren't involved.'

'No, Father, I wasn't involved, but I don't believe my husband is to blame.'

'Isn't to blame? From what I've heard, he was every bit to blame. My fellow priests and I want him out of the colony altogether. We've enough trouble in this godforsaken place without someone stirring up hatred like he did. And you can tell him that for me.'

'I'm sorry, Father … I'm sorry, Father, I don't know your name.'

'Flynn, Mrs Cameron. Father Flynn.' The priest was backing towards the door. 'If I were you, ma'am, I'd keep your husband on a very tight rein. Some of my parishioners are not beyond taking the law into their own hands. You know what I mean?'

'Thanks for your advice, Father Flynn,' Cordelia said as she watched the priest turn his back and head for the door. 'Oh, one last thing, if I might, Father.'

'What is it?' Flynn looked back over his shoulder, one hand on the architrave.

'Where would I find Father Lovat? What parish is he in?'

'He's not in a parish. He runs the seminary, St Mary's, in town.'

Thirty-three

Dear Father Lovat,

Please excuse my boldness in writing to you. We met some weeks ago at the rest home in Surry Hills. You were filling in for the Church of England chaplain at the time. We had a brief discussion about our respective losses, my child and your sister and brother, and about anger with God. I know you must meet many patients and quite likely have forgotten about me, but I do wonder if my husband and I might call on you sometime at your convenience.

Yours sincerely,
(Mrs) Cordelia Cameron

The letter was dated 26 August. Father Charles Lovat received it on the 30th. It was sitting on his desk when he returned to his room after a day of teaching.

Dear Mrs Cameron,

I do remember our meeting at the home, and our conversation about the losses of which you speak. I would be happy to receive you and your husband at the seminary when it can be arranged. I am busy teaching for the next two weeks and my weekends tend to be taken with supplies in different parts of Sydney. There is a week's break in classes starting this September 28th. Might I suggest that a day during the following week would be most suitable? I could meet you anytime between 9 a.m. and noon, or after 3 p.m. until 5 p.m. Just let me know what is most suitable for you.

Yours in Christ,
(Rev.) Charles Lovat

'Are ye sure ye want me there? Ye know I really don't like men of the cloth. Not after everything.'

'I know you're not comfortable in their company, Samson. But nor am I, perhaps even less than you. But this man is different, and I think it would do us good – both of us – to speak with him.'

'About Elizabeth?'

'About Elizabeth. And anything else we might like to discuss.'

'Like what?'

'I don't know, Samson. Let's just see what happens.'

On the 30th day of September 1838, the cab drew up outside

St Mary's Seminary in Macquarie Street, Sydney. Cordelia had arranged for Mrs Cartwright to look after the children. She had fed Gracie and put her down just before leaving. They left home at half past nine. They were arriving at a quarter to ten for a ten o'clock appointment with Charles Lovat.

'Thank ye,' Samson said as he paid the driver. 'So, we'll see ye here at eleven o'clock.'

'Yes, guv'nor,' the driver replied, reaching for the change.

'That's all right, lad,' Samson said. 'If ye're here on time, ye can keep the change.'

'Thank ye, sir. I'll be here. Goodbye, ma'am.'

Cordelia nodded in the driver's direction. Samson took her arm, and they walked together through the gates of the seminary.

'That was very generous of you, Samson – especially for a Scotsman.'

'Aye, well, ye'll know the Scots have a reputation for their generosity.'

Samson tightened his grip on her arm and took note of her reaching her spare hand over and resting it on his own hand. He felt a rare sense of being at one with her. She seemed at peace with the idea of meeting this priest again, he thought. *The wells of a woman's heart!*

'So, you've come for confession, I suppose?' the amply fed woman said as she opened the door, her Irish accent giving away her loyalties. *Not likely*, Samson thought.

'No,' Cordelia replied. 'Could you let Father Lovat know that Mr and Mrs Cameron are here to see him?'

'Hmm,' the Irish woman grumbled as she stood back and

pointed towards a bench seat inside the foyer. 'Well, you should be here for confession is all I can say. Anyway, I'll leave that to the Lord to sort out. Take a seat. Father Lovat will see you soon.'

'Thank you,' Cordelia said, taking Samson by the hand before he could put the 'old biddie' in her place. 'You're too kind.'

The lady walked towards a door opposite the front door, mumbling to herself. She entered the door and closed it behind her, casting one last, distinctly unfriendly glance in their direction as they were seating themselves on the bench.

'Do ye think this might be a mistake, Cordelia?' Samson whispered. *What does Cordelia want with this unfriendly lot?* he wondered.

'No. I'm sure it's not. And don't be so negative!'

'I'm sensing it might well be an ambush.'

'Hardly, Samson. I'm sure the Catholics have more on their plate!'

'Well, just to be clear about it. I'm not going to confession.'

The door that the Irish woman had entered amidst much grumbling opened to reveal the tall, dark-haired, friendly-looking gentleman that Cordelia had described. He was wearing a black soutane and matching cape, with a large clerical collar around his neck. Cordelia stood up, leaving Samson still planted firmly on the bench.

'Father, thank you so much for seeing us,' Cordelia said, accepting Charles Lovat's extended hand. She gestured in Samson's direction. 'This is my husband, Samson Cameron.'

'Welcome Mrs Cameron, Mr Cameron.' Father Lovat's hand remained extended for Samson.

'Reverend.' Samson stood and took the priest's hand.

'Please, won't you step into the parlour?' Lovat was pointing to a door to one side of the foyer.

Once inside, he showed them to two high-backed wooden chairs on one side of a small table. They were facing a single identical chair on the other side. Samson was struck by the relative simplicity of the furniture compared with what he had become used to in the Presbyterian offices. The furniture was also lighter in colour, a cedar brown instead of the dark wood of his former employment. Only the smell was the same, that of well-polished timber on floors, tables, and chairs. The wall was bedecked with large-framed portraits of popes and bishops and the like. *No sign here of any British royalty*, Samson thought. He felt more at home than he'd thought he would.

'Would you like a drink?' Their host was hovering over the chair opposite them. 'Water, or tea perhaps? I can have one of the ladies prepare something if you would like.'

'Oh, no thank you, Father,' Cordelia replied, looking to Samson to check on his concurrence.

'No, thank ye, Reverend.'

'*Father*,' Cordelia whispered, looking crossly at Samson. 'You should call him Father.'

'Oh, that's perfectly all right, Mrs Cameron.' Charles was taking his seat opposite them. He levelled his gaze at Samson. 'Call me anything you like. Just not late for dinner, as my father used to say.'

Cordelia chuckled. Samson took in the twinkle in the priest's eye, the warm smile on Cordelia's face. *What's going on with this priest's good humour, and why does he seem to have such instant rapport with my wife?*

'Thank ye, Reverend. Ye see I was taught that I have only one da.'

'Of course. Of course. I grew up in a part of England where Catholics were forbidden to call their priests *Father*. So, I can well understand.'

'I knew you weren't Irish, Father. But the nurse in the nursing home insisted that you must be.'

'Oh, I know it causes much confusion. Most of the Catholic clergy here are Irish, so there's a certain expectation.'

'Where do you come from, Father?' Cordelia asked. 'I'm from Leominster in Herefordshire.'

'Lancashire. I was born in Preston and grew up in Pemberton. But I know Leominster quite well. When I came back from Rome, I was appointed to the Jesuit school in Llanrothal. Do you know it?'

'I recall my father speaking of it. I think he had some business interests there. So, you were in Rome, were you, Father? How wonderful. My father always promised to take us there, but we never made it.'

'Ah, yes, it's a wonderful place. I was very happy there.' Samson noted the faraway look and wistful tone in the priest's voice. *Hmm, a priest with a few secrets to tell, I'll warrant*, he thought.

There was a brief silence before Cordelia broke it. 'Why did you not stay, then, Father? I mean, Rome versus Sydney Town. There's not much competition, let's face it.'

'Well, it's the old versus the new, isn't it?' Lovat replied, smiling gently. 'All part of God's Kingdom, so we go where we're told.'

'Truly, Father?' Cordelia persisted. 'You truly wanted to come here?'

'Didn't you, Mr and Mrs Cameron?'

'Well, yes, but …'

'But what?'

'Well, for us, it was a business proposition.'

'And for me,' the priest said, twinkle in his eye. 'God's business proposition.'

Cordelia was gazing far too warmly into the priest's smiling eyes, Samson thought. *Time to change the subject.*

'So, ye truly believe, do ye, Reverend?'

'Aye, Mr Cameron,' Father Lovat replied, chuckling as he imitated the Scottish accent. 'Aye, I truly believe.'

Cordelia let out a loud chuckle. 'You continue to impress us, Father. You even understand my husband's foreign tongue.'

'Aye, it's what I grew up with, ye see.' Samson could tell that Lovat was enjoying himself. 'My father was Scottish. Well, born in England, should I say, but Scottish in every other way. His own father was a Highlander. And his father's father was actually a Jacobite.'

'Truly?' Samson jumped in enthusiastically. *Maybe this priest isn't so bad after all.* 'So was my da's da!'

'Well, there you go, then.' Lovat slapped the table, laughing. 'You have more in common with a Catholic priest than you might ever have expected.'

Cordelia joined in the laugh. Samson smiled, looking from the priest to Cordelia next to him. He noticed her watching the priest intently. She seemed unusually content.

'Now, to what do I owe this pleasure?' Lovat brought the laughter to a halt. 'Is there something I can do for you?'

Cordelia was opening her mouth to speak. Samson jumped in ahead of her. 'So, I presume ye've heard about the riot, Reverend.'

'Samson,' Cordelia scolded. 'We didn't come here to talk about that.'

'That's perfectly all right, Mrs Cameron. I have heard about it, of course. The whole of Sydney Town has been talking about it. Even the Governor. He was here yesterday speaking with my bishop about it all.'

'We're so very sorry, Father. My husband is getting the blame for it, but …'

'Say no more, Mrs Cameron. No-one knows the religious

politics of this town better than I – except perhaps my bishop. And may I say, we also know about Irish hot tempers? My bishop is an Englishman as well, you see. Not as good as being Scottish, I know, but the next best thing.'

Samson ignored the intended humour. 'Thank ye, Reverend, but does yer bishop know how nasty his Protestant friends are?'

'Well, Mr Cameron. They're not really his friends and nasty might be a wee bit harsh. They're just very devoted to their own denominations, let's say. Believe me, there are Catholics who also forget from time to time that they're meant to be Christians first and foremost.'

'Ye know what happened, then?' Samson said.

'*Know* might be a wee bit arrogant, Mr Cameron,' Lovat said slowly, seemingly picking his words carefully. 'But let's just say I'm fairly certain my guess wouldn't be too far out.'

'Thank you, Father.' Cordelia glanced at Samson. 'I'm sure my husband is as grateful as I am to hear you say all that. You do know he has lost his job in the Presbyterian Offices because of all this?'

'No, I had no idea.' The priest turned his gaze to Samson. 'I thought you were an actor, Mr Cameron. What other job did you have?'

'I—' began Samson, but Cordelia was on a mission.

'Samson is an accountant, Father. He learned accounting in his father's business in Edinburgh.'

Does she think I canna speak for myself?

'Is that so, Mr Cameron? So, you're out of work, then?'

That's better. A bit of respect from the priest, at least. 'Aye, Reverend.'

'But what about your acting?'

'Well, I doubt somehow I'll be doing any more acting in this town.'

'We hope to go to Adelaide at some point, Father,' Cordelia cut in. 'We've been asked to consider setting up a theatre there, but it's still a little uncertain – and with a growing family, a new baby and all – well, Adelaide is a long way away.'

'Indeed, it is. Well, listen to this. I believe God speaks in strange ways. Just yesterday – after my bishop filled me in on his conversation with the Governor, in fact – I was speaking with him about the need for some additional administration for the seminary, including someone to manage the accounts. This is something I've been doing since I arrived here late last year – on top of my teaching, I might say. It was manageable at first but as the seminary is growing – now a school for young lads as well as a theology hall for student priests – it's all getting a bit too much for me. And to be honest, I'm not much of an administrator. Never was. Terrible with numbers. I wonder if you would consider a job of that sort?'

'Working for the Catholics?' Samson said, feeling a grin spread over his face. 'What would my da and grand da say?'

'Samson!' Cordelia scolded. 'Don't be so rude. We'd be delighted, Father, if you would have us. Why, I would help out as well, in any way I could.'

'I doubt the lady who let us in here would be very happy about it,' Samson said.

'Mrs O'Driscoll?' Charles Lovat chuckled. 'Oh, don't worry. She scolds me regularly as well.'

'Because ye're not Irish?' Samson was sniggering.

'Possibly. And I haven't even told her about my Scottish heritage yet.'

'Well, perhaps it's best ye don't,' Samson said, laughing.

Lovat chuckled again, pulling his fob watch from his soutane and opening the cover. He looked up. 'Are you sure you wouldn't like some tea?'

'No, Father, thank you,' Cordelia replied. 'We have to get back to the children.'

'Oh, I'm so sorry. Here, I've been taking up your time talking about myself. What was it you wanted of me, anyway?'

Cordelia was quick to jump in. 'Father, please don't apologise. It's been wonderful getting to know you better and if you're serious about giving Samson a job, that would be a true godsend. But' – she stopped for a moment – 'but I had wanted to carry on the conversation we had in the home about bereavement and anger with God. I was so comforted by what you said, and I suppose it forced me to open up about losing our little Elizabeth, something I think both my husband and I have buried, in our grief, and just hoped we could act our way out of.'

'Ah, yes, I recall our conversation. It's important to come to grips with tragedies like that. Otherwise, they just rattle around inside, eating away at our soul. There are no shortcuts.'

The room fell silent. Samson could see Lovat's eyes welling as he looked at the table in front of him. The priest lifted his head to see them both staring at him through their own tears.

'So, when do you need to be home for the children?'

Thirty-four

ON THE FIRST DAY OF November 1838, Samson began working as Financial Manager of St Mary's Seminary. He inhabited an office next to Charles Lovat, working from eight o'clock to half past five on Monday to Friday and half past eight to one o'clock every Saturday.

'What do ye think about that heathen working in the seminary?' Father McEnally asked. They were in the office of the Diocesan Vicar General and Assistant to the Bishop, the Very Reverend Dr Ullathorne.

'Father, lower your voice, please. I assume you mean Mr Cameron, in which case he's only two doors down.'

'I dinna mind what the blighter hears. The one who mocked us all. The Holy Church, the Pope. What on earth is he doing here?'

Samson was aware that his presence had caused some con-sternation among some of the clergy and layfolk, but it was as well the walls were thick enough to prevent him from hearing the extent of it.

'Making fun of everything that's precious to us and we reward him with a well-paid job. Why, from what I hear, even the Presbyterians didn't want him after that disgraceful performance.'

'I see what you mean, Father, but it's not my decision. Father Lovat spoke about it with the bishop, and his lordship agreed.'

'Well, can ye no speak with him? The bishop, I mean. Are ye no' his main advisor?'

'Yes, but Father Lovat does have a certain sway with the bishop,' Ullathorne said, raising his eyebrows.

'Too much sway, I'd say!'

Ullathorne nodded in silence, a surly grin on his face. He reached for his pipe. 'Tell me, Father, how do the other priests feel about it?'

'Same as me, Doctor. Same as me.' McEnally shifted awkwardly in his chair. 'Not to mention the laity.'

'Oh, really? I haven't heard about that?' Ullathorne placed the pipe in his mouth and struck a match on the table between them.

'Oh, yes. Believe me, sir, it's caused a great deal of anger out there.'

Ullathorne took a puff and looked quizzically at his fellow priest. 'Truly? But how would ordinary folk even know who's working in the Church Offices?'

'Well, I'm not sure.' McEnally shifted again, turning his head away. 'Perhaps it's been mentioned in the odd sermon.'

Ullathorne took the pipe from his mouth and leant forward. 'By others, you mean, Father? Naturally, you wouldn't be sharing church business with your congregation, now, would you?'

McEnally looked up and fully gazed at his superior. 'Perhaps not, Doctor, but I'm frankly not sure I would see any problem if

I did. I mean, the lay folk have a right to know when a heathen is working for their church.'

'I don't believe Mr Cameron is a heathen, Father. As far as I know he's a Christian. Presbyterian, I believe.'

'Well, isn't that the same thing?'

'Not quite, Father. Not quite!'

As time went on, Samson became increasingly aware of the opposition to his appointment, opposition normally led by the Irish clergy. He had heard that Dr Ullathorne was regularly confronted by clergy claiming to represent the people in protesting against the appointment, not just of a Protestant but one who was widely believed to have made fun of everything Catholic on his one infamous performance. Dr Ullathorne would report these meetings to the bishop, who would then speak to Charles Lovat.

'I've had another complaint about your Mr Cameron, Charles,' Bishop Polding said, offering his favourite priest a whisky.

'No, thank you, my lord.' Lovat held up his hand. 'What is it this time?'

'The same old thing. If we needed someone to run the books, we should have given it to a Catholic.'

'So, nothing about the performance at the Royal Victoria?'

'Oh, that too, of course. What are your own feelings, Charles?' Polding took a sip.

Lovat leant forward in his chair, shaking his head. 'Mr Cameron is a model employee is all I can say. He truly is. He has taken a huge load off my shoulders, and he's always been respectful to a fault.'

Polding was studying the contents of his glass. 'Mmm. All right, that's good.'

'My lord, if this is all causing too much trouble, I can ask Mr Cameron to resign.'

'Oh, I don't believe that will be necessary. Frankly, if my fellow priests are not complaining about this, they'll be grumbling about something else.'

Polding chuckled. Lovat snuffed and shook his head again.

Once a month, on a Saturday after work, Cordelia would meet Samson in his office. From there, they would go to the parlour for a light lunch with Charles Lovat, where they would talk over a myriad of things, including their respective losses, and how to deal with them without losing faith in God.

Occasionally, Cordelia would ask to have her own time with the priest.

'Well, it's a kind of confession,' she said once when Samson asked what they spoke about. 'It's not confession because I'm not a Catholic, but I do feel cleansed as they say confession is meant to do.'

Samson learned not to ask too many questions. He was just happy to have Cordelia in a more peaceful place.

On one occasion, the three of them spoke about the various Christian denominations, what they have in common and what separates them.

'I sense ye're quite different from most priests, Reverend,'

Samson said, having just listened to Father Lovat's pensive musing on what his faith meant to him.

'Different from most priests?' Lovat looked down at his clenched hands. 'Perhaps I am, Mr Cameron, but it's not something I deliberately cultivate.'

There was a moment's silence before Cordelia spoke. 'Why do you think that is, Father?' Samson noted his wife's sensitivity to the priest's mood. 'That you might be different, I mean?'

'I don't really know, Mrs Cameron.' Lovat looked her in the eye and smiled. 'I've always just tried to be the best priest I can be, the best Christian I can be. I learned that from my father. He was a good Christian man, but he was also an intelligent man, a scientist in his own way. So, he taught us to trust in our own judgement. We children, I mean. Not to simply take orders from above, as it were. But I suppose it's easier sometimes if you do.'

'In the church, you mean?' Cordelia asked.

The increasing ease between his wife and the priest left Samson feeling that his presence was superfluous.

'Yes, or the army.'

There's that familiar glint in the eye, Samson thought. He jumped in. 'I imagine the church and the army should be quite different, should they no?'

Lovat turned to face Samson. The glint was gone.

'Different from each other, you mean? Perhaps, Mr Cameron, but all organisations need order, I suppose, so those who question orders can prove difficult, regardless of the organisation.'

'So, ye question the church's orders? Is that what ye mean?'

Lovat lowered his gaze and smiled, as if inwardly. 'Oh, not the fundamentals.'

'So, ye never doubt there's a God, Reverend?'

Father Lovat leant forward in his chair and steadied his gaze on

Samson. 'Oh, Lord no! I believe firmly in God. I can't remember a moment when I doubted that. Even as a child!'

'Ye're fortunate, then.' Samson sat back in his chair and turned his head away.

'Why fortunate, Mr Cameron? Do you doubt there's a God?'

Cordelia and the priest sat silently looking at Samson, head bowed and wringing his hands.

'Would ye think I was damned if I said *aye*, Reverend?'

'No, Mr Cameron. It's not for me to judge whether anyone is damned. I'm not sure I believe anyone can be damned if we believe in an all-merciful God.'

The two thespians sat in silence watching the priest, sensing he had more to say on the subject.

'That said, I do think that God sometimes makes it difficult for us to believe in him. Like when you lose a child, or me a sibling, or …'

There was another moment of silence as they waited for the priest to finish his sentence.

'Go on, Father,' Cordelia eventually said. 'Or what?'

Lovat looked up and smiled. Cordelia smiled back. *That connection that I've never had with her*, Samson thought.

'Oh, perhaps that's for another day,' the priest said, standing up and breaking the mood. 'I do enjoy our chats, I must say. There aren't many people I can speak with so frankly.'

'Even though we're not Catholic?' Samson said, as he and Cordelia stood.

Charles Lovat let out a short chuckle. 'Perhaps it's because you're not Catholic!'

'By Jove, I really do like that man,' Samson said as they walked to the cab. He was interested to gauge her reaction.

'Who would ever have thought Samson Pearce Cameron would say he liked a priest?' Cordelia squeezed his hand. 'A Catholic one at that.'

'Aye. I'd have lost a lot of money if I'd taken a bet on it.'

'He is a lovely man, though, isn't he?' she said as Samson was helping her up onto the running board. 'I wonder what his story is.'

'What do ye mean?' Samson sat next to her and signalled the driver to begin the journey.

'I mean why he's really here. Why he's not in Rome, or England at least.'

'I think he's here because those were his orders.'

'But he seemed to say he doesn't follow orders all that well. Didn't he say that?'

'Aye, he is a wee bit of a mystery, I admit.'

'More than a wee bit, Samson. I'd love to know more about him.'

'Then, perhaps ye should ask him. I sense he'd tell ye anything if ye ask.'

'Do you really, Samson?'

Cordelia grabbed him by the arm and squeezed it.

'Aye,' Samson replied as he turned his head to watch the hustle and bustle of Macquarie Street.

'Perhaps I will, then, Samson. Perhaps I will. Next month.'

They both fell silent, lost in their own thoughts as the cab bumped over the cobblestones, turning from Macquarie into Elizabeth Street on its way back to Woolloomooloo Hill. Samson glanced at her hand clinging tightly to his arm. What was she thinking about, to keep her quiet for so long?

Thirty-five

'I WAS WORRIED WHEN MR Cameron didn't arrive at work this morning.' Charles Lovat was standing at the Camerons' doorway.

'Oh, thank you so much for coming, Father. The doctor's with him at present, but he's about to leave. Won't you come in?'

It was Saturday of the following month, the next assigned time for Samson and Cordelia's scheduled lunch at the Catholic seminary.

'Only if I'm not imposing, Mrs Cameron. Is Mr Cameron unwell?'

'You're not imposing at all, Father. It's lovely to see you, and Samson will be especially pleased.' Cordelia closed the door and ushered him to the settee. 'He's all right, thank the Lord, but he was attacked last night on the way home.'

'Oh, my heavens. Attacked by whom? Do you know?'

'He suspects it's the same mob that caused all the trouble at the theatre.' Cordelia sat on a chair facing him. 'The Irish mob, you know.'

'Oh, I did read where that Flannery fellow was out of prison – yet again. Are the police doing anything about it?'

'The police don't know at present, but the doctor says they should be informed.'

'Why, of course they should be. They're an unruly mob, and with their leader now out to stir up more trouble. I've actually had my own run-in with them.'

'Truly? But aren't they …?'

'Catholics?' the priest scoffed. 'Well, they would claim to be.'

'But they would threaten a priest? I simply don't understand the Irish. Pardon my rudeness, Father.' Cordelia began to stand up. 'Would you like a cup of tea?'

'No, no. I have to get back. I'm travelling to Richmond this afternoon. I'll just wait and say hello to Mr Cameron.'

Cordelia sat back down. 'He'll be so pleased to see you, I know. Why are you going to Richmond, Father? If you don't mind me asking.'

'Not at all. My brother and his family live there. He's a school headmaster. He's arranged for me to say a special Mass there tomorrow.'

'Oh, I didn't know you had a brother here. How wonderful for you. It could be so lonely otherwise.'

'Yes, I'd love to see more of Thomas and his family, but life is so busy for both of us.'

'Did you come out together from England?'

'No, he came some months before me. From Ireland, in fact.'

'Why from Ireland?'

'Well, he is Irish actually. We're half-brothers, you see!'

'Oh, I'm so sorry.'

'What about?'

'All the things I was saying about the Irish.'

'That's perfectly all right.' Father Lovat laughed. 'Be assured, Thomas would agree with you on all that.'

'Even though he's Irish?'

'Especially because he's Irish, I imagine. He knows them far better than we do.'

Cordelia chuckled. She looked across and smiled at the priest, who smiled back – albeit a little awkwardly.

'Can I be honest with you, Father?'

'Please.'

'I'm intrigued by you. As Samson said, you are so different from what one imagines a priest to be.' Cordelia hesitated, gauging the priest's reaction.

'Go on,' Lovat said, the twinkle in his eye masked by a hint of embarrassment.

'Well, Mr Cameron also calls you mysterious,' Cordelia said, hesitating again.

'Mysterious?' He raised one eyebrow. 'What on earth does he mean?'

'I'm not sure, but I somehow know what he means. You are most certainly different.'

'Ah, yes, I think we've established that. Is it a good thing or a bad thing, do you think he means?'

'For Mr Cameron, all good. He's had most unpleasant experiences with clergymen, so being different can only be a good thing, so far as he's concerned.'

'One down …' Father Lovat said, slightly blushed.

'What do you mean, Father?'

'One down. Two to go. Is it a good difference for you – or a bad one?'

'All good,' Cordelia replied, smiling as she gazed at the priest.

'Believe me, it's good for both of us. We've truly valued getting to know you. In fact, it's been something of a godsend.'

'Godsend?'

'Yes, a godsend. Not only for the job you arranged but in every other way. You've restored our faith – such as it is – in the church. Indeed, in people. We were starting to doubt there were any good people in the world, and then you came along, and …'

'And?'

'Some of our talks – I call them confessions – have been very important to me. I think you know that.'

'Well, I'm honoured. Thank you for saying these things.'

'I'm just so pleased I've been able to. I feared I might not get the chance and then you'd be gone – or we'd be gone.'

'Are you going somewhere?'

'Oh, not immediately.' Cordelia relaxed into the easier conversation. 'But I know Mr Cameron will want to get back on the stage at some point, as do I, and our chances of doing that in Sydney seem limited. Especially after last night. I fear for Mr Cameron's safety. Even for our children's.'

'That's sad. I'll be sorry to lose Mr Cameron if that happens. He's been a fine worker. Just what I needed.'

They sat in silence. They could hear the doctor's muffled voice coming from the bedroom. Then his footsteps moving towards the door.

'It sounds as though the doctor might be leaving,' Lovat said, looking across at Cordelia, who lowered her head.

'And me?' she asked, looking up and catching his eye.

'And you what, Mrs Cameron?'

'Would you be sorry to see me go too?' Cordelia replied, her face blushing pink as she spoke.

'Ah …' The priest was looking down at his hands as if trying to find the right words.

'Mrs Cameron,' the doctor said as he opened the door. 'Oh, I'm sorry. I didn't know you had a guest. Good afternoon, Reverend.'

Lovat stood up. 'Good afternoon, Doctor.'

'Dr Smart, this is Father Lovat from the Catholic Church.'

'Pleased to meet you, Father,' Smart said as he stepped towards the priest with his hand outstretched. 'I don't believe we've met.'

'Father Lovat has been very good to us, Doctor,' Cordelia said, glancing at the priest with her face still blushed. 'How is my husband, Doctor?'

'Well, he won't be needing the good priest just yet, So, that's the good news. But he will be sore and sorry for a week or two. He certainly has some bruising around the chest and back. There could even be a cracked rib or two. I'll have to wait and see how the bruising goes before knowing for sure.'

'What happened exactly, Doctor?' Father Lovat seemed happy for the distraction.

'Well, I'm not sure of the details and Mr Cameron seems disinclined to fill them in, so I'll have to defer to Mrs Cameron.'

'All I know is he was attacked by a group of people when he was walking through the park next to Elizabeth Street, near—'

'An Irish mob,' Lovat interrupted. 'I think that's what you said before, Mrs Cameron.'

'Oh, truly?' Smart said, looking in Cordelia's direction. 'I hadn't even heard that detail. So, is this all related to the riot at the theatre last year?'

'We don't really know that, Doctor. Mr Cameron was a little delusional when he finally made it here.'

'But, Father, you seemed fairly certain.' Smart turned to face the priest.

Lovat glanced in Cordelia's direction. The look in her eyes told him that he had said too much already.

'I was perhaps just putting two and two together, Doctor. I can't really be sure.'

'Well, regardless, I have to report this assault to the authorities, and they will no doubt get to the bottom of it.'

'Is that really necessary, Doctor?' Cordelia said. 'It seems no harm was done in the end. Mr Cameron just needs to be more careful when walking home.'

'Ma'am, it is necessary. We take pride that Sydney is becoming a safer town, unlike in the past, and incidents like this threaten that reputation so essential to luring more British subjects here. I'm sure Father Lovat would agree, even if for different reasons.'

'Different reasons?' Lovat asked.

'Well, I'm assuming that all the churches are committed to building a Christian civilisation here. Isn't that true?'

'Of course.'

'Then you can see the need for the authorities to take this matter up and clean out the vermin.'

'I suppose.' Lovat glanced across at Cordelia.

'I'm sure Father Lovat agrees with you, Doctor. And so do I, for what that's worth. I wonder if Father Lovat would mind accompanying you to the police station.'

Thirty-six

'Did ye know it was Father Lovat who complained to the police?' Father McEnally said, his grizzled look demanding his superior's attention.

They were again in Ullathorne's office.

'Yes, I had heard that, Father.' Ullathorne was casually tapping his pipe on the ashtray. 'But I'm told he was only accompanying the doctor. It was the doctor who took the matter up with the constabulary.'

'All the same. Doesn't that tell ye something about Father Lovat's loyalties?'

'Loyalties?' Ullathorne looked up.

'Yes, loyalties. He favours his heathen friend over his fellow Catholics.'

Ullathorne took a deep breath. 'Well, let's not forget that it was these same Catholics who were guilty of assault – allegedly.'

'All the same.' McEnally turned his head away.

'So, you're not denying it, Father?'

'I don't know and frankly I don't care. Cameron got all he deserved.'

Ullathorne placed the pipe firmly on the desk. 'You don't care that a felony was committed? Is that right, Father?'

'The Good Lord works in mysterious ways, is all I can say.' McEnally was looking his superior in the eye.

'Are you suggesting that the Lord approves of violence, Father?'

'Violence begets violence, Dr Ullathorne. Doesn't the Good Book tell us that?'

'I'm not sure it does, Father. Perhaps you can point out the chapter and verse.'

McEnally fell silent, head down.

'Chapter and verse, Father!'

'I'll have to get back to you on that,' McEnally said, facing Ullathorne with an embarrassed smile.

'Mmm, when you locate your Bible, you mean?' Ullathorne was staring hard at the priest. 'If you have trouble finding one, why not ask one of the Protestant clergy. They seem to be more familiar with the Bible than your Irish colleagues.'

'Perhaps that's because they have nothing else to lean on, Doctor.'

'Meaning what, Father?'

'Well, they don't have the Church, do they?'

'I think they might disagree with you on that, Father. They have their own churches.'

'Heathen churches.' McEnally shifted in his chair, casting an evil eye in Ullathorne's direction. 'That's what the Holy Father calls them.'

'Truly, Father? My, my, you are a fund of unusual information. Is that in the Bible as well? The one you seem unable to locate?'

'Well, it might as well be, sir.' McEnally's face was flushed with anger. 'It might as well be because it's the truth.'

Ullathorne and McEnally sat glaring at each other in silence. McEnally looked away first. He moved to stand up.

'All I can say, Dr Ullathorne, is that you should warn Father Lovat that there will be no end of trouble so long as he keeps that heathen in his employ.'

'Sit down, Father,' Ullathorne growled, as he half stood up. 'Sit down and listen.'

McEnally sat down heavily and huffed. He stared at Ullathorne, his eyes ablaze with fury. Ullathorne took a deep breath, steadying himself before speaking.

'Father, let me make it very clear that if you or your fellow priests have any power over these troublesome thugs, then you should exercise that power to ensure there is no further trouble of the kind that befell Mr Cameron.'

Ullathorne looked, steely-eyed, at the priest across the table.

'Is that clear, Father?'

'Can I ask ye what the bishop thinks about all this?'

'Exactly as I do, Father. Be assured of that.'

'So, he'd not be interested to hear from his priests about it all?'

'I'm certain that the bishop will always be open to listening to the voices of his priests, but not to any condoning of violence. Do I need to make myself any clearer about this, Father?'

'No. But I think both you and the bishop perhaps overestimate the power we priests have over this element in the Irish population.'

'What are you saying, Father?'

'Just what I said before, sir. Father Lovat should know that his continuing employment of that heathen Scotsman is putting both him and the Scotsman at risk.'

'I'll be so sorry to see you go, Charles,' Bishop Polding said, shaking his head as he took a final swig of the only rough whisky the Catholics could afford. 'I just can't believe you're being driven out.'

'I didn't say I felt like that, my lord. Just that it might be best all around. Between all the tension over Mr Cameron and the difficulties I've been having with the clergy training, I think perhaps God is calling me to other pastures.'

'Well, who am I to take the Lord to issue?' Polding was studying the remnants in his glass. 'I've just been so delighted with what you've done here. Having someone of your calibre in the colony was beyond my most optimistic expectations.'

'Thank you, my lord.'

'And my loss is Yass-Goulburn's gain. I'm certain you'll make a fine pastor.'

'I hope so, my lord. It's not something I've done all that much. Only a short supply or two when I was in Rome. But I did enjoy simply being there for people in their need.'

'Indeed, Charles. There are times when I feel I'd love to do that kind of work too.'

'I believe you, my lord.'

They sat for a moment, smiling warmly.

'Have you told the Camerons?'

'That's my next job. I'll go straight around and let Mr Cameron know.'

'Please let him know he'll be welcome to stay on if he wishes.'

'Thank you, my lord. That's most generous. So, you're not worried about all these threats?'

'Not at all, Charles. Not at all. They just spur me on to do the right thing.'

'I thought ye might end up doing this, Father.'

'So, it's no surprise?'

'No, I was just saying to Cordelia that I thought ye'd be moving on soon.'

'Why is that, Samson?'

'Ye're too good for them, Father.'

'Meaning?' Charles Lovat asked, casting a quizzical eye in Samson's direction.

'Meaning I've come to see how some of these priests, and even some of the student priests, treat ye. They should be kissing yer feet for all ye do for them, but they dinna appreciate what they have in ye. I truly wonder what's wrong with them.'

'Perhaps there's nothing wrong with them, Samson.' Lovat paused, playing with the spoon on his saucer. 'I suppose it comes down to different ideas about being a priest, about being a Christian even.'

'Aye, and even different ideas about God.'

'Perhaps you're right, Samson. Perhaps you're right!'

'Well, we can't stay, can we?' Cordelia said.

'I know, but Father Lovat did say the bishop said I can stay in the job.'

'But would you want to work with any of those other priests?'

'No.'

'So, what do we do, then? Contact that gentleman in Adelaide?'

'Ye do seem keen to get to Adelaide, darling. Should I be worried?'

'Don't be ridiculous, Samson. I have no wish to see Mr Leigh, if that's what you're implying. No wish at all. It's just that Adelaide seems to be the only place we can go at present. Surely you agree!'

'Aye. Ye're right. And I'm sorry to scratch the sore, darling. I just need to know ye feel comfortable going to Adelaide. After all …'

'After all, nothing. There's nothing to talk about and there's no sore, thanks to Father Lovat.'

Samson wondered if she was going to tell him more about her 'confessions' with Charles Lovat. He watched her in silence. She was looking intensely at her sewing. He could see her eyes glistening. He waited expectantly, hopefully. Until she spoke, still attending to the sewing.

'I was ready to go to Adelaide before you started this job, remember, and it's your best chance of getting back on stage.'

'And yer best chance, too, darling.'

'I've thought of that, although …'

'Although what?'

'I'm not so sure I really want to.'

'Truly?'

'Yes, truly. I'm a little out of practice, you know.'

'Cordelia Cameron out of practice?' Samson chuckled. 'I dinna think so, darling. Ye were born to be on the stage.'

'Well, not according to my parents. They said I was born to be a good wife and mother – of many children!'

'And ye're that too. Ye were born to be both.'

'And you're a born diplomat, Samson Cameron.'

'Ye might be among the wee numbers who think so, darling. Scotsmen and diplomacy dinna go so well together, ye know.'

Samson smiled fondly at Cordelia. She looked away. He watched her until she turned to face him.

'Am I a good wife, Samson?'

'Of course, ye are, darling. The best. And the best ma too.'

'I'm not sure I'm the best mother, Samson, but I am enjoying motherhood more than I ever thought I would. I'm really enjoying Gracie. She's such a darling, and I only wish I'd not been so busy on the stage when the boys were smaller. And …'

Cordelia turned away again. He could not see her eyes, but he could see that she was shaking slightly. He moved closer and sat next to her, placing his hand on her shoulder.

'And what, darling?'

'I don't know, Samson,' she replied, choking on her tears. 'It's silly, I know, but I sometimes wonder if we hadn't been so busy – if we hadn't even come out here in the first place – would Elizabeth …?'

Samson pulled her around and took her in his arms. He cradled her head on his chest, his head buried in her hair. They held tightly and wept quietly together. Samson was the first to speak.

'Ye canna afford to think these things, darling. What will be will be!'

'I know. I know, but it's hard not to have these thoughts sometimes.'

'I understand. I have them too.'

'Do you, Samson? Do you really?'

'Aye. There are times when I think we should have stayed where we were. We'd have had family and friends around us. Way more than we have here. And ye'd have been the finest actress in all of Britain.'

'Oh, I don't care about any of that. Being a mother is so much more important and I'm happy enough here. Despite all the challenges, I've actually felt more at home here in Sydney than anywhere since we arrived in the colonies.'

'Truly, darling? Why?'

'Why? I suppose it's because we've made some true friends here.'

He looked down at her as she took the handkerchief from her blouse and wiped her eyes.

'Like who?'

'Oh, I don't know. Father Lovat, I suppose.'

'Aye, he's been a real friend to ye, hasn't he?'

'He has, Samson,' Cordelia said, her voice muffled against his shirt. 'To both of us.'

They sat in silence. He could hear her deep breathing, occasionally a tiny sob.

'What did he say to you?' Cordelia asked.

'Who? Father Lovat?'

'Yes.'

'Oh, just that he'd *caill mi.*'

'What?'

'That he'd miss me.' Samson chuckled.

'That's nice. It's good of him to say he'll miss you, isn't it?'

'Aye.'

Cordelia was silent for a time before speaking again. 'And what about me?'

'What about ye, darling?'

'Did he say he'll miss me?'

Thirty-seven

SAMSON WROTE IMMEDIATELY TO HIS contact in Adelaide, a Roger Goodfellow who had made his fortune in importation, starting in camel farming and, more latterly, in real estate. His boast was that he had the ear of anyone in Adelaide who mattered, including the Governor, and that the Colonial Secretary was a personal friend. A few days into September of 1839, Samson had his reply.

How quickly can you be here? was the postscript.

In the rest of the lengthy letter, Goodfellow explained that he had purchased a parcel of land in the middle of the town, on which he planned to erect a playhouse, Adelaide's first and, according to him, promising to be the finest in all the colonies. He was waiting on an architect to arrive from Scotland, so he was not certain when it would be ready, *But, Mr Cameron, if I can be assured of your imminent arrival, I have other options. I was sincerely hoping to open a theatre season at the beginning of summer.*

After consulting with Cordelia, Samson wrote back immediately and gave Goodfellow their assurance. They would be in Adelaide by the end of the month and ready to perform by the summer.

It was in fact a few days into October 1839 when Samson had his first meeting with Goodfellow, a lavish lunch at the Grosvenor Hotel with the Colonial Secretary, Robert Gouger, and a local trader with an interest in establishing the arts in the town, Donald McEntee. Gouger had asked McEntee to work alongside Goodfellow in managing arrangements for the new theatre, McEntee to look to the artistic side, while Goodfellow would serve as the business manager. It was at the lunch that Samson was told of the abandoned warehouse that was being turned into a temporary playhouse. It was also to be named the Royal Victoria Theatre in honour of the new young Queen, while the theatre being built would be named The Queen Victoria. Goodfellow was throwing a lot of money at the renovation of what all would come to know affectionately as 'The Royal' to ensure it would be ready for a mid-November opening.

'So, you'll be ready, then, Mr Cameron?' Goodfellow said, lighting up yet another cigar.

'Oh, aye, Mrs Cameron and I know the play well.'

'*Othello?*' Gouger chimed in. 'Oh, that's wonderful!'

'*Othello?*' Samson blurted out, banging his glass on the table louder than intended. 'I thought we were doing *The Stranger.*'

Goodfellow and Gouger looked to each other, seeming to wonder who should speak first. It was Donald McEntee who took advantage of their indecision.

'I'm sorry if there was any misunderstanding, Mr Cameron.'

McEntee glanced from Samson to Goodfellow to Gouger and back again. 'But the Governor insisted it must be Shakespeare. I was certain Mr Goodfellow had made that plain to you.'

'Oh, I thought I'd mentioned that, Cameron,' Goodfellow said, wriggling in his chair as he took a giant puff on the cigar. 'I was sure I had. We're told that the Governor's wife has fond memories of seeing *Othello* in London.'

'It's not a problem, is it?' McEntee said, staring at Samson.

'No. No. I'm sure it'll be fine,' he replied, hoping the look on his face hid his true feelings.

'Splendid,' Gouger said. 'Then be assured, your wife and your good self will have the "keys to the city", as they would say in the old country. No expenses spared. Isn't that right, Mr Goodfellow?'

'Indeed,' Goodfellow chortled as he added to the pile of ash that had missed the cigar tray sitting next to his plate. The starched tablecloth was the victim of his clumsiness. 'Anything to please the Governor's wife.'

The three Adelaide men joined in the chortle. Samson smiled absently. *How do I break this news to Cordelia?*

'Me play Desdemona?' Cordelia scoffed.

'I thought ye'd done it before, darling.'

'When I was seventeen, like Desdemona herself, yes! But I'm old enough now to be her mother.'

'I'm afraid we've no choice. The Governor's wife wants *Othello* and that's that!'

'Well, I'm not doing it. I really wasn't entirely convinced I wanted to do Mrs Haller again – or anyone for that matter – but playing a foolish nubile? No, I won't subject myself to any more onstage ridicule! We'll have to find someone to be Desdemona to your Othello. There must be a young actress somewhere who could do it.'

'In five weeks? I'm not sure – unless she's done it before.'

'Yes, unless she's done it before,' Cordelia said, emitting a tiny snort and looking Samson in the eye. 'And we both know someone who's done it before, don't we?'

'Who?'

'You know who, Samson!'

'Grace?'

'Precisely. Weren't you the one gloating over the article in the *Geelong Advertiser*? How long ago was that? No more than two months?'

'Aye but …'

'But what, Samson? She'll do it if you ask her.'

'I dinna even know where she is, Cordelia.'

'Well, find out. That shouldn't be too hard. Start with Geelong. She might still be there. Or didn't you say she comes from Adelaide?'

'Aye, or somewhere in South Australia. She mentioned that her father got into the whaling business, and they moved to some nearby island for his work.'

'I'll find out for you, Mr Cameron,' McEntee said. 'But are you certain Mrs Cameron won't do it? I feel the Governor's wife might be disappointed.'

'Aye, I'm sure.'

'Very well, then. Just wait here.'

Samson sat in McEntee's office, scanning the flyers on the wall.

Choral recitals, operas, orchestras, ballet. London, Paris, Edinburgh, Berlin, Vienna, Edinburgh, New York, Rome, Edinburgh.

'I get the sense ye might be from Edinburgh, Mr McEntee,' he said as his host re-entered the room.

'Oh, I see you've picked my bias. Yes, I was born in Edinburgh.'

'But ye dinna have the accent.'

'No, I was a child when we left.'

'A wee bairn, as we say,' Samson said, nodding and smiling.

'Oh, yes. Very wee. I have no memories of the place, although I feel as though I know it. My father, especially, never really got over leaving there. He even spoke of going back, but my mother used to say she preferred the climate here. "Go back and freeze if you really want," she used to say. "But I'm staying here with the children."'

'Aye, and she's right, for sure. But it is a bonnie place, all the same.'

'So, you come from there, do you, Mr Cameron?'

'Aye, my grand da moved there during the Clearances.'

'Where from, if I might ask?'

'From Duthil, in the Highlands. My da went back for a time. "The Highlands are in my blood", he used to say. He remembered growing up there.'

'And you went back with him?'

'No. My ma stayed in Edinburgh with the wee bairns. Only my older brother went with Da. He stayed there when Da came back to Edinburgh.'

'So, you're a Lowlander, as they say there?'

'Not really. A Highlander in my heart.'

'Highlanders and Lowlanders.' McEntee chuckled. 'Oh, the Scots would truly rule the world if only they'd unite.'

'Aye, but I think we rule anyway.'

'Yes, no doubt,' McEntee replied, smiling broadly. 'Anyway, I think we might have solved your problem. One of my staff tells me that Grace Bellingham is currently with her family on Kangaroo Island.

'Kangaroo Island … is that far away?'

'No, not at all. It's quite a short trip by boat. There are ships coming back and forth quite regularly. They're always open to a paying passenger or two hitching a ride.'

'No, you should go alone, Samson,' Cordelia said. 'We can't really drag the children there and, besides …'

'Besides what, darling?'

'Oh, you know. You have a way with Grace, and I'd only spoil it.'

Thirty-eight

SAMSON DISCOVERED THAT THE BELLINGHAM dwelling in
Kingscote, Kangaroo Island, was quite well known in the com-
munity. Her father had been lured from Van Diemen's Land
when whaling first began on Kangaroo Island some years before.
Samson was on a boat within days. He enjoyed being back on the
sea, even in a basic whaling craft. There was a late spring drizzle
in the mid-afternoon, when the vessel pulled up to the dock.
The sight and stench of whale carcass cuttings was something
he would talk about for years to come. He alighted with a small,
one-night-away valise, and took directions to the home. It was a
ten-to-twelve-minute walk up a small muddy incline. The hovels
and tents to be found near the dock gave way to an open field and
finally a handful of slab huts on both sides of the track, a couple
whitewashed, one with a thatched roof.

The haves and have-nots even here.

Samson was reminded of a fishing village he had visited once
as a child on the West Coast of Scotland. He remembered the

unpretentious good folk who lived there. *So, Grace is nearby*, he thought, feeling a familiar warmth in his heart. He was surprised at his own sense of excitement at the prospect of seeing her again.

Recognising the dwelling from descriptions jolted him back to reality. The last frosty conversation with Grace came back to him. He wondered all of a sudden just what sort of reception he should expect.

'Oh, Mr Cameron,' the portly lady said at the door. 'I'm Grace's mother. What a pleasure to meet you. Grace has spoken so highly of you. She's down near the water. If you follow the road back to the dock and turn right. There won't be too many down there on a day like this.'

Samson felt a nervousness overtake him when he saw her from a distance. She was strolling near the gently breaking waves. A young gentleman was by her side. He wondered if he should disturb them. *But I've come so far, and Grace is our only hope of putting on the play in a little over a month.* He stepped onto the beach and strode towards the pair.

'Mr Cameron, what on earth are you doing here?' Grace said as she spotted him, a mix of shock and embarrassment on her face.

'I'm sorry to disturb ye, lass, but I need to talk with ye.'

'I presume you know this gentleman, Grace,' the young man said, stiffening his whole body as if ready to defend his companion.

'Oh, yes.' Grace reached out to take Samson's hand. 'This is Mr Cameron, the actor I owe so much to. Mr Cameron, this is Charles Folley, the son of one of my father's friends.'

Samson released his hand from Grace's grip and extended it towards Folley, who reciprocated. They exchanged greetings.

'You said you need to speak with me, Mr Cameron?' Grace said, smiling. He saw the welling in her eyes.

'Aye, if I could have a word with ye sometime today.'

'Of course, how long are you here?'

'I hope to be on a boat back to Adelaide tomorrow.'

'Goodness, so soon.' Grace turned to Folley. 'Charles, do you mind if we talk again tomorrow? I'd better attend to Mr Cameron. Heaven knows what news he has for me.'

Samson could see that Folley noticed her blushing.

'Ah, certainly, Grace dear.' Folley took her hand in his two hands. 'If you're sure you're all right.'

'Of course, I'm all right, Charles. This is Mr Cameron, my dearest friend – well, apart from you, naturally.'

'Then I'll bid you good day and I'll see you in the morning. Should I come around ten o'clock, or even earlier?'

'Ten o'clock will be good, thank you, Charles.'

Folley let go of her hand and extended it to Samson.

'I bid you good day, sir. I assume you'll see Miss Bellingham home safely.'

'I certainly will, sir. It was braw to meet ye.'

'That means it was good.' Grace was smiling at Folley as she laid her hand on Samson's arm.

They strolled alongside the water in the direction of the dock. They saw Folley striding away, turning around a couple of times, no doubt to see them becoming smaller and smaller figures. He would have noted Grace's arm wedged into Samson's.

'I can't believe you're here.' Her voice was trembling.

'I wasna certain ye'd want to see me again. After last time.'

'Oh, I'm so sorry, Mr Cameron. I felt such a fool afterwards.'

'No, Grace. I was the fool. A right proper *amadan*, as my da would have said!'

They walked in silence past the dock and moved into a wooded area alongside the water.

'So, how is Mrs Cameron?'

'Oh, she's well.'

There was another prolonged period of silence.

'Is she still in Sydney?'

'No, no. She's in Adelaide.'

'Oh!'

They walked a little further.

'Why Adelaide?'

'We're performing in Adelaide. At the new Royal Victoria Theatre. Did ye not know?'

'Why would I, Samson?' *That sharpness that comes from nowhere.* 'Do you think I keep an eye on you, or something?'

They had reached the end of the track. To walk further would mean stepping into the water. They stood looking back at the lights around the dock starting to flicker as dusk was falling.

'I'm sorry, Mr Cameron. I'm being a fool –yet again! Aren't I?'

'I dinna know, Grace. I dinna know. Did ye think …?'

'Did I think what?' she butted in. 'That you'd come to tell me you'd left Mrs Cameron? That you'd come to your senses? That you'd like me to marry you?'

There was another awkward silence. Samson cleared his throat, readying to speak.

'Why would you think such a ridiculous thing?' Grace cut him off. 'Why on earth?'

She turned to face the opposite direction. Samson placed his hand on her back, feeling her deep, unsteady breathing.

'I'm so sorry, Grace. I thought perhaps …'

'You thought I'd be over all that nonsense,' she spat out. 'That I'd have grown up, perhaps?'

Grace wouldn't look at him. Samson pulled his hand away.

'No, but that ye might have found yerself a special someone, like that bonnie lad.'

'Charles?' Grace shrieked then fell to laughing. '*Charles?*'

'Well, I dinna know, but he seemed a fine young man to me.'

'Then you can have him, Samson,' she scoffed. 'You can have him!'

'He seemed very fond of ye, lass. That's all I'm saying.'

'Oh, well, you're right about that. Poor Charles has been fond of me since we met through our fathers some years ago. He'd marry me tomorrow if I let him. Have my first child in nine months and one day if I let him. The second about eleven months after that if I let him.'

'Is that so bad, lass?'

'What do you mean, Samson?'

'Well, is it such a bad idea?'

'So, I shouldn't care about my acting career? I shouldn't care about my independence?'

They stood in silence again. It was dark by now. Samson saw Grace turn her head towards him, noticing the moonlight glistening in her eyes.

'I shouldn't care that I don't love him?' she said sternly. 'Is that what you're saying?'

'No, lass!'

'And don't call me lass!' She took a step forward and started banging her fist on his chest. 'I've told you that before. I'm Grace, remember? I'm not a lass. I'm an adult, just like you. A fully-grown woman. Would you please treat me like one – finally?'

Silence again, as she continued tapping her clenched fist on Samson's chest. Her head was turned to one side, looking out over the water.

'Are you going to say anything?' she whispered. 'Or are you going to just stand there?'

'Then I think ye should call me Samson.'

Grace burst into laughter, turning her head towards him, and resting it over the clenched fist still on his chest.

'You are the most infuriating man I've ever known, Samson Cameron.'

He placed his arms around her and drew her head closer to his chest.

'And ye're not the first one to say that, la— I mean Grace.'

He could feel her chuckling, her head turning in frustration. They stood like that for a few minutes. Without a word, she stepped away.

'Enough! That's enough! Why did you come here, Samson? Except to torment me?'

'I dinna want to torment ye, Grace. Ye're such a bonnie lass – sorry, *lady*.'

'Call me lass again and I will hit you, *Mr Cameron*.'

'*Samson*,' he corrected her.

'Samson,' she chuckled, shaking her head. 'Anyway, I need to get home. My mother worries when I'm out after dark.'

They began walking back towards the dock. Together but several feet apart.

'So, why did you come here, Samson?' she said, as if merely to break the silence. 'I would have thought you'd both be relieved to have me out of your life.'

'Not at all, Grace. Not at all.'

'So, why then?'

'It doesna really matter. It was a mistake. I didna realise ye still felt the way ye do.'

'Truly, Samson.' Grace was shaking her head and laughing. As if to belittle him he thought. 'Tell me anyway. Were you going to offer me a job? To fill in for Mrs Cameron, perhaps? Poor, indisposed Mrs Cameron.'

Samson remained silent as they turned into the track leading to her home. They could see her mother standing in the lit doorway.

'I'm sorry, Samson. I'm not a very nice person, am I? But please do tell me why you came.'

They stopped some thirty yards short of the Bellingham home. Samson turned to face her.

'They want me to do *Othello*.'

'*Othello*? Why, I've just finished a season of *Othello*.'

'In Geelong? I know, Grace. I know. I've been reading the rave reviews.'

'So, you do keep an eye on me, then?'

'Aye. Is that all right?'

'Yes, I don't mind at all. In fact, I'm quite touched. Does Mrs Cameron know?'

'Aye, of course. It was her idea that I should come here to ask you.'

'Ask me?'

'Aye. To play Desdemona.'

Grace stood shaking her head. He could hear her sniggering.

'But I imagine that won't be happening,' he said quietly.

Grace's mother was calling.

'I really must go. It was lovely to see you again, Samson. I truly do wish you and your family all the happiness in the world. But …'

'I know, Grace. I know. Goodbye.'

'Goodbye, Samson.'

They turned away from each other. She to her home, him walking back towards the dock.

'Samson,' she called. 'Where are you staying tonight?'

He turned and called back. 'I dinna ken. I'll find something near the dock.'

'You can stay with us if you wish. Mother will make up a bed.'

'Thank ye, but I shouldna impose on ye.'

'It won't be an imposition, Samson. It's just common decency, seeing as you came all this way. My mother would want you to stay. I know that for a fact.'

'Thank ye, lass. Sorry, Grace. And thank yer ma for me. She must be a fine lady if ye take after her.'

Samson turned and continued walking towards the water. He sensed that she would be watching him disappear into the night.

Samson found some bare lodgings in a small tavern close to the dock. In the morning, he hastened to the vessel already in half sail and straining at its moorings. *That stench again.* It was raining heavily, and the wind was fearsome. Samson could barely see the end of the gangplank as he made the last turn towards the ship. Clenching the valise with one hand and steadying his hat, head down, with the other, he was battling the wind wanting to blow him backwards. His progress was suddenly impeded by someone standing in his path. He almost knocked her down.

'Grace, what are ye doing here, lass? Ye'll get yer death of a cold.'

'Yes,' she said, reaching out and holding the hand carrying his valise.

'Aye, what, Grace?'

'I'd love to play Desdemona – as long as you're playing Othello.'

'Truly? But I thought …'

'That I can't be a professional? Well, you just watch me!'

'Grace, I … I …' he stuttered.

'Say no more, Samson. I'm honoured that you would come all this way to ask me. How could I say no?'

'But are ye free? Available?'

'I have no commitment until Launceston next Easter. So, I'm yours until then – if you'll have me.'

'Of course, lass. *Grace*. Of course I'll have ye.'

Grace stretched her arms around him. He dropped the valise and held one arm around her. The other hand was gripping the hat that threatened to be blown back to Adelaide if he let go.

'Thank you, Samson,' she whispered.

'Thank ye, Grace. Ye're the one doing me the favour.'

They stepped apart, still holding hands.

'I mean thank you for continuing to forgive me,' she said, tears and raindrops dribbling together down her cheeks. 'When do you need me there?'

'There's naught to forgive, Grace. Can ye be there this week?'

'I'll be on a boat in a couple of days.'

'And ye can stay with us if ye wish.'

'Thank you, but that might not be wise. I have an aunt and uncle in Adelaide. I'll be fine. They'll be thrilled to know I'll be on the stage there.'

'I'm so excited to work with ye again, Grace. And I know Mrs Cameron will be excited as well.'

'Thank you for saying so, Samson.' He noticed the gentle smirk on her face. 'Even if it's not true!'

Samson smiled as he let go of her hand, picked up the valise and strode against the wind towards the boat. He turned to see her standing, drenched but smiling widely.

'Ye look happy, lass,' he shouted against the wind.

'I'm deliriously happy, Samson,' she called back. 'You've no idea how often I've dreamt of working with you again.'

'That's wonderful, but dinna get sick now.'

'No, I won't get sick. Fate could not be so cruel.'

'Ye know I've never played Othello,' Samson shouted.

'Good,' she shouted back. 'So, I'll be in charge this time.'

He smiled and waved one last time before turning away. She waved back, then stood dripping wet until he finished climbing the gangplank. When he reached the deck, he looked back to see her turn and walk away.

Thirty-nine

'MR GOODFELLOW CAME TO SEE you while you were away,' Cordelia said as she greeted Samson at the door of their cramped lodgings in North Terrace.

'Aye, do ye know why?' He reached over and kissed her on the cheek.

'No, he wouldn't speak with me but …'

'But what?'

'He seemed quite agitated. Or is that just who he is?'

'No. Not at all.' Samson slumped down on the nearest chair. 'Cocksure is more how I'd describe him.'

'Well, that's interesting, then. He was desperate to see you. Seemed quite put out that you weren't here. I said you'd make contact as soon as you were back.'

'Aye, well I'll contact him tomorrow.' Samson began to stand. 'For now, I just need a wash and a rest.'

Cordelia grabbed his hand and pulled him towards her. 'I'd go now if I were you, Samson. There's too much riding on this. If something has gone wrong, what are we going to do?'

'I canna go like this.' He pulled away and pointed to his dusty shoes and trousers.

'Frankly, Samson, I don't think Goodfellow would notice if you were naked. He seemed quite preoccupied with whatever was concerning him. And I did promise that you would go immediately.'

'Oh, if ye think so, darling. Do ye mind if I leave my valise here then? I'll unpack when I get home.'

'Of course. I'll guard it with my life.'

'It's not worth yer life, darling.' He reached over to kiss her again. 'I'd rather have ye. I can always buy another valise, but there's only one Cordelia Bouchier.'

'Enough of your smooth talk, Samson.' She turned her head away.

'Only for yer ears, dear.'

'Are you sure?'

'I'm sure.' Samson was heading for the door.

'How did things go with Grace?'

'Good.' He looked back over his shoulder.

'So, it's not only for my ears, then?'

'What?' *Here we go again.*

'The smooth talk.'

Samson blew a kiss and exited the door.

The smile quickly left Cordelia's face. She slumped her head on the back of the chair and turned to face the window. She felt the warmth of the tears forming and slowly oozing out to fill her eyelashes. She shut her eyes and allowed herself a few moments of subdued anxiety.

'Oh, Cameron,' Goodfellow said, jumping up from his desk as Samson was ushered into the office. 'So pleased you're here, man. Please take a seat.'

Samson took the extended hand and was guided to the high-back chair on the opposite side of the desk. Goodfellow hurried back to his chair. An apprehensiveness overcame him as he watched the rotund figure lift a cigar from the box and light it, then, looking over at Samson, raise the box and gesture with it towards him.

'Sorry, Cameron, would you like one? I can't remember if you indulge or not.'

'No, thank ye.' Samson shifted in his seat.

'Look, old man, I won't beat around the bush. I have a bit of a problem.'

Samson said nothing, simply raising one eyebrow as a concession to his readiness to listen.

'It's all a tad embarrassing, frankly, and I'd appreciate your discretion.' Goodfellow paused, casting an appealing glance in Samson's direction.

'Aye, sir. I'm sure I can give ye that.'

'Oh, that would be a relief.' Goodfellow took a deep breath, followed by a raucous cough as he dispensed the cigar ash somewhere in the vicinity of the overburdened ashtray. 'I frankly would prefer it if no-one knew about this, especially the Governor and the Colonial Secretary.'

Samson watched as Goodfellow tapped on the desk and puffed especially vigorously on the cigar. It was as if he did not quite know where to begin. Samson pondered on the extent of the man's unattractiveness, on his father's hatred of what he called 'new money', those brought up with no breeding who chased money-making and revelled in the power it gave them, albeit never able to shake off their heritage.

'I'm not sure where to begin, so I might just get straight to the nub of the matter. Is that all right with you? You probably don't need to know all the gruesome history anyway.'

'Getting straight to it would be braw, sir.'

'Very well, then, Cameron. I'm in some financial strife.'

The words cut through to the worst scenario Samson could have imagined. All the way in, he had assured himself that there must be some more beneficent reason for Goodfellow's concern. But here it was. And he had just abandoned a secure position to move his family to Adelaide to risk the inherently meagre security that always accompanies the theatre business. Just coaxed Grace to abandon other opportunities and opt for loyalty to him for what would likely be less financial reward and possibly less security in her own future.

'Financial strife?' Samson repeated, attempting to exude calm.

'Yes, my accountant has been warning me, but I suppose I thought he was being a tad over-dramatic. You know what accountants can be like.'

'Aye, I'm one myself.'

'Are you? Really? You're an accountant?'

'Aye, that's actually how I supported my family in Sydney when the theatre business turned sour.'

'Well, well,' Goodfellow said, sitting back in his chair and taking an unusually deep puff on the cigar. 'Yes, that might actually help us here.'

'How so, sir?'

'Well, at least you have some understanding of money and perhaps between us, we can work something out.'

'Between us?'

'Well, yes. We are in this together, after all. Don't you agree?'

'Ah, aye, though I thought ye'd be taking care of the finances. That was what I thought we'd agreed.'

'Yes, well, the truth is I've overinvested in restoring the Royal and building the Queen's at the same time. It's taken more than we anticipated and now the bank is refusing to provide any more finances until the current loans are paid back.'

'So does that mean the new theatre won't be ready as ye'd promised?' For the first time, Samson was unable to hide his agitation.

'Oh, it might take a little longer but even when it's finished, it's all the other things. Fittings, props, ticket sales, salaries.'

'*Salaries*?' Samson blurted out, thinking of Grace having put her faith in him. 'Ye mean ye dinna have any money to pay the players?'

'Just at the moment, no, but I'm sure we can work something out.'

'Work something out?'

'Well, yes, I wondered if you might have some of your own capital that you could put up.'

'Sir, I've just given up secure employment to come here. Moved my family at great expense to be here. Placed a bond on rented premises so I could be here. Trusted in yer good word to be here.'

Samson stopped talking, breathless. His head was spinning.

'Well, now, there's no need to be acrimonious about it, old man. I've done my best here and I'm sure there's some way around it all. I just need a little time, you know.'

'Aye, but time to do what? There's no time.'

'Time to get some cash flow. You understand about cash flow, surely. You're the accountant, so you say!'

'Cash flow? Ye mean ye've not enough finances to even make a start?'

'That's what I'm saying, so we just need some benefaction or a loan to tide us over for the first few weeks, months at the most, and I'm sure we'll be fine after that.'

'What about the Governor? Surely?'

'No, the Governor has made it clear from the start that there would be no government money for any of this. I've even prevailed upon his wife to put a bit of pillow pressure, let's say, but he's one to play things by the book and he insists that government money can only be expended on essentials. Infrastructure, services, those sorts of things.'

'The Colonial Secretary? Surely he has contacts.'

'Same thing. They're like two sides of the same coin, those two.'

Samson shook his head in exasperation. 'Well, what about Mr McEntee?'

'Head in the clouds, Cameron. All talk. He'll jump in when things are up and running, but he won't put up a penny to get them started. Not sure he has a penny to put in anyway!'

'Which leaves?'

'You, sir! Cameron, you have capital power. You'll know what I mean by that!'

'Tell me.' Samson was breathing out loudly through his mouth as he shook his head.

'Well, from all I know, your theatre ventures in Van Diemen's Land were most successful. Is that not true?'

'Aye. For the most part!'

'Then, you and your wife are assets in that sense. You'd represent good capital for any bank looking to lend money. They'd know you're a sure thing!'

'So, ye're suggesting …'

'Precisely! You secure a loan that will cover the first few weeks of production, and we'll cut a deal to ensure you get a fair share of the returns so you can pay back the loan. What do you think?'

Samson was peering down at the floor. Silent. He could hear Goodfellow's chair squeaking as he shifted around in his own chair.

'I'll need to speak with my wife.'

'Your wife?'

'My wife.'

'Truly? That's most unusual,' Goodfellow said, a confused wry smile flashing across his face. 'I thought as an accountant—'

'My wife,' Samson said sternly, standing up and extending his hand. 'I'll be in contact soon.'

'Very well, then.' Goodfellow was snorting and shaking his head. 'Do let me know what your wife decides.'

'She'll not decide, sir. We'll decide together. That's how it is with us.'

'Modern marriages,' Goodfellow chuckled. 'You'll have to forgive me, Cameron. In my day …'

'I forgive ye, sir. And, by the way, do ye truly think I could get a loan? From any bank?'

'Of course, Cameron. I'd see to it.'

'I think we should set up our own company,' Cordelia said, nodding her head as she contemplated the blue and white chequered counterpane that lay over her.

Despite Samson's best efforts, he had woken her when he arrived home late. Cordelia insisted he tell her everything about the meeting with Goodfellow.

'A company?'

'Yes, why not? It's something we've always wanted, and then

we wouldn't be so dependent on the good or bad graces of the Goodfellows of this world.'

'Do ye think we could manage it? It's a whole lot of extra headaches.'

'Well, you have the accounting skills, and I think I have a pretty good business head, don't you?'

'I think ye have the prettiest head I could ever imagine, darling,' Samson said, his smiling eyes glistening with warmth.

'Smooth talk again!'

'Only with ye, darling, as I said!'

'It had better be, Samson, as I've said before!'

'Ye know so.' He reached across and kissed her on the cheek.

'Mmm.' Cordelia pushed him away so hard he fell back and onto the floor.

'Darling,' he said indignantly as he lifted himself up.

'Sorry, Samson. I didn't hurt you, did I?'

'Just a wee bit.' He was dusting himself down.

'And here was me thinking you Highlanders were a rugged lot.'

'Well, we are when it comes to wielding a sword, but not when wrestling with a tiger.'

'Just you remember I'm a tiger, husband dear. A very protective tiger! You know what I mean?'

'Aye, darling. I know!'

'Good. So, when does the little hussy arrive, anyway?'

So, it came to pass that Samson and Cordelia formed a theatrical enterprise, The Cameron Company. They secured a loan without any help from, and avoiding all advice given by, Goodfellow, which greatly displeased him. They then negotiated to take responsibility for the entire cost associated with all productions at the new theatre, receiving a hundred per cent of the profits and offering Goodfellow a fee to cover the rent.

'You can't be serious,' Goodfellow said, spraying ash more widely than normal across the desk.

'I've been told to say to ye *take it or leave it*.'

'But what's in it for me, then?'

'Good rental return and …'

'And what?'

'My silence.' Samson cocked an eyebrow and smiled.

'Well, you leave me with little choice at this late stage. Let's sign on this basis for six months and then re-negotiate.'

'Twelve months will be wonderful.'

'Nine.'

'Twelve. Take it or leave it, sir.'

'Twelve it is. And not a word to the Governor or Colonial Secretary about my situation.'

'Ye have my word.'

'The word of a Scotsman?'

'Even better: a Highlander.'

Goodfellow signed the prepared contract, then passed it over the desk to Samson's waiting hand. Samson dipped the quill in the inkwell, signed and lifted the papers.

'And who told you to tell me that?'

'Tell ye what?'

'To take it or leave it?'

'My wife. I'll get her signature and bring the contract back this afternoon.'

'Modern marriages,' Goodfellow grumbled, shaking his head as he watched Samson move through the doorway.

Forty

Mr Cameron's Othello surpasses even the best renditions from the old world, according to none other than Lady Gawler, the Governor's wife. This theatre critic agrees with Her Excellency's judgement, albeit with less exposure to comparisons. It is, after all, the first time the eminent thespian has performed this role in the colony. Nonetheless, it is difficult to imagine a rendition that would better capture the multifarious moral themes intended, and the range of performative expressions needed to manifest them. Be it in the form of a master tactician, a jealous rage, a supplicant partner, or a helpless lover pleading for attention, Mr Cameron's acting prowess must be the envy of the best performers in the entire British Empire. In this critic's view, the only more outstanding performance – and it was outstanding – was in Miss Grace Bellingham's Desdemona. It has come to my attention that Miss Bellingham was commissioned quite late in the piece to play the part, it being intended initially for Mrs Cordelia Cameron, who has been indisposed of late. The Royal Victoria Theatre owners and managers must be hoping that Miss Bellingham is allowed to grace the stage in this and other roles for many months to come. Dare one say this would be Grace's grace!

So read a theatrical article in the *South Australian Gazette* on the morning of the 24th day of November 1839.

'Well, Madame Bellingham's done it again,' Cordelia said, looking up from the newspaper.

She moved baby Gracie from one breast to another, then looked away and out the window.

'I have to go back to the theatre, darling,' Samson said softly. 'There's a few wee things we need to go over for tonight.'

'Imperfections?' The baby stirred and gave out a small cry. 'Not according to the *Gazette*.'

'No, just a wee thing or two Grace thought we could have done better.'

'So now she's a director as well. Being the best actress that the world has ever known isn't enough. Is that it?'

'Goodbye, darling.' He moved to the door, head down.

'Samson,' Cordelia called as he was about to close the door behind him.

'Aye,' he replied, holding the door ajar.

'Please do congratulate Grace on her performance.'

'Aye, darling.'

'I mean *all* her performances, the ones on the stage and the others!'

Samson closed the door behind him, saying no more.

Forty-one

OTHELLO RAN FROM NOVEMBER 1839 to April 1840, with breaks over Christmas and Easter. There were three performances each week, with a variety of other plays and recitals interspersed on other nights. Samson and Grace did not miss a performance in the lead roles of *Othello*, and Grace played a starring role in virtually every other play and recital, in some cases alongside Samson. In May of that year, a short season of *The Wonder* began. It was a play about the Irish potato famine of 1729. Samson managed and directed it but stood aside from the acting to appease some of Cordelia's concerns about the amount of kissing between the two main characters.

'Wasn't she meant to be going to Launceston by Easter anyway?'

'Aye, but she managed to re-negotiate. She'll go later.'

'I wonder why on earth she would prefer to stay here?'

Samson smiled and moved towards her. She was sitting at the kitchen table darning a sock. He put his arm on her right cheek and turned her head towards his lips advancing from her left side.

He was aiming for her cheek, but she turned her head further, so to lock their lips together.

'Speaking of kisses,' he said, chuckling as he took a deep breath and righted himself.

'Well, just you remember where you get the best ones, won't you, husband?' Cordelia went back to focusing on her handiwork.

The Wonder finished in mid-June and the Company took a long-awaited winter's break that was supposed to last until late September, when Grace would be finished in Launceston and the new theatre would finally be completed. At last, a season of *The Stranger* was to begin at that time. In mid-August, Samson received a letter from Grace, saying she had cut short the Launceston commitment because her mother had fallen ill soon after her parents had relocated to Port Lincoln, a fast-developing settlement on the southern Eyre Peninsula. She apologised but said she might not be ready to reprise the role of Mrs Haller by the September date and could someone else fill in until she was ready.

'How would ye feel about doing *The Stranger* again?' Samson had just returned from a meeting with Donald McEntee.

'What part?' Cordelia's eyes widened with anticipation.

'Mrs Haller, of course.'

Cordelia burst into a scoffing laughter.

'Has your little madam finally tired of you, dear one?'

'Her ma is ill. She's in some place called Port Lincoln and doesna know if she can be here in time.'

Cordelia sat, shaking her head, worrying a skein of wool. She sniggered, studiously avoiding looking in Samson's direction.

'What do ye think, darling?'

'So, the understudy finally gets her chance? Is that it?'

'Honestly, Cordelia. Ye know it's yer part. It always has been. I was just talking with McEntee. He's excited. He said ye're the one he wanted all along.'

'Oh, be quiet, Samson. Just let me take all this in.'

'Aye. It's just that I know everyone'd be so excited if ye did it.'

'Including that horrid man at the *Gazette*?'

'Ye know what critics are like. Just look at what they've said about me at times.'

'I suppose that would mean you could play Mr Solomon, wouldn't it?'

'Aye, just like the old days. Would it no be braw?'

'Let me think about it, Samson.'

In early September, Cordelia suffered a bout of what the doctor described as melancholia, rendering her bedridden. Samson arranged for a maid who came every day to care for the children, cook and housekeep.

'I'm sorry, Cameron,' McEntee said. 'Very sorry for Mrs Cameron's indisposition, but you did say she would do it and, on that basis, we've already advertised. We've had enormous interest, even from across the colonies. We've ordered the props and everything. It will just have to go ahead. Isn't there anyone else who can play Mrs Haller?'

'There just might be.'

'Oh, spare me, Samson,' Cordelia shouted from her bed. 'Surely, not this again?'

Samson shut the bedroom door. 'Well, what else can we do?'

'Wasn't she supposed to be looking after her mother in – what was the name of that place?'

'Port Lincoln.'

'Yes, there. Wasn't that why you asked me in the first place?'

'Her ma died, darling. I told ye that.'

Cordelia turned her head away. 'No, you didn't. When did she die?'

'Darling, please keep your voice down,' he whispered. 'The week before last.'

'The week before last?' Cordelia spoke more loudly than ever. 'How did you find out so fast? Carrier pigeon?'

'She told me herself.'

'When? Where? Where is she?'

Samson moved closer to the bed, finger to his lips. 'Here in Adelaide. I told ye that too. She was here on Monday wondering if she should stay.'

'Oh, no, you didn't tell me that, Samson.' She was shaking her head. 'You did not tell me that.'

'I was sure I did. Perhaps I forgot.'

'Yes, I think you might have forgotten that little detail. Anyway, surely there's someone else. What about Lucy Willis? Wasn't she going to be my understudy?'

Samson sat on the side of the bed, looking into her eyes. 'Aye, but Lucy's never done it. This is the first time in Adelaide, darling. It has to be a really good performance, and we know Grace can do it. Not as well as ye play it, but she can do it.'

'Oh, spare me the patronising, Samson.' Cordelia turned her head away. 'And I suppose that means you'll play Mr Solomon?'

'Aye, I think I must, darling. There's no-one else ready for it. We let Fergus go when we thought ye were playing Mrs Haller.'

Cordelia turned to face him, wry smile on her face. 'Duty calls? Is that what you're saying?'

'Aye.'

'And the kisses?'

'I can delete them if ye like.'

Cordelia turned her head and snuffed.

'No, I wouldn't want to spoil things for Madame Bellingham!'

So it came to pass that *The Stranger* ran as the main performance until just before Christmas that year, with Samson and Grace again in the lead roles. As it happened, they were still performing in the old Royal because the Queen Victoria was yet to be finished.

Grace returned home for Christmas, writing in mid-January that she had to stay in Port Lincoln to look after her father.

'What will we do, Cameron?' McEntee asked. 'The play is meant to start again in a week. 'Are you sure Mrs Cameron can't be convinced now?'

'I'm quite sure. The lass is in confinement.'

'Oh, I didn't realise. Another child on the way, then?'

'Aye.'

'And how is Mrs Cameron in other ways?'

Samson lowered his head before speaking. 'Ah, well, she's out of bed, which is braw. But she always worries when she's with child. Ye know we lost a child. And she blames herself.'

'All right, then, Cameron, you know your own business best.

But what are you going to do? Isn't there anyone else at all? Who was the understudy?'

'Lucy Willis.' Samson was shaking his head.

'What? Is she not up to it, Samson?'

'She's away until Easter, but she's not good enough anyway. Not after Grace.'

'You really are fond of that girl, aren't you?'

'She's a bonnie actress.' He lowered his head to hide the look on his face.

They sat for a moment in silence. McEntee was looking at him, smiling.

Samson finally looked up. 'And the new understudy has never played the part.'

'All right, then, what thoughts do you have?'

'I think we should postpone *The Stranger* until the Queen's opens. Make a fuss about how exciting that will be. In the meantime, I can arrange a series of recitals. We have some really good singers in the Company, and I can probably get some others from the other colonies.'

'Mmm.' McEntee was rubbing his chin. 'I'm not certain how the Governor's wife, or even the public, will react to that.'

'Well, they have no choice, do they?'

'Governors and their wives, and even members of the public, tend to believe they have many, Cameron, and it's the job of minions like you and me to make them happen.'

'Is that what we are, sir? Minions?'

McEntee chuckled. He lifted his pipe from the desk and began to fill it with tobacco.

'Perhaps me more than you, sir.' He was casually stoking the pipe. 'Anyway, why don't you draw up a plan that I can quickly take to the relevant parties, and we'll see where we go from there?'

Hence, from February through to May of that year, 1841, The Cameron Company put on a series of recitals, mainly singing, interspersed with the odd orchestral event and the even more occasional poetry recital. The highlight came in late March when Samson convinced Cordelia to offer a one-night reprise of some of her best-known songs.

'Oh, I don't know, Samson. I haven't done this for a while.'

Samson looked at her fondly. 'I think it'll take no more than a wee few seconds before ye feel right at home again. Where ye belong.'

'Do you really think I'm good enough?'

Her vulnerability stirred sadness and cherishment in Samson's heart. 'Darling,' he said, shaking his downturned head. 'There's no-one as good as ye are.' He looked up and into her eyes. 'Ye know that, d'ye no?'

'Well, I did once. Until you-know-who came along.'

'Darling, ye-know-who canna hold a candle to ye. Ye know that too.'

He watched as she raised a handkerchief to her nose, wiping it before looking up. 'Thank you, husband, for saying that, but we both know it's not true – and so do those who write in the *Gazette*, remember?'

'That's all just what they call colonial jealousy. Grace is one of their own. Ye're the old enemy. That's what all that's about.'

'Still, there's a lot of people who read that horrid newspaper.'

'Well, it's up to ye, darling. The doctor thinks it's a good idea. He thinks ye need something like this.'

'Does he now? So, you've been talking about me behind my back, have you?'

'Only beautiful things, darling! Only the best of things!'

Samson's attempt at a warm smile was met with something more subdued. He turned towards the door.

'So, what do I tell Mr McEntee?' He pulled on the door and turned around to face her.

'Tell him I'll think about it.'

The city was treated to a special night last evening when Mrs Cordelia Cameron graced us with several of her most famous numbers. Never have our cultural caste been more generous in their applause. Deservedly so. Mrs Cameron reminded us of what we have been missing since her forced confinement. We can only hope and pray she will be back on the stage as soon as the doctors consider it wise.

'And ye were worried about the *Gazette*.' Samson handed her the newspaper.

'I admit I'm very pleased.' Cordelia was smiling and extending her hand.

'Pleased ye did it?' He took her hand and kissed it.

'Yes, I am.' She brought her other hand forward and held it over his own. 'I have only one quibble.'

'What is it, darling?' He sat on the bed, moving closer to her.

'Why did he have to use the word "grace"?'

They burst into laughter as he leant forward to kiss her on the lips.

'I think ye should do it again. Will I tell Mr McEntee?'

'Oh, perhaps. Let me think about it.'

'Ye know what he'll think that means.'

'Well, perhaps best not to tell him then. Let me see how I come up from this one.'

'Are ye weary, darling?'

'I'm exhausted, Samson. Thoroughly exhausted.'

As it was, Cordelia did not perform again before the birth of another son on the 20th day of July 1841.

'I'd like to call him after you, Samson,' Cordelia said, tears in her exhausted eyes.

Samson sat on the edge of the bed and touched the baby's cheek. 'If that's what ye want, darling. Ye've done all the work here.'

'But you would like that, wouldn't you?'

'Aye, I think it'd be braw! What about his middle name?'

'Well, if he's named after you, he should be named after you. Samson Pearce Cameron. Such a special name. More famous by the day. So, there should be another. And perhaps another after that.'

'That's bonnie of ye, darling. I'd be honoured.'

'All right, then.' Cordelia lay back against the pillows and closed her eyes. 'Anyway, thank you for coming. I know you have to get back to the theatre. Tonight's the last performance in the old one, isn't it?'

'Aye.' Samson stood up. 'They start taking all the props over to the Queen's in the morning. Everything. Even the seats are going across.'

Cordelia's eyes snapped open. 'Truly? I thought they'd purchase new seats for the Queen's.'

'Aye, well, I think they've run out of money. It all cost a lot more than they thought,' Samson was edging towards the door. 'I'd best go. I'll see ye tomorrow.'

'You don't want to hold the baby?'

'Oh, I suppose.' Samson hastened back towards the bed. 'Just a quick one. Ye know I'm always afraid I'll drop them.'

'But you never have, now, have you?' Cordelia lifted the baby into his outstretched arms.

Forty-two

ON THE FOLLOWING SATURDAY FORTNIGHT, the 7th day of August 1841, the new Queen's Theatre opened its doors to the long-awaited reprise of *The Stranger*. As Donald McEntee had predicted, the audience came from far and wide, including from across colonial borders. Among the audience members were theatre critics from all the colonies except for Western Australia. Even Queensland, a near three-thousand-mile ocean voyage, was represented. Over the next two weeks, articles would be written in all major colonial newspapers extolling 'the finest theatre in the Southern Hemisphere', 'the most exquisite theatrical performance of any so far in the history of the colonies', 'the sterling acting and directing of Mr Samson Cameron', and 'the belle of the theatrical ball, Miss Grace Bellingham'.

'I can never go on stage again, Samson.' Cordelia was juggling the feeding newborn, with a three-year-old asking why she couldn't still feed from Mummy, and two boys, five and seven years old, fighting over whose turn it was to play the ship's captain, whose the pirate.

'What was that, darling?' Samson said over the din.

'Children!' Cordelia shouted with a rarely heard sternness. 'Please! Mummy and Daddy are trying to talk.'

The baby's head reared away from his mother's nipple, his face contorted and reddened with fear, his mouth wide open readying himself to protest in the way babies know best. Then the sound that can drown out all other sounds.

'See what you've done!' Cordelia snapped as she cradled the wailing baby to her chest. 'Boys, go to your room immediately. Gracie, sit up here next to Mummy and don't be silly. You're not a baby anymore.'

'Is there anything I can do, darling?' Samson appeared as hapless and helpless as normal in these situations.

Gracie fell to her knees as her head collided with the chair next to her mother. She began to wail as though trying to compete with the baby. Cordelia ran her spare hand through the little girl's hair.

'It's all right, darling. Mummy didn't mean to shout.'

'Should I see to the boys?' Samson began moving in the direction of their bedroom.

'Yes, see if you can do something with them,' she replied in a tone that predicted the inevitable futility of sending her husband on a childcare expedition.

'And what was it you said, darling?' he called back as he was passing through the door.

'Don't worry. We'll talk about it later.'

'Mr Cameron, we need to be paid what we're owed,' Jeremiah

Sutcliffe said, looking around at the assembled group for support. 'That's all. We're not asking for bonuses, although some of us feel we could, granted the success we keep reading about.'

Sutcliffe was the conductor of the orchestra. He had quickly become the spokesperson for the musicians, actors and behind-the-scenes staff when they began to share their common concern that their pay was being increasingly delayed. It was the 15th day of December 1841. There were only three performances left in that year.

'Aye, I know,' Samson replied, wiping his brow with a handkerchief. 'We just need to wait until the money's been counted by the bank.'

'Counted by the bank?' Sutcliffe said, shaking his head in disgust. 'Well, if that's the only problem, tell them I'll round up volunteers who can help them in their counting.'

'Sir, I've a sick young child who needs her medicine.' Cecily Chalmers, a budding actor with several non-speaking parts in the play, chipped in. 'And I can't afford it until I'm paid.'

'How long is this bank-counting business going to take?' Sutcliffe added. 'None of us are wealthy, sir. You do understand, surely?'

'And Christmas is coming, sir,' Charlotte Webdale, seamstress and make-up artist, added her voice. 'You must know what an expensive time that is for all of us.'

'Even Grace?' Cordelia asked. 'What does she have to say about all this?'

'She doesna know.' Samson was carefully avoiding Cordelia's enquiring stare.

'What? She doesn't know that you have a revolt on your hands?

Does the girl live in another world? Isn't she worried about being paid? Doesn't she have an ageing parent she cares for?'

'She's been paid,' Samson replied, back turned and barely audible as he fossicked in the desk drawer.

'Oh, I see. Of course, how stupid of me. Naturally, Grace would be the pampered one.'

Samson continued the fossicking, making out he hadn't heard her.

'What are you looking for, Samson? Can I help?'

'I thought we had some cash in here. Didn't ye say we needed to put some aside for a rainy day?'

'Yes, and we did. Until you took it all last week for some unknown purpose. Remember? The rainy day has come and gone, dear one!'

Cordelia watched as Samson stood, head down, fists on the chest of drawers. He knew she was pondering on whether to say what she wanted to say. He was motionless, conscious of his deep, unsteady breathing.

'Or was the rainy day one Miss Bellingham?' she finally uttered, disregarding her caution.

'Well, she is more important than the others, isn't she?' Samson turned to face her. 'Without the lass, we have no performance.'

'But they're all important, aren't they? Without Mr Sutcliffe, you have no-one to conduct the orchestra. Without Mr Craig, no-one to manage the props. Without—'

'I know. I know.' Samson stopped to inhale a deep breath. 'I know.'

'What's gone wrong, Samson? I thought everything was under control, especially with your accounting knowledge.'

'I know. I don't know. I …' He choked on his words mid-sentence.

Cordelia stood up and moved towards him, placing her hand

on his back. He turned and drew her head to his shoulder. They stood in silence for a while. She patted his back as he snuffled, trying to restore his breathing.

'What is it, Samson? What are you not telling me?'

Samson said nothing, but his cheek on the top of her head told her that he was shaking.

'I dinna know. I just dinna know how it happened. I thought everything was under control. But then, the curtain needed replacing and audience numbers were down in those two rainy weeks and—'

'The curtain?' Cordelia took a step back and looked into his eyes. 'In a brand-new theatre?'

'Aye, because it came over from the Royal, just like everything else, but it was hopelessly inadequate for the new stage's size.'

'Of course, it would be, but surely the curtain is Goodfellow's responsibility.'

'I thought so too, but he said the contract makes it clear that everything in the new stage area is the responsibility of the Company.'

'And does it?'

'I dinna know. I canna find my copy.'

'Samson, this is not like you. We need to fight this. Goodfellow is a highly suspicious character. We know that.'

'Aye, but I had no choice. We needed the curtain, and if he wasna going to do anything about it, then I had to.'

'So how much did all this cost?'

'A hundred and forty-three pounds.'

'What? That's exorbitant! Did you get other quotes?'

'No, I was told Bingham and Sons were the only people who could do the job.'

'Who told you that?'

'Goodfellow.'

Cordelia shook her head in disbelief.

'Of course he did. Samson, truly!'

'We need to speak with you, Mr Cameron,' Sutcliffe said as the curtain came down on the second last performance.

'Can it not wait?'

'No, sir. We insist. And we want Miss Bellingham here this time,' Sutcliffe replied with sufficient loudness to ensure Grace, retreating as he spoke, heard him.

'You want me where, Mr Sutcliffe?' Grace was turning back to face him.

'Over here will do.' Sutcliffe was pointing to a spot somewhere next to Samson. He then swivelled his head around as he called to the supporting cast, orchestra members and others streaming onto the stage to ready it for the next evening's performance. 'Everyone, Mr Cameron wishes to speak with us. Please gather around.'

'What's all this about, Samson?' Grace whispered.

'It's of no concern to ye, lass,' he whispered back, noting that Sutcliffe's head was turned away. 'Ye can go. I can deal with it.'

'Thank you.' Grace squeezed his arm. 'I'm very tired.'

She turned to walk offstage, stopping only when Charlotte Webdale stood in her way.

'Please stay, Miss Bellingham.' Charlotte was holding the young actor's elbow. 'It's important you be here for this.'

'Ah, of course, Charlotte, if you think so.'

Grace turned around and walked back to stand by Samson's side.

He touched her shoulder. 'I said ye can go, lass.'

'I think they want me to stay.' She was looking into his eyes and smiling. Samson could tell that she saw the pain in his own eyes.

By this point, the cast and crew had assembled. Cecily Chalmers had been assigned the duty of making sure the audience had left, by peering through the slit between the two curtains. She turned her head towards Sutcliffe and nodded.

'All right folks,' Sutcliffe said in a loud voice. 'Gather around. Mr Cameron has agreed to stay and hear our demands.'

'Demands?' Grace mouthed to Samson, having caught his attention by tugging on his sleeve.

Samson smiled before turning back to face Sutcliffe.

'Mr Cameron,' Sutcliffe said in a way courting no favour. 'We need to know if the banking situation has been resolved. Are we to be paid or not?'

'I'll be going to the bank tomorrow to sort everything out,' Samson replied, avoiding Sutcliffe's eye by scanning his head across the group. 'I promise ye, ye'll all be paid in full.'

As he turned back towards Sutcliffe, Samson caught Grace's puzzled and concerned look. He smiled and rested his hand on her wrist.

'Well, that's good then.' Sutcliffe's eyes were scanning the assembled group. 'Let's agree then to meet here at three o'clock tomorrow to receive our pay or, as we have agreed already, if we are not all paid in full, then tomorrow night's performance will be cancelled.'

'Cancelled?' Grace blurted out, glancing sideways at Samson before turning back to face Sutcliffe. 'Cancelled? We can't cancel a performance at such late notice.'

'We can and we shall, Miss Bellingham.' Sutcliffe stared piercingly at the young actress. 'It's all very fine for you. We believe you've already been paid in full. But the rest of us have not, and we have families to look after, expenses to cover.'

'And Christmas is coming,' Charlotte added.

'Precisely,' Sutcliffe said. 'Christmas is coming. Mr Cameron, are we agreed?'

'Aye, we're agreed!'

'I had no idea there was such a problem, Samson,' Grace said as they walked along, arm-in-arm. 'I was just saying to my aunt the other day how good you were with paying your staff on time.'

'Thank ye, Grace. Ye always see the best in me, lass. Ye've been such a bonnie friend.'

'More than a good friend, I hope, Samson,' she replied, squeezing his arm.

'Aye, ye are, dear. Ye truly are.'

'It means so much to me to hear you say that, Samson. There've been times when I've had occasion to wonder.'

'Wonder what?' he said, stopping and looking her in the eye.

'Wonder if I've been a good anything to you … or just a burden, a silly young thing with a …'

They were in a darkened spot on the road, mid-distance between two flickering streetlamps. Samson stepped forward and cradled her head against his chest.

'That's my fault, Grace, my dear. I've not always been straight with ye.'

'Oh, no, not at all.' He could feel and hear her unsteady breathing. 'You've always been wonderful to me. So good, so caring.'

'Not as good as I should have been.' His chin was resting on the top of her head, her fluttering hair tickling his cheek. 'Not as good.'

'But you have, Samson,' she whispered, choking back the tears. 'Why you've even risked the Company to pay me in full when you obviously couldn't afford it. That's how much you look out for me. You've always looked out for me.'

Samson chuckled. 'That's not looking out for ye, Grace. That's just good business. Ye're the star of the show. Everyone knows that. I'm just being a crafty businessman looking after his most important asset.'

Grace was silent for a moment, nestling her head further into his chest. He tightened his hold until she spoke. 'I just hate to see you suffering like this. That was so ugly tonight. Mr Sutcliffe has no right to treat you like that, threatening to call off the show. What a hide! Why, there'd be nothing for any of them if you weren't here putting on the show of the ages.'

'Thank ye. I sometimes think ye're the only real friend I have.'

'What about Mrs Cameron?'

'What about her, Grace?'

She said nothing. They stepped back from each other and kept walking. Some yards along the road, Grace stopped again and turned to face him.

'Samson, how confident are you of getting the money you need from the bank tomorrow?'

'Oh, I dinna really ken. Ye know what banks are like.'

'I do, and that's why I want you to know that I will hand over whatever money I can so you can pay the staff.'

'Oh, Grace, ye truly are the bonniest of lasses, but I couldna let ye do that.'

'But I want to, Samson. I want to. I've done it before.'

The last sentence was like a bolt of lightning finding its target.

'When have ye done it before?'

She quickly lowered her head, saying nothing.

'Grace, when have ye done it before?' he said, holding her shoulders firmly.

'I'm sorry, Samson. I vowed never to tell you but—'

'In Hobart Town?' he butted in. 'When I was in debtor's prison? Was that you who paid the lawyer?'

'Yes, it was. Are you angry with me, Samson?'

'Oh, my heavens,' he said, pulling her into his arms. He felt her squeezing in so tightly, it seemed there could be no space for an atom between them. 'I had no idea. I'd always wondered. Of course I'm not angry. How could I be? I'm just overwhelmed. How on earth did ye afford it?'

'Oh, I borrowed it – from my parents, some friends. It wasn't so hard.'

'Well, I must pay them all back.'

'They've been paid back,' she whispered.

'Then I must pay ye back, ye darling lass.'

'I don't want you to do that, Samson.'

'But …'

'But nothing, Samson. It's something I chose to do, and I want it to stay done.'

'But it's such a remarkable favour, Grace. No-one has ever done me such a favour.'

'It wasn't a favour, Samson,' she said, pulling away and looking up at him. He could see the glow of the lamplight flickering in her tears. 'It wasn't a favour.'

'Then …?'

'You don't need to ask. Just let it be. And speaking of favours, I have only one to ask of you.'

'Of course, anything.'

'Please don't tell Mrs Cameron.'

Samson nodded as they turned and continued walking forward, in silence. They arrived soon after at Grace's aunt and uncle's house.

'There ye go, ye darling lass. And thank ye again – from the very bottom of my heart.'

'Goodnight, Samson.' She reached up and kissed him on the cheek.

Grace began to walk up the short flight of steps to the door. He watched her stop and turn around to see him still standing where she'd left him.

'Speaking of Mrs Cameron,' she said.

'Aye.'

'Shouldn't she take my place in the play?'

'I dinna think she wants to.'

'But it would help with the finances, wouldn't it?'

'What do ye mean? Why?'

'Well, I'm really taking the money she should be getting and then you'd have enough to pay the staff.'

'I dinna see it like that. I'd pay anything to have ye do it, Grace. I wouldna have it any other way.'

Grace fell silent, looking down at the steps between them. She looked up with a huge smile on her face and eyes welling up. She ran back down the few steps and planted a kiss on his other cheek. Before he could react, she turned and rushed up the steps, opened the door and disappeared inside. Samson was still standing watching the door before turning and continuing his walk home.

The following day, Samson met with the bank manager, who

agreed to provide a cash loan against the intake from future performances, so long as Roger Goodfellow was prepared to go guarantor by placing the deeds to the Queen Victoria Theatre in the bank's hands. Samson discovered that Goodfellow had earlier on refused to do precisely that in order to secure his own loan with the bank. Annoyed at Goodfellow's persistent deception, Samson made a quick trip to his office, bank papers with him, to negotiate an agreement to the bank's terms.

'Well, I suppose I have little choice, Cameron, granted this is where my rental return is coming from.'

'I'm pleased ye see it this way, sir. If ye could just sign here … and here.'

Along with almost cleaning out The Cameron Company cash account, the loan provided enough to fully pay the staff what was owed to them. The final performance of the year went off without a hitch, although tensions remained high between Samson and the staff.

'They're just so ungrateful, Samson,' Grace said as they stood again at the bottom of the steps to her aunt and uncle's place. 'I just can't believe it. Even after you paid them in full.'

'It's about trust, Grace. They've lost their confidence in me.'

'Well, they shouldn't have. They're never going to find a better, more generous boss than you, Samson!'

'Thank ye, Grace. Ye're my bonniest fan, aren't ye?'

'That's one way to put it, Samson.' Grace reached up and kissed him on the cheek. This time, she remained on tiptoes while the kiss lingered.

He stood frozen before deciding to reach out to hug her. Before he could, she quickly turned and raced up the steps.

'Have a very happy Christmas, Samson,' she called as she turned back to face him.

'Bonnie Christmas, Grace,' he replied, catching the look in her eyes of fondness mixed with hurt.

She turned into the open door and was gone from sight.

Forty-three

CHRISTMAS CAME AND WENT THAT year. Samson took the family to a beachside house where they spent New Year's Eve. The year of our Lord 1842 was upon them.

On their return home, a letter awaited.

'It's from Mr McEntee,' Samson replied to Cordelia's query. 'He says he wants to see me urgently.'

'Shakespeare? Lady Gawler wants Shakespeare again! Is that a command?'

'Well, Samson, when it comes from Government House, I think we call it a request.'

'So, *Othello* again?'

'Well, it was very good, but I sense she would like to see something different. Something new! What about *The Merchant of*

Venice? She says she saw a splendid performance of it in London and would love to grace Adelaide with it.'

'Does the Governor's wife have any idea how much work it takes to put on a new play?' Samson was wringing his hands and shaking his head. 'I mean few of my current players have any experience in Shakespearean work and none, including myself, have performed in *The Merchant*.'

'Oh, I thought you had, in Hobart Town.'

'No, I did some backstage work on it, but I've never performed in it.'

'Oh, well, I'm sure it wouldn't be all that difficult to—'

'Excuse me, Mr McEntee, but do you really have any idea how much work is involved – and in such a short time?'

'Of course I do, Cameron, but the Shakespeare-loving Lady Gawler *is* the Governor's wife and, you know, we can't risk losing royal patronage.'

'Aye, well, perhaps it'd be braw to lose royal patronage.'

'Spoken like a true Scot,' McEntee chuckled. 'Look, if you need an extra couple of weeks to get things ready, I'm sure we can do that.'

'What are ye talking about, man? An extra couple of weeks? We'll need months to prepare for a play that no-one has done before. Can we just do *The Stranger* until Easter, as we planned, and that will give us time to work on a new play?'

McEntee took a deep breath as he looked down at his desk. Samson waited for a response to what he thought was an eminently reasonable request.

'Cameron,' he eventually said, looking up into his eyes. 'I'm sorry but we can't have any more performances of *The Stranger*.'

'What are ye saying?' Samson's eyes were on fire. 'What are

ye saying? Everybody is ready. We have the props, the orchestra. Grace is coming back especially to do it. She rejected an offer from Geelong to be here. What's the problem?

'The Governor's wife …'

'Oh, truly, I'm coming to despise this woman. I thought she really enjoyed *The Stranger*. That's what ye said yerself, did ye no?'

'Yes, well I did. But I gather some group of women has gotten to her with a different point of view.'

'Oh, dinna tell me. Some Christian group of women?'

'I think that might be the case, Cameron. Lady Gawler is quite involved with the church, as you know.'

'We've had this before. In Hobart Town, many years ago. And what does the Governor think about all this?'

'Samson, when it comes to these kinds of things, I sense that the Governor follows his wife's dispositions. I have heard him say that in matters of state, he makes the decisions, but in everything else, his wife rules.'

'So, I suppose there's no point in trying to speak with him.'

'I don't believe so.'

'And nobody else has a view?'

'No!'

'Even though any Shakespeare play won't bring the same financial returns as *The Stranger*? We know that from experience.'

'Well, Samson, the sad truth is that no-one, other than your good self, will be too worried about financial returns. Least of all the Governor's wife. I'm afraid any shortfall will fall on your Company.'

'Well, please make sure to thank Lady Gawler for her concern.'

'Did you tell him about the bank loan, Samson?' Cordelia asked.

'No. It's none of his business.'

'Samson, if we can't run *The Stranger* until at least Easter, we won't even be able to repay the loan much less pay the staff. We'll go broke. And Adelaide's theatre life will be like a desert. Don't you think he might see that as his business?'

'Aye, I know. One would think so.'

'Well, what are you going to do about it?'

'I think we should leave Adelaide and go back to Launceston. Ye know they made us an offer some time ago.'

'Yes, but we're committed to Adelaide. Didn't we sign a contract?'

'Aye, to do *The Stranger* until Easter and then re-negotiate. That's what the contract says, and they've broken it. So, we have no obligation to any of them. Goodfellow, McEntee or even the Governor's wife. The Laird bless her soul!'

'But what about the loan?'

'Well, our friend, Goodfellow, went guarantor so I suppose he can sort things out with them all, including the Governor's wife. I canna say I have much sympathy for any of them.'

Cordelia was silent. She was looking at her book. Samson watched as her mind was ticking.

'You're right, Samson. We can't let those hypocritical women win these battles. And besides, I'm a little bored with this pretentious place, so why don't you renew contact with our friends in Launceston?'

Samson went to her side and sat next to her, reaching over and kissing her on the cheek.

'I love ye, Mrs Haller.'

'I'm not Mrs Haller, Samson,' she replied, pushing him away. 'Are you sure you're not confusing me with someone else?'

By good fortune, only two days later, a letter arrived from Mrs Anne Clarke, a theatre manager with whom Cordelia had worked in England. Unbeknown to them, she was in the process of taking up a position in Van Diemen's Land as colonial theatre manager. She was writing with an offer to sponsor a season of Cameron Company performances in various parts of the island.

'I truly do think the Laird is calling us home, darling.'

'I always get worried when I see you turning to religion, Samson.' Cordelia was moving to his side as he stood at the kitchen table. 'But, on this occasion, I'm delighted.'

'Where do ye think we should live? She says we can choose, so long as we know we'll need to travel.'

'Well, where were we happiest?'

'Launceston, of course.'

'Launceston it is!' Cordelia said. 'I'll be pleased to have an ocean between us and our unhappy memories here.'

'Have they really been so bad, darling?'

'Bad enough,' Cordelia replied, her voice choking.

'But you can't, Cameron,' McEntee said as he hastened to his feet, leaving papers flying off his desk. 'You're committed. Under contract. Have you spoken with Mr Goodfellow?'

'No, Mr McEntee, but I've spoken with our lawyer. He says if ye've broken the contract, we're free to go elsewhere, and that's precisely what we're doing.'

'Well, we'll see about that.' McEntee's fiery eyes were darting everywhere except to face Samson. 'You can't get away with this.'

'If ye wish, our lawyers can fight it out. Regardless, we'll be on the boat to Van Diemen's Land next week.'

'Have you written to all the staff about our move?' Cordelia was standing by Samson's shoulder as he sat at the desk.

'Aye. I'm just finishing the last one now.'

'Including to Grace?' Cordelia was pinching his shoulder.

'Ouch, darling. Ye have greater strength than ye think,' he replied as he reached to soothe the pain.

'Sorry, but answer my question.'

'No. I think I need to do that personally.'

Cordelia was silent. He could hear her drawing an extra deep breath.

'I mean I need to go to Port Lincoln to speak with her,' Samson continued, as he tried to catch her eye. 'Is that all right with ye? I'd only be gone a few days, especially if I can catch the right boat.'

'I suppose so, Samson. We'd hate to offend the little darling, wouldn't we?'

'Well, she has been a very special friend, ye know? Even more than ye realise, believe me!'

'Oh, I do, Samson. I do.' she released her grip on his shoulder and turned to walk away. 'How could I ever forget it?'

The house at Port Lincoln was a decided step up from the slab hut on Kangaroo Island. Made of stone with a slate roof, it was one of eight cottages that sat halfway up the gently sloping knoll that looked down on the settlement.

'Samson, what on earth are you doing here?' Grace stood at the doorway, staring at him. She coughed and raised a handkerchief to her mouth. 'Come in, please. Get out of the heat.'

'Thank ye, Grace.' He brushed past her outstretched arm.

'Well, don't I at least get a kiss?' she said as she closed the door and turned to face him, smiling expectantly.

'I'm sorry, lass.' He stepped towards her and kissed her lightly on the cheek before stepping away.

'I swear I never know where I stand with you, Samson.' She was shaking her head and huffing quietly as she lowered her outstretched arms.

'I'm sorry, Grace. Did I do something wrong – except for calling ye "lass"?'

'Nothing more than usual, Samson.' She cast a steely look in his direction. 'What can I do for you? I take it you're not here because you've left Mrs Cameron and want me to take you in?'

'Laird, no. Laird no. Why would ye even think …?'

'Oh, it doesn't matter. Why would I even think it? I suppose because I'm a very foolish woman. Too foolish for words.'

Samson was taken aback by her harsh tones. *I thought we'd moved past that stage*, he thought. He took a step backwards, watching as she looked down and coughed, then lifted her head and looked him squarely in the eyes.

'So, to what do I owe this pleasure, Samson?'

'I'm sorry, Grace. I should have warned ye I was coming, but I wanted to let ye know in person what's occurred.'

'Of course, Samson. Forgive me. My father's been so unwell, and it's all been such a strain since I came home. And then I picked up this awful summertime flu. So, I'm really not at my best. Please do forgive me. Come into the sunroom and tell me why you're here.'

Grace stepped towards Samson, taking his arm and guiding him into the next room.

'Can I get you a cup of tea – or perhaps something to eat? Have you eaten?'

'Aye, I'm fine, lass,' he replied as he moved to the chair Grace had been pointing to.

'Samson!' Grace said firmly, stopping him in his tracks.

He turned around.

'Samson, for the very last time, will you stop calling me *lass*?' She was breathless, choking on the words. She began to cough uncontrollably. He stood and watched helplessly until she gained control of her breath. 'How many times do I have to say it? I'm not your lass, do you understand? I'm a grown woman with feelings. Very strong feelings in your case. And even if that means nothing to you, it means a lot to me.'

'I, I …' he said helplessly, taking a step or two towards her.

'Stop!' Grace was holding her hand up in the form of a sergeant major. 'Don't touch me, Samson. I couldn't stand it. Just say your piece and go.'

'Are you all right, dear?' a feeble voice came from somewhere in the house. 'Is someone there?'

'It's all right, Daddy,' Grace called back, clearly suppressing her anger. 'Someone is here but he's just going.'

Grace sat down in the farthest chair from the one assigned to Samson. She gestured for him to sit down.

'I dinna want to cause any trouble, Grace,' he said softly as he backed up into the assigned chair.

'No, you never do, Samson,' she replied, letting out a scoffing chuckle. 'You never do. Anyway, what is it? Do you need me back early? If so, I'm not sure I can. With my father, you know?'

'No, it's the opposite, Grace. We dinna need ye back at all.'

'What? What's happened? You do realise I turned down a very good opportunity in Geelong to stay with you.'

'I know. I know. That's why I wanted to let ye know in person.'

Samson brought her up to date with all the events of the past weeks.

'So, you're going back to Launceston?' She was drawing her handkerchief to her nose. 'That's the long and short of it, is it?'

'Aye. I'm afraid so, but there'll be a place for ye if ye want it. I'm sure I could arrange it.'

She sat in silence, studying the floor, occasionally shaking her head and wiping her eyes.

'No, I don't think so, Samson. I've been thinking a lot about my future since I came home. I've actually been thinking of writing to you to say I didn't think I could come back.'

'Truly?'

'Yes, truly. Samson, I do appreciate everything you've done for me. I've learned so much from you and you've been like a second father to me.'

He watched her choke on the final words. He sat and waited to see what would come next.

'But the truth is I have a father. I don't need a second one. I need …' Grace broke down and sobbed, her head fully in her hands.

'Is that you crying, darling?' the feeble voice called again.

She pulled herself together, taking a deep breath. 'No, Daddy. It's all right.' She offered Samson a half smile.

'I think I should go,' he said softly, standing up and taking a step towards the door.

Grace nodded, standing up and smiling as she took his arm and led him to the door.

'I'm sorry, la … Grace,' he said as he turned the door handle.

She burst out laughing. 'Samson, call me *lass* if that's what you want; if that's how you truly see me.' She held him by the arm and placed her head on his chest. 'I should just accept that. I know I should. My head tells me so – all the time it tells me so!'

'Grace …'

'Hush, Samson!' She lifted her head and looked up into his eyes. 'I'm just so sorry you've had to put up with me like this so often. When I'm prepared to be professional, I can steel myself to do the right thing. As I did for those many months in Adelaide. But when you surprise me with your visits, I just get so excited and my guard slips. Dear Samson, please forgive me. Yet again!'

'It's I who need forgiving, Grace.' He drew her to him again. 'I'm the fool who's always putting his foot in it. Making the wrong move. I really thought I should come and tell you this news personally, but I suppose it would have been better if I'd just written a letter.'

'No, no. I do appreciate you coming all this way. And I'm sorry for being so ungrateful.'

'Grace.'

'Yes,' she said, stepping back and looking him in the eye.

'In other circumstances …'

'Stop, Samson,' she replied, stepping back and raising her arms as if to hold back the tide. 'Please stop. Please don't say another word. Not another word that might haunt me until my dying day.'

Samson nodded, turned towards the door and opened it. Grace followed him, wiping her eyes. They stood in silence for a moment in the half-open door, bracing themselves against the blustery mid-summer wind. Samson stood immobile, looking at her, pleading for a cue for the next move, hoping for a right one at last. Grace read the signs and stepped forward, putting her arms around his body. He put one arm around her shoulder, while stroking her hair with the other hand.

'Darling, is the door open?' the feeble voice returned. 'It's breezy in here.'

'Go now,' she whispered as she pulled away. 'And good luck in Van Diemen's Land.'

'Thank ye, Grace,' he replied as he placed his hat on his head and turned towards the dock. 'Launceston will always be there if ye want it.'

'Thank you, Samson. I'll think about it.'

She watched him striding away. He turned his head and waved.

'Oh, Samson, wait,' she called and disappeared into the cottage.

She appeared a moment afterwards, running towards him with a small parcel in a paper bag.

'I almost forgot. I was going to post it to you but seeing as you're here. Sorry I didn't have time to wrap it properly.'

'Thank ye. What is it?'

'It's a book. You can look at it later. Just think of me whenever you read it.'

'I shall.'

'Promise?'

'Aye, lass, I promise,' he said, reaching his arm out and hugging her.

'Farewell, Samson,' she said as she pulled away.

'Farewell, dear Grace.'

Samson turned again towards the dock.

'I love you, Samson,' she called from behind.

He stopped and turned fully around facing her. He hesitated. *Should I go back one more time?* He remained where he was and smiled. 'I know, *lass*. I'll never forget ye, ye know.'

Grace burst into laughter, shaking her head as she blew a kiss.

Samson nodded, a broad smile on his face. Yet again, he turned and made his way towards the dock.

The wind was as blowy near the water as the last time he had trodden this path. Only this time, it was a far hotter wind. He recalled how on that last occasion Grace had surprised him, standing in his way and so coming back into his life. Maybe – just maybe – it would happen again sometime.

He climbed the gangplank, looking one last time over his shoulder, before taking a seat on the upper deck of the vessel. Just in case! He was alone there, the only passenger foolish enough not to take sanctuary below decks.

As the boat pulled away towards the open sea, he strained his eyes one last time in the forlorn hope that he might at least catch a final glimpse of the lass who had come to fill his heart in a way so unintended yet so richly.

When all hope was gone, Samson took to the inside. There were only four other paying passengers, two parents and a young boy and girl. He nodded in their direction and headed to a seat furthest away, choosing to sit alone with his thoughts and his gift. He opened the paper bag to find a new collection of the works of Percy Bysshe Shelley. He had introduced Grace to Shelley's prose and poetry, telling her about the elocution prize he had won at school when reciting 'To a Skylark'. He quickly went to the contents page and then turned to the poem.

> Hail to thee, blithe spirit!
>   Bird thou never wert,
> That from Heaven, or near it,
>   Purest thy full heart
> In profuse strains of unpremeditated art.

Higher still and higher
From the earth thou springest
Like a cloud of fire;
The blue deep thou wingest,
And singing still dost soar, and soaring ever singest.

Samson realised he must have been smiling when he saw the young boy staring at him. Samson winked and he looked away. He went back to the title page to see when the book was published. His eyes alighted on the words in ink.

To My Skylark
Ever soaring
All my love xx

Samson had much to think about on the journey back to Adelaide, much about life's mysteries, the alternative paths it offers. The choices we make.

'So, how did it go?' Cordelia asked as they sat at the dinner table on his return.

'Aye, braw.'

Forty-four

ANNE CLARKE WAS AT THE George Town dock to meet them off the boat from Adelaide. It was mid-March of 1842. She arranged for a carriage, large enough for their growing family and luggage, to take them on the thirty-mile road journey to Launceston.

'I love it,' were Cordelia's first words as they pulled up outside their new house in the upper reaches of George Street, overviewing the township of Launceston in the valley below. 'I never want to move from here, Samson.'

It was a single-storey sandstone dwelling, with three good-sized bedrooms, a veranda on three sides and a small garden in the front bounded by a white picket fence. Anne Clarke had arranged for an interest-free loan to be made available to them for resettlement.

Mrs Clarke left them to settle in while she returned home to Hobart Town. By arrangement, she would return at the end of the month to discuss theatre plans from there.

'So, you've seen the Victoria Theatre?' Anne Clarke asked as she placed the two lumps of sugar in her tea. 'What do you think?'

Samson opened his mouth to respond. Cordelia cut him off.

'It's splendid. More than adequate.'

Samson had already confided in Cordelia that the former blacksmith's workshop at the rear of the Kangaroo Inn was too small, and the acoustics could be a problem.

'Wonderful.' Mrs Clarke stirred her tea. 'And you're happy to manage it for now?'

'Yes, certainly.' Cordelia jumped in again. Samson knew she didn't want him sharing his anxieties about getting into the management side of things again.

'Splendid,' Mrs Clarke replied. 'Let's talk about itineraries, then. Have you heard of *The Bushrangers*?'

Cordelia looked confused. She turned her head to Samson who smiled and waved his hand. *You're telling the story, darling.*

Cordelia rolled her eyes before turning to Mrs Clarke. 'You mean the bank and stagecoach robbers?'

Mrs Clarke chuckled. 'No, I mean the play, *The Bushrangers*, by Henry Melville.'

Cordelia looked again to catch Samson's eye.

'I think I might have heard of it,' he said, casting a self-satisfied smile in Cordelia's direction.

'Well then, you will have heard that it has been very popular in Hobart Town these past few months. Mr Melville has made quite a name for himself, buying newspapers and stirring up the establishment. He's a very fine writer, you know.'

Samson and Cordelia looked to each other and then towards Mrs Clarke, who had paused while she took a sip of tea. Samson was about to speak.

'But'– Anne Clarke interrupted – 'and I will have to rely on your discretion here, you understand?'

'Of course,' Cordelia replied, while Samson nodded.

'Well, the truth is that Mr Melville has been unhappy with the quality of our performers. I've been dealing with this for a while. But things have come to a head of late and Mr Melville is threatening to withdraw his support – why, even to pen an unfavourable review in one of his own newspapers. That would be disastrous for the entire future of theatre in the colony.'

'We didna know any of this. What's the trouble?'

Mrs Clarke was in the process of lifting the cup to her mouth. She stopped, cup hovering some inches away, and stared in his direction. 'Well, there are a few problems, but the main one has been Jonathan Leigh, the principal actor, hero of the play. I believe you might know him?'

She maintained the pose of a statue, the cup remaining just a few inches from her mouth. Only her eyes moved from Samson to Cordelia and back again. Samson noted the slightest of surly smiles and mix of enquiry and mischief in her eyes. Cordelia was stunned into silence, her face flushed, unsure where to look.

'I believe we do,' Cordelia finally replied, turning to face her husband. 'So do you, Samson. Remember we did a very short season at the Court House some years ago?'

'Oh, aye, I do recall,' Samson said as casually as he could manage, in one of his poorer performances. 'But did he no spend some time in prison?'

'Well, let's not hold that against him,' Mrs Clarke said, chuckling as she finally took a sip of her tea. She looked Samson in the eye. 'After all, Mr Cameron. Even the most eminent of people can find themselves in that situation. Would you not agree?'

'Indeed,' he replied, ignoring the pleasure all this was clearly giving the woman. 'But I did hear that Mr Leigh had been released.'

'Did you, Samson?' Cordelia was looking over at her husband. 'From whom did you hear that?'

'Ah, I think Grace might have said something.' He was avoiding his wife's stare.

'I see.' Cordelia was smirking. 'My husband is referring to—'

'Grace Bellingham,' Mrs Clarke said excitedly. 'Oh, I know her. I saw her perform here in Launceston some time ago. I even travelled to Geelong to catch her again. What a gifted performer! Voice like an angel!'

There was a moment of awkward silence as Samson looked at Mrs Clarke, smiling and nodding, and Cordelia looked down and drew a deep breath.

'Yes, she is a gifted performer,' Cordelia finally conceded. 'In every imaginable way, a natural performer!'

'And you agree, Samson, don't you?' Anne Clarke cast a concerned look in his direction. 'You seem to have some reservation about her.'

'No, she's a fine actress. As good as any who could hope to replace my wife.'

'Anyway, tell us more about Mr Leigh,' Cordelia jumped in, ignoring the most recent drift in the conversation. 'After all, we were talking about him, I believe.'

'Ah, yes, of course,' Mrs Clarke replied. 'We were indeed. Well, there are some obvious problems with our Mr Leigh. For one, some would say he's a drunkard. Now, I'm not qualified to cast that judgement. To my mind, he performed admirably, and his drinking didn't impair the role. Indeed, I would argue it enhanced it, granted the hero he was playing, a fictional bushranger called Fawkes. Harry Fawkes is himself not meant to be an overly admirable character, in my view at least. A bushranger, after all, can hardly be so, I'd have thought.'

'So, what was the trouble, then?' Samson asked.

'Well, the problem is that Mr Melville has a view that the Fawkes character is not as ignoble as Jonathan Leigh portrayed him. To Mr Melville, Harry Fawkes is a true Van Diemen's Land hero, against the establishment but not as the anti-hero that was Leigh's interpretation. In a word, he thought Leigh diminished Fawkes, rather than elevated him.'

'Was Mr Leigh made aware of this?' Cordelia asked.

'Oh, yes, many times, but he would always say "But listen to the audience; they love me."'

'And did they?'

'Well, yes and no. Overall, it was a highly popular performance with the people. The people, mind you, but not so much with the critics, and certainly not with Mr Melville.'

'I'm not sure ye can take much notice of the critics,' Samson observed.

'I agree, except that they did influence Mr Melville and some influential people.'

'What did they say?'

'Well, Mrs Cameron – and I hope this won't offend you – but an article in *The Colonial Times* said something along the lines that Jonathan Leigh had as much of an idea of acting as the average beetle.'

'Why should I be offended?' Cordelia said in an indignant voice. 'Why on earth would I be offended?'

Anne was silent, as was Samson. Cordelia's head was down, studying her teacup. The awkward silence lingered. Mrs Clarke glanced in Samson's direction.

'That's actually quite funny.' Samson attempted to lighten the mood. 'I dinna see why my wife would be offended, but the poor man himself must have been, surely?'

'No, not at all,' Anne Clarke replied, seizing the opportunity to recover the situation. 'Water off a duck's back. "Another tankard, mate", would have been his response. But it did add to the pressure coming from Mr Melville.'

Samson chuckled along with her, taking note that Cordelia's head remained down, she clearly not willing to join in the banter.

'So, where does all that leave us?' Cordelia finally said in a way that brought all frivolity to a shuddering halt. 'Is the play going on or not?'

'Well, it's been delicate.' Mrs Clarke jolted herself back into her normal no-nonsense persona. 'But I think we've resolved to keep going with it until Easter. That's when Leigh's contract is over. The play has been promised to all the major centres in the colony, including here in Launceston, and Mr Leigh assumes he'll be along for the ride. Mr Melville insists that can't happen, and so that's where you come in.'

'Ye want us to perform *The Bushrangers*?' Samson asked. 'Ye know we dinna even know what it's about, and we dinna have any support players. We left them in Adelaide.'

'Yes, yes, I know all that. Look, it's a very simple play, as you'll see when you view the script. Only seven roles, and several can be done by the same player. You could get by with as few as four players.'

'Well, I did think we'd be doing something much simpler. Ye know that Mrs Cameron hasna performed for quite a while, and we've a growing family.'

'What did you have in mind, Mr Cameron? That you'd just get up and do a song and dance once a week?' Mrs Clarke sat forward in her chair, placed her cup on the small table in front of her, and stared him down. 'You do realise that I have gone out of my way to bring you here – at significant expense, might I say?'

'Aye, ma'am, I know—'

'And you are in quite a bit of debt, I hear?'

Samson sat, pale, mute.

'Oh, we're most grateful, Mrs Clarke,' Cordelia jumped in. 'We truly are, and we'll be happy to do whatever you have in mind. Won't we, Samson?' She turned to face him, urging a response.

'Aye, most certainly!'

'Good, I assumed you would be compliant,' Mrs Clarke said, sitting back in her chair and letting out a deep breath. 'Granted your circumstances!'

'So, tell us a little more about the play.' Cordelia rested her hand on Samson's arm.

'Why don't I go one better and get Henry Melville to speak with you about it?'

Three days later, Samson and Cordelia were sitting listening to Henry Melville expostulate on his favourite work. Melville was nothing if not enigmatic, some might say a living contradiction. Born into wealth in England and travelling to Van Diemen's Land in 1828 in a style that most who journeyed there could only dream about, he established some of the colony's earliest newspapers and steadily subsumed much of the competition. He lived in one of Hobart Town's finest residences in Sandy Bay and held lavish parties for the elite. That was one side of the enigma. The other side, that Cordelia and Samson came to see that evening, was of a despiser of the establishment, his sympathies clearly with the struggling poor, many of them former convicts, and with an unusual conscience about the plight of the Indigenous population.

'When did you arrive here?' Melville asked.

'In 1833,' Cordelia replied.

'Mmm. And did you ever hear about the Black War?'

'I believe we have,' Samson replied. 'We were told early on about the trouble with the Blacks.'

'If by "trouble", you mean murder, rape and pillage, then that's an accurate description of what George Arthur perpetrated on our native population.'

'The Governor?' Cordelia queried, wide-eyed. 'I was to understand he was a man of some conscience.'

'Well, I'm not sure where you would have gained that impression, Mrs Cameron. Admittedly, he was crafty in skirting the blame for much of his misdeeds, but that he knew exactly what he was allowing, if not plotting and planning, for the native population is without doubt.'

'I believe things have not been so good for these people,' Samson said.

'Not so good, you say,' Melville replied, a wry grin flashing across his face. 'You could say that. They've been all but wiped out.'

'Why do we not know more about this, then?' Cordelia asked. 'We're both avid readers, but I have to say the extent of what you say – be it true – is news to me.'

'Well, ma'am, I assure you of its truth, and you would have read about it in my newspapers had you been here in the last few years. But I'm afraid they don't go past the shores of Van Diemen's Land, and even here they've been restricted and blocked where the establishment can manage it. And as for the other colonial governments, well, they have made certain I don't get a foothold in their territories. Even here in this colony, I've had to learn to be careful. I've had several lawsuits brought before me because of stories I've printed, and even had my press vandalised at one point.'

'Truly?' Samson said. 'It's a wee bit like the stories from the Clearances.'

'The Highland Clearances, you mean?'

'Aye. My grand da had all sorts of tales of what the English did, the mass murders followed by suppressing anyone who tried to tell of them.'

'Oh, of course, I hadn't made the connection with your Scottish background. You would have an especial appreciation of what's been going on here. English authorities do these things wherever they go, it seems.'

'Oh, aye. Governments, armies, churches. They're all the same!'

'Indeed, Samson – do you mind if I call you that? – I'm becoming more and more excited at the prospect of you acting in the role of Harry Fawkes. He represents the one who is prepared to call out the authorities. He's a hero and antihero in one. A vagabond and a saint.'

'Vagabond and saint!' Cordelia chuckled, as she turned to face Samson, wry smile and all. 'I'd say that's an apt description of my dear husband, Mr Melville.'

Samson returned the smile before turning back to face Melville. He noted the quizzical look on his face.

'As ye can see, Henry – ye don't mind if I call ye Henry? – my wife thinks only the best of me.'

'Ah, yes, well, I'll take you at your word, Samson,' Melville replied, smiling. 'So, I take it you're disposed to taking on this role?'

'I think I like this Harry Fawkes even though I've never met him!'

'Splendid. Splendid. Well, let's get to work then.'

'Just before we do,' Cordelia said, stopping them from standing up. 'About Mr Leigh?'

'Oh,' Melville replied, his face quickly losing its amiable appearance. 'I suppose Mrs Clarke told you about all that.'

'Ah, yes,' Cordelia said, carefully avoiding Samson's glare. 'What will happen to him?'

'Well, if I were a betting man,' Melville replied, looking down to the floor. 'I would guess he would go back to his old ways.'

'Old ways?' Cordelia couldn't hide the slight blushing.

'Yes, ways given to perfidy might be the best way to put it.'

'Perfidy?' Samson said after a moment of silence.

'A gentle way to speak of deceit, untrustworthiness, philandering.' Melville was studying the floor, seeming to be careful in choosing his words. He looked up and stared straight at Cordelia. 'A thorough cad, one might say.'

Cordelia looked down, saying nothing.

'But you won't have to worry about him, I assure you.' Melville cast a smiling glance in Samson's direction. 'Either of you!'

Starting after Easter in Launceston, *The Bushrangers* began its northern Van Diemen's Land season, with Samson in the lead and dominant role of Harry Fawkes, vagabond and saint, and Cordelia playing three of the minor roles, as well as standing in for Anne Clarke as the theatre manager and director, while Mrs Clarke was principally working in Hobart Town. Cordelia also provided pre-performance and intermission singing by demand.

'The house was crowded to excess', reported the *Launceston Courier* of 28 April 1842, with an especially strong endorsement of Cordelia's role in the audience's 'general satisfaction'.

'Are ye all right with all this work, darling?' Samson asked one Sunday evening after an especially hectic week. 'I know ye wanted to spend more time being a ma. And here ye are, busier than ever.'

'Well, needs must, Samson. What else can we do? I could stay out of theatre altogether and mother the children, but then how would we feed them? One has to make these choices in life. I just hope we can get on top of our financial situation, so one day I can be the mother I want to be.'

'I believe I must be the most fortunate man in the world that I have ye, my darling.'

'Thank you, Samson. I do quite like it when you say things like that – all too rarely, I might say.'

Samson was about to open his mouth to challenge the claim but thought better of it.

'Are the bairns all right with the way things are, do ye think?'

'Yes, they seem to be doing well with Mrs Livingstone looking after them. She's a lovely grandmotherly type who gives them great care and keeps them under her thumb. They're probably doing better with her than they would with me, to be honest. I love being a mother but I'm not sure I'm a natural at it. Whereas Mrs Livingstone was born to be a mother and grandmother. We're lucky to have her.'

'So ye wouldn't be wanting to have any more bairns, I suppose?'

'I didn't say that, Samson. I most certainly did not say that!'

The Bushrangers ran for six weeks in Launceston before moving to George Town for four weeks, Zeehan for three weeks, and thence to

Queenstown for three weeks before returning to Launceston for a further six weeks. There was barely a week in between each season, during which time they had to move the family, Mrs Livingstone in tow, and set up in a new, normally less-than-fully-adequate venue. Henry Melville was a prominent audience member for the opening performance in each town. They always looked forward to whatever time they could spend in their home in Launceston.

'He's delighted,' Anne Clarke reported when she came to visit them in Queenstown. '"Godsend" was the word he used to describe his elation. He wants us to talk about a Hobart Town season and then possibly look to the mainland after that.'

'That's splendid,' Cordelia replied. 'So, things have been smoothed out with Mr Leigh, then?'

'No, they couldn't be worse.' Mrs Clarke was shaking her head. 'He's wanting to sue everyone from the Governor to the newspapers, especially Mr Melville's ones, and even threatening to use his influence with the workers to have us shut down. Nothing we didn't expect, mind you.'

'Truly?' Samson replied. 'He sounds like what my da would have called a *buaireadh*.'

'I'm not sure what that means, Samson,' said Mrs Clarke, chuckling. 'But if it means Jonathan Leigh is a serial pest, then I agree.'

'That's quite enough,' Cordelia butted in, unsmiling. 'What are you doing about it, then? Are you worried that he could shut everything down?'

'Oh, I doubt it. Frankly, he's just a – what does Henry call him? – "blustering braggard". I quite like that, I must say.'

'So, if we come to Hobart Town, do ye think we'll be safe?' Samson said, glancing aside to Cordelia. 'Ye know we have wee bairns?'

'Oh, perfectly safe. Mr Melville has some very good friends in the constabulary.'

'Well, that's reassuring,' Cordelia said, looking across at Samson before turning back to face Mrs Clarke. 'But there's something we do need to talk about.'

'Surely,' Mrs Clarke replied, wide-eyed and expectant. 'What is it?'

'Well, we are fairly certain we're going to have another mouth to feed in the not-too-distant future.'

'What? Another child?' Mrs Clarke blurted out before checking herself. 'Oh, I'm sorry, but I mean, don't you have—'

'Four,' Samson butted in. 'Aye, ma'am, four wee bairns and we wouldna want any less. In fact, we clearly want more.'

Samson and Cordelia sat in silence, staring the theatre manager down, awaiting her next move.

'Oh, well, of course. I'm sure that's wonderful news,' she finally uttered, a fixed smile on her ruddy, perspiring face. 'Yes, congratulations.'

After some negotiation, an agreement was signed between Anne Clarke's enterprise and the Cameron Company that saw additional returns of revenue to the Camerons and further support for the management of the Hobart Town season that ran from October 1842 through to late March 1843. Cordelia's roles on stage were relieved in the 1843 parts of the season so that she could prepare for the impending birth.

'I must say I'm quite enjoying my pregnancy this time, Samson,' she said after the last show.

'I know ye are, darling. It's as though this is yer first time.'

'It's because I feel so well. I'd just come to assume that carrying a child meant being an invalid for nine months.'

'I was starting to think the same. I actually thought we mightn't have any more for that reason. So, it's braw to see ye looking so well.'

'I actually think we could have lots more.' He noted the glow in her eyes as she spoke. 'Lots more to look after us in our dotage.'

'Aye, darling.' He sat down next to her and took her hand in his own. 'Ye can have whatever ye want.'

Throughout the Easter holidays of 1843, they moved the family back to their favourite home in Launceston where, on the 11th day of May of that year, Catherine Nairne was born. She was almost nine pounds in weight, the happiest and healthiest baby so far.

Forty-five

Over the next ten years, Cordelia did have the 'lots more' children that she desired, with seven pregnancies producing four live births, all born in either Melbourne or Geelong in what would become, in 1851, the independent Colony of Victoria.

Henry Melville finally managed to get the toehold for his business interests, mainly newspapers and theatre, on the mainland, starting with the closest settlements in Victoria, just across Bass Strait. At the time of his first incursion, Victoria was still governed by New South Wales. When, in 1842, the New South Wales Colonial Secretary first called for tenders for theatre companies to be established in Victoria, Melville was deliberately excluded on the grounds of his alleged 'seditionary dispositions'. It was from a discussion between the governors of Van Diemen's Land and New South Wales, Major Cumberland and Sir George Gipps, that this ban was finally lifted.

'I couldn't speak more highly of the Cameron Company's work, George,' Cumberland said. 'But if you want them, you'll have to accept Henry Melville into the mix.'

Governor Gipps accepted his peer's advice, and so the Cameron Company set up in the Eagle Tavern in Bourke Street, Melbourne, for a season of *Rob Roy* in mid-1844.

'The compromise was that we don't do *The Bushrangers*, at least for a while,' Melville announced on his return to Launceston. 'Apparently, Governor Gipps is no fan of bushrangers.'

'Doesna he ken that the real Rob Roy was a kind of bushranger?' Samson was chuckling. 'Or that's what the Sassenachs say anyway.'

'I'm not sure the good Sir George knows much about the real Rob Roy. After all, that's all about the Scottish Highlands, a world away from the colony he's trying to manage.'

Rob Roy, a personal favourite of Samson's, was followed by a season of *The Widow's Victim*, selected by Cordelia. She had performed in this play in Leominster many years before. This took them through to Christmas and the New Year of 1845.

'I love Melbourne,' Cordelia said, as they strolled down Collins Street one Sunday, their five children with them, two in prams. 'And the children are happy here. I want to stay if we can.'

'Aye, it's a wee bit like Edinburgh. Just not quite so cold.'

'But warmer than Van Diemen's Land,' Cordelia said, mocking a shiver. 'Oh, my heavens, going back there after Adelaide was difficult.'

'Aye, and to think ye wanted to go back home.'

'To England? Oh no. I never could now.'

On the first day of February 1845, the Company reprised *The Stranger*, with the two thespians in their old and favourite roles, Cordelia as Mrs Haller and Samson playing the part of Mr Solomon. It ran to rave reviews for eight months.

The only problem is the inadequate venue. How these fine actors can tolerate The Eagle Tavern is beyond this commentator. When will our Sydney-based governance recognise Melbourne's need for a decent theatre?

So wrote the theatre critic in *The Melbourne Advertiser* in April 1845. By the end of that year, the Queen's Theatre Royal had been built in Queen Street, taking its first performance just before Christmas, the inaugural play being *The Bushrangers*. Henry Melville had contributed significant funds to the new theatre and so had some influence over the schedule of performances.

'I feel as though I can now die in peace,' he confided to Samson.

'Ye canna die yet, Henry. Not until we perform it in Sydney.'

Melville laughed. 'I could never wish to live so long, Samson,' he said with a wink.

Demand for a new season of *The Stranger* was so strong that a further season was planned for May of that year, 1846. Just before Easter, Cordelia announced that she was pregnant again.

'Don't look at me like the cat that spilled the milk, Samson. Just write and see if she's available.'

'I dinna think she is, darling.'

'How would you know, Samson?'

The conversation went back and forth. Samson was disinclined to call on Grace again. He felt that they had left things in a good place back in Port Lincoln and it was a chapter of his life best left closed.

'What about Winifred Shaw?'

'What about her, Samson?'

'Do ye think she could carry Mrs Haller for a season?'

'Well, she's been a very faithful understudy and apparently done well standing in for the odd rehearsal. And so long as you're there to carry your part, I suppose …'

'Well, I was actually wondering about Timothy Easton as Mr Solomon.'

'What, two understudies carrying a whole season? I'm not sure. But why, Samson? Don't you want to keep on doing Mr Solomon?'

'Not without ye, darling!'

'Well, that's sweet, but there's no need for that. Why, if I was happy for you to be working alongside Grace, I'd have no problem with you working with Winifred. Kissing her even! I don't see her as your type, frankly!'

'Ye're my only type, darling,' he said, returning her cheeky grin. 'I just think perhaps it's time we thought about the future for the Cameron Company. I mean, we canna go on forever, can we?'

'We're hardly in our eighties, dear. I'm sure you have many more years onstage.'

'Aye, but running the Company is becoming a bigger job all the time, and we have the bairns to think of, and …'

'And what, Samson?'

'I'm tired, Cordelia. Ye've had yer rest from the stage, but I've been acting now for fifteen years with hardly a break. Ever since we left Britain.'

Eventually, Samson won the argument. Cordelia was never fully convinced about his motive, and for good reason. Secretly, he doubted whether he could be a convincing Mr Solomon with anyone other than Cordelia or Grace. It had been during a quiet read of his works of Shelley, a book that he kept well out of sight, that he came to that realisation.

So, after some pleading from Samson, the season of *The Stranger* was postponed by six weeks to provide enough time to bring the new cast up to the standard expected of a Cameron Company performance. The opening night was June 15th.

The disappointment we all felt when Mr and Mrs Cameron's absences were announced was well and truly overturned by the splendid performance of Miss Winifred Shaw and Mr Timothy Easton.

—*The Melbourne Advertiser*, 17 June 1846.

'Did you see *The Advertiser* this morning?' Cordelia said as Samson walked in after the evening performance.

'Yes, darling.'

'It seems we're dispensable.'

'Aye, and that's all good for the Company.'

On the 18th day of October 1846, Cordelia gave birth to a girl almost as heavy and healthy as Catherine.

'I believe ye should have yer own, just like I have Samson.'

'What? Call her Cordelia? Won't that be confusing?'

'No more than having Samson and wee Samson.'

'So, wee Cordelia?'

'Aye, why not?'

Young Cordelia was christened in the Scots Church in Collins Street on the 24th day of October by the Reverend Dunmore Lang.

'It was a bonnie ceremony, wasn't it?' Samson said as the carriage drove them away.

'Yes, but I'm still sorry Father Lovat couldn't be here. He was in Ballarat just last week.'

'I doubt the Reverend Dunmore Lang would have let him in the door, darling.'

Cordelia maintained contact with Charles Lovat who, as pastor of Yass, would periodically move through the lower reaches of his parish, one that extended from southern New South Wales well south of the Murray River that marked the boundary between the old colony and the newly minted Victoria. Their correspondence had begun with an annual Christmas card and occasional letter but had increased over the years as Cordelia sought more and more counsel. All Samson knew or cared about was that it seemed to make her happy.

The Cameron Company became a mainstay of Victorian theatre for the next fifteen years, moving mainly between Melbourne and Geelong, with occasional touring performances in Ballarat, Bendigo, Shepparton, and Echuca. There was an extended season of various performances in Geelong throughout 1848, during which year Cordelia was pregnant again.

'No, I don't think so, Samson,' Cordelia said when it was suggested she might make a guest appearance.

'But they'd love to see ye, darling.'

'Let's just leave it as it is,' she replied, putting an end to the conversation.

When the Company was performing in Geelong and Samson needed to travel from Melbourne, he would stay in a local guesthouse run by an elderly childless couple, Mr and Mrs Nesbitt. They always treated him like the son they had never had for themselves.

'I think I'll come with you next time you want to stay down there, Samson.'

'That'd be wonderful, darling. The Nesbitts would love to meet ye. But what about the bairns?'

'John can be in charge. He's a very mature fourteen-year-old.'

'Fourteen? Is he really?'

'Yes, darling. Remember the celebration you missed?'

'Oh, aye. When I couldn't get home from Geelong.'

'Yes, dear. That one!'

Cordelia regularly made the trip. She enjoyed Mr and Mrs Nesbitt fussing over her.

'I do love my parents, Samson, but I sometimes wonder if I'd have been a happier person with parents like the Nesbitts.'

It was a telling reflection and one he felt certain would have been shared with Charles Lovat.

It was on one of Cordelia's overnight stays at the Nesbitts that she went into premature labour. On the 24th day of November 1848, Isabella was born in their guesthouse.

'Oh, how embarrassing.' Cordelia was cradling the infant to her breast. 'Have you apologised for me? For us?'

'I'm sure there's no need, darling. They thought it was braw that new life came into the world under their roof. That's what they said.'

'How gracious of them. I have such little memory of it. Was Mrs Nesbitt here?'

'For all of it, darling. I think it was one of life's highlights for her.'

'Was anyone else here?'

'Well, the midwife, of course. You do remember her, surely?'

'Vaguely. Ever so vaguely. It was almost as though I dreamed my way through it.'

'Aye, well ye were screaming in pain at one point, so she gave ye something to calm yerself down.'

'Really, what was it?'

'I dinna know, but it worked. Everything went smoothly then.'

Cordelia closed her eyes, exhausted. Samson moved to take the sleeping baby from her, when she woke with a start.

'Samson, was Grace here?'

'No, darling, she wasna here.'

'Why do I feel as though she was? I was sure she was here.'

'No, she wasna but ye were calling out to her at one point.'

'Was I? What was I saying?'

'I dinna think ye'd want to know, darling.'

'What do you mean, Samson? What on earth do you mean?'

'Darling, ye were a wee bit delirious last night. Perhaps it's best forgotten.'

'What do you mean, Samson? Did I disgrace myself?'

'Just a wee bit, darling. Ye were shouting at Grace. Telling her to get away, to leave ye alone. Ye said some not very genteel things to her.'

'Oh, my goodness, did I?' Cordelia was moving the now wakened baby from one breast to the other. 'What was I saying?'

'I dinna think ye'd want to hear. Let's just say ye were calling Grace's virtue into question.'

'Oh, no.' Cordelia's eyes welled up. She was shaking her head. 'I think I remember now. I do hope she never finds out.'

'I'm sure she won't but even if she did, ye know she's a bonnie lass. One of the best.'

Cordelia fell silent again, eyes closed, Isabella sucking gently, falling in and out of sleep. Samson sat in the chair watching them, feeling content with how his life choices were unfolding. The Company was thriving, his family growing, Cordelia was in a contented place, and an unexpected opportunity in the most bizarre of circumstances to defend Grace's virtue had just come his way.

His mind wandered to Grace as he relaxed in the chair. *I do hope all is well with her*, he was thinking as he began to doze. He was woken sometime later by Mrs Nesbitt bringing him a cup of tea.

Forty-six

Samson and Cordelia would live to endure burying a child for the second time. On the 10th day of May 1850, young Cordelia died at the age of three.

'I can only say I wish it was *this* Cordelia,' Cordelia said, pointing to herself, on the night of the funeral. 'To lose a child once is a tragedy. Twice, it's a nightmare!'

'Aye, and folks really think there's a Laird. No decent Laird would do this.'

'Don't blame God, Samson. We were warned.'

'What? That she was delicate?'

'That she would never get better here. That she needed warmer climes.'

'Aye, so it's my fault then, is it no? I was the one who wanted to stay here.'

'Oh, there's no use blaming ourselves. I'm as guilty. I should have insisted.'

'Is there anything I can do, darling? Is yer friend, Father Lovat, anywhere nearby?'

'No. He's stationed somewhere in Sydney now. He says he's too unwell to travel anymore.'

'Do ye think ye'd like to visit him?'

'In Sydney?'

'Aye. I could care for the bairns if ye'd like to go.'

'Samson!' she replied, looking at him and emitting a small chuckle.

'Aye, I know. Well, perhaps we could find someone else to care for them.'

'I'll think about it, Samson. Thank you for your thoughtfulness. I'll write to Father Lovat.'

Despite several overtures by which they suggested they might meet, it never happened. Cordelia and Charles Lovat's relationship remained purely one through correspondence, a relationship that appeared to sustain Cordelia through some of her most difficult challenges. Samson was never privy to what passed between them; Lovat's letters to her were always placed carefully in a spot where he could not accidentally stumble on them.

Over the next four years, Cordelia would conceive four times and bear two more children, being Donald Henry on the 2nd day of March 1851 and Ellen on the 11th day of December 1852. Both children were born in Melbourne, and both to a woman in her forties. Ellen was born prematurely, and grave fears were held for her surviving even a few hours. When the immediate danger period passed, they saw her turning into a remarkably similar copy of young Cordelia's fragility. By the age of five, she was showing signs of following young Cordelia to an early grave. The thought of burying a third child weighed on Cordelia to the point of despair.

'We have to go, Samson.' It was on the evening in the dead of the especially cold Melbourne winter of 1857. 'Or I am, at least, with the children.'

'Aye, I know, darling. We canna take the risk again.'

'Good, then how soon can we go?'

'I dinna know. It depends on where we go. Sydney, perhaps? Is that far enough to the north?'

'We can ask the doctor what he thinks. But would you want to go to Sydney? Our experiences there were not so memorable.'

'Oh, I could contact Mr MacTavish and see if I could get my old job back.'

'What? After working for the Catholics there? I doubt it, Samson. Perhaps we should make contact with Father Lovat and see if he could arrange something.'

'I dinna think Father Lovat has much influence there anymore. I hear the Irish clergy have really taken over in Sydney. Perhaps we should do something entirely new. Be brave!'

'No-one could ever accuse you of not being brave, Samson. What are you thinking?'

'Well, it's warmth ye want for our bairn, is it no?'

'Yes, for all of us, I think, but especially for Ellen.'

'Then, what about Queensland? North Queensland? They say it never gets cold there, even in winter.'

'Oh, that's brave all right. But what would you do, Samson? I don't think there are any theatres in North Queensland.'

'Then, what if we were to start one?'

'Perhaps you're right. Isn't there talk of Queensland becoming its own colony?'

'Aye, I think it's close. The New South Wales Parliament is setting up a process for its separation.'

'Then they'll be looking to establish their own theatre, surely?'

'Aye, and we could be in on the ground floor.'

'On the ground floor,' Cordelia mused. 'As we always are.'

Epilogue

SAMSON SAT IN HIS FAVOURITE chair on the spacious western-facing veranda of his 'Queenslander' home in Mackay, northern Queensland. It was late afternoon, the sun low in the early Autumn sky. He was enjoying the peace and quiet after his eightieth birthday celebrations of March 14th, 1890. He pondered on the day's proceedings, notebook in hand, pencil at the ready. He had only recently taken to keeping a diary. He began jotting down memories that he might write up properly in ink later on.

All seven of the surviving children and most of their own families had made it to the special lunch organised by Gracie, Catherine and Isabella, who all lived nearby and regularly tended to their elderly parents. With their help and encouragement, Cordelia had left the bed where she spent most hours of the day to sit at the opposite end of the table. *Just like the old days*, Samson wrote. A pity she doesn't remember them, he thought.

His mind was cast back to the beginnings of their journey to the Antipodes.

All I ever wanted was for us to be a pair of thespians, he wrote.

A pair of thespians now a pair of octogenarians, he thought, a wistful smile on his face.

He thought back to the Christmas of 1857, when they had wound up their commitments in Victoria and began to plan the move to Queensland. Part of the plan had been to travel via Sydney so Cordelia could meet with Charles Lovat. A month before they left, she had received a 'return to sender' from a letter she had written. He recalled the look of apprehension on her face when she asked him to make enquiries with the Catholic Offices in Melbourne, and the grief she could not hide when he broke the news to her that Lovat had died in June of that year. When the boat docked in Sydney, she had refused to set foot on shore.

Samson thought back to the first year or so in Queensland, which was marked by several attempts to gain a foothold for the Cameron Company. When nothing was forthcoming, he had again settled for an accountancy position, this time with an auctioneering business in Mackay. Then, a year or so later, Queensland had separated from New South Wales to become its own colony, leading to renewed moves to establish theatre in various towns and cities, especially Brisbane. They had often been approached to ascertain their interest in re-establishing the Company or participating in some other way, but it always involved a move to Brisbane and taking some financial risk. He jotted a note or two to this effect.

In the mid-1860s, an especially attractive offer had come their way. Samson recorded that it involved the prospect of *Othello* being staged in a revamped Brisbane warehouse, to be named the Empire Theatre. They were told that the wife of the Governor of Queensland had a close friend in South Australia who had extolled to her the virtues of the Company's rendition of the play. On this recommendation, they were approached to play the lead roles, at least for the opening weeks, while another company would manage the production, and a consortium of businesspeople would take full financial responsibility. Cordelia declined because of failing health but she encouraged Samson to accept the offer, telling him she had noted signs of despondency in him about his life as an accountant. She even suggested he should write to Grace to see if she might be free to play Desdemona and told him how she saw a renewed spring in his step when he agreed to do so.

It had been some years since he had heard from Grace, the last occasion being a letter telling him that she and Charles Folley were married and living in Adelaide. He found the address and wrote, full of hope. A letter of reply came back some eight weeks later, in Folley's hand. He wrote to tell of Grace's death in childbirth some months beforehand. It would have been their fifth child, Folley had added. Samson recalled the devastation he would never disclose to anyone, declining the Brisbane offer and refusing all entreaties to perform from that time forward. He wondered what to write – should he? Could he? He held the pencil aloft, then put it down and closed the notebook.

The Van Diemen's Land Thespian rested his head on the back of the chair and dozed until Catherine came and helped him inside.